Rita Bradshaw was born in Northamptonshire, where she still lives today. At the age of sixteen she met her husband – whom she considers her soulmate – and they have two daughters and a son, and a young grandson.

Much to her delight, Rita's first attempt at a novel was accepted for publication, and she went on to write many more successful novels under a pseudonym before writing for Headline using her own name.

As a committed Christian and passionate animal-lover – her two 'furry babies' can always be found snoring gently at her feet as she writes – Rita has a full and busy life, but her writing continues to be a consuming pleasure that she never tires of. In any spare moments she loves reading, walking her dogs, eating out and visiting the cinema and theatre, as well as being involved in her local church and animal welfare.

Rita's earlier sagas, ALONE BENEATH THE HEAVEN, REACH FOR TOMORROW, RAGA-MUFFIN ANGEL, THE STONY PATH, THE URCHIN'S SONG and CANDLES IN THE STORM, are also available from Headline.

The Most Precious Thing

Rita Bradshaw

headline

First published in 2004
by HEADLINE BOOK PUBLISHING

First published in paperback in 2004
by HEADLINE BOOK PUBLISHING

3

ISBN 978 0 7553 0621 3

Typeset in Times by Palimpsest Book Production Limited,
Polmont, Stirlingshire
Printed and bound by
CPI Group (UK) Ltd, Croydon, CR0 4YY

Headline's policy is to use papers that are natural, renewable and
recyclable products and made from wood grown in
sustainable forests. The logging and manufacturing processes
are expected to conform to the environmental
regulations of the country of origin.

HEADLINE PUBLISHING GROUP
A division of Hodder Headline
338 Euston Road
LONDON NW1 3BH

www.headline.co.uk
www.hodderheadline.com

To my big sister, Tonia, who shares the memories of childhood – remember who used to eat her selection boxes for breakfast, dinner and tea on Christmas Day? – the joys and sorrows of being grown-up, and the prospect that we're both getting steadily older!

I love you, Sis.

Acknowledgements

I owe much to numerous sources for the background material regarding the Depression and Second World War, but special mention must go to the following: *Life in Britain Between the Wars* by L.C.B. Seaman; *Southwick* by Peter Gibson; *Durham Miner's Millennium Book* by David Temple; *Tommy Turnball* by Joe Robinson; *Our Village, Memories of the Durham Mining Communities* by Keith Armstrong; *Sunderland's Blitz* by Kevin Brady; *English History 1914–1945* by A.J.P. Taylor and *British History* edited by J. Gardiner and N. Wenborn.

I would also like to thank those grown-up children and grand-children of the old miners, who generously shared stories, experiences and memories of the strikes and marches their forbears endured, and of their stalwart womenfolk who worked from dawn to dusk with a fortitude we can only marvel at now. Truly they had little time to dream . . .

When Ev'ning does approach we homeward hie
And our Domestic Toils incessant ply;
Against your coming home prepare to get
Our work all done, our House in order set,
Bacon and dumpling in the pot we boil
Our beds we make, our Swine to feed the while;
Then wait at door to see you coming home,
And set the table out against you come.
Early next morning we on you attend;
Our children dress and feed; their clothes we mend:
And in the field our daily task renew,
Soon as the rising sun has dry'd the dew.
Our toil and labour's daily so extreme,
That we have hardly ever time to dream.

Mary Collier (washerwoman), 1739

Part 1

The End of Childhood

1925

Chapter One

'His mam's done everything she can to stop this wedding. You know that, don't you?'

'Aye, I do. You've told me often enough.'

'I hate her and she knows it, but I don't care. Upstart, she is. I said to Walter, your mam is an upstart and as tight as a tadpole's backside, and that's watertight.'

'What did he say?'

'He agreed with me.'

That didn't surprise her. Carrie McDarmount grinned at her elder sister and Renee smiled back, her full-lipped mouth wide. Walter was fair barmy about Renee; if her sister had said black was white he wouldn't have argued.

'She might rule the rest of them in that house with a rod of iron but she's not starting any carry-on with me. I'll soon send her packing with a flea in her ear. I would, you know.'

'I don't doubt that for a minute.' Carrie was laughing now, her mouth – smaller than her sister's but just as full and bow-shaped – opening to reveal a set of perfectly even white teeth.

'The cunning old so-an'-so tried to make out she wanted us to wait because of the strikes and such, said it wasn't a good time to think of getting wed with the slump worsening. I said to Walter, when *will* be a good time as far as your mam's

3

concerned then? We live at the wrong end of the street, that's the thing. And then there's Da.'

Renee's voice had hardened on the last words and now Carrie wasn't smiling. She had never understood the antipathy between her father and his eldest child but ever since she could remember their rows had rocked the house. There was Billy, who at sixteen was just a year older than herself and two years younger than Renee, and then the twins, Danny and Len, the babies of the family at seven years old, and never a cross word with their da, but Renee only had to walk into the same room as him and there were ructions. Their mam said it was because the pair of them were like peas in a pod under the skin, and maybe she was right.

'And you needn't frown at me, Carrie McDarmount.' Renee tossed her head, causing her wedding veil to flutter like a trapped bird. 'I've nothing against a man having a drink, but Da! He can't hold it, you know he can't, and it'll be the same old story later, him dancing and singing and acting the cuddy, likely as not in the street, and poor Mam not knowing where to put herself.'

'Renee—'

'No, don't come out with your endless string of excuses for him, not today of all days. Knowing he's going to show us all up as usual has taken the edge off me wedding day, and that's not fair. I don't know why you stick up for him like you do, I don't straight. He's big enough and ugly enough to look after himself.' Renee's voice trembled slightly as she finished her tirade and, as always happened when her sister's brash façade slipped a little, Carrie immediately softened.

'Oh, lass, don't take on.' She sprang up from the edge of the old iron bed she shared with Renee and put her arms round her sister who was sitting on a hardbacked chair in

4

front of the spotted mirror fixed to the back of the wardrobe door. 'Look, I'll try and keep an eye on him once we come back to the house, all right? See if I can stop him drinking too much. How's that?'

'No you will not.' Renee gave the slender figure a hug, her own voluptuous and well-padded curves straining against the cheap satinette of her wedding dress. She sniffed loudly, before pushing Carrie away, saying, 'I want you to enjoy me wedding day, Caz. Do you hear me? You're not going to look after anyone. I wish you could've been my bridesmaid, lass, but with what it cost for the dress and then the bits of furniture we've bought . . .'

'I know, I know.' Renee's use of the pet name told Carrie she was forgiven. 'I didn't expect it, honest. You've had more than enough to do with making your dress anyway.' She stood back a pace, surveying her sister in the long-sleeved, high-necked shimmering gown. 'You look bonny, Renee. Just bonny.'

'Walter's mam's managed to let me know she thinks a white wedding's a waste of money.' Renee wrinkled her nose, her brown eyes taking on their normal wicked sparkle. 'She was referring to the cost, of course; she doesn't know the horse has been out of the stable for some time. She's such a cold fish she probably doesn't think a woman could like a bit of making on. How she's managed to have four bairns is beyond me.'

Carrie smiled wryly but said nothing. The sisters shared a bedroom in the cramped terraced cottage in Sunderland's Southwick district. The curtained-off area provided just enough room for the pallet bed that the twins slept in, top and tailed; Billy slept on a desk bed in the sitting room. The enforced intimacy meant it was not Carrie's mother but Renee who had explained to Carrie what the blood on her nightgown meant some twelve months before. Renee had also gone on to expound a little about the birds and the bees when she had seen her sister's total ignorance of the facts of life, adding airily that she and Walter had been doing 'it' for some time, and that there was nothing to be frightened of. 'Don't say nowt to no one though,' she had warned after she had sorted out a chunky homemade linen pad with ties each end for her younger sibling. 'Mam and Da'd go mad if they knew.'

'But . . . but if doing it makes babies,' Carrie had asked, bewildered, 'what if you have a bairn, Renee?'

'Don't you worry your head about that. There's ways and means.' Renee had nodded her head mysteriously, leaving her sister more confused than ever.

No baby had materialised, and now it was Renee's wedding day, a day that had had their mother fretting for months. With a strike every other week at Wearmouth colliery – or so it seemed to the womenfolk – and shifts being cut, and their da and Billy and the other miners being locked out at the drop of a hat, Carrie knew her mother relied on every penny her daughters brought home from their work at the firework factory across the river. When Renee had first got Carrie and her friend Lillian set on alongside her the year before when the girls had left school, Carrie had given her mother all her weekly wage of seven shillings and fourpence, only accepting the return of one shilling and fourpence when her mother had absolutely insisted.

Now Renee's contribution to the family pot, already halved since her engagement as she began her bottom drawer and saved towards furniture, would stop altogether. Her mother's housekeeping had been stretched to the limit the last months as she'd endeavoured to put the odd penny or two by for the wedding feast.

Renee rose to her feet, fluffing out her short veil. 'I have to say I shan't be sorry to leave this house. You'd have thought it was a funeral we were getting ready for rather than a wedding, and Mam's begrudged every stick of furniture we've bought for our place.'

'She hasn't begrudged you it, Renee. She's pleased you've got a few things together, she told me so. It's just that she's at her wits' end half the time trying to manage on what comes in.'

Renee shrugged meaty shoulders. 'Aye, well, be that as it may, we all have to look out for number one in this life. I tell you, lass, I don't intend to end up like Mam. Walk into any pit house round these parts come evening and what d'you find? A blazing hot fire, heavy, damp, stinking clothes hanging all over the place and a tired woman who looks double her age. Walter might be a miner but he already knows I'm not the sort to drop a bairn every year and worship the ground he walks on. We've an understanding, me and Walter, and whatever his mam says, or ours for that matter, I'm not giving up me job just because I've a ring on me finger. I want to enjoy being married and have a bit of a life, and you can't do that if you're stuck with a bellyful on a miner's wage. Look at Gran and Granda, both gone well before their time thanks to the pit.'

Carrie nodded. She'd heard it all before and she wasn't about to argue with Renee, not on her wedding day. Besides, she agreed with Renee in part. Their da had been an orphan and was brought up in the workhouse, but their mam's parents, Gran and Grandad Cain, had lived only a few doors away till three years ago. Then Granda had died in an accident at the pit and within three months Gran had succumbed to a heart attack, brought on by years of overwork and the many miscarriages she'd endured after their mam, Gran's only child, had been born in the first year of marriage.

Carrie smiled into the plump, attractive face in front of her and said briskly, 'Come on then, lass. You ready?'

'Aye, I'm ready.' But then Renee caught hold of her sister, her voice thick as she said, 'We've had some right good cracks in our time, haven't we, lass? Pillows over our faces often as not so's not to wake the lads. That's the only trouble with Walter, he hasn't got much of a sense of humour.'

'You two will be fine.' Carrie hugged her again. 'Now come on, Da's waiting and Mam and the lads have been left ages. I'll have to be nippy to get there before you at this rate. And no arguing with Da once I'm gone, mind. This is one time I'm trusting you to be all sweetness and light, our Renee.'

'Huh!' They were both laughing. 'That'll be the day.' Renee hitched up her ample bosom with her forearms, smoothed her dress and exhaled loudly. 'I just hope Norman Finnigan has managed to borrow his uncle's horse and trap like he said. Walter's slipped him a few bob but you never know with Norman.'

'I'll go and see if he's here yet.' Carrie left the bedroom and Renee followed just behind her, both hands holding her long skirt clear of the bare floorboards.

As the girls entered the kitchen the man sitting in a decrepit rocking chair in front of the warm range turned his head towards them.

'Here she is, Da, and doesn't she look bonny? I reckon Walter will burst a blood vessel when he sees her.' Carrie's voice was bright and still holding a thread of laughter but her eyes were pleading with her father, and Sandy McDarmount was well aware what his youngest daughter was asking. Be kind, say something nice. Don't mention the cost of the new finery again or how Renee's time would have been better spent

8

putting the money into something for the house she and Walter were renting.

His eyes lingered on this favourite child, the light of his life as he privately put it, and not for the first time he asked himself what he would do when Carrie made her choice and began courting. No one would be good enough for his bairn, he admitted ruefully, no one from round these parts any road. It wasn't just that she was blossoming into a real beauty, skin like peaches and cream and eyes of such a deep blue they almost appeared black at times, it was the tenderness of her, the warm-heartedness to all and sundry. There were plenty who preached about going the extra mile but few who would walk it when push came to shove, but his Carrie possessed a generosity of spirit that made him fear for her at times. She even brought out the best in Renee, and that was saying something.

He forced himself to smile at his eldest daughter and his voice was jocular as he said, 'Burst a blood vessel? Probably half a dozen, I'd say. You look pretty as a picture, lass.'

Renee stared at her father. She couldn't remember a time when everything about the small, walrus-moustached man in front of her hadn't irritated her to screaming pitch, and it was on the tip of her tongue to say, 'Don't overdo it, Da,' but instead, mindful of the day, she smiled back and pretended to curtsey, making the three of them laugh.

Carrie darted across the living room, opened the front door and peered up and down the street before giving a little squeal. 'He's coming! Norman's coming, Renee. You'll have to make him wait a few minutes to give me time to get to the church. Oh, where's my coat? I left it on the chair by the door.'

'Here, lass.' Sandy reached out to a small cracket tucked by the side of the range and handed the coat to her. 'It got moved when old Mrs Duncan brought in a plate of somethin'. Can't

9

go more than a step or two without havin' to sit down now, poor old gal, but she makes a canny seed cake.'

'Aye.' Carrie paused in the act of pulling on her coat, a coat which had fitted her perfectly three years before but which now was at least six inches too short and had her arms sticking out of the sleeves in a way she knew looked ludicrous. She turned to survey the square kitchen table, resplendent in its Sunday cloth and groaning under a load of food the likes of which it hadn't borne in years. 'Aren't people kind? Everyone's brought something.'

'Everyone from this end of the street,' Renee put in flatly. She caught her father's eye as she spoke, and for once the two were of like mind.

To those who didn't live there, James Armitage Street might look like a street of identical, small, single-storey terraced houses with three rooms and a scullery but its inhabitants knew that the top end was considered vastly superior to the bottom end. The top end led out into Fulwell Road and the cricket ground and then a sprawling farm or two, while the bottom bordered Cornhill Terrace and eastwards the grid of mean streets stretching north from Wearmouth colliery. Those at the top end would tell anyone that this area was almost lower middle class – didn't a policeman live just a few doors away? And there was a professional family or two in Hawthorn Street and Clarendon Street, which were only separated from James Armitage Street by Fulwell Road. And how many bairns from the bottom end passed to go to Houghton Secondary or, if they did pass, could be spared by a family eager for another wage-earner? Not many. Oh no, not many. And Walter's family lived within spitting distance of Fulwell Road.

This last fact had been at the forefront of the minds of all the women who had popped in that morning with 'just a little

10

something for the table, lass'. Them at the top end might think they were God's gift and gold-wrapped with it, but they'd soon see the bottom end knew how to put on a good spread and look after their own.

'You'll wait a while so I can get to the church before you?' Carrie asked again. She grinned her thanks as Renee nodded and then she dived out of the door into the frosty December air. It had snowed heavily on and off all through November and the first week of December, thawing slightly, freezing, then snowing again, until the ground resembled a skating rink and Sunderland infirmary's trade in broken limbs trebled. Olive Sutton, Walter's mother, had been like a dog with two tails, according to Renee, taking every opportunity to remind all and sundry that she had said a December wedding was a mistake and that it would have been better to wait until the spring. Renee had become tight-lipped and snappy, especially when she returned home after an evening at Walter's.

And then, thank goodness, Carrie thought as she hurried along in the bitterly cold morning, a persistent thaw ten days ago followed by fresh dry winds and weak winter sunshine had taken care of every last flake of snow. Suddenly Renee had been all smiles again and an uneasy excitement had taken hold of the house. It was a shame that in the last twenty-four hours the weather had turned raw once more, with the sky so low you could reach up and touch it, but it wasn't snowing yet, that was the thing, and Renee could have her horse and trap and turn up at the church in style.

Carrie smiled to herself and blew hard on hands already turning a mottled shade of blue. She'd set her heart on that, had Renee, and it would be one in the eye for Walter's mam. As was often the case when her mind touched on Renee's future mother-in-law, Carrie's next thought was, with all she's got, a

11

lovely family and a nice home and all, why does she have to be so crabby all the time? Mr Sutton wasn't nasty or bad-tempered, salt of the earth she'd heard her da describe Walter's da more than once, but *her*. And like her mam said, Olive Sutton had nothing to be uppity about. Wasn't her man a miner born and bred, and hadn't the bairns all played together and gone to the same schools, and didn't their Lillian spend more time at the McDarmount household than she ever did in her own?

'Yoohoo! Carrie!'

It was as though the thought of her best friend had conjured her up. Lillian was beyond the end of Cornhill Terrace on the old village green straight ahead. She was jumping from one foot to the other, not so much to get Carrie's attention as to keep warm, and now she came running across, firing a barrage of questions as she did so.

'Where on earth have you been? I thought you were going to be late! Do you know there's only five minutes to go? Where's your Renee? Is anything wrong? Didn't Norman turn up?'

Carrie didn't interrupt the flow. When Lillian reached her she smiled, her voice warm as she said, 'Thanks for waiting for me, lass. Everything's fine. Renee just wanted to talk a bit after I'd helped her get ready.'

'She's goin' to turn up, isn't she?'

'Course she's going to turn up, don't be so daft.'

They grinned at each other and then hurried on the way Lillian had just come, past the chapel and the Green. Not until they came to the end of Town Street and the Holy Trinity Church was in front of them did their pace slacken.

'Our Walter and your Renee getting married.' There was a lilt in Lillian's voice and her plain, good-natured face was alight. 'That means our families are linked, you thought of that? We'll both be aunty to their bairns.'

'Give 'em a chance, they aren't even married yet.' They were giggling as they reached the church door and had to wait a moment or two to compose their faces before they entered Holy Trinity.

Carrie loved the feeling the inside of the church always gave her; its familiarity never failed to cheer her. She had been coming with her parents and the rest of the family on Sunday mornings for as long as she could remember. Church in the morning, Sunday School in the afternoon in the old National School at the bottom of Stoney Lane, and then there was the Boys' Brigade, the Girl Guides, the Girls' Friendly Society and the church choir at various times during the week. All her friends were in the same groups and she had never questioned this, or why it was that the bairns who went to St Hilda's, the Catholic church, were barely known to her, in spite of there being plenty up and down the street. Sunday School treats, Christmas parties, concerts held in the Mission Hall at Low Southwick, whist drives, fêtes, parish teas were all tied up with belonging to Holy Trinity, and going along to the Church Institute – again held in the old National School – to play table tennis and other games had been part and parcel of her childhood.

Both girls quietly sidled up the aisle, smiling at each other before they slid into the seats their respective families had saved for them.

'Everything all right, hinny?'

Her mother's voice was hushed like everyone's was in church. Well, everyone but her da, Carrie qualified silently. However he tried, her da couldn't seem to whisper and her mam had long since given up attempting to get him to lower his voice.

Carrie smiled and nodded at her mother who was sitting with

the twins either side of her. They had disgraced themselves earlier that morning by arguing over some comics they had swapped with Archie Flack, two doors up. It hadn't been the squabble that had caused their long-suffering mother to whip down their trousers and apply her hand with devastating vigour to each small backside, but the fact that the altercation had suddenly degenerated into a dogfight punctuated with words their mother would have sworn on oath neither of them had ever heard, just as Mrs Hayes, the verger's wife, had called with a plate of ham and egg pie for the table. Neither of the small boys raised their heads now but Billy, seated next to Len, winked at Carrie. She smiled and looked away.

Carrie sat staring ahead for a few seconds, nerving herself for the moment when she would glance across the aisle to the Sutton pew where Walter's parents, his two brothers and Lillian were sitting. Walter and his best man, Joe Gill, were stiff figures in the row in front. Her stomach quivered when she turned her head, her eyes passing over Mr and Mrs Sutton, Lillian and David – at eighteen the youngest Sutton brother and a childhood playmate and friend – before her gaze came to rest on the object of all her dreams and desires for the last twelve months.

Alec Sutton. The most wonderful, the most handsome lad in all the world. Although he wasn't a lad, not really, not at twenty.

Carrie swallowed, knowing she was staring shamelessly but unable to look away. It was rare she got the opportunity to feast her eyes on him like this; normally it was just a quick shy glance and a muttered hello in the street if he happened to pass her coming to or from work. He always looked so smart on those occasions, his clothes immaculate and the trilby hat he'd taken to wearing of late perched at a jaunty angle on his head. But then he didn't work down the pit like his da and brothers, she reminded herself, as though her thoughts had been a criticism of the others and her own menfolk. Alec could afford to be always well turned out.

Carrie suddenly became aware of a small movement; her eyes left Alec's profile and were caught and held by those of his mother. Deep blue eyes met cold glassy green, and such was the expression on Olive Sutton's unprepossessing face as she purposely let her gaze move up and down the young girl in the opposite pew, that Carrie could feel her cheeks burning. She quickly turned her head away.

Oh, she hated Mrs Sutton, she agreed with Renee on this. Walter's mam had a way of looking at you that made you sort of shrivel up inside. She was cruel, spiteful.

Suddenly the excitement of the day drained away, along with the thrill of the new dress she was wearing under her old coat, the coat Mrs Sutton's face had reminded her was faded and shabby. She should have bought a coat, she told herself miserably, her mind going back to the lunch hour a week or so before when she had been browsing in the Old Market in Sunderland's East End, but the dress had been so bonny.

She had virtually pounced on it when she'd spotted the eggshell-blue brocade material among the usual motley collection of second-hand clothes. The feel of the rich cloth beneath her fingers told her the dress was a good one, even before the stallholder assured her it came from one of the big houses Hendon way. 'Only put it out ten minutes ago, lass, an' it's a bargain at three bob. You couldn't buy the material for less than three times that, I'm tellin' you straight. Quality it is, from one of them fine London shops. You seen the label? Here, look. Beautiful dress, eh, lass? Beautiful.'

Carrie had agreed with him. The dress was beautiful, but

three shillings was still three shillings and she was saving every penny she had left from her one shilling and fourpence, after she'd bought her toiletries and stockings and slipped the twins a Saturday penny, for a new winter coat.

She'd stood dithering for more than ten minutes, the dress still clutched between her fingers and the stallholder, sensing a sale, keeping up a steady stream of banter. Perfect though the dress would be for Renee's wedding, she could buy a new lace collar and cuffs for her Sunday dress and make do, although the Sunday dress was two years old and showed where the hem had been let down twice. It was long overdue for being consigned to weekday use. In the end she'd bought the dress simply because she had not been able to bear the thought of walking away without it.

A rustle from the back of the building announcing the arrival of the bride cleared Carrie's mind of everything but Renee, and the next moment the organ had struck up and her sister was walking up the aisle on the arm of their father. Carrie turned along with everyone else to watch, thinking again how bonny Renee looked, sort of glowing. A beautiful bride.

Carrie had walked into the fields beyond the Carley Hill Waggonway the day before, collecting ivy, red hawthorn berries, nipplewort and the seed vessels of rosebay willowherb and beaked parsley to make a wreath to hold Renee's veil in place. She had worked on it for hours until she was satisfied the delicate ring was a thing of beauty. Now she was aware of a choked feeling as she recalled Renee's ecstatic pleasure at the surprise gift and the way her sister had cried and hugged her. For the first time it dawned on her just how much she was going to miss Renee's buoyant presence at home.

Carrie blinked hard, telling herself not to be so silly. She would still see her sister every day at the firework factory, and Pilgrim Street, where Renee and Walter were renting their house, was only a ten-minute walk from James Armitage Street. She and Renee would still have their cracks, and Renee had already said umpteen times she must come and visit them often. Yes, she was being daft, likely because Mrs Sutton had made her feel funny, but she wouldn't give Walter's mam the satisfaction of ruining the day for her. She was going to have a lovely time, she *was* or her name wasn't Carrie McDarmount!

'Look here, I'm tellin' you, Paddy, Mick'll knock Gussie Hogg into next weekend. Wind an' water, Silksworth's bloke.'

'Says you.'

'Aye, says me, an' if you're not of like mind it might be better for you to get your backside down to Silksworth an' ask if they want a hewer.'

'Don't you come that tack with me, Ned Sutton. I'll put me money on Mick same as the rest, but it don't mean I can't see what's under me nose. Gussie Hogg's a mean 'un an' his right hook is vicious. He'll take Mick out in the first round, that's all I'm sayin'.'

'You're sayin' a sight too much if you ask me.'

The two miners' voices were rising, and as Carrie and Lillian saw Olive Sutton put a hand on her husband's shoulder, squeezing it until her nails were digging into his shoulder if his pained expression was anything to go by, Lillian said flatly, 'By, lass, me da's going to be in for it when we get home. He's verging on mortalious and me mam won't let him forget that in a hurry.'

Carrie said nothing but the irony of the situation didn't escape her. Here was her da, sober as a judge even with the drink flowing, and poor Mr Sutton well and truly pickled.

17

Remembering the times – and they were many – when Lillian had made no reference to the fact that her father had been singing in the street with enough gusto to wake the dead, Carrie now said quietly, 'It's a wedding, lass. Everyone gets tipsy at a wedding.'

'Aye, well, you try telling that to me mam. She's a bitter pill as you well know and she don't hold with gambling neither. He must be three parts cut to talk about the fight like that.'

Poor Mr Sutton. Carrie glanced at Lillian's father again. He was a good-looking man, short and stocky and with a mass of thick curly hair which was still as black as the ace of spades and nut-brown eyes which surveyed the world from under brows as bushy as her da's moustache. Everyone knew Mr Sutton liked to bet, everyone except his wife that was, and her da said it was Ned Sutton's passion for boxing that had stopped him murdering his shrew of a wife years ago. Without that the man would have nothing, her da had argued when her mam had murmured it wasn't right to keep Olive in the dark about her husband's gambling.

Every pit had its own boxing champion, even the different religions had them, and they were very nearly all Irish by birth. The fights were real sporting events and because they represented the honour of the pit everyone was expected to support them, again according to her da, so Ned Sutton had a point. The boxers would train, members of the community paid for tickets to see the fight and the purse could be as much as a golden guinea.

Billy had been to a few fights in the two years since he had been down the pit, and when Carrie had said she couldn't imagine the easygoing, mild Mr Sutton enjoying such violence, her brother had laughed fit to burst. 'What?' he'd mocked. 'You don't know the half, lass. He goes fair barmy, calling the bloke from the other pit all the names under the sun and insulting the referee right, left and centre. How do you think he got that black eye last week? You didn't believe the story about the pit prop, did you? He'd been yelling at the two in the ring that it was supposed to be a fight not the last flaming waltz and that he could do better with one hand tied behind his back when a big fella from Harton way got fed up with listening to him and laid him out cold. One of our lads then took this bloke on and before you knew it all hell was let loose. Damn good night, that was,' her brother had added reflectively – and quite mystifyingly as far as Carrie was concerned.

'Here, Carrie.' Lillian nudged Carrie in the ribs and brought her attention back to herself. 'You ever tried sloe gin?' And then because she knew the answer, she continued with hardly a pause, 'I've nabbed a bottle me granny brought. What say we oil our wigs with the rest of them?' She nodded at what Carrie could now make out was a bottle-shaped lump under her cardigan.

Carrie grinned into the plain little face, a spirit of recklessness taking hold. They had been packed like sardines in this room and the scullery, and at times one person pressing past another had only been achieved by indrawn breath, but not once through the hours since the wedding ceremony had Alec so much as smiled at her. David, along with Mr Sutton and others, had told her she looked bonny in the new dress but as far as she was aware Alec hadn't even noticed she was there. He thought she was a bairn, that was the thing, but she wasn't. She would be sixteen in just over six weeks' time, the same age Renee had been when she'd started courting with Walter.

'Where are we going to drink it?' Carrie whispered into Lillian's ear. 'Da'd go mad if he caught me.'

'Our house, of course. Everyone's here, aren't they?' Lillian's voice had a gurgle in it, and as Carrie inclined her head in agreement she was giggling too. They held on to each other as they squeezed out of the room.

From his vantage point across the other side of the living room David Sutton watched the two girls leave and this was not by chance; he had been unable to take his eyes off Carrie all day. He shifted suddenly where he was leaning against the wall and the beer in his half-full mug slopped over the side with the abrupt movement.

He was daft, stupid, he should have said something months ago. Why hadn't he? And the answer came back as though spoken by another voice. Because you know full well she don't think of you like that, man. You're a friend, not a lad, as far as Carrie's concerned. Right from a little bairn they'd had a bond which had made her confide all her upsets and woes to him, but that wasn't the same as liking him in *that* way. He didn't see any sign of that.

Did Carrie have a lad in mind? It was something that tormented him often through the long night hours when his body wouldn't let him sleep, usually when he'd seen her at her home when he'd called to go for a jar with Billy. If she did have a lad, Lillian didn't know anything about it, that much was certain. He had casually broached the subject once or twice with his sister, and Lillian's answers had been enough to satisfy him on that score. Mind, that didn't mean Carrie wasn't soft on someone. She wasn't one to wear her heart on her sleeve, Carrie. Never had been.

David rubbed his hand over his face and took another swig of beer, glancing across the room again. This time his gaze was caught by Alec as his brother threw back his head and laughed at something Madge Patterson was saying. At seventeen she was a saucy piece, Madge – if she hadn't been their cousin he would have used a stronger term – and she liked Alec. But then all the lasses liked Alec, and David knew that a few of them who were no better than they should be had proved it. Alec only had to lift a little finger and the lasses were queueing up for the privilege.

David shook his head at himself, disturbed momentarily by the bitterness the thought held. He should get himself a lass, he told himself, and then maybe he could sleep as soundly as Alec at night. Here he was at eighteen and he'd never so much as kissed a girl, and more than one lass had let him know they were willing to walk out with him. He might not be an oil painting but he wouldn't crack no mirrors either.

He finished the last of the beer, his gaze still fixed on his brother whose bright eyes and flushed face bore witness to the fact that he had been drinking a drop of the hard stuff along with the ale, and that he was well on the way to being plastered. Alec was the only one in the family who could get blind drunk and not feel the lash of their mam's tongue. Couldn't do no wrong in their mam's eyes, could Alec, and yet from a bairn it'd been him who had been the cause of all the mischief and unpleasantness in the house, with Walter and himself picking up the tabs, of course, David thought sourly.

Damn it. Again David shook his head, irritated by the inner carping. If he didn't like how things were, why didn't he get out from under his mam's roof – it didn't occur to him here that he had left his father out of the equation – out from the area, maybe even out of the pit? There were other pits, and there were other ways of life too, especially down south. He was young; if he was ever going to make a break, now was the time.

He had listened to his da and the other older miners talking,

21

and he believed their predictions that the next year was going to be like none they had seen before because the coal subsidy ended in May. When the coal-owners had told the government they were going to increase miners' working hours and reduce wages, the government had started paying them a subsidy rather than tell them they weren't allowed to do that, but there hadn't been a man or boy down the pits that hadn't known they were living on borrowed time. His da maintained the government, especially Churchill and his gang, together with the coal-owners and the owners of every other industry in the country, wanted to destroy the unions, and in May all hell was going to be let loose. So wouldn't it make sense to get his backside out of it before the worst happened? Aye, it would, he felt it in his bones, and when all was said and done, there was nothing to hold him in the slowly dying north.

Immediately the thought mocked him as the image of a young girl with shining chestnut hair and midnight-blue eyes sprang into his mind.

Carrie had looked so bonny today, grown-up, different. He groaned deep within himself. He should have *asked* her. He would, he would speak up and to hell with it; at least he would know then, once and for all. When she and Lillian came back from wherever they'd taken themselves off to, he would take Carrie aside and speak what was in his mind. His guts twisted with a mixture of apprehension and excitement as he continued to hammer home the decision, his gaze focused on the door and his beer glass forgotten in his hand.

Chapter Two

As always when she entered Lillian's house, Carrie found herself marvelling at the difference to her own home. True, both had three rooms, a scullery, and a fair-sized paved backyard with the privy at the end, which was cleared by hand each week, and in both dwellings water was from a tap in the yard and heating and cooking by the range in the living room, but there any similarity ended. And, strange as it would seem to most folk, Carrie admitted, she much preferred her own home, shabby and threadbare as it was.

She stood just inside the back door, looking round the Suttons' antiseptic-clean scullery and its row upon row of shelves laden with various items, those in boxes bearing neat labels. There was always an overpowering smell of bleach in this room, enough to make your eyes water at times. The tin bath was propped against one whitewashed wall and next to this stood a small table with a shelf beneath it, the upper part holding a bowl and other utensils, the lower scrubbed and scoured pans.

'Come on.' Lillian took her hand, pulling her through into the living room where the smell of burning coal from the big black leaded range didn't quite disguise the lingering odour of bleach from the flagstones beneath their feet. Here there was no old battered saddle with great darned flock cushions you

23

could curl up on, and no creaking rocking chair placed at an angle to the range so the man of the house could toast his toes on the fender after a hard day down the pit. Instead the only seats were six hardbacked chairs with stiff upholstered bottoms, grouped round a table which always boasted a white cloth over the oilcloth beneath. A china cabinet stood in one corner and a small dresser in another, and the lace at the window was starched into permanent billows. The full, dark brown velvet curtains made the room always seem dark even on the brightest summer day.

The enormous thick clippy mat in front of the range at home – a lovely warm place to sit and dream and look into the flickering flames of the fire, even if it did collect the dust and bits – was represented by a thin fringed rug at Lillian's, and Carrie never trod on it without feeling she shouldn't. Lillian had told her once that her mother always made the men strip off their pit clothes in the yard before coming into the scullery where the bath would be standing filled with water, and when Carrie had enquired what if it was raining or freezing cold, and didn't they ever bathe in front of the fire, Lillian had just shrugged, saying, 'That's me mam for you,' as though it was sufficient explanation.

It was from that day that in her bedtime prayers Carrie had started to thank God each night for her own mother. She had always known a miner's life was hard and a miner's wife's no better, but now she noticed her mother's cheery singing and her chirpy chatter as she went about her tasks of scrubbing, washing, ironing, cleaning, polishing and baking, in a place nearly always steamy with clothes drying and pans boiling, and always smelling of sweaty boots and coal dust. And if her mother wasn't busy darning in the evenings or finishing some ironing or preparing meals, she'd have her box of old rags out and would be working away on the clippy mat she made each year in time for Christmas. The old one would then be moved into one of the bedrooms, and the one from the bedroom was transferred to the scullery.

'Sit down, lass.' Lillian pushed her down on one of the hardbacked chairs before producing the bottle hidden under her cardigan like a magician pulling a rabbit out of a hat. She looked at Carrie, her brown button eyes bright and her mouth stretched in a wide smile. 'Me granny swears this is the best drink this side of heaven. She's known far and wide for her sloe gin, is me granny.'

'Won't the bottle be missed then?'

'Not the way they were all guzzling the beer, not to mention the whisky me da took.'

Lillian had fetched two mugs as she'd been talking and now she poured a generous measure of the dark liquid into each. She handed Carrie hers and said, 'Bottoms up, lass,' before plumping down on a chair on the opposite side of the table.

'Ooh, it's nice, sort of . . . blackcurranty. No, not blackcurranty, it's . . . What does it remind you of, Carrie?'

'Sloes?'

It wasn't particularly witty but both girls were convulsed with laughter again, and they continued to titter as they sipped at the deceptively innocuous drink.

Some time later, when the level in the bottle had dropped to half, Carrie became aware of a wonderful sense of contentment and happiness. How could she ever have thought this room was cold and unwelcoming? she asked herself. It was bonny, so bonny. Everything was bonny. Suddenly the ever present spectre embodied in the words 'locked out', which had first entered her life four and a half years earlier when every colliery in the country had been closed and padlocked against its workers to force the miners to accept reduced wages, harder working conditions and longer hours, was gone. The bairns she and Lillian had passed on the way to the house, little mites of five and six who had been lugging a half sack of coke they'd collected from following the coke cart for hours and picking up the pieces that rolled off, ceased to tug at her consciousness. Life was a beautiful thing and anything was possible if only you wished hard enough.

She stretched her legs out in front of her, admiring the brocade of her dress across her knees; the folds of the material shone in the mellow light of the oil lamp Lillian had lit when they'd first come in. Glancing at her friend she saw Lillian was pouring them both another measure of sloe gin, her brow furrowed in concentration and both hands on the bottle as though it weighed a ton.

'There, lass.' The task accomplished, Lillian fell back against the unyielding wood of the chair, her mouth fixed in a wide grin. And when she raised the mug to her lips only to miss her mouth entirely, pouring the contents down the front of her dress, Carrie found herself laughing with her friend as though she'd never stop.

Neither of them heard the back door open or the footsteps in the scullery, so when Alec's voice cut through their laughter and brought both girls' heads jerking to the doorway, Carrie's fright caused her to slop the remainder of her drink all over the pristine white tablecloth. 'What the hell . . .' Alec's voice died away as he surveyed his sister and little Carrie McDarmount and the severely depleted gin bottle which told its own story.

'Ooh you, our Alec. Look what you've made Carrie do.' Lillian tried to rise to assist Carrie who was desperately mopping at the stain with her handkerchief but she found her legs wouldn't hold her. She subsided into her seat again, and said plaintively, 'I'll get wrong from mam now an' it's all your fault.'

They were stewed, the pair of them. Even in his own intoxicated state Alec could see the girls were totally inebriated. He stared at them, his mouth open in a slight gape. His mam would skin Lillian alive if she came home and found them like this.

Carrie stared back, but in spite of the dawning dismay at the pickle she was in she found herself thinking, oh, but he looks grand in that dark suit and white shirt. He was so handsome, so perfect, she loved him so much. He had to ask her to be his lass one day, he just had to.

'I don't need to ask what you've been up to, do I?' Alec's voice held amusement chiefly, but when he added, 'Mam's going to have your hide for this, Lil, you know that, don't you?' the benign expression on Lillian's face changed to one of fuddled alarm.

'You won't tell, Alec?' Lillian managed to pull herself up and stood swaying slightly, one hand held out in supplication to her brother. 'Please, please, Alec, say you won't.'

'What about all this?' He gestured towards the stained tablecloth and the gin bottle, his gaze moving over Carrie's flushed face as he did so. She was still staring at him, and when he read the look in the deep blue eyes he found himself smiling slightly. So that was the way of it, was it? She was sweet on him. He looked harder at the young girl and found he liked what he saw. Some time in the last weeks and months his sister's little friend had become all grown up. Why hadn't he noticed that before? She was going to be a beauty if he wasn't mistaken, with that russet hair and wonderful creamy skin.

'I'll . . . I'll get out the spare tablecloth an' put this in to

27

soak. If you say you spilt something on it, Mam won't go for you, you know she won't. *Please?*'

Lillian stumbled towards her brother, tripped on the rug and would have gone head first into the range but for his hands shooting out and steadying her. She began to cry maudlin tears. Alec shook his head impatiently. 'All right, all right, cut the blubbering but I shall want payment for this, mind. I've a good few socks ready for darning and a couple of shirts minus buttons, and you know what Mam's like when it comes to mending. Once in a blue moon if we're lucky.'

'I'll do it tomorrow, I promise,' Lillian gabbled emphatically. 'Aw, thanks, man. Thanks, Alec.'

'Get yourself to bed before you break your neck.' He pushed her towards the door. 'I'll see to the cloth before I walk Carrie back, all right?' And then he picked up Lillian's mug, held it to his nose and sniffed. 'By, Lil, this is Gran's brew, isn't it? You've started at the deep end sure enough,' but his eyes were on Carrie as he spoke and he was smiling.

She smiled back, nodding at Lillian as her friend said a subdued goodnight and disappeared, and then watching Alec as he stripped the cloth off the table and took it through to the scullery. He returned a moment later, fetched a new cloth from the dresser and spread it over the oilcloth. 'There.' He grinned down at her and she felt her heart thudding frantically. 'Good as new.'

She had wanted to say she'd help him but the old shyness was rendering her dumb. Pull yourself together, say something intelligent, she told herself frantically. Show him you're not a bairn but as good as all those lasses who set their caps at him. 'I . . . I'm sorry about the cloth. You' – she was going to say you made me jump but changed it to – 'startled me,' thinking it sounded better.

'Did I?' His smile widened, showing white teeth, and she was close enough to see he had a tiny chip on one of the front ones.

Somehow it made him more human, more approachable, and she found herself saying, 'Thank you for not giving us away to your mam.'

'My pleasure.'

Carrie hadn't moved, mainly because she didn't trust her legs to hold her. She had picked up the bottle and the two mugs while Alec changed the cloth, and now she proffered them to him. 'Here. I don't know what you want to do with the bottle.'

He took it from her and shook it, his eyes tight on her face. 'Not much left.' He pulled out the chair next to hers. 'How about we finish it off before I walk you home?'

Walk her home. Alec Sutton was going to walk her home. The words had the magic ring of dreams about them. She stared at him as he sat down and gestured for her to place the mugs on the table. 'I . . . I don't want any more.'

'Course you do.'

As he poured two more measures into the mugs Carrie wanted to make a protest, but the tone of his voice and his manner had been so friendly and warm she didn't like to. She watched him as he drained the contents of his mug but made no attempt to lift her own. This was her moment, her opportunity, and nothing like it would happen again. What could she say, what could she do to make him really notice her?

When he reached out and lifted her chin she felt her heart jump with the thrill of his touch, and then he whispered, 'You're beautiful, lass. Do you know that? Got a lad, have you?'

'No.'

She was looking right into his eyes and it made her dizzy,

along with the wonder bursting from her heart. He was going to kiss her, she knew he was, even before he whispered, 'You should have,' and bent forward, putting his mouth on hers.

He smelt faintly of smoke but overriding this was a nice smell, like the eau de Cologne Renee bought but sharper. She had never been close to a man wearing aftershave before – her father and Billy and the other miners she knew would have scorned what they saw as womanly titivation – and it added to the trembling that was spiralling through her body. His lips were warm and firm, and when he stood up, drawing her with him, she didn't object.

'You're lovely, Carrie.' He was holding her in the circle of his arms now, so close she could feel the pounding of his heart under his shirt, and she felt engulfed in the height and breadth of him. She shivered, and as he stroked her hair from her brow his voice was thick as he murmured, 'You're cold. Let me warm you, lass,' and then he was kissing her again.

Carrie knew she was being kissed, really kissed for the first time in her life, and at first the floating, dizzy feeling was all that registered. It was some moments before she became aware that his hands were moving all over her body and now the kissing was of such an intensity that it frightened her. 'No . . .' She tried to pull away a little. 'Don't, Alec, please. I don't want—' Her breath was cut off by his mouth which had become hard, grinding, and his leg was behind her knees as he twisted his body and brought her falling to the floor with him on top of her.

For his part Alec was conscious of her struggling beneath him and of hands beating against his chest, but the quantity of alcohol in his system and not least Madge Patterson's provocative teasing earlier had inflamed him to the point where he only knew he wanted release from the burning in his groin. He pressed one hand across her mouth and with the other fumbled for the hem of her dress. When it was up round her thighs he wrenched at her knickers with such force that they tore away from one leg.

'It's all right, it's all right, it's all right.'

His voice was like a chant, and in spite of her blind panic and fear Carrie could make no impression against the strength of the hard male body crushing her against the floor.

'It's all right, it's all right, it's all right . . .'

But it wasn't, for she was suddenly pierced through with pain, ravaged by it as he pounded away at her with hoarse groaning until, with one final convulsive thrust, everything became very still.

Carrie wasn't crying, the shock was too great. She lay wide-eyed, staring up at Lillian's mam's whitewashed ceiling, her mind numb but her body hurting. And then, as the head which had dropped to nestle in her shoulder moved, she came to life, pushing at Alec with shaking hands as she tried to hotch back away from him.

He stirred again with a low groan, levering himself up on to his knees to adjust his clothing. When her legs were free of him Carrie rolled over on to her stomach and pulled her dress down. Then she realised she was without her knickers. Oh, God, oh, God, help me. He'd done it to her, Alec Sutton had taken her down. What would her mam and da say?

'Carrie?' It was tentative, but when she scrambled as far away as she could get before she turned to face him, his tone changed. His voice was rough as he said, 'Don't look at me like that, you wanted it same as me.'

She was shaking from head to foot as she sat staring at him,

31

her teeth chattering so much she found it difficult to speak. 'I didn't, you know I didn't.'

'Look, the first time is always . . . Well . . .' He rubbed his hand across his mouth as he got to his feet, glancing down at the torn remnants of her underclothes before he said again, 'You wanted it.'

'Stay away from me.'

The shrillness of her voice as he made a move towards her brought him to a halt, but now there was real aggression in his manner when he ground out, 'Don't come this lark, not with me. You can't lead a man on and then leave him nowhere. Look, no one need know.' He reached down and before she could blink he had thrown her knickers on to the fire where they flared briefly before being consumed by the flames. 'There, it's done with. Let that be an end to it.'

An end to it? He had . . . Had he said an end to it? Was he mad? Carrie struggled to her feet, nausea and dizziness making the room swim. She watched him gather the mugs and gin bottle and disappear into the scullery again.

She was still standing in exactly the same spot when he returned, and as he glanced at her white face and stricken eyes his voice was softer, with a wheedling note. 'Look, it's done now, lass, so don't take on—' And then he froze, his head turning towards the scullery as the sound of voices reached them. 'Quick, out, it's me mam.'

Before she knew it Carrie found herself in the street with the front door closing against her, vaguely aware that he had pushed her out of the house after thrusting her coat into her hands. She stood, swaying slightly and making no attempt to put her coat on in spite of the raw east wind. He'd said she'd led him on, that she'd wanted him to do that to her but she hadn't, she *hadn't*. She stared down the dark street, her eyes

32

dry but burning. She had wanted him to kiss her but not the rest of it, and he must have known. She had fought him, hadn't she, struggled, tried to call out? How could he have imagined she wanted him to do it then?

She began to walk, still holding her coat against her chest. When she reached the junction with Collingwood Street, she left the main road and skirted round to the narrow track running at the back of the houses. She needed to get to her backyard and go to the privy, she told herself numbly, waves of nausea making her feel faint. If she just kept putting one foot in front of the other she could get there and slide the bolt and be safe.

The odd flake of snow was spinning in the icy wind; the biting cold and black night was all part and parcel of the desolation which had claimed her. Her father didn't like her walking the back lane once it was dark, but tonight any shred of nervousness was gone. Nothing could be worse than what had already happened. She stumbled along, and it wasn't until she was almost home that she thought to pull on her coat, shrugging it on with hands that were frozen and had little feeling.

She had only taken one step into the backyard when the sickness claimed her, wave upon wave of retching culminating in an attack of vomiting which left her kneeling on the flagstones utterly spent, tears streaming down her face.

'Carrie? Carrie, lass, get up. Come on.'

When David's voice sounded above her head she made no effort to move, and kept her eyes tightly shut. They would say she was bad now if anyone found out, a loose bit like Eva Barber or Muriel Price who went to pubs together and painted their faces. Only last week she had seen Mrs Gray and Mrs Weathergill from a few doors up spit at Eva as she'd passed them, and when she'd told her mam and da about it over dinner that night, her mam had pursed her lips and shaken her head, saying, 'I've no sympathy for the lass. Anything she gets she's brought on herself and that's a fact. Different lad for every day of the week and staying out all night as often as not. She'll be the death of her poor mother, you mark my words.'

And when Billy had winked at her and said casually, 'Eva's not so bad, I was thinking of asking her out myself,' their mam had rounded on him, her voice tight as she'd said, 'Over my dead body, lad. Over my dead body. You'll have a decent lass, pure, untouched, or she won't be welcome in this house.' Billy had laughed then and patted their mam on the hand. 'Keep your pinny on, I was only funning. I wouldn't touch Eva with a bargepole. Who'd want other men's cast-offs anyway?'

And now, thought Carrie, she was like Eva, defiled, dirty. She could still feel where Alec had touched her, hurt her, and she was all sticky between her legs, and with all that lot in the house she couldn't even have a washdown.

'Carrie, come on, lass, get up out of it, you'll catch your death.' David was kneeling beside her and he reached out to help her up.

Carrie surprised them both by the fierceness with which she said, 'Don't touch me, don't you dare touch me.'

David froze and for a moment there was absolute silence, only the sound of faint laughter and voices from within the house breaking the stillness. 'What's the matter, lass?' He spoke very quietly. 'Someone hurt you?'

Oh, she mustn't let him guess, she mustn't let anyone ever know. She forced herself to stand up, wiping her mouth with the back of her hand. 'I . . . I was silly, it's my own fault. I had a drink, sloe gin, and it's made me feel bad.'

He had risen with her, and now, in the shadowed night, she was aware that he was peering at her and she was glad it was too dark to see clearly. 'Is that all?' he asked quietly after some seconds.

Carrie drew in a deep, shuddering breath. 'Aye, yes.' She pushed her hair back from her face with a shaky hand. 'Isn't that enough?'

David frowned. There was something wrong here, something not quite right. She might have been drinking but . . . 'Look, lass, if there's something else, you can tell me. We're friends, aren't we?' He didn't make the mistake of trying to touch her again.

Carrie nodded slowly, her chin deep into her neck. What would David say if she told him what was in her mind at this moment? That lads, men, were a race apart, possessed of the power to so hurt and destroy that she didn't feel she could ever refer to one as her friend again. 'It's just the drink,' she muttered, willing him to go back into the house or to the privy which he must have been making for. 'That's all.'

David stared at the bowed head and wished he could see her face. She was shivering so violently it was like someone with the ague but she didn't seem to be aware of it. And it was obvious she wanted to be alone. But how could he leave her out here in this state? 'You're cold.' He slipped off his suit jacket and placed it round her shoulders, careful that his hands made no contact with her flesh.

The small act of kindness was nearly Carrie's undoing. She gulped once and then again, her body aching and her heart sore. How could this have happened to her? It was Renee's wedding day, it was supposed to be a happy day, wasn't it? She licked her dry lips, her head pounding, and then visibly flinched as the back door opened. But then her father's voice said, 'Carrie? Is that you? Your mam an' me was wonderin' where you'd got to.'

'Da.'

It was a soft whimper, and immediately the small stocky figure was at her side. 'What is it, lass? What's wrong?'

For a quivering moment she almost blurted out the truth but something outside herself, born of humiliation and shame and guilt, warned, *don't say a word, not a word about Alec. Blame it on the drink. Just the drink.*

'I . . . I feel bad.'

'Bad?'

She reached out to him, clinging like a child to the one man she could trust. 'We . . . it was Granny Sutton's sloe gin. I've been sick.'

She was still trembling violently in spite of David's jacket and she felt her father stiffen, but his voice was matter-of-fact when he said, 'You go in an' lie down, lass, get yerself to bed, eh? That lot in there are makin' moves to go so it won't be long afore it's quiet, an' you'll feel a mite better in the mornin'.'

'Da—'

'Go on, lass, go on.' When she would have said more, Sandy put her gently from him, pushing her towards the back door. 'I'll be in in a minute an' you'll be better in the warm.' He took the jacket off her shoulders and handed it to David without a word.

The door had barely closed on the slender, bowed figure when Sandy ground out, 'I ought to bash your face in, David. She's not sixteen yet an' you're plyin' her with sloe gin? What's your game?'

'What?' David stared at the man he had known and respected all his life and for whom he had genuine affection. He had umpteen uncles on his father's side and several more on his mother's, but he'd always known that if he was in trouble and couldn't get to his da, Sandy McDarmount would be the next best thing. He had been working on the screens – the conveyor belts that sorted the splintered coal and stones from the main coal – for six months before he got to go down the pit, and but for Sandy taking him under his wing that first day he doubted he could have stood it. From the moment the cage had begun its mad descent, tearing faster and faster into the bowels of the earth as though it had gone out of control, he had been scared witless. When the gate of the cage had clashed open with such a bang he'd almost filled his pants, it had been Carrie's father who had guided him along the roadway to his place of work, saying all the right things to a terrified lad of fourteen who had just fully realised he was a hundred-odd fathoms or so beneath the ground. He hadn't known at that point he would have been considered soft if his own father had looked out for him but that it was acceptable for someone else to take a newcomer on. He had just thanked God for the gravelly-voiced, ginger-haired little man staring at him so fiercely now.

With the past in mind, David's voice was even and controlled when he said, 'Hold your horses, man, this is not what you're thinking. Let me explain.'

'Explain be damned! No explainin' would take away what I've seen with me own eyes. That was your jacket round her, wasn't it, eh? An' I don't see no other blighter here with us.'

'Now look—'

'No, *you* look, lad. She's little more than a bairn an' as good as gold, my lass. There's plenty in that street out there' – he thumbed in the direction of the road – 'who are ready and willin' for some sport, but my lass isn't one of them and she's not tasted liquor afore neither. You'd better stay out of my way for a while, I'm tellin' you straight.' And with that Sandy turned and stomped back into the house, ignoring David's appeal for him to stay.

This was rich, this was. David glared after the older man, anger and irritation vying for first place as he pulled on the jacket that had provoked the accusation against him. All he'd done was to try and comfort the lass, and now he was being blamed for it all. Should he follow Sandy into the house and have his say? Pride said yes, reason said no. Carrie's father was upset, and thinking what he did he might well be inclined to act first and ask questions later. It was Walter's wedding day, and any unpleasantness would mar the occasion. No, he would wait until he saw Sandy on the Monday morning shift, by which time Carrie would probably have set her father straight anyway.

After standing for a while longer, David walked out of the backyard into the narrow lane beyond, hands thrust deep into his trouser pockets. He wasn't thinking about Sandy now or the unfairness of what he had been accused of, his thoughts were centred on the young slip of a girl he had loved all his life, or that was what it felt like. He couldn't rid himself of the feeling there had been more to her evident distress than having too much to drink; the way she had gone for him for example, that wasn't the Carrie he knew. *Had* something happened?

His stomach muscles tensed and he halted, oblivious of the snowflakes swirling in the wind. For a moment back there he had thought she was frightened of him, and there had been what he could only describe as a haunted look about her.

He began walking again, the knowledge of his inadequacy to measure up to the occasion that had presented itself rising like bile in his mouth. He had to face it, he was nothing to Carrie McDarmount, nothing beyond a friend and hardly that if the truth be known. Once you got to a certain age it was accepted you didn't have friends among the opposite sex. You were either walking out with a lass or you weren't and there was an end of it. And he very definitely wouldn't be courting Carrie if her reaction to him tonight was anything to go by.

Damn and blast it. He stopped, turning to look back the way he'd come. For two pins he'd go back and have it out with Sandy and to hell with them all.

He could hear old Sep Heslop cleaning out his pigeons on the other side of the wall as he stood hesitating, talking to them as if they were bairns. Lived for his pigeons, did Sep, them and his pipe and baccy. Winter and summer Sep would choose to be out in his backyard with the birds rather than trapped inside with his wife and ten bairns. And there were plenty like Sep if the talk down the pit was anything to go by.

For some reason the thought of the old miner diffused his anger, sadness settling on him instead. He wanted more from marriage than a hot meal on the table when he got home from work and a body beside him in bed. He'd as soon cut his throat and be done with it if he thought he'd have to endure what his da had put up with for years.

He took his cap off and banged it against his leg to clear the snow, ramming it back on his head as he turned and walked on. Maybe it was as well he'd had his answer from Carrie without even having to ask the question. He could start to make plans now, and come spring he'd be ready to move down south or maybe even further afield, America perhaps or New Zealand. His da had a cousin in New Zealand. He could make his fortune and then come back and show Carrie McDarmount what she'd missed out on. That was what he'd do. The world was bigger than Sunderland and there were more fish in the sea than Carrie. Life was what you made it, wasn't it? He repeated this to himself several times before he reached his own backyard, and his face was grim.

Chapter Three

It was at the end of January when the gnawing fear Carrie had been trying to put to the back of her mind ever since the night of Renee's wedding was confirmed.

She had told herself that the non-appearance of her monthly over Christmas was down to the shock of what had occurred, but on the last Saturday in January something happened which made it clear she couldn't pretend to herself everything would return to normal in time. She felt she'd been living in a vacuum the last weeks, making the right responses and striving for normality when in fact she had been screaming inside and terrified she might bump into Alec Sutton.

She had blamed her early nights and lack of desire to go out with Lillian in the evenings on the after-effects of the chill which had confined her to bed for a few days after her walk home in just a thin dress, but she knew she couldn't keep that up for ever. And so, when Lillian offered to treat her to a birthday tea at Binns in Bishopwearmouth, Carrie had forced herself to smile and sound grateful.

The two girls had a lovely cream tea in Binns restaurant. Lillian presented her friend with a card and little brooch in the shape of a C, before they left to spend time window-shopping in the big shops in the High Street. The night was bitterly cold, made bleaker by thick damp fog which turned the street lights into hazy gold circles and made visibility poor, but they'd promised to do some shopping in the Old Market for their mothers so they were waiting until the meat and fruit came down in price. Lillian had a list of items Olive Sutton had asked for, but Joan McDarmount had just whispered to her daughter, 'Anything you can get real cheap will do, hinny. You understand?'

Carrie had understood. With Renee's wage gone, and her da off sick due to a runaway tub which had gone over his foot, crushing it so the blood had seeped out between the lace holes of his boot, every farthing she and Billy brought in was precious. Her mother had kept a clooty bag on her da's bad foot for days, but the flour bag filled with hot bran was taking the swelling down only slowly. Her da still couldn't force his boot over the black bloated flesh even though he'd tried until the sweat had poured off him.

The two girls took their time wandering through the Old Market, standing listening to the barrel organ for a while and sharing a bag of hot chestnuts cooked in a brazier coke fire with the little monkey dressed in a red suit and tiny pillar-box hat. Some of the stalls had paraffin heaters which smelled homely and warmed the air under the covered roof, and the sweet stalls gave off sugary, burned-toffee odours along with the sharper scents of aniseed and winter mixture. There was masses to see as always and the stallholders, most of whom Carrie knew, were as good as any music hall act, especially when they were engaged in shouting rude remarks about each other in good-natured rivalry.

Carrie was tired, she seemed to have been constantly tired the last week or two, but for the first time since Alec's attack she found herself relaxing into all the hustle and bustle going on around her. Prices were coming down at last, and soon she would be able to purchase a bag of broken kippers and some fat bacon bits she had her eye on, along with a couple of bags of bruised fruit and browning vegetables which went for next to nothing as the stallholders cleared their stock for the weekend.

Lillian was buying a pound of sausages and pork ends from Soldier Sammy's meat stall – so called because the ancient warrior was a veteran of the Boer wars as the row of medals pinned to his green, ragged jacket proclaimed – and Carrie stood a few feet away, listening to Sammy's ongoing repartee with his rival, Hattie, who kept a pease pudding and faggot stall.

'I've heard there's a few more cats missin' round your way then, Hattie, m'dear. Nice flavour to them faggots is there?'

Hattie, who was as round as she was tall and who had arms the size of a circus strongman's, pulled the man's cap she always wore more firmly down on her springy grey hair and glared Sammy's way. 'Less of your lip, Sammy, else you might find it's twice the size.'

'How d'ye mean, lass?'

'Don't you come the lass line with me, not after your 'sinuations about me faggots.'

'Ee, lass, lass, you cut me to the quick.'

'Aye, an' I might finish with that an' all.'

Customers were handing over plates and dishes for them to be filled with hot food for their suppers, and Carrie was smiling along with everyone else at the entertainment when a sudden waft of cooking from Hattie's stall came her way. Her stomach turned over and the queasiness that had attacked her at odd times the last few days returned with renewed vigour.

She just had time to call to Lillian that she had to get some fresh air and dive out into Coronation Street before the nausea

43

overcame her and she lost the cream tea. When Lillian came hurrying to find her she was leaning against the wall, wiping her mouth with her handkerchief.

'You all right, Carrie?' It was a silly question and Lillian must have realised this. Her next comment was, 'You look like death warmed up, lass.' It was meant to be comforting, as was the patting on Carrie's shoulder. 'You should have said before if you felt bad. We needn't have stayed this long.'

'I . . . I wanted to. To get a few bits for Mam.'

Lillian nodded. She knew the situation in Carrie's home and it was typical of her now when she said, 'You tell me what you want and I'll nip back in. I've got most of what Mam wanted now anyway. I'll make sure I get it at the right price an' all.' She stepped back a pace from Carrie as she spoke, adding, 'By, you're as white as a sheet but it can't be what we had at Binns 'cos I feel fine. You've been all out of sorts since Christmas, haven't you?'

'Aye, I have.'

'You ought to go and see old Ma Bradley, she'll put you to rights. Remember when I had the bellyache for weeks and weeks and she made up one of her potions? Wild foxgloves and all sorts went in it, so me mam said, but it worked, and it didn't taste too bad neither. Go and see her, Carrie. Me mam says Ma Bradley's better than any doctor. Seven and six for them to walk through the door and a couple of bob for any medicine they dish out, but Ma Bradley's happy if you slip her sixpence. Everyone swears by her.'

Carrie nodded. She had missed her period and she knew what that meant; she couldn't ignore the truth any longer. When you stopped having your period you were going to have a bairn and that's why she had felt ill lately. All the potions in the world wouldn't cure what she had. She looked into Lillian's

44

concerned face and said quietly, 'I'll go and see her in the next day or two.'

'Promise?'

'Aye, aye, I promise.'

Once she was alone again she stood quite still with her back pressed against the wall and one hand to her throat. What was she going to do? Her heart was thumping fit to burst. She couldn't just carry on, she had to *do* something. And the answer came so clearly she suddenly realised she had been anticipating this moment for days, ever since the nausea had begun to make itself felt. *She had to tell Alec.*

Carrie shut her eyes tightly, taking a gulp of the soupy grey air. If she told Alec she was having a bairn he would have to marry her, wouldn't he? She began to tremble, the hand clutching her throat working convulsively and the other dropping across her stomach before she brought it sharply away, her whole being recoiling from the thing growing inside her. And that was how she thought of it, as a thing, something dirty and horrible brought about by an act that had been dirty and horrible. How could she ever have thought she loved Alec Sutton? She must have been stark staring mad.

The chill of the foggy air made her shiver but she felt too desolate to go back into the warm womb of the market. She had to tell him, there was nothing else she could do, and if they were married straight away no one would know about the bairn. Folk would just think it had come early and even if they suspected something they wouldn't know for sure. But what would her mam and da say? She'd have to tell them. She moaned, deep in her throat. And if she was married she'd have to lie with Alec Sutton, let him . . . She swung her head to the side. She couldn't, she wouldn't be able to bear it, she'd rather kill herself. No, no, she wouldn't. She

45

lifted her head, gazing up into the opaque sky as her thoughts tumbled on.

She was scared by the thought of dying but she didn't want to live either, not with this thing growing inside her and the thought of Alec being able to touch her whenever he wanted. Oh, if only she could just go back to Renee's wedding day, to the person she had been then. That girl seemed like a stranger now. And whatever happened in the future, there would be some who would whisper she was a trollop who had gone to the altar with her belly full, even if they didn't say it to her face.

When Lillian bounced out of the market a few minutes later, pleased as Punch by her bargaining prowess, she was slightly aggrieved at the lack of enthusiasm when she showed Carrie her purchases. Her tone reflected this when she said, 'Look at these veg, lass, they're still as good as when they were pulled, and there's enough bacon bits here to make a couple of pans of broth and then some. Old Jimmy threw in the pig's trotters for nowt an' all, and they're big ones.'

'Thanks.' Carrie took the bags and her change. 'Thanks very much.'

Somewhat deflated, Lillian reminded herself that her friend was middling – you only had to look at Carrie to see that. Silently the two girls walked to the tram stop. This made it all the more surprising to Lillian when, having alighted from the tram in Cornhill Terrace before walking to the bottom of James Armitage Street, Carrie continued past her own house, saying, 'I'll just pop in and thank your mam and da for their card before I go in.'

'What?' Lillian had stopped at Carrie's doorstep and she had to hurry to catch up. 'Ee, you don't have to do that, lass, not with you feeling bad. They won't expect it . . .' Her voice trailed away. Carrie wasn't listening.

What was she going to say to Alec if he was at home? And how could she bear to be in that room where it had happened? Carrie's mind went blank for a moment. When the blankness passed the first question she asked herself was, can you do this without letting Mrs Sutton suspect something's wrong? She answered this immediately. What did Mrs Sutton matter now anyway? She couldn't let more time go by, not now, not after tonight. Something had changed as she'd stood outside the market and the last vestige of hope had gone. She had to face this, she couldn't pretend any more. And part of facing it was acknowledging that Alec Sutton didn't care a fig about her; he hadn't even tried to see her again or sent her a note asking if she was all right . . .

Carrie gazed ahead down the dark terraced street, the bricks stained by smoke and grime from the collieries and factories and hundreds of house chimneys, and her face was grim.

If he was in she would ask him, very politely, if she could have a word with him outside, and his mam could think what she liked. If he wasn't home she would leave as soon as she could and wait on the corner of Collingwood Street. That way she would see him from whichever direction he came. But whatever, she *would* tell him. He might not care about her, and she felt she hated him, but with a bairn on the way everything was different.

Alec wasn't in. When the two girls entered the aseptic environment Lillian called home, only Olive Sutton looked up from where she stood ironing, and again the smell of bleach was overpowering. She ignored Carrie, looking directly at her daughter as she said, 'What time do you call this, miss?'

'We waited at the market, you know, for stuff to come down.'

'No need for that, we can afford to pay our way, I'm sure.'

Lillian's mam was being nasty. Carrie stared into the sharp-featured face in front of her. Mrs Sutton knew full well her da was off sick and money was short and this was her way of rubbing it in. For a second the churning feeling the older woman's antagonism always wrought in her was paramount, and then Carrie's chin lifted and she mentally braced herself to speak to Olive.

'I came to say thank you for the birthday card, Mrs Sutton,' she said flatly.

Aye, and pigs might fly. Olive Sutton stared at the girl who had ceased to be merely an irritant years ago and was now a constant thorn in her flesh. Thought she was the cat's whiskers, did Carrie McDarmount, and no doubt the chit had been hoping Alec or David would be at home. Man mad, like her sister, with the same come hither look in her eyes, but she would see her lads rot in hell before she let another of them marry a piece of McDarmount scum. But she knew how to get under this one's skin.

Olive smiled thinly. 'And how's your da's foot, Carrie? Surely he's back at work now.'

'Not yet, Mrs Sutton, no.'

'Dear, dear. How long does it take for a bit of bruising to go down?' There was no mistaking her meaning, and Olive noted the sudden flush in Carrie's cheeks with some satisfaction. She'd bet her last farthing that the only thing wrong with Sandy now was his back – it stuck to the bed of a morning. But this dimwit standing in front of her, blue eyes ablaze, would never see it. The Pope, Archbishop and King all rolled into one, Sandy McDarmount was, according to Carrie.

'My da can't even get his boot on yet and he can hardly go down the pit barefoot.' Carrie's tone was such that if Lillian had spoken in the same manner Olive wouldn't have been able to keep her hands off her. As it was, Olive contented herself with glaring her dislike before turning her gaze on her daughter. 'You, get yourself to bed, and don't think you're going to the social after church tomorrow neither.'

'Aw, Mam.'

'And don't "aw, Mam" me, madam, not unless you want to feel my hand across your mouth.'

Carrie knew she had better go. Mrs Sutton was just going to take it out on Lillian like she always did, and she didn't want to get her friend into any more trouble. She turned on her heel, only to become still as Mr Sutton walked in through the scullery, with Alec and David behind him.

It had been bad enough to be in the room that carried memories of such abasement and Carrie had been stifling her panic through the altercation with Lillian's mother. Now, as her gaze was drawn to Alec's face, she became rigid with burning humiliation and bitterness. He looked the same lad she had always secretly loved and admired – handsome, smiling, carefree. How could he look the same after what he'd done to her? She stared at him but he was looking past her at his mother, and after a short, tense silence it was Mr Sutton who said, 'What's going on?' and his eyes, like Alec's, were on Olive.

'Going on?' Olive's voice was sharp. 'Nothing's "going on" as you put it. I've just told your daughter I won't have her coming in at this time of night, that's all.' She didn't add, not that it's any of your business, but the tone of her voice said it for her.

Ned continued to stare at his wife, his words slow, deep and flat when he said, 'I thought she was doing some shopping for you.'

'So? That doesn't give her leave to stay out all hours, does it?' And then, as Olive's gaze moved past her husband to the two young men standing behind him, she said even more sharply, 'I thought you and David were attending some union meeting the night.'

'We met in the street a couple of minutes ago, Mam.' It was Alec who spoke and his tone was one of appeasement. 'I've been in town like I told you.'

'Right.' Olive nodded, her face softening as she looked at him.

Carrie sensed immediately this explanation had pleased Mrs Sutton although she didn't understand why. It seemed to infuriate Mr Sutton, however, who muttered, 'Aye, wouldn't be seen dead with us, would you, lad?' He took a deep breath but whatever he had been about to say was pre-empted by Lillian.

'We went to the Old Market, Da,' she chimed in, 'me an' Carrie, and waited till they started clearing up. That's why we're late.'

Lillian's face was trying to convey what she didn't like to put into words, and now Carrie said quietly, 'It was my fault, Mr Sutton. I wanted to wait.'

'Oh aye?' Ned nodded at her, his face smiling even as he thought, of course, that's what this is all about. Olive's turning the knife as only she can. By, he'd swing for her one day, he would straight. 'Makes sense to me, lass. I like a woman who's canny with her money.'

She had to say something to Alec right now. Carrie wanted to put her hand over her heart which was beating so violently she was sure they would all notice, but before she could steel herself to look at him again, he spoke, a lilting note in his voice.

'Want to know how my bit of business in town went then,

Mam?' And before Olive could respond, he continued, his gaze sweeping over all of them as he thrust his thumbs into the pockets of his waistcoat, rocking on his heels with mock dignity. 'You are now looking at the fiancé of Miss Margaret Reed, spinster of this parish, although not for much longer if I have my way.'

'You asked her?' Olive's face was alight, her voice high.

'Aye, I asked her.' Alec was laughing. 'After I'd spoken to Mr Reed in his study, all very formal and above board.'

Miss Margaret Reed. Alec worked for a Mr Reed who owned a string of gents' outfitters throughout Monkwearmouth and Bishopwearmouth. Only a few months ago Olive had been full of how he had been promoted to manager of his particular shop . . . Carrie's mind was working after a fashion but curiously she didn't seem able to feel anything. She knew she was staring at Alec but he was looking everywhere but at her. It struck her he hadn't once looked her full in the face since he had walked into the house.

'And how was he, Mr Reed? When you asked him like?' Olive's voice was bright, eager. It didn't sound like her at all.

'Said he'd been expecting it. He thought Margaret had made her choice some time ago, and of course they've always made me very welcome at the house.'

It didn't occur to Carrie until some time later that none of the others present had said a word, and such was her state of mind she couldn't have said how Mr Sutton and his other two children had taken Alec's news. She felt strange, tingly, but when she moved, her feet seemed like lead and her head dizzily light. *You can't pass out, not here, not with Alec Sutton looking on.* 'I have to go.' Her lips felt numb as she spoke.

'You all right, Carrie?' It was David who spoke, and when she looked at him she saw his eyes were tight on her face.

'No, she's not,' Lillian answered her brother. 'She felt bad at the market, didn't you, Carrie? That's one of the reasons we were late back,' she added with a sidelong glance at her mother.

'Bad?'

'It was nothing.' Carrie brushed David's concern aside with a flap of her hand. 'And I really do have to go.'

'Make sure you tell your mam there's going to be another wedding soon, and a right grand one I don't doubt.' Olive made no effort to keep the satisfaction out of her voice. Walter might have married beneath him, but Alec had more than made up for his brother's shortcomings. Alec and Mr Reed's daughter! This would show the McDarmounts and some others hereabouts she could name that the Suttons were a cut above. By, it would.

Carrie didn't acknowledge Olive's words but turned dumbly away, opening the front door and stepping out into the foggy street without answering Mr Sutton's subdued, 'Ta, ta, lass.' Blindly, she began to walk, but instead of stopping when she reached her own doorstep she passed the house without a turn of her head, continuing into Cornhill Terrace and then on to Southwick Road.

Alec was going to be married. He had been courting Miss Margaret Reed and now he was going to be married. The refrain was beating in her brain like a drum.

She passed the smithy on the corner of Southwick Road and then turned into North Bridge Street, the shopping bags still clasped in her hands and her head bent low into her neck. She hadn't made a conscious decision about where she was going and what she was going to do, but her steps were steady as she walked towards Wearmouth Bridge.

There were few people about, the thick fog had seen to that, and when eventually she reached the bridge she continued along the pavement into the middle of the massive structure. She had seen someone fall from here some years ago when she had been going home with her da after watching the East End carnival procession. She had been tired and her da had been carrying her on his shoulders, so she had seen the man jump before her da did. There had been shouts and cries and people running over to peer into the water, but her da hadn't let Renee or Billy join them. He had hurried them past the spot so fast her sister and brother had been crying that their legs hurt before they reached Southwick Road. She had cried for the poor man though.

From her vantage point high above the crowd she had seen his face quite clearly in the moment before he had launched himself into the river, and his expression had returned to haunt her in nightmares for months. Her mam and da had tried to soothe her, telling her it had been an accident and that the man had probably been rescued by one of the boats frequenting the water at the time, but she had heard them talking when they'd thought her asleep the following night on the evening the *Echo* had published an account of the suicide.

'Poor so-an'-so,' her da had said. 'Lloyd George might have talked about a land fit for heroes, but what did that poor blighter find waitin' for him when he comes home minus an arm? That he's straight into the dole queue, that's what, while them as sat nice an' comfy at home durin' the war makin' money get knighted. Damn profiteers! The last straw was when his wife an' kids went into the workhouse, accordin' to the paper.'

She'd heard her mother murmur something, and then her da had replied, 'Nor could I stand it, lass, I tell you straight. Seems he was a stretcher-bearer an' lost the arm savin' I don't know how many; got the Military Medal, his wife says. Takes a lot of them things to fill your bairns' bellies an' keep warm though, don't it?'

At the time, despite the awful circumstances of the ex-soldier, she'd wondered how anyone could come to a point in their life where they would actually choose to kill themselves; to decide to end their life before their allotted span.

She leaned over the iron railings, staring down into the curling misty darkness below.

And now she knew.

The bags were heavy and she drew back, placing them at her feet before once again leaning against the barrier. It wasn't very long ago that she'd been happy. Sometimes she'd felt so filled with joy and happiness – like when she had been in the fields Carley way and a heavy frost had draped a blanket of diamond dust over the hedgerows, or when the sun had set in a sea of red and gold and purple. She'd felt then that she would burst if she didn't express the feeling inside her. She would never feel like that again.

She couldn't see the water in the blackness of the night but she could picture it. She shivered. Did it hurt to drown? Well, she'd soon know, wouldn't she?

'You ailin', hinny?'

A hand tapped her on the shoulder and Carrie jumped violently. She swung round to find one of the fishwives who frequented the dock areas after dark peering at her. The woman's lined face was painted and her head uncovered, showing the brassy colour of her hair, but the eyes in the world-weary face were kind. It was to these Carrie replied. 'No, no. I . . . I'm just having a rest. My . . . bags are heavy.' She gestured to the shopping at her feet.

'Aye, well, I wouldn't tarry too long, a nice little lass like you. There's all sorts about this time of night. You get yerself home.'

A nice little lass like her. Carrie stood staring at the woman

54

but for the life of her she couldn't speak. Something of what she was feeling must have shown on her face, because after a long moment the fishwife said softly, 'There's nowt so bad you can't deal with it, hinny, an' I should know. The sea's taken everyone I ever loved, me man an' me three lads, but you can't let it beat you, not in here, see?' She placed her hand on her shawl above her heart. 'You have to fight back, that's the nature of things.'

'And if you can't?'

'Oh you can, hinny, you can. You take life by the scruff of its neck an' bash its face in, it's the only way.' There was another pause and then the woman said, even more softly, 'Is it a bairn, lass? You in the family way?'

And, surprisingly, Carrie found she could tell this stranger quite easily. She nodded, saying, 'It was only the once, I didn't . . . I mean I hadn't done it before.'

'Once is all it takes, lass, for some. The lad, won't he marry you?'

'I was going to tell him tonight but when I was at his house he told his family he'd asked someone else to marry him. The thing is, there was a wedding and I had too much to drink and we just . . .' Her voice trailed away.

The woman showed she understood when she said, 'The swine, takin' advantage of a bit bairn. How old is he, lass?'

'Twenty.'

'An' you?'

'Sixteen. It's my birthday today.'

'Lass, you tell him what's what, betrothal or not, an' if he still drags his heels, you get your da to sort it. You do have a da?'

Carrie nodded.

'Any brothers?'

She nodded again.

'Then you do what I say an' keep away from the river an' all. If anyone should be standin' here, it's that swine, right?'

Carrie's eyes opened wide. The woman knew. After gulping hard, Carrie reached out her hand and touched the woman's arm. 'Thank you,' she said quietly. 'You've been very kind.'

'Aye, well, there's plenty who'd say someone like you shouldn't be seen talkin' to someone like me, an' perhaps they're right at that. Now you get yerself home an' come mornin' you have it out with this lad. Here.' She bent down, lifted the bags of shopping and passed them to Carrie. 'Don't you worry, hinny, it'll all work out right in the end.'

No, no, it wouldn't. Even as she smiled and then turned and walked away from her good Samaritan, Carrie knew she wasn't going to tell Alec. He didn't care about her. That being the case she wasn't going to force him to marry her. And she couldn't let her da know either. He'd beat the living daylights out of Alec, she knew he would, and with Renee married to Walter and Mr Sutton and the others working with her da and Billy down the pit, there would be ructions. She had to get away, but how, and where to? Where could she go so that the stigma of her having a bairn wouldn't touch her family? Down south? Perhaps a workhouse down south and then once the baby was born she could leave it there and escape, and no one here need ever know.

She walked on, her head whirling with one impossible plan after another, but in the few moments before her father hailed her – having come to look for her and being half out of his mind with worry due to the lateness of the hour – Carrie realised that although nothing had changed, she wouldn't think about the river again. Added to which, now she knew she wasn't going to marry Alec Sutton and let him touch her and use her like he had the night of Renee's wedding, she was glad. And that might be barmy, she admitted silently, her chin rising a notch, but whatever, she *was* glad. Seeing him again had made her feel sick to her stomach.

Chapter Four

'So, you've got what you always wanted then?'

The door had hardly closed behind Carrie when Ned spoke, his brown eyes narrowed as he stared into Alec's face.

'What does that mean?'

'You know what it means, lad. You'll be doin' right well for yourself with Reed's lass an' her the only one. Mind, I dare say that thought's crossed your mind an' all.'

'You saying I'm only marrying her for the money?'

'Well, doesn't this take the biscuit!' Olive now joined in the fray, her voice vicious. 'Any other man would be congratulating his son on making such a match, but you!'

'Aye, me.' Ned glared at his wife. 'The common workin' man, the pit yakker, who's put clothes on your back an' food in your belly for donkey's years.'

'And I'm supposed to be grateful, is that it?' Olive's thin eyebrows rose. 'It's no more and no less than what any man should do for his family. It's your duty.'

'Don't talk to me about duty, not you.' Ned's voice was bitter. 'Not after the dance you've led me over the years. Nothin' has been good enough for you, has it? An' you've done all you can to make him' – he jerked his thumb at Alec – 'as connivin' as you. Pushin' him, always pushin' him since he was at the breast. By, I've even had it in me to feel sorry for the poor blighter at times. You convinced him he was too good to go down the pit afore he could walk, an' everythin' that's followed can be laid at your door.'

'Is that so? Then it's all credit to me, Ned Sutton, that one of your lads is in a good job with prospects and promised to the boss's daughter. Is that what you're saying?'

'I'm *sayin'* he's put out a line an' reeled in that poor lass like you did me twenty-three years ago, an' with about as much feelin' an' all. An' if history repeats itself her life will be a livin' hell.'

There was no sound in the sitting room now. Lillian was still standing exactly where she had been when Carrie had left, and Alec and David were either side of the range, Alec near his mother and David just behind his father.

The noise of Ned's teeth grinding broke the silence, and in the seconds before he turned and stomped out of the room, all three children looked from one parent to the other without speaking. The back door banging brought Olive to life. She fairly leaped into the scullery, wrenching the door open and yelling into the yard, 'Aye, you go! And I'm bolting the door behind you so think on.'

'You're not, Mam.' David's voice came from deep within his throat and in any other circumstances the look of amazement on his mother's face would have struck him as comical. He shouldered her out of the way, stepping into the yard.

'*What did you say?*'

'I said you'll leave this door alone till we get back, whatever time that might be.'

'Why, you—' Olive's rage choked her, causing her to take a pull of air before she bit out, 'You'd take his part against me?'

David made no direct answer to this. Instead he said, 'I'm

60

warning you, Mam, if it's locked I'll break it down, and damn the neighbours,' before he took off after his father at a run.

Olive stood by the open door for some moments before she closed it and walked back into the living room, her face hot with temper. She looked first at Lillian, who immediately lowered her gaze to the flagstones at her feet, and then Alec. 'You heard what your brother said? *Him* warning *me*? The ungrateful little scut! I've worked my fingers to the bone for years and that's all the thanks I get. Well, I know how things stand with him now, don't I? He's nailed his colours very firmly to the mast. I shan't forget this night.'

'Mam, Mam, don't upset yourself.' Alec's voice was soothing and he put an arm round the stiff figure of his mother. 'Don't let either of them, David or Da, spoil my news, eh? Come on. To hell with what they think anyway. You know Da's never liked it because I wouldn't follow him blindly down the pit like the others, and as for David, he's just plain jealous. Mr Reed's daughter is a catch and he knows it. But they don't matter, neither of 'em, not to us. They never have, now have they?' He gave his mother a comforting little squeeze.

'The years I've done without myself and put you bairns first.' It was plaintive.

'I know, Mam, I know.' Alec led his mother across to the table, pulled out one of the chairs and pushed her down on to it. 'I'll make us a nice cup of tea and while it's mashing I'll tell you what Margaret's mother wants for the wedding, shall I? She's set her heart on a do at the Grand and no expense spared. What do you think of that?'

'The Grand?' Olive was smiling again. 'Oh, lad.' She caught hold of her son's hand, beaming up at him, and neither of them noticed when Lillian left the room.

*   *   *

61

'Tell me again what she said, and word for word, mind, from the time you caught sight of her in North Bridge Street.'

'For cryin' out loud, woman.' Sandy twisted restlessly in the bed but his voice held no real irritation. The truth of the matter was that he was worried sick himself, he admitted silently. His lass hadn't been right since Christmas, all white and wan looking, and he could swear she was thinner than ever. The East End was still a hotbed of consumption and other things, and with that damn firework factory being located so close to the docks . . . 'You noticed her coughin' at all?' he asked his wife abruptly, frightening Joan to death in the process.

'Coughing? Oh, Sandy! Our Carrie? You don't think . . .' Joan sat bolt upright in bed, one hand clutching the neck of her faded red flannel nightgown.

'Lie down, woman, you've pulled all the covers off, an' no, I don't think! I was just askin', that's all.'

Joan slid down beside him again, her cold feet automatically finding the warmth of his body which was better than any stone water bottle. Although the room was in total blackness she knew he was rubbing his hand round his face, something he did when he was troubled. She pressed closer to him, one arm round his wide thick chest. 'What did she say?' she asked again.

'I've *told* you.' And then, when Joan said nothing, he sighed. 'She was walkin' steadily, not hurryin', just steady like, an' I hailed her an' asked her what the hell she was playin' at, worryin' us both to death. An' she said she'd had to wait longer than she thought at the market for the sell-offs. I asked where Lillian was an' she said she'd made her go home 'cos of her mam bein' liable to play up if the lass was late. I said you were fair out of your mind an' she said she was sorry but she wanted to get the best prices she could, an' then she went for me for comin' out to look for her with me foot bein' bad.'

'How does it feel now?' Joan asked softly. He'd insisted on going himself even though it had taken him a full minute to force his boot on and there had been no question of lacing it up.

Again she felt, rather than saw, the irritated flap of his hand. There was silence for a moment and then Sandy said, 'You'll have to talk to her the morrer an' get to the bottom of it.'

'I've tried, you know I have.'

'Aye, I know, lass, I know, but we can't carry on like this.'

Joan nodded, murmuring, 'Aye, all right.'

His arm came round her and he pulled her close into his side. 'Now you get to sleep, lass, an' don't worry, all right? I'm not havin' you make yourself bad over this. Whatever's wrong with the bairn I'll sort it.'

Joan made no answer to this, but she reached up and kissed the stubbly square jaw before lying quietly again.

Don't worry, he said, and there was him beside himself. There had been plenty who'd said she could do better than Sandy McDarmount when she'd started walking out with him – her own mam and da included – but none of them saw the man she knew.

True, she'd come near to braining him with the frying pan on occasion when he was well-oiled and playing the goat, but he wasn't a drinker like some she could name. The trouble was, Sandy only had to have a pint or two to be falling over and the drink always made him silly.

She knew plenty who could sit down and drink all night and then get up and walk out of the door as though they'd been supping water, or others who regularly got so drunk they couldn't speak. They'd stagger home, flopping down on to the hearth, there to sleep right through until the buzzer sounded for the next shift, often with their bairns stepping over them where they lay. Nothing was said about them of course, because 'they could hold their drink'. Her lip curled in the darkness. How she hated that phrase. A man could come home and knock ten bells out of his wife and bairns, but because he hadn't made a fool of himself outside, that was all right. Well, she wouldn't swap her man, not for all the tea in China she wouldn't. He was all heart, was Sandy, in spite of playing devil's faggarties at times.

She'd seen him give his last bit of keepy-back money he'd earmarked for baccy to the ex-soldiers who'd been too badly injured to get a job after the war, and who came round the doors selling bobbins of thread and bootlaces. And only she knew how it affected him when he recognised one of the blind ones who walked up and down queues playing battered old fiddles or mouth organs as ex-comrades from his early days down the pit, along with the ones with no legs who sat on mucky pavements outside the theatres, drawing pictures of animals and birds and scenes from the Bible with chalk.

Sandy stirred beside her. 'You reckon our Renee might wheedle it out of the bairn if you have no joy?'

'Renee?' Joan blinked, striving to keep her voice matter-of-fact when she said, 'She might. Aye, she might at that. I'll put it to her the morrer if I get nowhere.' By, he must be worried to suggest bringing Renee in, normally the mere name of their eldest was like a red flag to a bull, Joan thought, her brow wrinkling in the darkness.

And it was this last which guaranteed she lay awake with her mind buzzing until dawn was breaking.

At the other end of the street, David, too, was enduring a sleepless night. Strangely, it wasn't the fact that he'd walked the streets with his father for over two hours before he could persuade him to return home which was now keeping him tossing and turning, or that Alec had still been awake when he'd entered the bedroom he shared with his brother, and in the resulting row – albeit in low, hushed voices – they'd both said unforgivable things. Rather it was the memory of how Carrie had looked in the few brief minutes before she'd left that had really disturbed him.

He hadn't seen her since the night of the wedding, and there had been little of the laughing-eyed, high-spirited girl he'd known all his life in the white-faced figure standing so quietly in the sitting room. Even allowing for his mother's barbed tongue and what might have gone on before he and his father and Alec had entered the house, his gut feeling was that something was terribly wrong with the lass.

His heart was thumping against his ribs, causing his breath to catch in his throat as yet again – as he'd done hundreds of times in the last weeks – he grappled with the events of that night before Christmas. He was certain now that something major had happened to Carrie. He would make sure he had a word with Lillian tomorrow before she left for church with his mother and find out exactly what had occurred at the market. His sister had spoken of Carrie being bad, but that could mean anything. He might even accompany the women to church, depending on what Lillian revealed, even though once he had started work he, like his father and brothers, only attended Holy Trinity on high days and holidays. But Carrie would be there, and it might be the best chance he'd have to take her aside for a minute or two.

A thought was hammering at the edge of his mind, a possibility he'd kept at bay by sheer willpower the last weeks because to give it free rein was unbearable. Now, as his muscles tightened in his limbs, so taut he could feel cramp beginning to work in one leg, he forced himself to relax. He loosened his joints one by one and breathed deeply, emptying his mind of everything but the physical state of his body.

It was proving to be a long night . . .

Chapter Five

It was beginning to snow as David stood outside Holy Trinity church the next morning, the flakes of white sharp in the keen north-east wind and the ground frozen rock hard beneath his feet. He could see Carrie some yards away standing with her mother and the twins, but as convention demanded he was in a group of men which included her father and brother, and the subject of conversation was the usual one – that of the anticipated fight involving the unions against the government and the coal-owners.

David had intended to walk past the men as he exited the church but Sandy had caught his arm, drawing him into the circle. After Carrie had told her father that he had had nothing to do with getting her drunk on sloe gin the day of Walter and Renee's wedding, Sandy had come to him cap in hand, and ever since had been at pains to make sure their relationship was back on its old comfortable footing. It was proving an irritant.

'I tell you, lads, if the government thought they could get away with passin' a law to prevent workin' men an' women gettin' educated an' thinkin' for themselves, they would,' Sandy was saying militantly. 'What say you, David?'

David nodded perfunctorily. If Carrie moved away from her mam, even for a minute, he'd go over.

'The owners have made up their minds to crack down on us:

the writin's been on the wall for years. With them so-an'-so's in Japan an' America an' the like producin' cheaper than us, our industries should have pulled their finger out an' come up with better or different, but what have they done? Gone on in the same way but demandin' we accept reduced wages an' increased hours so their profits aren't cut, an' safety is their last consideration. Luxury, that's become.'

'Aye, you're right there, man.' Another miner joined in, his rough-hewn, pockmarked face red with indignation. 'An' you say a word out of turn, just a word, an' they label us the "new red threat" an' "worse than the Hun". Lost a brother an' two of me lads in the last war, an' me leg's still peppered with bits of shrapnel where I copped it afore they brought me back to work the pit again, an' they dare call me a traitor to me country.'

'There'll be a fight come May, you mark my words, an' that Baldwin sittin' there like butter wouldn't melt in his mouth, an' the other 'un, Churchill, with cigars the size of a bazooka stickin' out of his gob, they'll both be at the front of it. Nowt but music hall acts, the pair of 'em.'

'Aye, but acts with the power to bring Britain to its knees, man. Don't forget that. Britain an' us too, I reckon.'

'What?'

The chorus of voices that greeted this last declaration suggested it was not a popular one, and in the general hubbub that resulted, which included phrases such as 'You're a bloomin' Jonah if ever there was one' and 'Strikes me you'd better make up yer mind whose side you're on, man', David made his escape.

Carrie had her back to him as he approached, but Joan McDarmount caught his eye and smiled at him, although he was too worked up to respond with more than a twitch of his mouth. 'Carrie?' He touched her lightly on the shoulder. 'Could I have a word?'

Perhaps because of the mental battle he'd had with himself all through the service which had left him thinking he didn't know which end of him was up, his voice sounded abrupt, even harsh, and as Carrie turned he saw that her expression was apprehensive. 'Hello, David.' It was low. 'I . . . I've been meaning to have a word with you. To apologise for how I was and my da getting the wrong end of the stick.'

Aw hell, she thought he was being prickly, that he'd come to get his pound of flesh for that night. He felt himself flush, the colour suffusing his face. This was off to a bright start. 'Forget it, that's not what I want to talk to you about.' And yet it was – the circumstances which had led up to him finding her in the yard anyway. The thought threw him; it wasn't going at all as he'd planned.

Carrie's mother was still standing by although she was tied up with the twins who were finding it hard to stand still for a few minutes, and now it came to him that he couldn't do this in front of inquisitive eyes and flapping ears. He had to get Carrie alone, it was the only way they could both talk frankly, and damn what anyone thought.

Carrie was smiling uncertainly although he noticed it didn't touch her eyes. 'Well, I'm sorry anyway. You were only being kind and I jumped down your—'

'Carrie, I need to talk to you privately. Can I walk you back home?' Her eyes widened momentarily as he interrupted her, and when she didn't answer, he said, his voice as low as hers had been but the tone urgent, 'Please? It's important.'

For a second he thought she was going to refuse. Then she shrugged her shoulders slightly and nodded. Turning to her mother she raised her voice to make herself heard above the twins who were now squabbling about something or other. 'Mam, I'm cold. David's going to walk me back.'

'Aye, all right, lass.' Joan smiled ruefully at the pair of them. 'Looks like the men'll be a little while yet. Why they have to start again on a Sunday is beyond me. You'd have thought they get enough union talk an' such of a weekday, wouldn't you?'

Neither of them made any reply to this. David said, 'Goodbye, Mrs McDarmount,' and Carrie smiled at her mother before they turned and made their way out of the church grounds. It wasn't until they were approaching the Green that Carrie said, 'What's wrong, David?'

His jaw tightened. Carrie's tone was casual, even offhand; he wasn't to know that this was a defence against the vulnerability she was feeling. In view of the fact he'd had to visit the privy umpteen times before he'd left for church and still his bowels were threatening to turn to water, Carrie's composure grated on him. Even walking at the side of her like this, her head just reaching his shoulder, he felt weak-kneed. He could hold his own with anyone, be they man or woman, his mam included, but when he so much as set eyes on Carrie he was suddenly all at sea. And he didn't like that. Gruffly, and without any preamble, he said, 'What's wrong? It should be me asking you that from where I'm standing. And don't say nowt either 'cos there's something.'

Carrie stumbled but recovered herself instantly, her head still lowered but her voice firm when she said, 'I don't know what you're talking about.' She'd suspected it would be something like this when he'd asked to walk her home; it wouldn't be so bad if she knew exactly what she was going to do, but her head was still spinning with the enormity of what had befallen her. The disgrace would break her da, her mam too, although somehow she knew her mother would come to terms with it in

70

time. But not her da. A hasty wedding was one thing, jumping the gun happened more than folks admitted and her da might just cope with that, but to be taken down and left with a bairn? She couldn't tell him, she had to get away, but how? And where to? She had no money and she wouldn't be able to work for long anywhere before she began to show.

'I don't believe you, Carrie. I know something's up.'

She forced a note of outrage into her voice, tossing her head as she said, 'I don't care whether you believe me or not, David Sutton.' And then, as she caught sight of two figures some way ahead, Carrie checked her steps, saying, 'Your mam and Lillian are up in front if you want to catch them up.'

'I don't.'

'I think you should.'

'Now hold on a minute!' He swung her round to face him with one hand on her arm, but when he saw the terror in her eyes he let go of her immediately, his voice raw when he said, 'For crying out loud, Carrie, don't look at me like that. I'm worried about you, that's all. It's not a crime, is it?'

She didn't answer but stared at him, unblinking, her face even whiter than the snowflakes which were beginning to fall more thickly. He recognised she was frightened, genuinely frightened of him. She was ramrod straight, and her expression caused him to gentle his voice. 'Lass, that night. You don't have to tell me the ins and outs, but someone hurt you, didn't they? Was it a lad? Did he attack you, Carrie?'

Her face crumpled even before he'd finished speaking, and as his guts twisted, his mind yelled the confirmation of his worst fears. He hadn't known till this moment how much he had been hoping he was wrong.

'Carrie?' It was soft, a whisper. 'Talk to me, lass. This is David. We're friends, aren't we?'

She made a deep obeisance with her head, the only sign she gave that she could hear him.

'Have you told anyone? Your mam? Renee?'

'No.' Her voice cracked, and he saw she had to swallow before she could say, 'I . . . It started out as just a kiss and then . . . then he wouldn't stop.'

'Who? Who wouldn't stop?'

She turned her face away, dipping her head so that her voice was muffled when she said, her voice thick now with tears, 'I'm having a bairn, David.'

No. The word spiralled in his head, freezing the thought process, so it was with some surprise he heard himself say, 'What does he say about that?' as though she'd just admitted to something mundane and ordinary.

'He doesn't know. There . . . there's no point. He doesn't love me. It only happened because we had drunk too much.'

'You have to tell him. You know that, don't you?'

'*No.*'

There was a ringing silence. Some children were playing on a makeshift swing attached to a lamppost on the north side of the Green, close to the Savoy Theatre which had bairns queueing for hours for the Saturday penny matinees, and in spite of the weather two little girls without coats were taking turns skipping with a piece of old rope, their hair matted, clothes filthy, chanting:

House to let, apply within,
As I go out, my neighbour comes in!
House to let, apply within,
A woman put out for showing her thing!

Carrie was little more than a bairn herself. David stared

72

across the settling snow, the Green quieter than a weekday when the noise of the collieries, shipyards and factories guaranteed grime and toil and noise in all the surrounding streets, and tall black chimneys pumped out fetid thick smoke. She'd said this lad wouldn't stop so she hadn't been willing to be taken down, but willing enough for a kiss. 'Do you love him?' Considering the words were wrenched from somewhere deep inside him, it didn't show in his voice. 'You said he doesn't love you, but do you love him?'

'I thought I did, before . . .' He saw the shudder she gave.

'And now?' He had to know.

'I hate him.' It was flat, definite.

David looked down at his hands where his fingers were rubbing against each other. He felt as if he'd been punched in the stomach and had to swallow his bile. 'He ought to take responsibility for what he's done, for you and the baby.'

'I don't want anything from him.'

'From who?' he asked again. 'Who did it?'

Her head came up and she wiped her wet face with the back of her hand before she took a deep breath. 'I can't tell you that. I *won't* tell you that.'

'And your mam and da? You'll have to tell them, Carrie.'

'Nor them.' Her answer was vehement.

'They'll insist on knowing.'

'It will cause too much trouble.' She was fighting the tears. 'And for what? He won't marry me, he'd probably even say he's not the father if he found out, and I couldn't bear—' She bit her lip. Her voice was more controlled when she said, 'I couldn't bear him to touch me ever again. And if he knew about the bairn, even if he wouldn't marry me, it's a link, don't you see?'

He'd had his answer as to whether there was the slightest

feeling left on her part. Knowing how she felt made it easier for him to say, 'Actually, I don't think I want to know his name after all.'

She was still looking at him, her long eyelashes spiky with tears and her mouth slightly open in surprise.

'That way I can think of the bairn as yours, only yours. Carrie . . .' He hesitated, his throat constricting so tightly he felt he was being strangled. What if she said no? What if she refused him? He swallowed before wetting his lips. 'There's a way out of this. You could marry me.' He was hot, sweating, and he could feel colour flooding his face again. She was staring at him as if he was mad. She probably thought he was. He might be.

She shook her head slowly. 'I don't understand. Why would you do that?' she asked, amazement in every word.

He stared into her face for some moments before he said softly, 'Can't you guess?'

No, she couldn't guess. How on earth could she guess? With anyone else she might have suspected it was some sort of cruel joke, but not David. David didn't have a cruel bone in the whole of his body. Carrie stared into the face of the lad she had always thought of primarily as Alec's brother. A nice lad, friendly, kind and quite good-looking in a rough sort of way, and again she wanted to cry. She bit the inside of her bottom lip hard, focusing on the pain to stop herself breaking down. She'd cried enough for one morning. But he hadn't drawn away from her in spite of what she'd revealed and she was so grateful to him for that, knowing there were plenty more who wouldn't be so generous.

For the first time since Alec had raped her, Carrie voluntarily reached out and touched a man other than her father, patting David's arm once as she said, 'Thank you for not hating me.'

'Hating you? Oh, lass, I could never hate you.' He stared at her, suddenly tongue-tied. The falling snow had coated her felt hat and the shoulders of her coat, framing her in a circle of white, and she had never looked so bonny. But she was carrying a bairn, another man's bairn, and a bairn conceived in blind lust, from the little she'd said. But he couldn't think of that now. If he dwelled on it he knew the feeling rising up in him, a feeling which urged him to force the name out of her so he could go and do murder, would take over. And that would ruin everything. It had happened. That was the crux of the matter. And although he wouldn't have wished it this way in a million years, it had presented him with his one and only chance of ever meaning anything to her. He would have liked to do it properly. To start courting her, taking her out on his arm to the music hall or the cinema, showing her off to all his pals. Then, once they were engaged, there'd be kissing and clarting on somewhere secluded and private, up near the old quarries like as not where most of the courting couples went after dark. But he'd have waited for marriage and the bedroom before he'd have asked for more than kissing. For Carrie he would. But it was too late for all that. And the folk round here, the old wives and the not so old lasses who had always been a mite jealous of her looks and all would crucify her with their gossip and spite and cold-shouldering. Her life wouldn't be worth living.

'Marry me,' he said again. 'As soon as possible. That way no one can be sure that the bairn didn't just come early when it's born.'

Her hand had fallen to her side and again she was staring at him with great blue eyes. 'David, that's impossible, you know it is,' she said haltingly. He must be feeling sorry for her.

'No, it's not. I . . . I think a bit of you, I always have.'

It was Carrie's turn to flush now. He liked her? In that way?

But he'd never said. She spoke the last thought out loud. 'If that's true why haven't you ever asked me out?'

'Because I knew I didn't have a chance, I suppose.'

'But . . .' She paused, unable to fully take in what he had proposed. And it was a proposal, she told herself shakily. He'd asked her to marry him, even knowing about the bairn. For a second hope soared, for one blinding moment she saw a way out of it all. And then reality kicked in. How could she expect anyone to take her as she was now? He might think he liked her enough but lads always wanted to be the first, didn't they? With the lass they married? And there was the bairn.

'But what?' he asked quietly. 'What are you thinking?'

'That you could have any lass you wanted.'

'Maybe I don't want any lass.'

'But the bairn? It would always remind you of how we started.'

Aye, it would. 'No it wouldn't.'

'It would, you know it would.'

She started walking again and he fell into step beside her. He wanted her, and if he had to stomach the bairn to have her, then so be it. Having Carrie as his lass had been a dream before this moment, a far horizon he'd always known deep down he couldn't reach but which he couldn't let go of. He played his trump card. 'What are you going to do if you don't marry me?'

'I don't know.' They had reached the far end of the Green and again she stopped, pulling her coat collar up round her neck. There followed a silence during which their eyes met and held, and after a little while she said again, 'It's impossible,' her voice trembling. 'I . . . I don't want to be anyone's wife.' And then, as his face changed, she said quickly, 'It's not because it's you, David, really.'

76

And she meant that. She had never really looked at him before this day, not in the light of a lad anyway, but now she saw he was rather handsome. Well, not handsome. There was something too strong and rugged about his face for it to be called handsome, but his eyes were lovely. Deep brown and almost velvety; kind eyes.

'Is it because of . . .' he found he didn't know quite how to put it, and finished lamely, 'making on?'

Her face was on fire now but she nodded.

'You don't have to worry about that,' he said flatly, hot colour flooding his own face. 'With the bairn and all I wouldn't expect—' He stopped. 'What I mean is, after it's born it'd be up to you. If you didn't want to I'd wait till you were willing.'

Her voice was very small when she said, 'What if I was never willing?'

How did he answer that? He stared stupidly at her, knowing he couldn't express what he wanted to say. If he'd been one of those educated types who had a way with words he might have been able to convince her. As it was . . . He'd like to be able to tell her he loved her, that he'd always loved her for as long as he could remember. Aye, he burned for her but that was natural, wasn't it? That was how it should be if a lad loved a lass, but that wasn't all of it. She was terrified, scared out of her wits at the thought of being married, and who could blame her after what had happened? But in the weeks and months ahead – if she took him – he'd be able to let her see she needn't be frightened of him. But if he tried to say all that, it would only come out wrong. Besides, a lad didn't talk of love – not in broad daylight on a Sunday morning, leastways.

The silence was lengthening and he knew he had to break it before he lost any chance he might have. He swallowed hard. 'I said I'd wait till you were willing and I mean it.'

'But it would all be so unfair on you—'

He cut short her protest. 'It's what I want, all right?'

She shook her head, murmuring, 'I don't know what to say,' but in that moment he knew it was done.

They were married in the same week the government announced it was to give two million pounds for the development of Kent coalfields, thereby whipping the unrest in the beleaguered north-east to fever pitch, but for once this latest tactic by the 'enemy' left Sandy McDarmount unmoved.

Since the Sunday afternoon following Carrie's sixteenth birthday, when she and David had confronted her parents with the reason why their marriage should be immediate, her father seemed to have aged twenty years. After his initial shock Sandy had leaped at David, and it had only been the younger man's quick reflexes that had saved him from the knock-out blow Sandy had attempted. Carrie had flung herself between them, but even with her mother and brother hanging on to her father's arms, it had taken some minutes before he'd calmed down.

'Don't blame David, Da, please. It wasn't like that.' Carrie had been beside herself, even though David had been adamant that no matter how things went with Sandy they must stick to the story that the child was his. It was the one and only condition he'd inflicted on her, that she should never reveal to a living soul that he wasn't the father.

David had told her it was for the child's sake; that if anyone knew the truth there was a risk that at some point in the future a careless word might reveal it to the child. This way it was tidy, he insisted. The child had legitimacy, her father would have no need to press her for a name she felt she couldn't give, and once they were married she had the protection of respectability. Wild horses wouldn't drag the real reason he had claimed parentage from him. It was one thing to jump the gun with a lass and get caught out; quite another to be held up as a laughing stock because you'd been fool enough to take on someone else's flyblow. And that's how folk would see it, he told himself. Oh aye, he knew full well what would be said if word got out. 'That young 'un, Ned's lad, hasn't got the sense he was born with. She made a cuckold of him even before he got her to the altar, silly daft so-an'-so.' Oh aye, he knew his own and the sort of gossip which would race round the backyards like fire in a corn field.

But if Carrie's father took it hard, David's mother became almost demented at the thought of another son marrying a McDarmount.

David had refused to let Carrie be present when he faced the furore he knew would erupt at home, and he was doubly glad of this when, in the resulting fracas – and due in part to his father speaking up for Carrie, for whom he had always had a soft spot – the bitter enmity between his parents reached new heights.

Alec, of course, had put in his two penn'orth when he'd arrived home from the Reeds' house in the middle of the row, his sneering gibe as to whether David could support Carrie in the manner to which she was accustomed causing his brother to tighten his hands into fists at his side.

David had refused to give a reason for the need for haste, merely saying it was what they both wanted and was nothing to do with anyone else, which had further inflamed his mother. When Olive had lost her temper completely and accused him of planning events purely to put a spoke in Alec's wheel with the Reeds, he had walked out of the door and spent the night on a friend's sofa.

But now the short service at Holy Trinity was over. Both

families had been briefly united in their endeavour to put a face on things and had attended the espousal – all except Alec, who had been unable to take another Saturday afternoon away from the shop so soon after Walter's wedding, or so he said.

No one commented on the abruptness of the vicar, who had clearly made up his own mind about the need for haste and had let it be known, albeit silently and with clerical dignity, that he was most unhappy.

Joan McDarmount could not understand Carrie's flat refusal to wear the blue brocade dress again for the wedding, emphasising several times that the beautiful garment at least gave some suggestion that this wedding was not a hole-in-the-wall affair. When Carrie returned the dress to the stallholder, exchanging it for an inferior article in nut-brown linen, Joan had found it difficult to speak to her daughter for a day or two.

It had been Renee who, although more than a little hurt by her sister's stoical refusal to discuss the reason behind the sudden nuptials, had bought a wide-brimmed cream hat and matching ankle-strap shoes for the bride, trimming the hat with a bevy of fresh flowers and using the remainder for a small posy for Carrie to hold.

This act of kindness, along with Renee's fierce warning to all and sundry at the firework factory not to make disparaging comments about the unexpected wedding, had upheld Carrie in her worst moments.

Lillian was clearly bewildered and disturbed by events but she had been tact itself, although Carrie had detected a slight withdrawal on the part of her friend. She told herself this was only to be expected in the circumstances. They had been used to doing everything together from when they were bairns, sharing confidences and hopes and dreams, and now everything had changed.

From her position at David's side, Carrie looked across her mother's living room to where Renee and Lillian were laughing with Mrs Symcox from two doors down. Ann Symcox, besides being a neighbour and recently widowed, was her mother's lifelong friend, and the only person to be invited to the ceremony other than the two immediate families. Carrie didn't know if her mother had divulged anything, but Mrs Symcox's attitude to her had been just as warm and pleasant as always.

Another gust of laughter from the three made Carrie lower her eyes. Would she ever feel like laughing again? she asked herself desperately. She couldn't imagine so at this moment. Every time she met her father's eyes the sorrow there smote her like a fist, and although her da still spoke to David for appearance's sake and to keep alive the façade of this being a normal wedding, his bitterness towards David was palpable.

A small untouched piece of wedding cake reposed on the plate in her hand, and she stared at it. The eight-inch cake, along with ham sandwiches and a cup of tea, had made up the sum total of the wedding breakfast. Everyone had been very careful not to compare it with the feast before Christmas, everyone except Olive Sutton, that was. David's mother had enjoyed putting the knife in more than once, and had done nothing but glare her rage all day.

'Chin up, lass.'

David's voice was low, and when he took her arm, linking it in his, Carrie forced herself not to flinch away. She had tried, she'd *really* tried to rid herself of the churning sensation she experienced every time he touched her, but still it remained. Even a pat on the hand from a male other than her da made her flesh creep. She was going doolally. She made herself look up and meet David's eyes, smiling at him. At this rate she'd be fit for nothing but the company of the other loonies up at the asylum.

'Another half an hour or so and we can go, then you can put your feet up. How are you feeling now?' he asked softly.

'All right.' It was a lie. The nausea which now often claimed her every waking moment hadn't let up all day, and she hadn't dared to try and eat anything. Far from gaining weight she had lost a couple of pounds every week since the middle of January, but the effort of trying to hide how she felt from everyone outside the house was the worst thing. She had been counting the hours to this day for the last week, deeply thankful for the unwritten rule which said a married woman should not work outside the home. That Renee had guessed how she felt and the reason for it was apparent in the fact that her sister had not tried to dissuade her from giving in her notice at work, even though since her marriage Renee was becoming more fervent by the day in support of equality for women both at work and at home.

It was another hour before Carrie left the house she had called home for the last sixteen years. She was feeling so ill and tired that the walk through the icy streets, banked high with frozen snow and lethal beneath the feet, would have been beyond her but for David's arm round her waist.

By the time they had walked the length of Southwick Road and turned into Black Road, which was near the pit head, she was light-headed, and David was cursing the fact that she hadn't eaten anything. They were renting a room in Brooke Street, one of the roads in the area known locally as 'Back of the Pit', which indeed it was, as the thick black grime clinging to every building testified.

After passing colliery square, a collection of miners' cottages on the east side of the road, they crossed over Wreath

Quay Road where the wind blew enough to cut you in half, and into Hay Street before turning into Brooke Street some moments later. The Back of the Pit was a community within a community, cut off from the rest of Monkwearmouth by the train station and North Bridge Street. It consisted of some of the most smoke-blackened dwellings in Sunderland, along with many small factories that all added their quota of stench to the sooty air.

Their new home was one room on the ground floor of a two-up, two-down terrace in the middle of the dreary street. Several of the houses shared a backyard which contained two dry privies, one washhouse with a coal-fired boiler and the communal tap. This supplied all the water for the households and the many families they contained. It was a world away from James Armitage Street.

In the days since they had settled on their lodgings, Carrie had been doggedly repeating to herself that they were lucky to have found somewhere with a downstairs room vacant. It would save having to lug buckets of water from the yard up the stairs, and the small range in the room had been an added bonus. The two rooms they had viewed before this one had both been on the first floor of each house, and both had had only a small fireplace with a bar across it for resting one pan on.

They entered the dark narrow hall and Carrie watched David open their door with the key their landlady – a large, plump, bustling type who lived in the other downstairs room with her three cats – had given them, and for a moment, having stepped inside, despair overwhelmed her.

The room was clean – they had been round the last two evenings and scrubbed it from top to bottom – but that was all that could be said for it. There were no curtains at the narrow sash window, just a faded paper blind which the last occupant had left. The meagre scraps of furniture were their own. These consisted of Carrie's bed from home which her mother had let them have with the proviso that if they got another one she wanted it back for Billy, along with its old lumpy mattress, grey blankets and two flock pillows. They had placed the bed under the window, and although it was only a three-quarter size it seemed to fill the room. Next to the range was a small, worm-eaten table holding a few pots and pans, items of cutlery, a sharp bread knife, two plates and mugs and a washing-up bowl – all courtesy of the local pawn shop, along with the big black kettle sitting on the hob. On the other side of the range a battered tin bath was propped against the wall. Mrs Symcox had given them this, having recently acquired a new one.

The flagstones beneath their feet were devoid of the smallest clippy mat, and apart from an orange box which was more than adequate to hold their few items of clothing – there were three pegs on the wall near the door for coats and hats – and an old patched armchair that was losing its stuffing, which David had bought for a few shillings from a pal, the only other items in the room were a dented brass coal scuttle standing in front of the tin bath and a large and rather ugly oil lamp above the range.

Carrie wasn't aware of the expression on her face as she glanced round what was now officially her new home, but when David said, his voice hearty, 'This is just to tide us over, lass, until we can get hearth and home together,' she nodded quickly.

'Aye, I know, I know.'

'It won't always be like this.' He took her two icy-cold hands in his, chaffing them gently as he spoke. 'You do know that?'

She nodded again, but now her voice was soft when she said,

'David, what you've done for me . . .' She shook her head. 'I can't ever thank you enough but I am grateful.'

'No, don't say that.' Her russet hair fell over her ears in silky waves and it rustled beneath her hat as she moved her head. The skin of her cheeks was a soft creamy white, porcelain pale.

Too pale, David acknowledged painfully. And she always went a shade whiter when he touched her. But that didn't matter. She was his wife, his *wife*, and in time he would make Carrie love him like he loved her. He just had to be patient, that was all. Ever since she had agreed to marry him he'd been tied up in knots, scared to death she would change her mind at the last minute and refuse to go through with it when push came to shove. But she had gone through with it.

He began to tremble inside as he surveyed the girl in front of him. And now her face was drained of colour and she was saying she was grateful to him. He didn't want her gratitude. He wanted—

He forced himself to let go of her hands, saying evenly, 'You're freezing, lass, and no wonder. It's like an ice-box in here. I'll light the fire. I set it ready yesterday so it'll soon take, and once that's going it'll make everything more' – he had been about to say bearable but perhaps that was clumsy – 'cheerful, eh?'

'Yes, thank you.'

Thanks again. He wasn't going to be able to stand this if she kept thanking him all the time. As he reached for the matches on the shelf above the range, there was a knock at the door. He turned to look at Carrie in surprise.

She, in her turn, stared at him wide-eyed before she walked to the door. She opened it to Mrs Bedlow, their landlady, who began to speak before Carrie could say a word.

'I thought you could both do with a nice cup of tea, the

85

weather bein' so bitter. Am I right, lass?' The tray in the landlady's hands held a pot of tea, a milk jug and sugar bowl, a plate of freshly baked buttered drop scones and a small saucer of jam.

'This is so kind of you, Mrs Bedlow,' Carrie said. 'Won't you come in for a minute?'

'Just a minute then.' Their landlady's voice lowered although Carrie had now shut the door. 'I thought I'd better say hello an' God bless you both, 'cos it's for sure them upstairs won't pass the time of day. Mind, I've no complaints 'cos they pay up every Friday regular as clockwork an' are as clean an' quiet as the fairies, but they're foreigners, see. Polish I think they are, or mebbe it's Russian, I forget now.' She nodded to David who had applied a match to the fire and was straightening, brushing his hands against his trousers.

Carrie smiled at Mrs Bedlow, taking the tray as she said, 'You'll join us in a cup of tea, I hope?'

'No, thanks all the same, lass, but I'm expectin' a happy event in the next little while. My Emilia is havin' her first an' I don't like to be too far away in case she needs me.'

'Emilia? Is that your daughter, Mrs Bedlow?'

'My daughter?' There was a wheezy laugh. 'God bless you, dear, no, it's me little tabby. The good Lord never blessed the late Mr Bedlow an' me with bairns. Mind you, perhaps that was no bad thing. How I'd have managed with bairns *and* my Charlie, I don't know. You only had to mention the word work and Charlie's back would go. But he was a good man at heart, an' with the lodgers an' the bit of washin' an' ironin' I take in we was never short of a bob or two. An' he liked cats.' She nodded, causing the enormous bun of white hair balanced above the round face to wobble alarmingly. 'Aye, he liked cats, an' that's the main thing, isn't it?'

'Yes, I suppose it is,' Carrie agreed weakly.

'Anyway, I mustn't stand here jawin' with Emilia needin' comfort, must I, but I wanted to say welcome and congratulations to you both.' She opened the door and turned on the threshold to say, as though bestowing a blessing, 'May your two shadows ever lengthen in the sun of happiness. Me an' Charlie had that said to us on the day we wed, nigh on forty years ago now, by me old da. Couldn't abide Charlie, me da couldn't, but you couldn't fault his wedding speech. Grand, it was. 'Bye bye then, an' if you need owt, tap on me door.'

When the door closed, Carrie turned in a daze to face David who had taken the tray from her and placed it on the seat of the armchair.

'He liked cats.' David's voice was choked, and then they both began to shake with small helpless tremors which intensified into muffled laughter, their hands tight across their mouths to stifle the sound.

It was some time before they could control themselves, and as David glanced into Carrie's eyes, bright with laughter, he blessed Mrs Bedlow. The day had ended in laughter. It was a start.

Part 2

Not a penny off the pay
Not a minute on the day.

1926

Chapter Six

'So it's begun then?'

'Aye, it's begun.'

Joan McDarmount stared at her husband who had just walked in the door from attending a union meeting. Sandy's voice bordered on the euphoric, but try as she might she couldn't see eye to eye with him over this General Strike business.

Four days ago at the end of April the coal-owners had closed every pit in the country, locking the miners out, just as Sandy and many of the old diehards had predicted. The owners' terms to the miners amounted to pre-war wages and an extra hour on the working day to boot. Their terms to the government amounted to no state interference in the running of the mines, all strikes to be banned by law and the state to take control of all funds belonging to the trade unions. The owners had declared war on their working force, and every union, regardless of what industry it was involved in, knew it.

The TUC had said they would back the miners to the last man, and this morning workers in almost every industry had laid down their tools, bringing the country to a stop. No buses and trains were running, factories were deathly silent, the docks were deserted and offices empty. And Sandy was cock-a-hoop.

'Don't look like that, lass.' Sandy walked over to Joan who

had resumed the task she'd been about before his entrance, that of kneading bread dough. 'You knew it was comin', it had to, didn't it? We can't sit under it any more. Three pounds eighteen shillings I was earnin' regular five years ago, an' what is it now? Two pounds if I'm lucky, an' that's before I'm docked with their trumped-up fines. With every worker in the country showing they're for us, we can't fail.'

'You said that in nineteen twenty-one.' Joan's voice was bitter. 'An' I tell you straight, Sandy, I'm sick of hearin' it won't happen again. Why shouldn't it? The other unions hung the miners out to dry then and nothing's changed in my book. They'll back down again, I feel it in me water. It might take days or weeks, but they won't stand with us for ever. Churchill and his lot are already trying to paint the miners blacker than the ace of spades, you know they are. Never mind the dole queues and families like that poor Mrs Cook's in Renee's street. Him out of work sixteen weeks and eight of them starving. Renee said although Mrs Cook's nursing her latest, all the food she'd had when Renee popped in that day last week was a cup of tea at breakfast time, and tea and two slices of bread and butter, provided by a married sister living near, at teatime.'

'Aye, I know, lass, it's wicked.'

'It *is* wicked.' Joan glared at Sandy as though he'd disagreed with her. 'Churchill might insist all things are bright and beautiful in Britain, but only for them born with a silver spoon in their mouth.'

'Which is why we can't lie down after this last lot, lass. You do see that, don't you?'

'Aye, aye, you know I do.' Joan's rigid stance crumpled and immediately Sandy put an arm round her.

'Come on, lass, come on. This isn't like you.'

'It's bairns like Carrie and David I'm thinking about. It's

only been the last couple of weeks she's been anything like after that awful sickness. I was never like that, not with my first. She's skin and bone, Sandy. Skin and bone. But for that landlady of hers keeping an eye on her during the day I don't know what I'd have done.'

'They're not bairns, Joan. Neither of 'em.' Sandy's voice was flat.

'And now, just when she's able to pick herself up a bit, this strike has hit.' Joan continued as though she hadn't heard him, although she was very aware of both the tone of her husband's voice and the way he had removed his arm from her shoulders at the mention of Carrie and David. 'What if all this grand talk of solidarity and such melts away like it did before? Two hundred pits closed in Durham alone and one hundred and fifty thousand men laid off, and there they are in one room with next to nothing and a bairn on the way.'

'Aye, well, it didn't have to be that way, did it? It was their choice.'

'Don't be like that, love.' Joan's voice was suddenly soft. 'They made a mistake, that's all. A couple of bairns who let things run away with them.'

'Aye, mebbe.' Sandy turned away and stood staring into the fire glowing in the range. They wouldn't be able to have a blaze like this much longer, not with the free coal finished. The thought came from nowhere and it made his voice even more terse when he said, 'But they lied to me, the pair of 'em, an' that's what sticks in me craw if you want to know the truth. I went grovellin' to that lad after our Carrie told me he was all above board, an' he let me, all the time laughin' up his sleeve.'

'It wouldn't have been like that, you know that at heart. They'd have been frightened, scared out of their wits most like. Carrie's a good lass, always has been, and David's not a bad lad.'

'I know what David is.' There was no hint of softening in Sandy's voice or manner. 'By, if anyone knows that, I know it now.'

'Sandy—'

'No, don't, lass. Don't try an' talk me round because it's a lost cause. I want no more to do with the lad an' if it wasn't for our Carrie I'd wipe the floor with him. As it is . . .' He sighed heavily. 'I won't show him the door if he comes with her, but that's the most I can say. I'm sorry, but that's how it is.'

Stubborn as the day was long. Joan felt a mixture of irritation and compassion as she gazed at her husband's face. He was torturing himself daily with the loss of Carrie, she could see it clear as crystal, but would he admit it? Would he heck. She knew from what Renee had let on, via Walter, that her husband and Billy were making life as unpleasant as they could for David down the pit, but what could she do about it? Nowt. Only pray and trust that somehow this would all work itself out. They said time was a great healer, and maybe Sandy would be different when the bairn, his first grandchild, came, but she doubted it. And he was drinking again.

She rubbed a flour-caked hand across her forehead, suddenly weary with the lot of them. She could have done without this at her time of life, by, she could, what with the weather not having let up since the New Year and the twins being confined to the house with chickenpox for the last week and more, driving her mad in the process. And Renee had turned as flighty as she didn't know what, refusing to give up her job and furthermore declaring she and Walter weren't looking to have any bairns for the time being. As for Carrie, she looked like death warmed up in that awful, stinking hole— No. She caught the last thought, her innate honesty forcing her to admit, no, it wasn't stinking. Clean as a new pin, more like, but still no place for her bright, bonny bairn.

'Lass, I can't be other than what I am.' Sandy had turned back to her again and now took her arm, drawing her round and into his arms. 'I'd like to be able to shrug it off, say it don't matter, but I can't an' it does.'

Joan swallowed hard. Aye, it did, she knew it did, and wasn't this part of what had made her take him in the first place? He felt things, he cared. And whatever he said, she knew it wasn't just the loss of Carrie he was grieving. He had liked young David, loved him even.

'Sandy?' She rested her floury hands on the shoulders of his old jacket. 'Promise me one thing, lad.'

'What?'

'Don't . . . don't have a drink the next little while. Not . . . till we're sorted.'

Sandy stared into the face of the woman he had loved since he'd first set eyes on her some twenty-odd years before. She had been bonny then, she still was bonny, but now her looks had taken on the weariness of all the women round about. She was canny, frugal, she could make a penny stretch to two and she had needed to often since the bairns had come, but never a word of complaint. There had always been something hot for him and the bairns come evening, be it broth with bare rib bones to suck at and new bread from a flat cake to mop up the last tiny drop when things were extra tight. She had always been a great believer in filling the belly and keeping the range going day and night so there was always somewhere warm to curl up near; the rest, even the rent money, she always said, came second. He didn't know what he would do without her.

'Aye, lass, I promise.'

'You mean it?'

'I've said, haven't I?' And then he did something unheard of in the middle of the day in broad daylight. He kissed her, hard and long, the sort of kiss kept for the night hours and the warmth of their double bed. And Joan kissed him back, her arms tightening round his broad shoulders. She hoped Carrie and David had the same sort of feeling she and Sandy shared, she thought suddenly, but she just couldn't tell. In fact she couldn't work the pair of them out at all if she was being truthful. Course, it was early days yet, and being caught out like they'd been didn't make for a good start in anyone's book, but all that taken into consideration, there was something she couldn't put her finger on in all of this.

A little earlier, in an effort to expel some of the twins' pent-up energy, made all the more volatile due to the fact the two small boys couldn't even play in the yard or back lane owing to the driving rain and howling wind, she had set them the task of scrubbing the floorboards and furniture in the bedroom they now shared with Billy. Mindful of this she pushed Sandy away from her, half smiling as she muttered, 'Give over, man, that's enough. And where's Billy? Didn't he come back with you?'

'A few of the lads have gone for a jar in the Tavern.'

'And you didn't want to join them?'

'I thought you'd be wonderin' what was what.'

Joan stared at him for a moment, and her voice was soft when she said, 'Aye, I was. Sit yourself down then and I'll get you a sup. There's a bite of sly cake I made not ten minutes ago if you're peckish. Or a shive of stottie cake with a bit of pork dripping.'

Sandy glanced across to the thick pastry covering an old dinner plate. It would be generously filled with currants and sugar inside, and no one made pastry like Joan. His mouth watered but he shook his head, saying, 'A cup of tea'll do for now.' They were all going to have to pull in their belts for as long as the strike continued, so he might as well start now.

Joan had an inkling of his thoughts but didn't press him, her mind only half on Sandy. Once upon a time David, as Billy's best pal, would have automatically come back here on a day like this one, but recent events had changed all that. Sandy had lost a lad he'd looked on almost as one of his own, and Billy the pal he'd been thick with since he could toddle. Who'd have thought it? As for her, she was missing her lass more than she would have thought possible. Renee's going had been natural somehow, and something of a relief, with her and her da always at loggerheads, but she felt Carrie had been ripped away from her. And with every Tom, Dick and Harry doing their sums from the day David and Carrie had wed in such a rush . . .

Joan finished mashing the tea, straightened her bowed shoulders and adjusted her thick linen pinny before she brought the teapot to the table. Enough, she told herself firmly. It didn't help anyone brooding like this, and she'd enough on her plate with four hungry mouths to feed and next to nothing coming in. And things'd get worse before they got better, that was for sure. Like her mam had always said, take life in bite-size pieces and it won't choke you, and if anyone had known the truth of that statement, her mam had, the troubles she'd borne in her time.

Alec Sutton was one of those who had been doing his sums of recent weeks since his brother's hurried wedding. At first he had been inclined to agree with his mother that David's bolt from the blue had been aimed to take the edge off the news of his engagement to Margaret, but this turn of mind had not lasted. There might be no love lost between himself and his youngest brother, but David was too canny to fuel speculation and gossip just to attempt to put his nose out of joint. No, there was more to this than that. But that the lass should be Carrie McDarmount, of all people . . . He would have sworn on oath that the girl had been a virgin when he'd taken her that night, and to his knowledge David hadn't had anything to do with her, or any other lass for that matter. But no one wed with such haste except for one reason.

It was the recollection of the stricken expression on Carrie's face just after he'd announced his engagement which prodded Alec towards the inevitable conclusion, causing him to take several deep draughts of air as his heart raced like a greyhound.

Was it possible? And the answer came, aye, it was. Too true it was. He'd been verging on mortalious that night, the last thing on his mind had been the possible consequences of taking her without due precautions. But if what he suspected was true, if Carrie *had* fallen for a bairn, what the hell was David doing marrying her?

Alec brooded on various scenarios, eventually deciding on the obvious one. Carrie was both quick-witted and pretty, and David was as green as they come. She'd seduced him into sleeping with her and then immediately declared he had to marry her in case she was pregnant; at least one of his pals had been caught that way. Now if a baby materialised she'd tell the poor fool it was his, and he would bet his last shilling a bairn *was* on the way. The crafty baggage. He found himself smiling. David would have been putty in her hands.

Whatever, he was off the hook. If this had turned out differently, if the chit had turned nasty, it might have ruined everything he'd worked towards the last couple of years. He'd have denied anything Carrie McDarmount said of course, but mud sticks. Margaret may be smitten with him but her father was a different kettle of fish. Sharp as a razor, Arthur Reed was. He'd got the mother eating out of the palm of his hand though, Alec thought complacently and everyone knew Arthur Reed wasn't a well man. Dicky heart, the rumour was.

Well, if nothing else, this was a salutary lesson in making sure he visited a certain establishment in the East End more regularly. There was always one of Ma Siddle's lasses available for him, and most of them were well worth the prices she charged. Moreover, Ma was discreet, which was why he'd decided to patronise her whorehouse over the others some years ago and he'd never regretted it. Aye, he wouldn't make a mistake like the McDarmount girl again, not now he was sitting pretty. He had to keep his eyes fixed on his prospects.

By, David was a dolt. With all his holier-than-thou preaching and such, his brother still hadn't had the sense to keep it in his trousers when she'd played him for a fool. What were the odds she'd allowed him near her just the once, claiming he was the first, and then played him like a violin afterwards? Idiot. His upper lip curled in a sneer as he compared his present position in life to that of his brother. Before he was finished he'd have a house on the outskirts, Hendon way perhaps or maybe Roker or Seaburn. A maid, a horse and trap, even one of those new-fangled automobiles which were becoming increasingly popular since the war. The solicitor, two doors up from the shop, had just bought himself the latest model of the Austin Tourer – he could see himself in that.

Alec continued to allow pleasant visions of the future to engage his senses, putting any further thoughts of Carrie and David out of his mind with the ruthlessness which was habitual to him. He knew where he was going in life and exactly how to get there. That was all that mattered. And the pangs of disquiet that had attacked his conscience now and again since the night of Walter's wedding became duller and duller, until they bothered him not at all.

Chapter Seven

'I'm sorry, David, but I have to do this. Please try to understand. It's for us, can't you see that?'

David stood staring at his wife. When he had walked in just a minute ago and seen Carrie huddled over her baking board on top of the rickety old table where their pans normally sat, he hadn't realised at first what she was about. Then he had seen the papers, paste powder, blue touchpapers and paintbrush and it had dawned on him what she was doing. He'd bellowed her name and made her nearly jump out of her skin, but after the initial shock she had eyed him resolutely, her soft mouth trembling a little but otherwise her stance firm.

'It's slave labour, making firework cases at home. You've always said that yourself.'

'I know.' Her chin went up and he knew he was in for a battle. 'But needs must.'

'You're not doing it, Carrie. Look at you, sweating and tired, and for what? What are you getting?'

'Five shillings for ten gross of crackers.' She heard him groan but ignored it, continuing, 'And I was lucky to get it, I tell you straight. There's always more willing workers than work available, I know that from what Renee has said in the past, but when I went to see Mr Fleming he remembered me from before.'

'*You went to see him?*'

'Aye, I did.' She'd known he wouldn't like it, but as she had said, needs must. Mr Fleming was a kind man at heart, and she knew he was aware of her circumstances.

Since the General Strike had collapsed, just nine days after it had started, the miners had been on their own. At first the lodge had paid ten shillings a week to their miners; that had lasted two weeks. Then it was five shillings a week and that had lasted three weeks. Then four shillings a week for one week and three shillings for three weeks. And then nothing. The lodges simply couldn't cope any more. It was up to each individual to do what he could and each family to manage the best they could. The fellowship dinners, once merry affairs organised by supporters, had become soup kitchens, and Carrie knew – as one of the original members of the Wearmouth Feeding Committee – the soup was now as weak as dishwater. People were starving, it was as simple as that, and when a family decided they had to go into the workhouse, no one blamed them. It was no disgrace to be a pauper, the only shame lay in being a blackleg.

The strike coming when Carrie was just beginning to feel relief from the constant sickness meant she had been able to get involved in all the fundraising. Brass band concerts, dances, raffles, lotteries, talent competitions, athletic contests, the inevitable boxing matches, coconut shies, skittles, darts, 'guess your weight', pony rides and a whole lot more had sprung into being. The sea's resources were pillaged. Women and children picked winkles, crabs, seaweed and anything else which was edible, and collected driftwood and coal washed up on the beaches. Sand was washed in buckets and sold to builders for a few pence; coal tips and rubbish dumps were combed for anything that could be burned, repaired or sold. Church halls were turned into knitting factories by miners' wives, using woollens scrounged and unwound to produce 'new' items. Men who had spent all their working life down the pit turned into temporary carpenters, decorators, tinkers, gardeners and much more. It was a common sight to see bairns following carthorses and picking up the manure, some even collecting dog faeces and dividing them into black and white bags – the colour being dependent on what the animals had eaten – which they sold to folk for their gardens.

But now a long, hot, hard August had drawn to a close and resources were spent. Carrie had watched David collect fish and vegetable scraps from the market and from people's bins, and walk miles into Chester-le-Street, and sometimes as far as Consett, to sell them to smallholders and people who kept hens and pigs. But now even this source of keeping themselves alive had dried up. The rent hadn't been paid in months. Ada Bedlow, now a firm friend, had declared it could wait, but it couldn't wait, not for ever. And yesterday, when she had called in her mam's and seen the twins, pale and washed-out and alive with ringworm and impetigo, and her mother barely able to open her mouth for ulcers, Carrie had known she had to defy David and go and beg for work at the firework factory. She would have done it weeks ago but for knowing how wretched it would make him feel. But his pride wasn't more important than their surviving, and that was what this had boiled down to.

Carrie knew a few of the miners – one or two who had worked shoulder to shoulder with David in the past – had given in, and these men were labelled blacklegs. More were being brought in from other counties too, and the bitterness was fierce. David, along with other men, often one from every family involved in the strike, was now engaged in day-to-day picket duty, but she knew from what he hadn't said rather than what he had that her father and Billy were still cold-shouldering him. It seemed incredible at a time like this.

With her father in mind, Carrie now said, 'Who was in your shift for picket duty?'

'Damn the picket duty.' David was not going to be deflected. His voice raw, he repeated, 'You're not doing it, Carrie.' Here she was, liable to have the bairn at any time in the next few days, and as big as a house, and she had not only defied the unwritten law that said she shouldn't be seen outside in the street, she had actually gone to the factory to ask for work despite what he had said some weeks earlier when she'd raised the matter.

At one end of the table were brown papers spread out and pasted. In her lap lay the cases already rolled; to the right of her was a pudding basin and paintbrush covered in paste. He had the urge to fling out his hand and sweep the lot on to the floor.

'David, but for Ada we'd be on the streets right now.' Carrie's voice was low but nonetheless determined. 'There's nothing in the cupboard to eat and not a penny to buy any-thing.'

'I thought Ada was picking up a few bits from Marleys for us yesterday?'

'No, I told her I didn't want her to do it any more. She . . . she let something slip the last time she brought stuff in. Apparently our credit stopped weeks ago, along with everyone else's round here, but she didn't want to tell us. She's been buying us food out of her own pocket and her without two farthings to rub together. The bread and cheese we ate this morning was the last of anything.'

'Marleys stopped our credit? By, that's ripe. Thought he was supporting us all as long as it took.'

'It's a small shop, David, and he's bairns of his own to feed.

They can't live on thin air, any more than we can. All the shops, even the Co-op, are the same. They're tired of it all.'

He stood looking at her, despair working a muscle in his jaw as though he had a tic. He felt sick to his stomach. All their efforts over the last weeks and it had come to this. And it had been *their* efforts, not just his. Even when Carrie had begun to show to the extent it wouldn't be seemly her working in the soup kitchens or helping organise the events, she had taken on knitting at home before people had run out of old woollens and such to donate in the last couple of weeks. And in a strange sort of way he thought the strike had helped to get them over the awkwardness of living together in one room. He still turned his back while she undressed and scuttled under the covers, and he'd not seen so much as a bare ankle since they'd been wed, but he didn't mind that as long as she was feeling more comfortable with him. Their joined purpose in seeing the cause succeed and unity of mind had brought them together a bit, he felt. Or maybe he was just fooling himself. Clutching at straws. And now she was proposing to slave away all day for a pittance, but a pittance, he had to admit, which seemed like a fortune in their present circumstances. Nevertheless . . . 'I'll do something, anything, but I don't want you working on them things.'

For a moment Carrie wanted to scream the truth at him, so weary did she feel. Since the strike had dragged on, people in work had got fed up with donating and lending and helping, and she couldn't really blame them. The same ones tended to get pestered all the time. Gardens were maintained to the last blade of grass, scissors and knives and garden shears had been sharpened repeatedly, and some housewives – the kind ones – had more tea cosies, doorstops and clippy mats than the big shops in Bishopwearmouth. He'd said he would do something, but the last few days he had tramped miles without so much as the whiff of a job.

With the government refusing to let the workhouse Guardians give coal miners a penny – if they wanted relief they could go into the workhouse with their families to get it, that was Chamberlain's attitude – there was nowhere else to go. And she would die before she went into one of those places, and work till she dropped on her feet before she saw her mam and da and the others go in. Walter and Renee were just about getting by on Renee's wage although they were weeks behind with the rent, but Renee could have helped their mam out a bit by pawning some of their furniture. But if her sister didn't want to do that, she didn't want to. She couldn't force Renee to help out at home and when she'd broached the matter with her, Renee had got very much on her high horse.

Carrie took a deep breath and spoke to David from the heart. 'I've had a couple of weeks of doing nothing and I can't stand it,' she said quietly. 'I'm not made that way, David.'

'You've kept this place clean and got us meals.'

'Which doesn't take more than half an hour at most.' With no coal to light the range, they'd been eating bread and cheese, and any food they could get from the market stalls at the end of the day, such as bruised fruit or the scrapings of cooked ham or chitterlings and dripping.

'But look at you.' The wave of his hand took in her swollen stomach and puffy ankles. 'And what about when the bairn comes?'

He knew immediately he'd made a mistake. She never mentioned the coming event; it was as though she had blocked it out of her mind, and any reference to the baby by him always got the blank dead look he was receiving now. 'I'll manage.'

It was final and David recognised it as such, even as he

continued to argue with her for a few minutes more. In truth, he didn't know what they were going to do. The last few nights he hadn't slept a wink worrying how he was going to provide food for them to eat, and they had nowt for the bairn when it came, not so much as a few rags to use for nappies.

From the beginning of the strike the miners' halls had given out second-hand clothing and boots, particularly for the bairns, when they knew the need was genuine but plenty of desperate families wouldn't ask for charity, despite the fact their bairns were running around in rags with their backsides hanging out and no shoes on their feet. Others had been up to get something or other more than once, some on the quiet and some militantly declaring to anyone who would listen that it wasn't 'handouts'. They were all owed something for the blood, sweat and tears they'd put in over the years, and were still putting in.

Of the two camps, David knew he was in the former. How his pride would stand up if he saw Carrie in boots with more holes in them than leather, and the baby without a stitch, was another matter, and he prayed it wouldn't come to that. His suit and one decent shirt and tie had long since found their way to the pawn shop, along with the dress, hat and shoes Carrie had been wed in. They both now only possessed the clothes they stood up in, which Carrie would wash and dry overnight when necessary.

He stood awkwardly staring down at her bent head as she rubbed soap over the metal roller she was using because it was sticking. Her hair was still as shining and silky as if she washed it every night in a fancy shampoo, and the curve of her long slender neck brought an ache to his chest and his loins. He still couldn't look at her without wanting her, and that in spite of her being so far gone and about to pop, he thought wretchedly. He'd die for her without even giving it a thought, and here he was standing watching her work herself to death. Maybe she would have done better without him after all; his good intentions seemed to have dragged her further and further down.

And then she looked up and smiled at him. 'There's some tea in the pot although it's a bit stewed. Ada brought it in earlier,' she said softly. 'She made out she fancied an afternoon cuppa with me and then wouldn't take the tray back, saying she'd forgotten she'd got a pot on the hob at home. I don't know what we'd do without her, do you?'

He forced himself to smile back although he was horrified to find he wanted to cry.

Perhaps something of what he was feeling showed in his face because the next moment Carrie pushed the baking board to one side, rose to her feet and touched his arm gently in one of the rare physical gestures she made now and then. 'It will all work out, David. The strike won't last for ever and we'll get through.'

He felt himself tense slightly as she touched him; he always did because if he didn't have absolute control of himself he knew he would grab her and crush her to him. Other times, when the desire sprang up so hot and strong it was unbearable, he would take a long walk, even as far as Seaham on occasion. The nights were the worst. Lying beside her as she slept, rock hard and his loins on fire for hours, he thought he'd go mad at times. But it was worth it. *She* was worth it. He still couldn't believe it sometimes when he opened the door and there she was, waiting for him to come home.

He swallowed, as if ridding himself of a piece of sharp stone, and said, 'I know, I know,' and in case she read what was in his eyes he turned and walked over to the bed where Ada had left the tray. There was a small plate of gingerbread beside the teapot, and again the lump in his throat threatened to choke him. In spite of everything he was a darn sight better off than his da; by, he was that, he told himself grimly. Alec and his mam had made it clear every bite his da ate was on sufferance, according to Lillian, and but for his sister insisting their da met her in her break at midday when she always made sure he had a good feed from the faggot and pease pudding stall or the meat pie stall in the old market, he'd have wasted away by now. Lillian said it had got so he wouldn't take so much as a mouthful at home.

Not that his da had said a word about it, in spite of them being on the same shift for picket duty and such. But he could understand that, David thought. He'd be the same if it was him. It was one thing to suffer such humiliation, quite another to bring it out into the open. He knew Lillian was worried about their da; every time she came round to see him and Carrie it was the first thing she talked about, and he had noticed a change in him the last weeks or so. His da didn't carry himself straight any more or whistle like he used to. It was almost as if something had gone, been extinguished inside, so that he was shrinking down inside himself. Damn this strike, they'd all be up the pole by the end of it.

He poured two mugs of black tea and took one across to Carrie, along with the gingerbread. 'Get this down you, lass,' he said roughly, his eyes resting on the batch of fireworks she had already made which were lying in a Riley's Toffee-Roll tin.

Carrie took the tea but shook her head at the gingerbread. 'I've had some, that's for you.'

Her wrists were so thin they looked as if you could snap them with the slightest pressure, and although her stomach was ballooning and her feet were puffy, the rest of her was as thin as a rake. He didn't believe she'd eaten anything since the crust of bread and small smidgen of cheese she'd had before he had gone out that morning. 'Eat it.' He put the plate in front of her. 'You've had your way about the fireworks, let me have mine in this,' he said with a smile to soften his words.

'Half each then?'

He moved his head impatiently. 'I don't want nowt. Eat it up and then I'll take the tray back to Ada in a minute or two.'

The saliva filled his mouth as Carrie reluctantly bit into Ada's homemade gingerbread. He had thought he knew what it was to be hungry in the past, but the strike had shown him different. He had only to think of inch-thick bread held in front of a glowing fire on the toasting fork for his stomach to grumble, toast with melting golden butter fresh from the farm or salty pork dripping from the butcher's.

Funny, but of all the food he'd had to do without in the last weeks, it was the smell and taste of toast he missed the most. Or maybe it wasn't so strange. Toast was part and parcel of the happy times in his childhood, the occasions when he'd spent days or weeks at his Gran and Granda Sutton's when his mother had got fed up with four bairns under her feet and had shipped himself and Lillian off to South Shields for a while.

He had loved it there, running wild for the most part in a way he was never allowed to do at home but always knowing Gran Sutton's small two-roomed cottage was there to go back to at the end of the day. A kettle always on the hob, hot bath water in front of a rich red, yellow and orange fire, a glowing oven shelf wrapped in old sacking to warm the pallet bed in front of the range in which he and Lillian slept, and the smell of nutty slack and leftover tea leaves dampening down the fire as they'd drifted off to sleep listening to his gran and granda talk.

When he was still knee high to a grasshopper he would go and sit with the retired miners on the bench outside the village hall. They would send him home when the sun was setting and it was time for dinner, chivying him off with a tiny clay pipe and a hap'orth of chocolate tobacco, like as not. There had been big fat mushrooms in the fields close to the village, along with blackberries and sloes in the autumn, and he could still recall the beauty of the glistening frost on the spiders' webs draping the hedgerows in the winter.

He had never wanted to go home, never. And when his da had come to collect them, he'd known the indefinable something that existed between his parents made his da feel the same. His gran would send them off loaded down with homemade toffee, as brittle as it was transparent, and she always hugged his da longer than she ever did anyone else.

And then there was home and his mam waiting for them with a tight mouth and hard hands, her fingers bruising him as she stripped off his clothes, bewailing the state of them until she and his da had the inevitable row. And real life would begin again.

'Here.' He came out of his thoughts to find Carrie had risen to stand in front of him, holding a piece of gingerbread to his lips as she said again, 'Here, eat it. Please.'

He stared at her, and when she blinked at him and then smiled he opened his mouth and she popped the morsel inside. He chewed and swallowed, watching her all the time, and then said thickly, 'Thank you.'

She nodded, their gaze holding for a few moments more before she resumed her seat. And suddenly, in spite of his hunger and concern and fear, he felt as if he'd been handed the moon, gift-wrapped and diamond-studded.

It was later that night, lying beside each other in the three-quarter size bed without touching, that he began to talk of Gran and Granda Sutton who had passed away a few winters before. He talked like he had never been able to talk to her before, openly and without restraint. The darkness helped, that and her soft rejoinders that told him she knew how it was with his mam and da, and how things had been at home. When he had finished, David felt hot at just how much he'd revealed about himself.

All was quiet for a time, and then Carrie said softly, 'You shouldn't have married me, David. You ought to have someone who can love you like you deserve to be loved.' What must it have been like for him to grow up knowing his mother didn't love him? And he had known it, she could tell even though he hadn't actually said so. Perhaps Lillian and Walter felt the same way, she didn't know, but she did know that the hurt in David had gone deep. He gave the appearance of being so sure of himself, so tough, but the kernel within the hard shell was tender. She wished it wasn't. She didn't want it to be, she thought suddenly, thinking in the same breath, you're back to front and never mind the pony, lass, that's what you are. But the more nice things she found out about him, the more he intruded into the part of herself she needed to keep separate from him, from any man.

She didn't know what she was going to do when the baby came. Of course it might not live, lots didn't or were stillborn. She barely knew a family who hadn't lost a number of bairns to sickness within the first few weeks of their lives or before their first birthdays. Her own mam had lost three between herself and the twins being born. She hoped it was stillborn, that would be quick and final. The thought of having to look at it every day and remember what had happened . . . She wouldn't be able to bear it. But first she had to have it, and from what she'd gathered listening to the chatter of the married women when they were engaged in possing the clothes and linen in the big wooden tub in the backyard or stoking up the boiler in the washhouse, the pain was terrible. But she didn't mind that; well, she did, but she could put up with it if it meant this thing inside her was gone. They said a child born in strife always had something the matter with it, a club foot or a twisted body; some were imbeciles like Nancy Gibb or Sally Prince who had big heads and gibbered and dribbled all the time, so what was hers going to be like, conceived in violence and horror? It would be a monstrosity, she knew it.

The bed creaked as David stirred at the side of her, and then he said, 'Don't say I shouldn't have married you, lass. For better or worse we made our vows before God and man, and' – there was a slight pause before he continued – 'I don't regret it.' He wanted to ask her if she felt the same but he was too afraid he would know when she lied. And again, because of the darkness he felt able to add, 'You'll feel better after the bairn's born. You're worn out and no wonder with this heat.'

She didn't care about the heat or the strike or living in this one room, none of it would have mattered if she could just have gone back in time to Renee's wedding day and the girl she had been then. But she couldn't say that. He wouldn't understand and even if he did she daren't go down that road. She mustn't think about it, she could get by if she didn't think about it.

'Goodnight, David.' She was lying on her side; with her belly so big she had found it was the only way to sleep these days and she always made sure she had her back to him although he had never touched her, except by accident or when he was asleep.

'Carrie?'

'What?'

Her tone was flat and David said quietly, 'Nothing, it doesn't matter. Goodnight.'

Why hadn't he told her he loved her when she'd said he shouldn't have married her? It had been the perfect opportunity to voice the words which forever hovered on his tongue but he just hadn't been able to spit them out. Oh, he was stupid, useless. Worse than useless.

He heaved on to his side, the movement abrupt. It was no good telling himself he didn't need to voice it, that actions speak louder than words. Lasses put great store by those words, according to Walter. The Christmas before last when his brother had been so well oiled his breath knocked you backwards, he could remember Walter telling him that Renee always made him say he loved her before she'd have any making on. Not that that had any relevance in Carrie's condition, of course.

But he needed to say it. It was the truth, and once said it would be up to her what she made of it. But at least he would know that she knew.

David didn't let himself add here, whatever happened, because to do so would give form to the ever present spectre sitting on his shoulder, the little voice that whispered, you won't keep her, you know that, don't you? One day she'll be gone. It's just a question of how soon.

Instead he forced his mind away from the still figure beside him, and thought about the march planned for the next morning. There had been many since the strike began, organised attempts to get people's attention, but almost from the first the police had had orders to stamp down hard on such tactics. Many good men had been thrown into jail for 'causing disaffection', in spite of the fact that at the best of times ragtaggle miners were no threat to well-fed, hale and hearty policemen on big strong horses who used their batons to great effect. On the last march three days before, it had been miners nil, police eight, with six miners knocked unconscious and two with broken legs. He could understand there being a few broken noses and bloody heads when they were trying to stop the police escorting the blacklegs into the collieries, but a peaceful march? And now quite a few of the younger lads were arming themselves with anything from hammers to lumps of lead piping, which worried him.

David frowned in the darkness. Still, all he could do was to stay close to his da and Walter so the three of them could look out for each other.

He turned on his back once more and regulated his breathing to induce sleep, but it was a long time coming.

When Ned and Walter knocked on the door the next morning, David was ready to leave.

Carrie smiled at them all as she came to wave them off from the doorstep, but her voice was troubled when she said, 'Look after yourselves, won't you.'

'Don't you fret, lass.' It was Ned who responded, adding, in an effort to reassure his daughter-in-law, 'We'll make sure the other fella comes off worse if there's a punch-up. How's that?' and he brandished an old table leg he had under his jacket.

Carrie's expression made David hustle the other two away. 'Me and Walter will be keeping him out of trouble, lass,' he called over his shoulder in an effort to lighten the moment.

'Keepin' me out of trouble?' Ned was indignant. 'An' who'll be keepin' you out of trouble while you're keepin' me, I'd like to know?'

Walter shook his head. 'Couldn't you see she was worried, man?' he asked with a glance at David. 'It didn't help showing her a cudgel, now did it?'

Ned was genuinely amazed. 'I thought it'd comfort her, knowin' I'd brought somethin' to protect us all with.'

David and Walter gave up.

Outside the colliery gates one of the union leaders gave the gathering a pep talk along the lines of 'fight the good fight' but no violence unless they were provoked, and then they were off. Along with other miners from Durham pits they were marching to Whitburn where a meeting had been organised on the beach.

David saw Billy and Sandy close by them at one point, but although he felt Billy would have liked to speak, Sandy's grim expression and quickening footsteps made it clear he was as bitter as ever.

When the march reached the beach, a mass of other miners had already congregated there. There were a few women scattered amongst the men, something David disagreed with strongly. A march was no place for a woman, not when things could turn nasty. And today the mood was sombre, he could feel it. Some of the men had got so worked up by recent events they were spoiling for a fight, and the line of policemen on horses at the top of the beach looked just as ready to get stuck in.

He glanced at them, noticing the way they were sitting quietly but all the time thudding their batons into the palms of their hands. And the horses were different beasts from the obliging animals they used down the pit. Great brutes these were, with teeth as big as pit props.

The men from the Wearmouth pit were the last to arrive, and now that they were all assembled, one of the union leaders from the Whitburn colliery stepped on to an orange box and began to thank everyone for coming. It was what the police had been waiting for. The miner hadn't said two words before the officer leading the police brought his horse right in front of the union official. The officer was accompanied by a constable on foot carrying a pair of handcuffs which he swung as he walked.

David sensed what was about to happen, but even as he turned to Walter and said, 'Let's get Da out of this,' the mounted officer began to shout that he was making an arrest under the Unlawful Assembly Act. One of the miners hit out and sent the constable sprawling. Then all hell broke loose.

The mounted policemen galloped into the throng, lashing out with their truncheons indiscriminately, their horses trampling men and women alike. There was yelling and screaming, the crowd bunched together, surging this way and that. David found he couldn't move. His father and Walter were only two or three people away, but hemmed in as he was he couldn't reach them. Then he found himself swept away in a press of bodies and it was all he could do to stay on his feet. Blood began to flow as people were beaten to the ground. Just in front of him he saw one young lad, who couldn't have been more than twelve years old, hit so hard his skull caved in. Bones were being smashed, people were being mangled under the hooves of the horses and were crumpling all around him, and still the assault continued. Those who could get away were scattering in all directions, some of them chased by police.

For a moment David caught sight of his father and Walter. They were scrambling out of the way of a mounted officer, Ned's cap gone and blood pouring from a gash above his eye, but then the ranks closed again and he lost sight of them. He tried to force his way in their direction and suddenly found himself in front of Billy. Carrie's brother was caught like a rat in a trap between two mounted police, and before David could do anything, the younger of the riders brought his truncheon down with all his might on Billy's head, laughing as he did so.

David saw his old friend's knees buckle but somehow Billy managed to stay on his feet, clearly more terrified of the razor-sharp hooves than the other officer who was raising his arm to strike. This individual was a big, thickset man whose arms were bulging in his uniform. This swine was going to brain Billy for sure.

David didn't think about what he was going to do; instinct took over and he grabbed the horse's saddle. He swung his body into the side of the beast, trying to dismount its rider, but it was futile. The saddle was tightly strapped on with buckles the size of a man's hand, but the policeman was distracted and began to hit out at David's hands. With the first policeman now belting the stuffing out of the people to the right, Billy had the few seconds he needed. Just as the agonising pain in his hands forced David to let go, a surge in the crowd pushed Billy away from the horses and out of sight.

A minute or two later David found his father and Walter, who had been looking for him. Ned was the worse for wear but still standing, and Walter was relatively unscathed. 'Let's get the hell out of this lot,' muttered Walter, but this was easier said than done. Eventually, however, they were running and stumbling back the way they had marched just a short while before, away from the screaming and shouting and smell of horse dung. When they reached the end of the bay, David came to a halt. He and Walter were more or less holding their father on his feet now. All around them miners lurched past, some blaspheming, others shocked into angry silence. The more able-bodied were helping and in some cases carrying those who were badly injured.

David wanted to know if Billy was out of the madness, Sandy too, but he couldn't see either of them in the chaos. And he and Walter needed to get their da home, that was the first priority.

They stood catching their breath, Ned supported between them, looking at the folk streaming past them. They were just ordinary men and women, solid working-class mining stock and their only crime was to want a reasonable wage at the end of the day. The world had gone mad.

A young man David knew quite well, who had been on the last shift with him at the colliery before the gates had been locked and barred, passed by, carrying his unconscious wife in his arms. David remembered this lass; she was a bonny piece and they had only been married twelve months come September.

'Look what they've done to her.' Jackie was sobbing, the tears mingling with the blood on his face. 'Smashed all her teeth in and broken her nose. Aimed straight for her face, one of 'em did.'

'Get her home, man.' David didn't know what else to say. And then, as Ned sagged more heavily between them, he said to Walter, 'Come on, Walt. That's the place for us an' all.' The pain in his hand was excruciating now and he was overwhelmingly thankful Walter was with him. He would never have managed his father otherwise. The walk back was going to be a long one.

Chapter Eight

When the knock came at the door shortly after David had left for the march, Carrie thought for a moment it was Ada. Then, when Renee's voice said, 'Carrie? It's me,' she rose hastily, put the baking board to one side and hurried across the room.

Carrie's smile of welcome died a quick death as she took in her sister's face. 'What's the matter?' She reached out to Renee who was clinging to the doorpost. 'Are you ill? You look as though you should be in bed.'

Renee continued to hold on to the doorpost for some moments, her face twisted in pain, and just when Carrie was wondering if she needed to call Ada to help her lift Renee across to the bed, her sister reached out her hand. 'I'll be all right if I can sit down,' she said shakily. 'Can you help me?'

Really frightened now, Carrie grasped Renee's arm, taking most of her sister's considerable weight as she guided her over to the bed. 'You need to lie down a minute, lass, then you'll feel better.'

After collapsing on the covers, Renee lay still for a moment. Her normally rosy face was colourless and her breathing was deep and ragged. Carrie knelt on the floor at the side of the bed, stroking the hair away from her sister's damp brow. She waited until a vestige of colour came back into Renee's cheeks before she said, 'What is it? Does Walter know you're ill?'

'Carrie, you've got to help me. I've . . . done something.'

'Done something?'

'Aye, and I know you'll think I'm bad but I had to do it. I'm not like you, I couldn't put up with—' Renee stopped, sucking in breath. 'I tried all the normal things – drinking gin, scalding baths and the like, but nothing worked. Then Elsie at work put me on to a woman she knows in the East End, a midwife.'

Carrie had stopped stroking her sister's brow, her hand frozen midway. She stared into the white face, unable to take in what she was hearing. The sweat was standing out like tiny teardrops on Renee's upper lip, and she knew her sister expected her to say something but no words would come.

'Don't look at me like that.' Renee turned her head to the side in one of the peevish flounces Carrie remembered from the past, but then Renee's knees came up with what was obviously a cramping pain in her stomach and she groaned horribly, writhing about for some thirty seconds before she relaxed again.

Carrie remained perfectly still. Renee had gone to see one of the backstreet midwives in the East End, the sort who were known for getting rid of as many babies as they delivered. Carrie couldn't believe her sister could have done such a thing. Since her marriage and the washdays spent round the communal poss tub Carrie'd had a rude awakening to some of the seedier facts of life, but even among the women in Brooke Street, the old wives who practised their dangerous art amidst filth and degradation were always spoken of in furtive whispers.

'It's Walter's fault,' Renee panted weakly. 'He promised me he'd be careful but since we've been wed he don't seem to care any more. A couple of times I've gone mad at him and he just shakes his head and smiles that silly smile of his and parrots out that there's worse things in life than a bairn.'

'Does he know you're expecting?'

'Course he doesn't know, haven't you been listening? He wants me to fall, I know he does; all his talk when we were courting about waiting till I was ready and it being up to me was just that – talk. I think he's done this on purpose. But I'm not getting stuck with a bairn, Carrie. I'd rather top meself. Life with Walter is bad enough but at least I've my job and my own money to enjoy meself with, or I will have when he's back at work. I want to live a bit before I'm put six foot under in a wooden overcoat. Have nice things and live in a nice house.'

'I thought you and Walter were happy,' Carrie said, bewildered.

'Happy? Huh! You don't know the half, lass. By, I've had my eyes opened all right. Just 'cos we're married he expects me to be the little wife with the dinner on the table and his slippers by the fire, and the next minute wanting me skirt to be over me head while he takes his pleasure. And another thing, he seems older than his da at times. At least Ned likes to go down the pub and have his betting on the side; all Walter wants to do is for us to sit at home and twiddle our thumbs of an evening. I had more fun when we were courting.'

Carrie sank back on to the flagstones, dumbfounded. She'd had no idea Renee was feeling like this. But then the only times she had seen her sister since they were both married was in the company of their husbands. True, Walter had popped round a few times during the day since the strike and both she and David had thought he seemed subdued, but then everyone was down in the mouth, struggling as they all were.

The next pain caused Renee to grip a handful of the bedclothes. She gasped and moaned her way through it, and when Carrie again began stroking her forehead, she opened

123

her eyes and said, 'I'm sorry, lass. I didn't intend to burden you with this.'

'It's all right.'

'I went to see this woman Elsie told me about a couple of evenings ago, but knowing Walter was away on this march today I thought I'd go this morning to . . . have it done. I went early, I said to Walter it was overtime and heaven knows we need some with him bringing in nowt' – her tone was bitter and it reminded Carrie of Olive Sutton when she talked about her husband – 'and then I was going to go home and it could've all been over before he came back. Either that or I'd have made out I came home from the factory feeling rough with the monthly. But, well, it wasn't like I expected.' And that was putting it mildly. She had expected to have to drink something which would scour her out, or maybe for the woman to pummel her about a bit, something along those lines, but the knitting needle had been like a blade being pushed up inside her. Ever since, she had been almost rent in two when the pains hit and scared out of her wits.

'How far gone are you?'

'I've only just missed me second monthly, so that's not like it's a proper baby or anything, is it?'

Carrie made no reply to this but her face must have spoken for her, because Renee again turned her head to the side, and her voice was querulous when she said, 'It's all right for you, Carrie. You don't mind being in the family way but I'm different.'

The urge to bite back was strong but worry for her sister overrode everything else. 'You ought to see a doctor, Renee. You know that, don't you?'

'No, no.' Renee was gripping her hand again. 'Please, Carrie, don't tell anyone, *please*. You're the only one I can trust and

124

I didn't want to be on my own. It's done now, nothing can change that, and the woman said it would be over within a few hours.'

'What if she's done something, damaged you inside?' Carrie extricated her hand and reached over to remove her sister's footwear as she spoke. Instead of brown or black boots, Renee was wearing shoes of patent leather, and her stockings weren't of wool but were soft and silky to the touch. For a second the thought of what these must have cost flashed through Carrie's mind before she told herself it was none of her business what Renee did with her wages. And her mam wouldn't have accepted the money anyway. Although a couple of bags of groceries left in the scullery . . .

'She hasn't damaged me, not like that,' Renee protested, adding a moment later, 'but even if she has I don't care as long as I get rid of it.' And then another spasm seized her. When it was over, she said, 'Promise me, lass. Promise me you'll say nowt to no one. If you don't I swear I'll crawl out of here right now if I have to.'

The next two hours were the longest of Carrie's life but eventually it was over. When Renee started to bleed she insisted on climbing off the bed and squatting over the chamber pot so nothing got on the blankets that might raise questions from David. Shocked and upset though she was with Renee, Carrie couldn't help but marvel at her sister's iron strength of will. But if she was truthful Renee's cold-blooded attitude about what she'd done made Carrie's flesh creep. She held her sister's hand, mopped her brow and fed her sips of water until her own back was aching fit to break and she felt giddy and weak, but inside she was thinking, I don't know her. This is my own sister and yet I don't know her, because I would never have thought in a hundred years she could do something like this.

Eventually Renee stood up and draped the cardigan she had been wearing across the chamber pot. Then she washed herself with the cold water and soap Carrie had provided – there had been no coal for the range for days. Finally she said, 'I'm going to the privy.' And she picked up the pot.

Dumbly Carrie stared at her, and as though in answer to an accusation, Renee said sharply, 'It's just like the monthly has come late and all at once. That's all.'

No, no it wasn't.

'You won't say anything? Not to anyone?' Renee's voice had become softer, pleading. 'I know you don't agree with it but it's done now. You won't let on?'

'You know I won't.'

'It's for the best, Carrie.'

'It was a baby.' She hadn't meant to say it, the words had just slipped out, but Renee's expression didn't alter.

'I don't see it like that,' she said flatly. 'I'm sorry, but I don't. And I'll tell you something else, lass. The time's coming when men won't have it all their own way and women'll be able to pick and choose whether they have bairns or not, ordinary, working-class women. This is my body and my life and I don't see why I shouldn't say what happens to both. It's not up to Walter.'

Carrie said nothing to this and after a moment Renee went out of the room. A moment later the back door into the yard creaked. Carrie looked across to the chair and the baking board. It seemed incredible that only a couple of hours ago she had been sitting there working, contemplating going to see the owner of the corner shop and asking him to extend their credit for a few more groceries, on the understanding she would pay a chunk off the slate with her first week's wages. It seemed as if an age had passed since then.

When Renee came back into the room she had her hand pressed over her stomach, but when Carrie said, 'Perhaps you should wait a while before you go home,' her sister shook her head. She slid the chamber pot, washed out and clean, under the bed, straightened and then walked slowly over to Carrie.

'I didn't mean to involve you in this, lass, but I was scared,' she said softly. 'I didn't expect the pain to be so bad.'

'I know.' To Carrie, she looked at this moment more like the old Renee who only let down her defences when the two of them were alone.

'We're still friends, aren't we?'

'Don't be daft.' Carrie hugged her, saying, 'Look after yourself the next little while.'

'I will.' Renee smiled but her voice was husky. 'You know me, lass. Look after number one because no other blighter will. Carrie,' she hesitated a second before going on, 'you and David, are you happy? I mean, it was so sudden and everything, the wedding, because of—' She flapped her hand. 'Well, let's just say I wasn't surprised when I found out you were expecting a few weeks later.'

Carrie eyed her sister steadily. She had known this conversation would come sooner or later, she was just surprised it had taken Renee this long. 'We're fine.'

'I'm glad.' Renee had obviously been hoping for more. 'I thought David would be happy, Walter said he'd suspected David had liked you for years, but you'd never mentioned him.'

'Didn't I?' Carrie shrugged. 'Perhaps I did and you weren't listening.'

Renee's hand went again to her stomach and she winced. 'I think I'll get along home, lass, and let Walter look after me for a change when he gets in. Although I could be half dead and he'd only notice if his dinner wasn't on the table,' she added with the bitterness which had so disturbed Carrie before. 'These stupid marches, what good do they do?'

Carrie watched her sister leave with deep sadness, and it was only when she was alone that she realised just how much the last few hours had taken out of her. If what Renee said was true and Walter really had deliberately tried to get her pregnant, even knowing how she felt about having a bairn, that was inexcusable.

She turned to survey the room, her eyes drawn to the rumpled covers on the bed and then the chamber pot beneath it.

But to do away with the baby?

She glanced across to the baking board as the reality of what had just occurred hammered in her head, and, her mind seeking temporary refuge in the mundane, she found herself murmuring, 'I must get on, else I won't get my quota done.' Earlier she had placed a damp towel over the papers which had been stiff and difficult to roll that morning, but now it would be quite dry. She'd have to dampen it again. But still she did not move.

Renee had got rid of her baby, but was she any different? She'd wished the child inside her dead a hundred times since Alec had forced her.

No, it *was* different. It was as if there were two arguments going on in her head. Renee was married and she had been courting Walter for over two years before they had wed. Their child had been conceived in love, or at least respectability. Renee might not have liked the end result but she had lain with Walter because she wanted to; her sister would be the first to admit she liked a bit of making on.

But a bairn was a bairn, wasn't it? No child asked to be born, its birth was a result of a man and a woman making on, and who gave anyone, even the mother, the right to take away a life or wish the unborn child dead? Why was it wrong for Renee to want her baby dead because she was married and the bairn was her husband's, and right for her to wish hers gone because of how it had come into being? Her hand touched the mound of her stomach. She was a hypocrite, that was the truth of the matter, but she couldn't help how she felt. Nevertheless, she had to face the fact that this bairn inside her was the innocent one in all of this, just as Renee's had been. But that tiny life had been extinguished now, flushed out and disposed of in the privy where the scavenger's shovels would deal with it.

She put her hand to her throat, the lump there threatening to choke her. Oh, Renee, Renee, what have you done? Carrie worked the skin of her neck for a moment, struggling to get a hold on the emotion beginning to swamp her.

She couldn't think of this now, not Renee's dead baby nor her live one. Her hand moved to massage her forehead where a pulse of pain was throbbing. She'd think about it later, when she was lying quiet in the darkness with only the sound of David's breathing disturbing the night. Then she could re-examine everything that had gone on and all that Renee had said, along with these thoughts about her own baby.

She made herself walk across to the lumpy old armchair, settled the small table holding the baking board in front of her and sat down with a heavy sigh. She must concentrate on getting as much work done as she could before she walked along to the corner shop. She'd make sure she allowed enough time before David came back; Mr Marley would be more likely to agree to let them have a few things on the slate if she went to see him herself. He was a nice man at heart.

The extent of her girth made working at the table difficult but there was nothing to be done about that. As her fingers began to move swiftly with monotonous regularity, Carrie became almost oblivious to the papers and paste in her hands. Her thoughts sped on. David wouldn't like it but she would continue making the firework cases at home even once he was in work. They had weeks of rent to clear for a start, but it wasn't only that. They had to get out of this one room and into either the upstairs or the downstairs of a house at some point; they couldn't stay here for ever. She *wouldn't* stay here for ever. Five shillings for ten gross of crackers might not be much in the way of things considering the hours involved, but it wasn't to be sneezed at either. And she would make every penny work for them, just like her mam had done at home. Like that fishwife had said to her the night she'd found out Alec was going to marry Miss Reed, you had to take life by the scruff of its neck and bash its face in. She hadn't felt much like doing any bashing lately, but maybe it was time.

Her fingers became still and her heart began to thump hard. She wasn't going to let Alec Sutton taking her down ruin her life, not while there was breath in her body.

And David? The thumping intensified. She knew if she was being truthful that she still had to steel herself if he so much as touched her hand. What about the rest of it, the making on which would be bound to happen once the bairn was born? She couldn't expect otherwise. How would she stand that? Fear and revulsion rose up in her throat but again she cautioned herself, saying silently, enough, enough. Don't think of this now. Wait till the bairn's born and see what happens. He's a nice man, you above anyone have had proof of that. Take it a day at a time. Just a day at a time.

Carrie was standing on the doorstep when David turned the corner of Brooke Street later that day. She had been standing

130

there for quite a while, ever since she had gone to see Mr Marley. It had been then that she had seen the first of the miners who were beginning to straggle back into Monkwearmouth, bruised and battered and bleeding, and had heard what had transpired on Whitburn sands.

David paused when he caught sight of her. Her shawl was wrapped round her body in a vain attempt to hide her swollen belly, and she was leaning against the doorpost as though she was spent.

Seeing her standing there, for all the world as though she was an ordinary wife and theirs was an ordinary marriage, drained him of all strength for a moment. Then he forced himself to walk on, trying to ignore the pain in his hand which was making him sweat, along with the sick giddiness which had been with him ever since he'd lost his footing in the crush shortly after the incident with Billy, and a passing policeman had thought it opportune to put the boot in. In contrast, Ned had seemed to improve on the way home, which was something to be thankful for because he doubted if he could have helped Walter much with their da the way he'd begun to feel. When he had left Walter and his father, he had continued on with men who lived close to him and he responded to their farewells without taking his eyes off the figure on the doorstep. He could see her face was as white as bleached linen, her distress apparent to him when he was still some good few yards away.

As he neared the house, she called, saying, 'Oh, David, David,' a moment before the bulky form of their landlady filled the space behind her.

'I've tried to make her come in an' take the weight off for the last hour an' more, lad, but she was havin' none of it,' Ada bawled as though he was two streets away rather than two houses. 'Stubborn as a field full of cuddies in their second wind, your lass.' And then, as he reached the two women, Ada added, 'Landsakes, lad. It looks like they've done a number on you.'

He obviously looked as bad as he felt. Carrie had gone a shade paler still. David stretched his mouth in what he hoped resembled a smile, his gaze on his wife as he said, 'I'm all right, Ada. Come on, let's get inside.'

'If you're all right I'd hate to see the poor blighters who aren't feelin' too good,' Ada returned, ushering the two of them inside and following them into their room. 'Damn pollises chargin' about on their horses an' thinkin' they can do whatever they like. There ought to be a law against 'em.'

David couldn't help but smile. Ada's plump face was perfectly serious and highly indignant which somehow made what she'd said all the funnier. He hadn't thought he could work up a real smile after what he'd seen the day and how he was feeling, but then he hadn't accounted for Ada.

'Sit down, David.' Carrie's voice was quiet but firm, and when she pushed him down on to the bed he found he was glad to sit back against the iron headboard. The last half-mile or so he'd begun to wonder if he was going to make it home under his own steam. 'Let me look at your hand.'

He was feeling peculiar, really peculiar now, but he held out his hand to her, feeling her flesh touch his very gently. His fingers had swollen to twice their normal size on the hand the policeman had hammered at, and he could feel the broken ends of the bones in his thumb and first three fingers. Only his little one still seemed intact although bruised.

'You've a nasty bump on your head,' Ada commented helpfully at the side of Carrie. 'Egg size, it is, an' there's a gash the size of a kitten's tail alongside it. You got any laudanum in the house, hinny?' When Carrie shook her head, Ada said, 'I'll go an' get mine, he'll need somethin' the night an' I always keep some

132

by for when me rheumatism's givin' me gyp. You're goin' to need a doctor for that hand though, lad.'

'We can't afford one, Ada.' Carrie didn't look at her as she spoke. 'David, my da broke two of his fingers last year and I helped my mam when she saw to him.'

This wasn't a question but he answered as though it was, saying, 'Aye, have a go then, lass.' He just hoped he wouldn't disgrace himself in front of the pair of them and give way to the nausea making his mouth water. He'd only broken fingers; he'd seen worse injuries every day down the pit and men still able to act the cuddy even as they were being stretchered away.

'What'll you need, lass?' Ada's voice was low now.

'Bandages, any clean rags will do, and some pegs for splints for each finger. Oh, and a flat piece of wood to fix the whole hand to at the end.'

'I'll go an' see what I've got.'

Ada bustled away, and when they were alone Carrie said, 'I'll be as careful as I can but it'll hurt, David. My da yelled a bit.' He hadn't, but she thought it would make David feel better if he had to. David's hand was twice, three times worse than her father's had been.

Once the little table was clear of the baking board and fireworks and had one of Ada's old towels spread over it, Carrie made David sit in the armchair, his hand spread palm down on the flat surface of the table. Along with the strips of linen and other things, Ada had brought a half-bottle of brandy. 'Always keep a drop by me for when I'm not feelin' too good,' she said, pouring a generous measure into a glass and handing it to David as she spoke. 'Nothin' like a spot of brandy for puttin' fire in your belly.'

David wasn't about to argue with this. He drank the neat spirit straight down, feeling it burn a path down his throat

133

and into his stomach where it took care of the nausea. After another glass, the debilitating sensation of faintness went too, and suddenly things didn't seem so bad.

It took an hour and a half, but by the end of that time Carrie had succeeded in bandaging his thumb and each finger to small wooden splints made from Ada's pegs. After she'd finished setting the individual breaks, she bandaged the whole hand to one of Ada's big flat wooden table mats with a picture of the late Queen Victoria and Prince Albert painted on it. These had been a wedding present and were the old woman's pride and joy.

Ada stood at Carrie's side the whole time she worked, passing her whatever she needed, and now, as the last piece of linen was tied tightly into place, she said, 'Well, lad, if the infirmary had done the job you might have got a more professional finish than havin' the old Queen an' Prince, bless 'em, starin' up at you but I doubt you'd have had such a bonny nurse.' And then, as Carrie tried to straighten up and almost fell over, she added, 'Steady, lass, steady. You're all done in.'

She was exhausted. Carrie felt a pain slice through her abdomen, pulling downwards, and in repudiation of it she rubbed her hands vigorously together, saying, 'David's the poorly one, not me. Shall I give him some of the laudanum now?'

'Wait a while, lass. The brandy's still holdin' the pain for the moment but he'll need everythin' he can get in an hour or two.'

He wished they wouldn't speak as though he wasn't present. He rose from the armchair, his voice gruff as he said, 'Thanks, lass, but Ada's right, you are done in. You've looked after me so now go and lie down a while.'

'The both of you take the weight off.' Ada scuttled about, gathering the remnants of the pegs and strips of linen. 'I put a couple of taties in the ashes earlier an' there's half a pot pie goin' beggin'. The pair of you need somethin' hot the night so no arguin', lass. All right?'

Carrie had opened her mouth to protest but when she glanced at Ada's compressed lips she was silent. Dimly, with a mixture of understanding and compassion, she had come to realise that beneath the old woman's bustling exterior lived a lonely soul who felt redundant most of the time now her Charlie had gone. She said simply, 'Thank you, Ada.'

'No need to thank me, lass. I just can't abide to see good food wasted, that's all, an' you'll offend me if you talk of thanks. I'll be back in a mo.' And with that she sailed out of the room.

David, his face unsmiling, stared at Carrie for some moments as she returned the baking board and firework material to the table but she did not look at him. Curiously, she suddenly felt very shy. She had held his hand and worked on his fingers for an hour and a half, but in a funny sort of way it had not seemed as intimate as now. When David spoke, his voice came from deep in his throat. 'It was nice to see you waiting for me when I came home.'

She stopped her arranging of the papers and paste, her hands becoming still. And then she raised her head and looked directly into his dark brown eyes. 'I was worried.'

'You were?'

She nodded, and then because the intensity in his gaze was causing her heart to race, she added quickly, 'I was worried about me da and Billy, Walter too. All of you.'

Her voice was dismissive, and but for the memory of the look on her face when she had first seen him outside and the note in her voice when she'd said his name, his courage would have failed him. As it was he conceded to her barely concealed panic by turning away, but his voice was still deep and soft when he said, 'Like I said when you were doing my hand, I think the others are all right but I'll find out when I've had me dinner. But . . . it was nice, more than nice, to see you waiting like that, lass. I just wanted you to know.'

And in the second before Ada came hurrying back with two steaming plates of food, he looked at her again and smiled.

The pavements were still hot enough to fry eggs on when David left the house an hour later. The dusty streets were full of barefoot, raggedy bairns playing in the last of the dying sunlight and women sitting or standing on their doorsteps as they chattered to neighbours now the evening meal was over. Everyone seemed skinnier these days, he thought, walking swiftly as the pervading smell from baking privies got up his nose. Skinnier, raggier, more desperate. Hens had stopped laying and had been eaten, pet rabbits and prize pigeons too in some cases. Poor old Sep Heslop had cried like a baby when he'd let his birds go to fend for themselves, and from what he'd heard, Sep's wife had nearly brained him when she'd learned he'd given them their freedom rather than presenting them for the pot. But the miners would win through in the end, he told himself grimly. They had to. Anything else was unthinkable.

He had reached the corner of Southwick Road and was wishing he had taken a dose of Ada's laudanum like Carrie had tried to persuade him to do before he left the house when he heard his name called.

'David, man. I was on me way to see you.' Billy was in front of him, his good-natured face more ruddy than usual. And the reason for this became clear when he continued, 'I wanted to thank you for what you did, man. Is . . . is that the result of it?'

David had been supporting his throbbing hand as he walked along. Now he dropped it to his side. 'It's nowt.'

'Look, I wanted to see you.' There followed an awkward pause, at the end of which Billy cleared his throat and said, 'All this the last months over our Carrie, well, I've had a bellyful.'

David raised wry eyebrows.

'Heck, man, I didn't mean—' Billy stopped abruptly, his face scarlet, and then when David smiled he gave a sheepish grin. There was an attempt now at jocularity in his tone when he said, 'You know me, always put me foot in it even when I'm trying to make things right.'

They stared at each other for a moment, and then David said quietly, 'You're a good pal, Billy, you always have been, and I can understand how you felt. I'd have been the same if it had been Lillian.'

'Aye, mebbe, but to my mind it's gone on too long, the way me da is an' all. I'd like to get back to our old footing, that's what I'm saying.'

'And Sandy?'

Billy shrugged uncomfortably. 'You know me da. He thinks the sun shines out of our Carrie, always has done, and he's a stubborn old so-an'-so.'

'Won't it cause trouble if he finds out you're consorting with the enemy?'

David's tone had been light but Billy's was perfectly serious when he said, 'I've told him what I think, and I was already feeling this way before today, I want you to know that.'

David stared at his friend. In spite of the two-year age difference they had always got on like a house on fire and he had missed Billy's sly ribbing and humour more than he liked to admit. He had known he would come in for some stick from Sandy and Billy when he'd shouldered the blame for the bairn, but he hadn't thought they would keep it up like they had, and lately he'd been thinking along the lines of damn them both, they would want him before he wanted them. But like he'd just said, if it had been Lillian . . . He stretched out his good hand. 'Let's go on from here then, shall we?' he said quietly. 'If that's what you want.'

'Aye, it is.' Billy's voice was eager and he gripped David's arm, adding, 'Would I be welcome if I called round any time?'

'Don't be daft, the door's always been open, man. Look, I'm going to check on my da, he copped a blow to his head, but Carrie's at home. Why don't you go and see her? She'd like that.'

'Aye, I will. Thanks, David.' Billy punched him lightly in the chest. 'See you later then, eh?'

Even before he entered the back door David could hear raised voices from within the house, his father's the loudest. He paused for a moment in the scullery before walking through to the sitting room where he stood in the open doorway, surveying the occupants.

His mother, Alec and Lillian were seated at the table where the remains of the evening meal still lay, but his father was standing in front of the range, facing the others like an animal at bay. 'You know nowt about it, nowt,' he was shouting, his face as red as a beetroot. 'Poncin' about in that damn shop like Lord Muck! You've never done a decent day's work in your life.'

Alec, in strict contrast to his father, was leaning back in his chair in a nonchalant pose, his long legs stretched out in front of him and his arms crossed over his chest. His voice, too, was casual when he said, 'That's a matter of opinion, but even if you were right, my "poncing about" brings in a sight more than you breaking your back down the pit does, and that's when you're in work. Face it, Da, no one is interested in the coal miners' dispute any more. People are only concerned about such things when they're being inconvenienced, and with coal coming in from Germany they couldn't care less about the miners. You're doing yourselves no favours acting like maniacs and attacking the police who are only trying to do their jobs, when all's said and done.'

'Like Da said, you know nowt about it.' David's voice was raw. Alec always seemed to have the power to enrage him, not least because his brother was so cocksure of himself.

'Little brother.' It was a slow drawl as Alec turned his head and noticed David. 'And sporting battle scars, I see. That must make you feel like a man.'

'Something you'd know nothing about,' David returned bitterly. 'How does it go, Alec? Oh aye. Yes, Mr Reed. No, Mr Reed. Three bags full, Mr Reed, an' how low would you like me to grovel, Mr Reed?'

Alec was sitting up straight now and for a moment it looked as though he would spring up and strike his brother. Olive must have thought so because she caught at Alec's arm, her voice low and deadly as she glared at David and said, 'You, keep a civil tongue in your head or get out.'

'Don't tell him to get out. This is my house an' I say who's welcome an' who isn't.'

'Oh aye?' Olive's gaze snapped from David to her husband. 'Your house, is it? And who's been paying the rent the last umpteen weeks and put food on the table, I'd like to know?'

'You . . . you she-devil.' Ned's words were low now but heavy with such bitterness, David saw his mother blink. 'All the years I've provided, workin' extra shifts when I could get 'em when things were tight, an' the minute I'm not bringin' in you throw it in me face mornin', noon an' night. You work or you don't eat, that's what you've bin sayin' for weeks without openin' your mouth.'

Olive did not deny this. Instead she turned her head to David again, saying, 'What's brought you the night? I'd have thought you'd had enough fun and games for one day. You all ought to be thanking your lucky stars you're not in Durham jail, if you ask me.'

Ned swore, a particularly base profanity which David had only ever heard underground, and he said quickly, 'I came to see if Da was all right. One of those maniacs nearly brained him and he was a bit groggy on and off on the way back.'

'Huh.' Alec made an impatient movement, shaking off his mother's arm. 'If you were so concerned you'd have been better off talking him out of going. But that's you all over, wind and water with half a brain.'

'At least I'm not prostituting myself.' He hadn't meant to say it, the words had just come from an inner knowledge inside himself as to how to really get under his brother's skin.

Alec's face was now bereft of colour, his lips drawn back from his teeth and his eyes like green flame. Again Olive was hanging on to him but now it was with all her strength as Alec tried to rise to get to his younger brother. 'Don't, don't, Alec. Remember you're going to dinner there tomorrow night and you don't want your face marked. Think of your position.'

'He thinks of nowt else, Mam. Didn't you know? I wouldn't be surprised if the lass has made a nice little collar and chain to lead him about with.'

As Alec flung his mother off him and sprang to his feet, Lillian screamed loudly and shrilly. It was Ned who leaped between his two sons initially, holding Alec off David with the stocky force of his small body, and then Olive caught hold of Alec again, pleading with him not to fight.

In the moment Alec had come for him David had known he was no match for his brother, not with one hand tied behind his back, as it were. Nevertheless he stood his ground and didn't give an inch, glaring at Alec over Ned's head before Lillian's whimpering cooled his rage enough for him to say, 'To hell with you, Alec. You're not worth it.' He turned. 'I'll see you, Da,' he called over his shoulder above Alec's wild threats, and then he was outside in the backyard. He stood for a few moments in the fetid, still air, aware he was panting and that his hand, which had got jostled in all the pandemonium, was giving him gyp.

He had burned his boats as far as his brother was concerned. He stood breathing deeply for a moment or two before crossing the yard and opening the gate into the back lane. And he wasn't sorry. He pulled his cap further down on his forehead. Tonight had been coming for a long time and they had both known it. Funny, but they had never been able to stand the sight of each other right from bairns.

He began walking, slowly at first and then more quickly. One thing was for sure, he'd miss seeing Alec and his mam like he'd miss a hole in the head. Lillian and his da had already got into the habit of stopping by Brooke Street now and again, so nothing need change there. The house in James Armitage Street had been full of strain and strife for as long as he could remember; it had never been a home. He'd felt more settled in one room with Carrie than he ever had living under his mother's roof.

The twilight was thick when David entered the house in Brooke Street to find Ada waiting for him, all of a twitter. Carrie's brother had gone to get her mam and Mrs Symcox,

Ada gabbled, her mam's pal who'd said she'd help at the birth. The baby was coming, and from the pains the lass was having it wouldn't be too long about it neither.

Carrie's baby was born at three o'clock the next morning. It was a fine healthy boy, with the sort of lungs that guaranteed he would get attention when he demanded it.

David was sitting by the fire with Ada in her crowded sitting room which smelt strongly of cats when Ann Symcox came to tell him the news, adding that the birth had been so quick it was like the lass had been on her fourth or fifth rather than her first. She didn't remark on the fact that Carrie had behaved somewhat strangely in the minutes after the child was born, first of all refusing to hold or see it, and then, when her mother had insisted, staring at the small screwed-up face and tiny limbs for what seemed like ages before she suddenly reached out and grabbed the infant, and burst into tears. But then a confinement, even a straightforward one like hers, took it out of you.

The range was glowing with coal provided by Ada when David walked through, and Carrie was sitting up in bed with the child in her arms. Mindful of the part he was expected to play, David sat down beside her, saying softly, 'How are you feeling, lass?'

She was flushed and had obviously been crying, and the sight of her tear-stained face moved him more than he would have thought possible.

Carrie didn't answer him directly; what she did say was, 'It's a little laddie,' as her fingers gently stroked the small downy head.

'Aye, I know.' David tweaked back a corner of the shawl – Carrie's shawl – which the child was wrapped in. He stared down at the little blotched face and squashed nose. He didn't know what he'd expected to feel, but in the event he felt very little. In fact it all seemed quite unreal. He found it hard to imagine that this tiny scrap had been in Carrie's stomach just hours before. 'He's bonny,' he said weakly after a few moments, becoming aware that her mother and Ann Symcox were waiting for some reaction from the proud father.

'He's a beauty.' Joan's voice bordered on the indignant.

'There's not a man alive who could look at a newborn babbie an' call it a beauty with his hand on his heart,' Ann Symcox said briskly, calling forth a grateful smile from David. 'But give it a day or two an' you'll see for yourself, lad. You've got reason to thank the Lord tonight, He's done you proud.'

For a split second David's eyes met Carrie's, and now his voice was of a quality which satisfied even Joan when he said, 'I know that, Mrs Symcox. I'm a very fortunate man.'

Chapter Nine

Alec married Margaret Reed at the end of September. The wedding was a lush, grand affair which was talked about for weeks afterwards by those who attended. David and Carrie were not of this number.

At the wedding breakfast the bride's father presented the newlyweds with the keys of a fine little house overlooking Mowbray Park. Mr Reed also announced that his new son-in-law would no longer be managing one of the Reed shops but would join him in overseeing the running of the small empire. The clapping and cheering had gone on for ages, and Margaret Reed had flung herself into her father's arms, her plain face aglow.

All this was related to Carrie by Renee, a bitter and simmeringly angry Renee. It appeared she had been carrying twins, one of which still remained despite the crude abortion which had taken the life of its sibling. It afforded Carrie's sister little satisfaction that she was making her husband's life hell as a result.

What were they going to do, Renee asked furiously, if the strike still hadn't ended by the time the baby was due? When she told Walter he would have to look after the child while she returned to work, he had flatly refused even to consider such a proposal. Bairns were women's work apparently, and if the three of them starved to protect his manhood, so be it. 'I hate him, Carrie.' Renee's voice had been full of a cold, black fury which had struck a chill in Carrie. 'I really, really hate him. Doesn't he see the only thing between us and the workhouse is my job?'

By November, Walter and even the most staunch union men were forced to admit they weren't going to win the fight. Everyone's credit had run out long ago. The last speck of coal and tiny cinder had been gathered from the tips, it was icy cold and there was nothing to make a fire with. Without the lifeblood of the range there was no heat to warm the house, no hot water for cooking or washing, nothing to keep out the raw winter chill. Everything that could be pawned had been pawned and whole families were starving, nature culling the weakest – the elderly and the very young – first.

Not a day went by without Carrie giving thanks for the fact that the child was such a good baby, crying only when he was hungry and smiling long before he was six weeks old. With Matthew at her side in a makeshift crib consisting of one of Ada's cabinet drawers, she worked from first light to late at night, the money she earned enabling them to buy coal for the range and food to eat. She had long since ceased worrying about the back rent. That would have to be dealt with when David was in work again, but until then it was enough to stay alive and well.

Since she had called round to see her mother one day and found the twins shivering under old newspapers, all the blankets in the house having been pawned, she had slipped Joan a few groceries each week. These, along with small contributions from any neighbours with menfolk in the factories or ship-building yards, and even from a reluctant Renee, had kept her parents, Billy and the twins alive. Nevertheless, Carrie lived in fear that the illnesses like consumption and pernicious anaemia which were rampaging through the mining community would strike one of her family, and it was only the fact that she had to eat enough to provide good milk for Matthew that stopped her from cutting out meals in order to give Joan more.

She loved the child. She hadn't imagined that such intensity of love could exist before she had looked into the small red face in the minutes after his birth. After all the agonising, all the nights when she had lain awake tormenting herself with what she would do when the baby was born, it had been so simple. He had needed her, for his very existence he had needed her, and he was so bonny, so perfect.

And still the strike went on.

In the end it was the state of the women and bairns that persuaded the Miners Federation of Great Britain to advise their members to go back to work. Lists of names went up on all the noticeboards throughout Durham. If a man's name was there, it would mean his family could eat. If it wasn't, it meant the man concerned had been labelled a troublemaker or agitator by the powers that be, and it didn't matter if he'd worked for the colliery for a lifetime.

David's name was on the list, along with Walter's and Billy's. Ned and Sandy's were not. Those who were allowed back, went back. They all knew they hadn't only lost the battle, they had lost the war.

'Lass, all I'm asking is that you see sense. I'm in work again, I can provide for us. You don't need to do this.'

'I want to do it.'

'And what I want counts for nowt. Is that what you're saying?'

Carrie looked up from the baking board. It was five days

147

before Christmas, she had been working since six o'clock in the morning and it was now just after nine at night. Her eyes were red rimmed, her breasts bulging with milk for Matthew's ten o'clock feed and she was very, very tired. It was on the tip of her tongue to scream a few home truths at David. When the miners' executive had conceded to the government's demands, the owners had agreed 'temporarily' not to cut wages below pre-April levels – except in Durham, Northumberland, Cumberland and North Wales. David had gone back to work a beaten man, his wage packet smaller and his working day longer. She knew it, he knew it, the whole country knew it.

Instead of being put on face work where a man could just about earn a living wage if he was lucky and hadn't too many dependants, David, like many others, was doing labouring work until there was an opportunity for face work. He fetched and carried, cleaned things, shovelled pony dung, oiled, greased, lifted, pulled, loaded and unloaded, and all for the princely wage of seventeen shillings and threepence. He knew, the same as everyone else, that a man could be sacked with no explanation and no comeback.

And he was enduring the humiliation which every working day held for her and the bairn.

The knowledge checked her tongue. Instead of shouting that they were neck high in debt which his wage had no hope of even beginning to clear and that she would like nothing more than to never see another firework in the whole of her life, she forced herself to take a deep breath. 'It won't be for ever,' she said evenly, looking full into his angry face. 'Please, David, don't take on.' They had been having this conversation for the last hour and it was a familiar one, but she was determined not to give in. They were going to rise up out of the mire if it took her last breath, and they needed every farthing she brought in.

That was an inescapable fact whether David chose to recognise it or not.

David was standing with his back to the range, his jacket lifted as he warmed his buttocks in the heat of the fire. It had been a pig of a day and he was exhausted, but it was the accident which had occurred shortly before the shift ended which had him all out of sorts. That, and the sight of Carrie working herself into an early grave, he thought sourly.

He'd been cleaning out the stables when he heard a scream, and he had known immediately the accident was a bad one. A miner could be half dead before he'd make a sound. Along with others, he'd run in the direction of the screams, copping a blow to his head on the roof of the workway which made him see stars for a while. It had been Kenny Lloyd, a big handsome hewer built like a circus strongman, and both his legs had been sliced off clean as a whistle below the knee by the steel rope of a tub. A stupid accident for someone as experienced as Kenny, but tired minds, weary limbs, poor visibility, misunderstandings, carelessness or faulty and worn equipment were creating more accidents than they'd ever had before the lockout. The months of the strike had ensured that timber had rotted, water had gathered and lots of gas had been released. The mine was a disaster waiting to happen, they all knew it, but to voice such sentiments would relegate the speaker to the blacklist of unemployables.

The memory of Kenny's horrified face as he had clawed for his severed legs, the feet still grotesquely encased in his big working boots, haunted David. He tried to shake it out of his mind and stared at his wife as she began working again. Carrie's quiet tone hadn't fooled him. He knew that the tilt to her small chin and the way her full mouth was set tight meant she wasn't going to budge on this, and the galling thing was that he knew she was right. They did need what she was bringing in, desperately, but damn it, he hadn't meant it to *be* like this.

He turned his head away, inadequacy tearing at him, adding to the torment in his body which was with him day and night. Several times recently he'd told himself he should just roll over and take her one night and be done with it, that no other man would have waited this long. But the memory of how she had looked that night in her da's backyard stopped him. He wanted it to be different for her the next time, *he* wanted to be different from the scum who had forced himself on her all those months ago.

The white knight on his charger . . . David's mouth curled in abrasive self-mockery. A white knight was meant to rescue the fair maiden from her distress, not add to it by working her to death.

The child made a soft mewing sound in its sleep at Carrie's feet, bringing David's gaze to the drawer and its tiny occupant. And that was another thing, he had expected to be able to have some feeling for the baby – it was Carrie's after all – but every time he looked at it his guts twisted. She'd admitted she had thought she loved its father once, and there was no doubt she loved the child passionately now it was here, so had that revived some of the old feelings for the man who had sired it? Did she wish she was with him right now, instead of stuck in this one miserable room, living hand to mouth?

Perhaps he should have asked the name of the father after all. In fact he still could. Certainly it would bring an end to the list of names which swirled round his head as he lay beside her each night, his body burning and his soul sick, but he knew he wouldn't be able to keep his hands off the bloke concerned. But it wasn't just that, not really. Once he knew his name, once it had been spoken between them, it would always be there, spoiling everything. Crazy, but that's how he felt.

Aw, to hell with it! He didn't glance her way again as he stomped across the room on his way to the privy, but the aggression in his movement was not lost on Carrie.

She sat staring across the empty room when he had gone, her hands idle. She knew what would ease some of the tension between them, but the thought of it brought a fear which constricted her throat and made her nauseous. A gurgle from the baby at her feet brought her eyes downwards, and she smiled as she saw the wide-open, smoky-flecked eyes looking up at her. Matthew's eyes were beginning to change colour, she thought. She reached down and lifted him on to her lap where he immediately rewarded her with a toothless grin. She prayed his eyes wouldn't be green, or at least not the clear vibrant green of his father. She had hoped he would take after her in his colouring but it was still too soon to tell one way or the other.

She hugged the child to her for a moment before opening her blouse and baring her breast to the eager little mouth. He fed lustily, gulping hard and making contented little sounds which again brought the corners of her mouth lifting.

Maybe things would work out between herself and David if she just let life take its course. Let it happen naturally.

She was shirking the issue and she knew it, but as she heard his footsteps approaching she kept her head down and didn't look up when he entered the room.

Christmas was a quiet affair. For the miners it meant two days without pay, for their wives it meant having to see their bairns do without even the tangerine, penny, pink sugar mouse and secondhand toy they usually managed to stuff into

151

a stocking on Christmas Eve. Everyone was glad when it was over.

When, two days before New Year's Eve, Lillian arrived on the doorstep with an invitation from Olive to see the New Year in with them, David's first instinct was to refuse. It was only when Lillian began to beg the pair of them to reconsider that he wavered. It was an olive branch, Lillian insisted – sister and brother oblivious to the unintentional pun until Carrie began to giggle – and she knew their mam wanted to see her first grandchild.

'Then she should have paid a visit, shouldn't she?' David responded. 'Or are you telling me there wasn't a time in the last four months she didn't have a minute?'

'I know, I know, but she's stubborn and maybe she thought you would throw her out.'

David snorted.

'She's been in a right two an' eight since she realised she wasn't going to be asked to the Reeds' New Year do,' Lillian confided. 'She's been longing to see their house. Oh, Carrie, please come.' Lillian turned her attention to her friend. 'It'll be awful if you don't. There'll only be Mam and Da and the neighbours, and maybe Walter and Renee, and I don't want Isaac to be bored.' Lillian blushed on the last words, not least because of Carrie's delighted reaction.

'Isaac? Isaac Wellburn? Are you walking out with him?' Carrie had suspected for a long time Lillian was sweet on the young steelworker.

In the end, mainly because she knew Alec was not going to be present, Carrie said they would accept. 'We could call in at my mam's for a few minutes first,' she suggested to David, and when he nodded without comment she sent him a grateful smile. Since the night of Matthew's birth they had become more frequent visitors to her old home on her mother's insistence. Her da made a fuss of his grandson and was forever bouncing the baby on his knee, but to Carrie's knowledge he had never spoken to David unless David spoke first. It saddened Carrie, but she consoled herself with the thought that at least Billy and David were back to their old selves, ribbing each other and acting the goat as though the last nine months had never happened. She longed for her da to come and visit them but had reconciled herself to the fact that this was never going to happen now.

It was snowing slightly when they left the house on New Year's Eve after sharing a meal with Ada in her room. Carrie had tried to persuade the old woman to accompany them to her mother's, but Ada would have none of it. 'I don't want to traipse about the streets on a night like this, hinny, besides which Emilia would never forgive me if I didn't see the New Year in with her.' Ada cast a loving eye on the little tabby cat who was cuffing her six remaining kittens about the room. The kittens should have long since followed the two Ada had found homes for, but the old woman had got so upset over the ones that had gone that she had decided to keep the rest – not something, Carrie felt, Emilia approved of. The little cat had made it clear she had no time for her offspring and was already fluttering her eyelashes at Spud and Jonah, Ada's two ginger toms who appeared ready and eager to fulfil their God-given role in life. 'I've a drop of the hard stuff for when the clock strikes twelve, an'' – Ada lowered her voice – 'a nice saucer of cream an' two pennyworth of cod bits for this lot, so we'll be as happy as Larry.'

All the public houses were doing a roaring trade as Carrie and David passed them, the strains of 'Bye, Bye Blackbird' and 'Black Bottom', the year's two popular hits, already wafting out into the bitterly cold air. David was carrying a sleeping Matthew, wrapped in a cocoon of blankets, and Carrie was clutching a half-bottle of gin – Ada's present to her mam and da – and a batch of teacakes she'd made that afternoon for her mam's table, along with another for David's mother.

In Carrie's old home the glow from the fireplace and the Sunday cloth on the table – recently retrieved from the pawn shop – couldn't hide her family's reduced circumstances. The Christmas decorations – coloured paper cut up and clipped into shapes and hung on a piece of string – were brave enough, but with just Billy working and her mam taking in washing and ironing for some of the big houses Southwick way, money was as tight as it had ever been. But quite a few of the neighbours were there and they had all brought something to help the evening along; the atmosphere was merry and all the bairns were beside themselves with excitement.

It was with some reluctance that Carrie left with David an hour later. Difficult though it was between David and her da, she knew it would be worse at his mother's and she was already regretting promising Lillian they would be there. But perhaps his mam would be different. Perhaps she really did want to pour oil on troubled waters, now she had a grandson.

It was snowing more heavily now, a carpet of white already settling on ground that was icy underfoot. David was again carrying Matthew, and he echoed her thoughts as he said, 'We're barmy turning out on a night like this for me mam, lass.'

'It's not for your mam, not really. It's for Lillian, and your da as well. He'll love having you there, you know he will, and Lillian wants us to be with her and Isaac. She's been sweet on him for ages, you know.'

'She shouldn't let me mam within six feet of him then,'

David said darkly. 'If anyone can put a spanner in the works, me mam can.'

'All the more reason for us to be there and try to stop it happening then, I'd have thought.'

'Stop my mother?' David looked at Carrie pityingly. 'You would have as much chance stopping a charging bull elephant as preventing her from doing and saying what she wants. Me da's called her a she-devil before now, and he hit the nail on the head. I tell you, whatever Lillian's said about olive branches and the like, here's one who's expecting nowt in that direction. Lillian's too soft with Mam, always has been. She lets Mam walk all over her.'

Carrie stared at her husband as they reached the Suttons' doorstep. This had all the makings of a wonderful evening.

Unlike the house they'd just left at the bottom of the street, there was no laughter and singing, nor rowdy shouts of welcome from the assembled company when they entered the spick and span sitting room after a perfunctory knock on the front door.

Mr and Mrs Kirtley from two doors up and their unmarried daughter who was well and truly on the shelf at thirty-four were sitting at the table, a cup of weak tea in front of the women and a small glass of beer in Mr Kirtley's hand. Opposite them sat Olive and Lillian, and across the room, standing with their backs to the range, stood Ned, Walter and a red-eared Isaac Wellburn, the latter looking as though he was wishing himself anywhere but his present surroundings.

Walter raised his hand, explaining Renee's absence by saying she wasn't feeling too good the night and had gone to bed early, but Carrie wasn't really listening to him. All her senses, every nerve and sinew in her body seemed to have frozen as she took in the tall dark man standing with one hand resting casually

155

on the shoulder of the young mousey woman sitting on the remaining chair at the table.

'*Carrie.*' Lillian jumped up like a jack-in-the-box.

But Olive cut in and said, 'Here you both are, and this is Matthew?' her voice effectively checking Lillian's impulsive dash. 'I don't think you've met Alec's wife. Margaret, dear, this is Alec's brother, David, and his wife and child.'

'How do you do?' Margaret's voice held no trace of dialect, and Carrie told herself she should have been expecting this from all Renee had told her after Alec's wedding. Mr Reed had apparently sent his only child, the apple of the old man's eye, to one of those posh expensive schools which specialised in turning out young ladies of distinction. Not a boarding school though, but an establishment close enough for his darling to come home each night. However, although her voice was upper-class and perfectly pitched, it was also friendly, even eager, and the plain sallow face with its slightly pockmarked complexion and pale blue eyes was smiling.

'How do you do.' Carrie smiled back, keeping her gaze fixed on Margaret's face although she was vitally conscious of Alec just behind his wife. And then she turned, took Matthew from David and busied herself with peeling away the blankets from the child while David made conversation with Miss Reed – although she wasn't Miss Reed any longer, she reminded herself, smiling at Lillian as her friend pushed her down into a seat.

'What a beautiful baby.' Alec's wife bent forward the moment Carrie was seated. 'Is he good?' And then before Carrie could answer, she continued, 'We aren't really meant to be here, my father will be vexed we're late but I think it only right and proper Alec sees his family on New Year's Eve, don't you? Have you seen yours?' When Carrie nodded, Margaret twisted in her seat and looked up at her husband. 'Carrie has been to see her family, dear. I told you, everyone does.'

'So you did, Little Miss Always Right.' Alec's voice was indulgent. 'Just so long as you make it clear to your father it was your idea to come, that's all.'

'Oh, I know how to handle Father.'

'Now that I don't doubt for a moment.'

While the two were talking, Carrie took the opportunity to glance at Alec. He was dressed very well, 'like some jumped up mine-owner' as David said bitterly later. The dark dinner suit and shining black shoes were of excellent quality, anyone could see that, and the thick tweed overcoat draped over one arm and the hat hanging loosely in his free hand equally so. Margaret hadn't taken off her dusky pink velour coat but it was unbuttoned, showing a dress beneath of exactly the same material but encrusted with rows of crystals on the bodice, and her feet were encased in cream kid shoes. They oozed wealth and power, and instinctively Carrie's arms tightened round Matthew.

Her gaze rested for a second longer on Alec, but she wasn't seeing the dark, handsome face with its startlingly beautiful eyes as it was now; her mind had superimposed the image of features savage with lust. She shivered, her whole being recoiling, and in that second he glanced at her over his wife's head. His face slowly lost its smile before he said softly, 'You have a bonny son.'

She inclined her head but said nothing, then turned to David as he bent down to take Matthew so she could take off her hat and coat. 'Thank you.' She smiled at him in the brief moment when both their hands were joined round the child on her lap, and he smiled back, saying, 'Lillian's getting you a cup of tea,' his head close to hers.

157

'So, David, what are your plans for the New Year?' Alec's voice was pleasant although cool as it cut into the moment.

David straightened, the child now in his arms, and he looked at his brother long and steadily. The seemingly amiable tone didn't fool him for a minute, he knew his brother too well for that. Alec was annoyed about something – probably the way they had last parted in this very room – and he was out to get under his skin, as only he could. Alec knew full well he was in no position to make 'plans' of any kind: none of the miners were. Earning enough to be able to pay the rent and put food on the table was all any of them could hope for these days, and he couldn't even manage that.

Margaret, too, sensed Alec's mood. Loving him as she did, she had noticed a change in him the moment Carrie and David had come into the house. She had gathered enough from remarks her husband had made that there was no love lost between him and his brothers, but it seemed this one in particular, David, was a thorn in Alec's flesh. His wife was beautiful though. Margaret let her eyes rest on the clear baby-smooth skin of the woman in front of her and knew a moment of intense envy. That hair and skin combined with the deep blue eyes were striking.

'We just want to enjoy Matthew for the moment, don't we, David?' Carrie's voice broke the gaze of the two men, and Margaret noticed that as she rose to hand her hat and coat to Lillian, her sister-in-law positioned herself so that she was between the two brothers and had her back to Alec.

The ensuing oohing and ahhing over the baby relieved what had threatened to become an awkward moment, but Margaret found she was watching David's wife more than the infant. Some time after their marriage Alec had told her one day that his brother had got the girl into trouble and this had been the reason for their hasty marriage. He had intimated that David's wife was no better than she should be and that his brother had got himself a handful, but the young woman sitting quietly at her husband's side didn't strike Margaret as a loose type at all. Quite the contrary in fact. But then, she had only met her tonight so how could she judge?

Margaret's pale blue gaze moved to the baby who was now in his grandmother's arms, and again she experienced a pang of envy. She hoped they would have a child soon. She didn't mind if the first one was a boy or a girl, although she knew most men wanted a son, but she longed to be pregnant with Alec's child. She glanced at her husband as the thought hit and saw his eyes were fixed on the infant. He would make a wonderful father. He was wonderful altogether.

Ten minutes or so passed before Alec made a move to leave. As Margaret was buttoning her coat, Alec turned to his mother and said, 'May I?' holding out his hands for Matthew.

Carrie froze for a second and then as Olive passed Matthew over, her heart jumped into her mouth. The baby gurgled and smiled as he did at everyone these days.

'He's taken to you, Alec,' Olive said. 'He knows you're his uncle, that's what it is.'

'Do you think so?'

'Oh aye. If you're a bit nervous with them they sense it right away, like dogs.'

In the ensuing laughter Carrie found her hands were bunched at her sides as she fought the urge to snatch Matthew away. She didn't want Alec touching him, not for a moment, but she could see what Olive meant. Alec was handling the baby as though he did it every day of his life, showing none of the male awkwardness that Walter and Ned had displayed.

Carrie stood stiff and staring, wondering if anyone else

could see what she was seeing. *They were so alike.* But of course everyone would assume this was natural in an uncle and nephew, and the baby wasn't unlike David. Under his soft baby features, Matthew had the straight Sutton nose and firm chin all the brothers had. Did David see the marked resemblance to Alec? She didn't dare glance at him.

But perhaps she was imagining things here, because she knew Alec was Matthew's father. Certainly she had dreaded this moment ever since the child had been born, and it had been a huge relief when David had flatly refused to attend Alec's wedding. Foolishly – she admitted now – she had been hoping that the bad feeling between the brothers would mean their paths would never cross, especially now that Alec had gone up in the world.

Alec was aware of Carrie's tenseness and it was all the confirmation he needed that his suspicions were correct. For his part, he was taken aback by the rush of emotion that flooded him when his son smiled up at him. It was one of the rare occasions in his life when he was experiencing regret. Not that he would have changed any of the decisions he had made regarding Margaret and his marriage, he assured himself silently, his eyes taking in each feature of Matthew's tiny face. He wanted what his marriage had brought him. But he would have liked this child to have come from a union between Margaret and himself, that was all.

'Give him here, you have to be off.'

When David took the baby from him, Alec was again unprepared for the wave of emotion that came over him. But this time it was resentment liberally laced with jealousy. As David held the infant against his chest and Carrie took her husband's arm, her other hand moving up to stroke the baby's head, he could have socked his brother on the jaw. Instead he contented himself with saying, 'He's a bonny lad, considering he was so early.'

Carrie's eyes shot to his face, and in the fleeting second before she dropped them, Alec thought, aye, he's mine all right. Even without the dates fitting so perfectly, he could read it in her eyes.

'What do you mean?' David's voice was flat but the edge to it was pure steel.

'Mean? Nowt.'

'Come on then if you're going, Margaret's father will be wondering what on earth has happened to you.' Olive's voice was brisk but there was a warning in it too. She didn't want a scene in front of the neighbours, not on New Year's Eve. Mr Kirtley had a very nice little hardware business and his daughter was a secretary in a solicitor's office. You didn't air any dirty washing in front of people like that, let alone Mr Reed's daughter. She didn't know what Alec was thinking of to come out with a crack like that.

When she had ushered Alec and his wife out of the front door and waved them off, Olive turned back into the room, her gaze going immediately to the baby. She hadn't expected to feel any affection for her grandson. Of all the children she had borne, only Alec had stirred her maternal love and this she admitted quite readily to herself. The others were at best an irritation and at worst a liability. And so she had been prepared to feel nothing for David's child, especially with the mother being Carrie McDarmount. But . . . She stared at Matthew who was now being dandled on Lillian's knee. He was a nice little thing with a ready enough smile; charm the birds out of the trees, he would, when he was a bit older. She couldn't remember David ever being like that.

161

Chapter Ten

The weeks since New Year's Eve had seen nothing but sleet and snow, and bitter, unrelenting cold. The sky was so low it seemed to rest on the frozen rooftops, and the masts of the ships in Wearmouth docks were lost in swirling grey mist which soaked through clothes and boots far quicker than ever rain did.

David had still not been taken on at the face and consequently was like a bear with a sore head. Matthew had only recently fully recovered from a cold which had made him fretful and miserable, and which had made Carrie's quota of fireworks twice as difficult to achieve. And Lillian was living in a constant state of nerves, convinced that each time she saw Isaac, he was going to finish with her – something she called round daily to discuss with Carrie.

The back lanes were a sea of mud which got traipsed into every house, the tall black chimneys of the factories and mines seemed taller and blacker, and the terraced streets surrounding the shipyards where the great hulls of ships rose above the houses were grey and windswept.

All this Carrie could have coped with fairly easily if it hadn't been for the fact that she knew David was very unhappy. Seeing Alec again had revived all the memories of the night of Matthew's conception, and although she tried not to let it show, she was petrified David would soon insist on the consummation of their marriage and that she wouldn't be able to bear it. She *wanted* to be a good wife to him, she told herself endlessly, but the act itself . . . They couldn't carry on like this much longer, though, that was for sure. She knew he sensed how she shrank from any physical contact and it wasn't fair on him, not when he was so kind and so good with the baby.

Things were still as far away from being resolved as ever one morning in early April when David shook her gently awake, his hand on her shoulder. Carrie opened her eyes to find him standing at the side of the bed, fully dressed, and with Matthew wrapped up in his arms.

'What is it?' She jerked into a sitting position, her hands instinctively reaching out for the child. 'Is something the matter with Matthew?'

'Nothing's the matter with Matthew.' He didn't pass the sleeping baby to her; instead, his voice lighter than it had been in days, he said, 'Get dressed. I want to take you somewhere and you'll need to be well wrapped up. It's the best day we've had so far but still nippy.'

'David?'

'Get dressed.' He wouldn't answer the question in her voice and turned away as he said, 'We'll wait for you outside. Don't be long, all right?'

What on earth . . . Carrie glanced at the window. It was still dark outside.

She dressed rapidly, pulling on her heavy black boots last of all. David had sat all evening a couple of nights ago repairing them for her with some leather, nails and a wax end he'd bought. He had borrowed the iron last and a hammer from a pal he worked with, and had been as pleased as punch when he'd come home and shown her what he was about to do. Her heart gave a funny little lurch now as she thought of it, and the way he'd ignored the holes in the soles of his own boots.

Outside, Carrie pulled her hat further down about her ears. Nippy, he'd said. It was freezing, but at least the morning was dry. 'Where are we going?' she asked as they began to walk.

'Wait and see.' He looked down at her and grinned. 'Have a bit of patience, woman.'

'Huh!' She wriggled her shoulders in pretended irritation, but inwardly she was thankful he seemed so cheerful. She would have turned out of their warm bed and walked miles for that alone.

Dawn was beginning to break as they neared Penshaw Hill, and now Carrie saw quite a few people were making their way to the top where the monument, modelled on the Temple of Theseus at Athens, had been built by public subscription as a tribute to John Lambton, the Earl of Durham, decades before. 'David, what are we doing here?' She tugged at his arm as she spoke but he didn't pause.

'Wait and see,' he said again.

They were passing a tinker's covered cart, a little tent shaped like a segment of sausage, with a fire hissing at the door and the horse cropping at grass a few yards away, and Carrie's mouth watered as the smell of cooking bacon wafted towards them. She was hungry, starving, and soon Matthew would be waking for his morning feed. What *was* David about?

They reached the top of the hill just as the sun began to rise in the east. Grazing cattle mooed below them and the birds were singing. Carrie wasn't asking any questions now. There was what she could only describe as a spirit of expectancy about the people gathered around her. Then, slowly, darkness came over all the land, as the moon came between the earth and the sun. The mooing and birdsong ceased, even the bairns who had been running about just minutes before were still and quiet, pressed into their mothers' skirts. It was breathtaking, uncanny. Carrie found herself clutching David's arm, her eyes wide and her breath shallow.

A slight arc appeared around the edge of the sun, then slowly, very slowly, more and more of the sun's rays hit the earth in a glorious display of the Creator's power. A child clapped, a woman to the side of them gave a deep sigh, and then everything and everyone came to life again.

It was a rebirth. Carrie gazed about her, her heart so full she didn't know how to contain the feeling welling up inside her. And she would have missed it but for David.

'A total eclipse of the sun.' His voice was very soft beside her. 'I thought you'd like to see it.'

'Thank you.'

It was an inadequate response considering how it had affected her, but something in her face must have satisfied him because his smile was very sweet as he said, 'You're welcome, love.'

Love. He had never voiced the endearment before but it had slipped out as naturally as if he often thought it.

Matthew began to wake up as they walked down the hill. He struggled out of his blankets and put both hands on David's shoulder, gazing at the trees and birds and cows. There were primroses and dog violets starring the grass here and there, and when David bent down with the baby and pointed to a delicate white daisy type flower saying, 'That's greater stitchwort, Matthew, or *Stellaria holostea* if you want the proper name,' Carrie's mouth dropped open.

He saw her expression and grinned at her. 'Surprised? Not quite the ignoramus you thought you were married to?'

'I didn't think you were an ignoramus,' she protested vehemently, colour flooding her cheeks.

'Good.' He stood looking at her for a moment before he said, 'You get more beautiful every day, lass.' And then immediately changed the subject. 'It used to be an interest of mine when I was a lad, flowers and birds and so on.' His offhand voice told her he was slightly embarrassed about the disclosure. 'I used to get books out of the library and come up here with them, seeing what I could find. Course, I don't suppose I always get the pronunciation right.'

'I bet you do.' She stared at him, wondering what it cost him each day to leave this world of light and colour and go under the ground into blackness and filth.

He shrugged. 'Don't matter one way or the other, does it? Don't alter the beauty of 'em if you don't say it right.'

'No, I suppose not.' She hesitated, and then said quietly, 'Would you teach me? When we've time, I mean.'

He was standing very still now, his eyes holding hers and seeming to draw her over the space between them, and it was a full ten seconds before he said, 'Aye, I'll teach you, lass.'

David was on the late shift that day. Once Matthew had had his last feed and was tucked up and fast asleep in the crib Ned had made from a few orange boxes, Carrie made several journeys to the tap in the yard. After heating the water on the range she filled the tin bath half full, then stripped off her clothes and sat down in the warm water. She sat there for some time, thinking about what she was going to do, and then as panic began to take over she concentrated on the task in hand, washing herself all over with the hard blue-veined soap which never seemed to lather. Once she was squeaky clean she began to wash her hair, persevering until the soap gave in and there was foam beneath her fingers.

When she was dry again, she spent some time rubbing her hair through her fingers, sitting in front of the glowing range wrapped in a blanket, wearing just her drawers and shift, her head bent towards the heat. After brushing the silky waves exactly one hundred times, a habit from childhood, she left it loose about her face while she pulled on the rest of her clothes and emptied the now cold bath, bucket by bucketful.

Once that was accomplished, she brought in more water for the shallow bath David had each night on returning home from the colliery. When the water was heated and the bath was ready, Carrie stood looking at it for a moment or two.

What would folk say if they knew she'd been married for twelve months and had never once seen her husband naked? She always made sure David's bath was ready when he walked in the door, but she would avert her eyes while he undressed and then gather up his work clothes and take them through to the backyard. She made sure she stayed outside beating the dust and grime out of them until he was dressed in his other pair of working trousers and shirt which they'd got out of pawn as soon as he was back in work. Well, that was going to change tonight. Her heart began to jump and race, and she shut her eyes tightly for a second.

If this was a new start, a rebirth, it had to begin as it was going to continue, and her mam had always washed her da's back for him.

There was a pan of hodgepodge simmering on the hob, and she'd baked some stottie cake earlier to mop up the gravy with. The bread and butter pudding would be ready as they finished that. She nodded to herself, glancing round the room once again and smiling despite her nerves as Matthew made a little snuffling sound in his sleep.

And then she heard the front door open and close, and knew he was here.

'All right, lass?' David's voice was quizzical and Carrie belatedly realised she was standing to attention next to the tin bath as though she was on sentry duty.

'Aye, yes.' Her voice was a little high and she coughed, clearing her throat before she said, 'Your bath's ready.'

'Aye.' His eyes narrowed for a moment, and he put his bait tin on the little table next to the tin of freshly made fireworks before he said, 'Somethin' smells good.'

'It's hodgepodge.' She knew the rich stew made with mutton, turnips, carrots, peas, onions, broad beans, lettuce and barley was David's favourite. 'And there's bread and butter pudding for afters.'

His eyebrows rose. 'It's not me birthday, is it?'

'No.'

'I thought for a minute we were celebrating something.'

Oh, if only he knew! Would he think she was forward, brazen, if she followed through with her plan? She stared at him, desperately conscious of the height and breadth of him and the overall maleness of the strong compact body in front of her. Well, she couldn't help it if he did. It was now or never, she would never be able to work up the courage again, which had first reared its head out on Penshaw Hill.

She was aware he was standing as though slightly non-plussed, and following the normal procedure she now turned away, saying, 'I'll take your clothes through to the yard when you're ready.'

She waited until he had sat down in the bath before she turned round, and the water was still swishing when she croaked –

momentarily poleaxed by the broad muscled shoulders and lean back on view – 'Would you like me to wash your back?'

He had been rubbing his legs with the soap before she spoke, but now he became absolutely still. All the ripples in the water died before he said, his voice sounding perfectly normal, 'Aye, thanks, lass,' and he stretched out the hand holding the soap.

She performed the task almost mechanically, one half of her brain registering the small, blue-black indentations which the coal stamped on those who had the temerity to plunder it, and the other concentrating on thinking of nothing at all. And then she had finished. She handed him the soap and gathered up his pit clothes. 'I won't be long,' she said and bolted for the door.

He was fully dressed when she re-entered the room, and she could only admire his aplomb when he said, 'I've cleared the table and the tea's mashing, all right? You dish up and I'll get rid of the bath water.'

Her taut body relaxed a little as she went about the normal everyday task of lading out the stew and pouring the tea, cutting shives of stottie cake and putting them on a plate in the middle of the small table. Then she sat down on the edge of the bed. It had been a bone of contention between them when in the early days she had insisted that he have the armchair drawn close to the table and she sit on the bed for their evening meal. It was only when she had pointed out that he was taller and bigger than she was and much more suited to the armchair that he agreed to use it.

When the meal was over and the dishes had been cleared away, she laid out the papers, pudding basin, paintbrush and blue touchpapers ready for morning. She watched David extinguish the oil lamp. When the room was dark she knew he would begin undressing, laying his clothes on the back of the armchair by feeling his way. He would don his nightshirt, and she her nightdress, and then they would climb into bed.

And there the pattern would be broken. She swallowed. If she could bring herself to do this. She pressed her lips tightly together, closed her eyes and bowed her head. She was not going to back out now. *She was not.* David was not like Alec. They might be brothers but they couldn't be more different.

A dart of memory, carrying the pain her first introduction to sex had brought with it, caused her to tense. It wouldn't be the same with David, it wouldn't.

She finished undressing, pulled on her nightdress and slipped under the covers a second before she heard him walk across the room and then climb in beside her. Again she repeated to herself, this was David. *David.* It would be different.

It was different. It was different from the first moment she stretched out a trembling hand and touched him, murmuring, 'David . . .' and then found she just didn't have the words to say anything more.

But she didn't need to. He turned towards her, slowly and firmly put his arms about her and drew her into him, stroking her hair for long minutes until she relaxed against him.

She didn't know quite what she had expected, she admitted to herself afterwards in the moments before she went to sleep in his arms, but it hadn't been his tenderness and comfort, the way he had brought forth from her feelings she had never dreamed she was capable of. In fact, she didn't know if it was right and proper to feel all that she had, for her body to be so . . . She couldn't find a word for the pleasure she had experienced. And if she thought about some of the things he had done in the time before he had actually taken her, she would never be able to look him in the face again.

But it had been nice. The word mocked her with its prim overtones, causing her to blush in the darkness. It had been very, very nice.

Part 3

An Uneasy Peace

1936

Chapter Eleven

'You're cutting off your nose to spite your face, Da. Can't you see that? You have to play the owners and the government at their own game.'

'Play 'em at their own game be damned!' Ned Sutton glared at Walter before taking out his all too apparent bad temper on a hapless potato beneath his garden fork. 'They've got us by the short an' curlies. They put us on short time an' then say we can't claim benefit unless there's been three consecutive days without employment, so what's the bettin' that on the third day we're given a day's work? The owners are in with the government, you know that as well as I do. An' them cocky little upstarts from the means test take the biscuit. They were round at poor old Amos's yesterday sayin' him an' his wife had to sell the clock, pillow cases an' sheets, everythin' that wasn't nailed down, afore he'd get a penny. I'd like ten minutes in a dark alley with one of them, I tell you straight.'

'Aye, well, it's rough on Amos, I know that, but it don't help no one you flying off the handle with the deputy this morning when he wouldn't say you were on for tomorrow. There's not much chance you'll even be given the odd day after the mouthful you came out with.'

'I've only had two days' work in the last six.'

'And if you don't get any more?'

'Aye, well, at least I'll know where I stand then, won't I?'

'In the dole queue, man. That's where you'll be standing.'

'If you're tryin' to be funny, you'll be off home with a split lip, m'lad, big as you are.'

'All right, that's enough, the pair of you.' David rose from where he had been perched on an orange box outside the door of the ramshackle hut on his father's square of allotment. Or, to be more precise, Amos Proudfoot's allotment, his father's old friend who in the last few years had become too debilitated with the miners' curse of pneumoconiosis to do more than sit in a chair and try to breathe.

In return for a few fresh vegetables, Amos had turned the allotment over to Ned six years ago, and it was David's private opinion that this act had saved his father's sanity. It wasn't just being able to work in the fresh air on a plot of ground that to all intents and purposes Ned could call his own that had been such a lifesaver, or being able to supplement the meagre diet they were forced to live on with fresh vegetables and fruit. It was more the fact that Ned could escape the house in James Armitage Street – or, to be blunt, the woman within – and come up here. Ned would sit for hours in the sunshine in the summer and autumn, and in the winter and spring he would huddle in front of a small fire enclosed in an ancient rusting brazier. Even when it was raining cats and dogs or snowing a blizzard, his father would find an excuse to be up here, sitting in the doubtful comfort of the hut made of corrugated iron, sacking swathed round him for warmth and the door propped open so he could survey his patch of land.

Mindful of all his da had to put up with at home, David's voice was benign when he said, 'It's no use you taking out your anger at what they've done to Amos by having a go at our Walter, Da. It *was* daft, you sounding off at Tom earlier, and wouldn't the owners and the rest of them just lick their lips to hear you two coming to blows? Eh?'

Ned surveyed his two sons with narrowed eyes before pulling his grimy cap – the colour long since having been consigned to the onlooker's imagination – down on to his forehead. His head moved in a series of small jerks before he said, 'Aye, well, that's as mebbe. Anyway, it's done now an' I've no intention of goin' to Tom Burns cap in hand, if that's what you're suggestin'.'

'Would we, knowing you?' David's grin brought forth a reluctant smile from Ned. 'Anyway, Tom is all right, not like some of 'em who are nowt but boss's lackeys. He don't hold a grudge, Tom.' David didn't add here that before he'd left the colliery earlier that day he had made it his business to inform the deputy of Amos's circumstances and how his father was feeling about his old friend. And Tom, a small upright bullet of a man who was a lay preacher in his spare time, had listened without comment before saying, 'Aye, I thought somethin' was gnawin' at his vitals. He's a good old boy, your da, Dave, so rest assured, no offence taken.'

Ned thrust a box of vegetables and fruit into David and Walter's hands. 'Here.'

Both the brothers knew it was their father's way of apologising for his rancour, and this was further reinforced when Ned drew a piece of brown paper out of his pocket and said, 'Sit yerselves down, the pair of you, an' have a smoke afore you leave. Our Lillian picked up these tabs after they'd had a meeting in the office this week, an' a few of 'em only half gone.'

David shook his head. He wanted to get home, besides which he had told his sister time and time again she was endangering her job at the firework factory by hanging about after there had

177

been a meeting with the bigwigs in the office and nipping into the room to empty the ashtrays into her bag.

As his father carefully peeled back the paper to display the heap of cigarette stubs, David said, 'I'm for home, man, and thanks for these,' he nodded to the box in his hands. 'Carrie said to be sure you and Mam come round tomorrow for the lad's birthday party. You and Renee and Veronica as well, Walter.'

'Aye, I know all about it, our Veronica's been on about nowt else for weeks, when she bothers to come home, that is.' Walter grinned at his brother. His daughter spent more time at David and Carrie's than she ever did in her own home, and he couldn't blame her. He only wished he could do the same. He had always thought his mam was a bitter pill, but Renee could match her any day.

Walter's smile faded as he watched his brother wind his way out of the allotments, the odd man here and there who was still working on his patch in the mellow August evening raising his hand or calling a greeting across the rows of vegetables and runner bean canes. He didn't know what he was going to do about Renee. And then he caught the thought, self-derision fierce as he followed it with, don't kid yourself, man. There's nowt you can do. She's made sure of that. She covered her tracks better than any Indian scout, did Renee. And really he had nothing to substantiate his suspicions, only the fact that from being ravenous between the sheets she'd turned into a virtual nun the minute she'd found out she was expecting Veronica. But he didn't believe that, knowing his wife like he did. If he wasn't getting it, who was? Because he'd bet his last farthing someone was. Someone at that damn factory, like as not. His hands knotted into fists.

'Lucky so-an'-so, ain't he?' Ned had followed his son's eyes, but there was no resentment in his tone when he said, 'He's got himself a gem with his lass, has our David. They might have got off to a shaky start in that one room at the Back of the Pit, but she made damn sure they didn't settle there. First that move to Monk Street an' then Dock Street. Natural homemaker, Carrie is.'

'I wish a bit of it had rubbed off on her sister.' Walter's tone was bitter.

Ned slanted a glance at his son out of the corner of his eye. 'Aye, perhaps you do, lad, but there's worse off than you. Look at Alec. Thought he'd have it all plain sailin' when he married Margaret, but there's her lost one babby after another an' sufferin' with what the quack calls nerves now. She never was no oil paintin' but she's skin an' bone an' lookin' as old as yer mam these days.'

'Aye, well, I've no sympathy for Alec,' Walter said tersely. Alec's wife might be highly strung and look like the back of a tram, but at least his brother knew where she was twenty-four hours a day and who she was with. All this supposed 'overtime' that came Renee's way was a sight too convenient in his opinion, and he didn't believe she'd bought the trinkets she produced now and again either. In the last nine or ten years since Veronica had been born, she'd been playing him for a fool. He'd bet his life on it. Proving it was something else.

'I'm not sayin' I've got sympathy for him, lad. He made his bed years ago an' can't quibble about lyin' on it, but I do feel sorry for the lass. All them times she's bin expectin' an' then losin' 'em afore her time. You've got your Veronica, an' David his lad; it must rub it in a bit, especially with our Lillian only havin' been married two minutes an' announcin' she's expectin' the other night. That'll be an end to me tabs,' Ned added reflectively, shaking his head as the thought struck.

'After havin' been waitin' for Isaac to set the date for the last umpteen years, she'll waste no time in producin' one after the other if she has her way. Four, she said she wants. You ought to have seen his face.'

Walter wasn't interested in seeing his brother-in-law's face. 'Let's hope he doesn't lose his job like the couple of million unemployed then,' he said sourly. 'They might think they're set up nicely now through waiting and saving, but it could change with the wind.'

'Mebbe, but Isaac's a canny lad. He's managed to get through the Depression this far without bein' laid off. Likely he can weather the storm.'

Walter's voice was dry when he said, 'And his da being the foreman at the works might help.'

'Aye, there is that, lad.'

David was whistling to himself as he walked home along the warm dusty streets towards Dock Street. Hearing him, one could be forgiven for thinking the sound was motivated by happiness or inward satisfaction, but this would have been wrong. It was a habit. Right from a little lad, however bad the situation at home between his parents or Alec and himself, he had whistled outside. It was his way of informing the world that everything was all right with him, thank you very much, and that he wouldn't appreciate any enquiries even if it wasn't.

There was the usual motley collection of bairns playing out late in the streets, engaged in the sorts of games he'd played. He passed a group playing hitchie dabber with boot polish tins filled with soil, apart from two little girls who obviously had a relative who worked at the glassworks, judging by the round pieces of mottled glass with a pattern on the top that they were proudly holding aloft. Mount-a-kitty, diabolo, swinging round the lamp posts with washing line ropes – nothing changed, David thought. One lad had just presented the lass of his choice, a snotty-nosed tyke with matted blonde hair, with a sherbert dab, and the look on the little boy's face brought back a memory from the past.

He'd been all of seven years old when he'd given Carrie his Saturday penny for Mr Errington's merry-go-round. The old man had lived along the back lane by the Co-op in Charles Street and had had a mobile roundabout pulled by a pony. He'd charged a penny a ride, and the five-year-old Carrie had been all wistful blue eyes as she'd watched the other bairns have a go. Her face had lit up when he'd put the money in her little hand but, if he remembered right, Alec had told on him that night. His mam had informed him that if he was daft enough to give his penny to the likes of Carrie McDarmount then he obviously didn't want it, and so it would be stopped forthwith until she thought he'd come to understand the value of money.

David paused, turning to look back to where the little girl was now shyly offering her small beau some of the sherbert.

His mam. Even then he had known she couldn't stand the sight of him. Not that she'd been over keen on Walter or Lillian either, but they had never answered her back like he used to and so had escaped the worst of her rages. And now she was making his da's life a misery again, since the talk of war had died down.

They'd all thought they were on the up and up a couple of years ago, when news had filtered through to the powers that be that Germany was building up her armed forces. The government had got windy, with the result that working pits all over the country had been expanded and re-opened, and the shipyards and armament factories like Armstrongs and Vickers had started getting busy again. All of a sudden, amid increasing rumours of conflict with Germany, miners were back on full time, even the 'troublemakers' like his da and Sandy were taken back. But it hadn't lasted, damn it. The last six months things were as tight as they'd ever been. Huge stocks of coal were lying dormant and the shipyards were on short time. Miners were getting laid off every day, and those who weren't were getting fewer and fewer hours. And to hear his mam go on, you'd think his da was the sole cause of the slump.

The sherbert dab apparently finished, the little girl darted off into the open doorway of what was obviously her home, leaving the lad staring after her, crestfallen, kicking disconsolately at the kerb with his boot.

Poor little devil. David wanted to walk back and tell the wee boy that faint heart never won fair lady and tomorrow was another day, but he didn't. He had enough problems of his own. He turned again and walked on.

There was bad feeling down the pit about whether the deputies should be taken on to the management side entirely. Every miner was hotly against the idea because deputies were responsible for safety down the mine, and there had already been a steep rise in injuries and deaths in the last years – the owners paid scant attention to improving working conditions. Feelings were running high and David thought they could be called out on another strike over the issue. And he didn't want that. Damn it, a strike was the last thing he wanted. Carrie was already bringing in more than he was now that they were cutting back on the shifts again, and he didn't mind admitting it was driving him nuts. He pulled off his cap and rubbed it irritably over his hair once or twice before replacing it on his head.

At least Carrie didn't show him up by going out of the house to work and telling all and sundry she was the main breadwinner like Renee did. By, he felt for Walter, he did straight. Renee had been a stroppy little madam before she'd got the job as forewoman at the firework factory, but the last five or six years she'd been so full of herself you'd have thought she was one step down from royalty. And she had no time for the bairn, even when she wasn't working. No wonder Veronica lived and died at their place. She was a nice little thing, Veronica, even if she did drive Matthew mad by following him about like a puppy.

The thought of Matthew deepened David's frown. He and the lad were chalk and cheese, he knew it, even though he'd always fallen over backwards to try and be a good da to him. Maybe he'd tried too hard. Bairns weren't daft, they sensed what was what. Or perhaps it was Carrie's love for the lad, which almost amounted to obsession at times, that had put a wedge between him and Matthew. Certainly the lad would never be disciplined if it was left to his mother. If Carrie had fallen for a child of his, would that have made a difference? Provided a balance perhaps? But it hadn't happened.

David thrust the sick feeling of disappointment aside, telling himself, as he always did, that they'd have their own child in time. They were still young; Carrie was only twenty-six, after all, and he was nearly twenty-nine.

He didn't acknowledge here that much as he wanted to be a father, it was the bond a bairn from their union would bring that was paramount in his desire to impregnate his wife. If he had examined the feeling beneath the natural longing for his own child, it might have brought to the surface the constant but deeply buried worry that one day Carrie would leave him for someone she really loved. Someone she hadn't *had* to marry. And this same brooding subconscious unease coloured his thoughts about her work, to the point where it had become a bone of contention between them on occasion.

183

'Yoo hoo! Mr Sutton!'

As he turned the corner of Zetland Street into Dock Street, David became aware he'd been called a couple of times without it registering. He turned, waiting for the big meaty woman who was panting after him and smiling as she reached him. 'Sorry, Mrs Mathen. I was miles away.'

'Hope it was somewhere a mite better than these parts, lad. That's all I can say.' Mrs Mathen put a hand to her heaving bosom and gasped a couple of times. 'I just want you to tell your Carrie our May loved them things she did for the bairn. With them strugglin' like they are, our May'd got nowt for the babby an' it made all the difference, your Carrie sendin' them little matinee coats an' all. She's a marvel, your lass. You tell her that from me.'

'I will, Mrs Mathen.'

'I said to my Nobby the other night, she's a marvel, Carrie Sutton. If anyone deserves to get on in this life, it's that lass.'

David was keeping the smile on his face with some effort now.

'An' he agreed with me, so he did. There's them that say an' there's them that do, Nobby said, an' that lass is a doer, God bless her, an' as bonny as a new morn into the bargain. An' that lad of yours, spotless as a new pin, he is. You never see him runnin' around with his backside hangin' out like some I could name.'

David was edging away now. 'I'll tell her—'

'An' her doorstep white as snow. Says a lot about folk, does that.'

'I have to go, Mrs Mathen. My dinner's waiting.'

'What? Oh aye, aye, lad, you go. You go. But mind you tell her what I've said.' Mrs Mathen hitched her enormous breasts with her forearms as she spoke. 'She's a marvel sure enough.'

As David walked on, the old woman's words were ringing in his ears. Mrs Mathen was right, Carrie was a marvel and none knew that better than he did. When the home work from the firework factory had dried up in the worst of the Depression, Carrie had already realised she had a knack for knitting and crocheting new items from old woollen garments she picked up at the Old Market for the odd penny or two and then unravelled. The compliments she'd received about Matthew's clothes had prompted her to try her hand at some modern fashion items for women, which she had then asked Renee to show to the girls at the factory. When everything had been snapped up like hot cakes, Carrie had taken it upon herself to approach a couple of the big shops in Bishopwearmouth to see if they were interested in selling her wares. The result of this had been a regular income which had proved a godsend, enabling them, with Carrie's careful budgeting, to get straight and pay off all their debts.

Once this had been accomplished, they had moved out of the increasingly cramped conditions at Brooke Street and into two rooms and a scullery which had seemed like paradise. A further move, two years ago, had brought them to their present accommodation, a two-up, two-down terraced house in Dock Street with its own privy and washhouse.

Oh aye, Carrie was a marvel all right, and it wasn't only Mr Mathen who had noticed how bonny she was either. David hitched the box of vegetables further under his arm as he reached his own doorstep and he was frowning. He didn't like the jealousy that reared its head when he caught a covert glance at Carrie from another man and read what they were thinking, but it was something he didn't seem able to get over.

He stood for a moment without making any move to enter the house. He was daft, a nutter. Why else would he let the very qualities which made her so special come between them time and time again? True she was bonny and warm and kind, but to his knowledge she had never so much as looked at another man, so why did he allow the inner questioning and doubt to get to him? Her work, first for the firework factory and then the clothing enterprise, had been to benefit them as a family, he knew that at heart. And where would they be without it? Would he rather they were still stuck in Brooke Street living hand to mouth just so he could say he was her provider?

David couldn't truthfully give himself the answer to that question because it would have been yes. Instead he reiterated for the thousandth time how he hated seeing Carrie work every minute God sent, her hands often knotted with cramp at the end of the day and her eyes sore. He made a sound low in his throat which could have signified anything.

Just as he was about to open the front door, he noticed Matthew come round the corner with several of his pals and it was clear from the way the boy was walking that he was holding something wrapped in his jumper.

'Da!'

Matthew's cry held an element of relief in it, and as David waited for the crowd of small lads to reach him, he noticed how tall Matthew was getting. It hadn't struck him before, seeing the boy every day, but he was a good head above his pals who were all about the same age. When the group was still a few yards away, David called, 'What have you got there?'

'It's a baby rabbit, Da.' As Matthew reached him, the boy unfolded the jumper just enough to reveal a tiny ball of fluff with a quivering nose and whiskers. 'Mr Dent was up by the old quarries an' his Jack Russell had gone down a hole and brought up the mother an' all the little 'uns. It'd killed them all 'cept this one an' so I grabbed it quick.'

'The dog bit him,' one of his friends supplied.

'It bit you?'

'Just a nip.' Matthew waved the concern away, his focus wholly on the baby rabbit. 'Can we keep it, Da? It'll die without its mam.'

David glanced at the insignificant little scrap. Matthew had been after having a pet of his own for some time now but Carrie wasn't too keen on the idea, mainly because she suspected it was a whim which would burn itself out once the boy had to feed, clean and take care of an animal. 'I'm not sure it's old enough to survive on its own, Matt.'

'But if it can?'

'Who's going to look after it? And by that I don't just mean stroking it and giving it some food now and again.'

'I will, I promise. I promise, Da.'

David stared down into the intense little face, his brows raised sceptically.

'Please, Da. I saved it and if I take it back it'll die.'

It was time the boy had some responsibility, David thought, and the way this had happened, with Matthew having, as he'd just said, saved the little creature, he was sure Carrie would be amenable. 'I'll talk to your mam, all right? And if she's happy about it we'll see about building a hutch and a pen in the yard where it can exercise. But I'm holding you to your promise. Pets need time and attention.'

'Aye, I know.' Matthew's face had relaxed. If his da was going to talk to his mam it'd be all right.

'Come on then. Say cheerio to your pals.' David opened the front door and stood aside for Matthew to step into the narrow hall in front of him. Then he called, 'Hello there.'

'Hello there, he says.' Carrie appeared in the doorway of the kitchen. She was only half joking when she said, 'I've kept dinner going for more than a couple of hours past when it should've been eaten, and all he says is, hello there. I thought you said it was going to be a quick word with your da.'

She hadn't noticed that Matthew had something in his bunched up jumper, and as the boy sidled past her and went into the kitchen, David said, 'Sorry, lass. Walter was with Da and we got talking. He was a bit down the night.'

'Walter or your da?'

He could have said both of them. 'Me da. Over that business with the deputy this morning. Mind, we had to talk round the trees and up the Khyber Pass before he'd let us raise it with him, but we got there in the end and he saw sense. He'll make it right with Tom in his own way now.'

In the kitchen, David placed the box of vegetables on the work table next to the sink. Matthew had seated himself at the kitchen table and was as quiet as a mouse, his big eyes fixed on his parents.

'Go and wash your hands, Matthew.' Carrie had already begun to ladle thick beef stew and dumplings on to three plates at the side of the range but she turned as she spoke, suddenly conscious of the boy's stillness. Her voice changed as she said, 'What have you got there?' Her eyes were on the jumper now resting on his bony knees.

'Ah, now we want a little word with you about that.' David smiled as he spoke, his eyes drinking in her peaches and cream skin and glowing hair, the soft mouth which even when it was trying to be stern, like now, was inordinately kissable. 'Go and get a cardboard box, Matt. There's one in the privy.'

Matthew took the hint to disappear and scuttled off without a word, whereupon David walked over to his wife, took the ladle out of her hand and drew both her hands to his chest. 'He's rescued a baby rabbit from someone's dog which had killed the mother and the rest of the brood. He wants to keep it and I think we should let him.'

Carrie stared up at her husband. One of the reasons – maybe the main one, she acknowledged silently – she had hesitated about getting a pet for Matthew was because of the confrontations between her son and David which would occur if the boy didn't follow through on his promises to look after whatever he had. She knew she was too easy with Matthew at times but he was a good lad at heart, although she had to admit in the last twelve months he'd begun to be something of a handful. He was so different to David, that was the thing. This hadn't been apparent when he was young, but lately . . . But she was glad David was championing the rabbit for Matthew; she'd just have to make sure the boy kept up to scratch with cleaning its hutch and so on. This last thought prompted her to say, 'What about a hutch?'

'I'll let him help me make one. It'd be nice to do something together, just me and him.'

The words brought a measure of gratitude along with some sadness, but her main feeling was one of sick panic. It had been some eighteen months ago, when Alec had come to David, cap in hand, that things had started to change between her husband and son, and Matthew had begun to challenge David's authority now and again. She had prayed David wouldn't be taken in by his brother's apparent desire to eat humble pie at the time, but Alec was clever. He'd gone on about Margaret's miscarriages and the difficult time they were having, how he had come to realise family was everything and bitterly regretted his estrangement from his youngest brother. David was so lucky to have a good wife and bonny child like Matthew, Alec had said wistfully. He'd give his eye teeth for the same. When Alec had gone, David had been very quiet for an hour or so, before saying, 'He's changed, you know. I never thought I'd see the day, but all this trouble with Margaret has knocked the stuffing out of him, taught him a lesson. What do you think?'

She had told him what she thought, and he had looked at her in surprise. 'Easy, lass, easy. It's not like you not to give anyone the benefit of the doubt.' She had realised then that she had to be careful. And Alec's behaviour had confirmed the suspicion she'd had for some time that he was aware Matthew was his child.

Before that day she could have counted the number of times she had seen Alec and Margaret on both hands, and those had been unnerving enough. To see Alec doing the benevolent uncle act and monopolising Matthew had given her the jitters for days afterwards. And she had been right to be wary.

She reached up to touch David's cheek and said quietly, 'Why don't you go and tell him he can keep the rabbit while I finish dishing up the dinner?'

'Aye, all right, lass.' He drew her into him, kissing her hard on the mouth, before muttering into her hair, 'You smell of apple blossom and strawberries, do you know that? Good enough to eat.'

'Go on with you.' She smiled at him, pushing him with her hand, but once he had disappeared into the backyard the smile faded. Was she the only one who realised the significance of Alec's timing? Didn't anyone else think it a little odd that the very week Margaret had been told by the top consultant her father had called in that it was unlikely she would ever carry a child full term, Alec had made peace overtures to David? But it was best they didn't. Whatever, Alec had set out to buy Matthew's affection eighteen months ago, playing the fond brother with David even as he furthered his aim to take David's place in Matthew's heart by indulging the boy shamelessly, and always putting David in the position of a killjoy. It wasn't fair. None of it was fair.

'Oh, Mam! Mam!' A little whirlwind burst into the kitchen as Matthew raced across and hugged her waist. Carrie smiled at David who had followed the boy into the kitchen. 'I'll look after it and clean it and everything, and me an' Da are going to get some wood for the hutch after dinner.'

'Are you now?' She smiled down into the handsome little face, the heavily lashed hazel eyes almost too beautiful for a boy and the rich brown hair just a couple of shades darker than her own.

'We're calling him Nibbles, aren't we, Da?'

'Aye, Nibbles it is.'

'And we're making the hutch with two compartments, a bedroom and a living room.'

'Lucky Nibbles,' Carrie said lightly, her mind registering that Matthew was smiling Alec's smile. Not for the first time she thanked the Almighty that her son's colouring was so different to his natural father's. In spite of all her worry, Matthew had inherited the McDarmount fair complexion and her hair; his eyes, although flecked with green, had enough brown in them for that colour to dominate. He resembled Billy more than anyone else, although she could see Alec's mouth more and more as the boy grew, and a certain devil-may-care tilt to Matthew's head of late that had caused her heart to come up into her mouth. He was changing fast, there was no doubt about it, and she lived in constant dread that someone sometime would point out the likeness between Matthew and his Uncle Alec.

'Can I bring him into the kitchen while I eat me dinner, Mam?'

'No you cannot.'

It was firm and brooked no argument and David laughed, ruffling the boy's hair. 'Nice try, son.'

Why couldn't it always be like this? Carrie pushed Matthew towards his chair and turned to the range. She would give anything for Alec to be out of their lives and gone for good.

Matthew bolted his dinner down, squirming about on his seat and watching every mouthful David took. As David finished his last forkful, Matthew said, 'Can we go now, Mam?' as though he and David were the same age.

Carrie smiled, shaking her head. 'Wait a minute.'

'Oh, *Mam*.'

Carrie walked across to the pantry. It was Matthew's birthday the next day and unknown to him she had baked a separate little cake when she had made his birthday cake, decorating it exactly like the bigger one. She said, 'Here, this is a happy-the-day-before-your-birthday cake.'

'Thanks, Mam.' Grinning from ear to ear, Matthew demolished the cake in ten seconds flat before sliding off his chair and pulling at David's arm. 'Come on, Da.'

'Matthew?' Carrie's voice was serious and brought the pair of them to a halt just as Matthew opened the back door. 'The rabbit isn't a birthday present, not really. You do understand it's a live creature and will be depending on you to care for it? The hutch will need cleaning out even if we're knee deep in snow.'

The brown head nodded solemnly. 'I know, Mam.'

'Can we go now, Mam?' David asked gravely.

Carrie wrinkled her nose. 'You're as bad as each other, you two,' she said, flapping her hand at them, but again, once the back door had closed, she stood quite still for some moments before starting to clear the table.

When she had washed the dishes in the tiny scullery off the

kitchen, Carrie walked through to the front room. This was not set out with a stiff three-piece suite, china cabinet and aspidistra, as most people would have expected considering there was only one child in the family and no lodgers to necessitate the room being used as a bedroom. It was Carrie's work room. The kitchen was the family room with a table, four hardbacked chairs, David's armchair and a small saddle with thick flocked cushions along one wall. It was here the three of them ate, sat in the evenings, washed and generally lived.

Although the front room held a drop-leaf table, four Georgian style chairs and two small pink armchairs with bobbles round the bottom, these were pushed against two walls and covered in piles of clothing. A bundle of woollens waiting to be unpicked, finished articles neatly arranged in piles and awaiting collection by Horwood's van, work in hand, and remnants of linen and rolls of cloth were piled high, and in front of all these stood an ancient table with a small sewing machine on the top and a chair tucked underneath it. Two clothes horses, one holding garments and the other draped with more cloth, completed the room, and the cream paper blinds with deep imitation lace on the bottom at the window were bordered by thick blue curtains, the same colour as the lino on the floor.

Carrie looked about her. In view of the number of people coming to Matthew's birthday tea the next day, she would need to clear all her work away into the big packing case in a corner of the room and rearrange the furniture so folk could sit and eat in here as well as in the kitchen, she thought. And there was still plenty of baking to do, the kitchen floor to scour and clean, lemonade to make with the lemons and sugar and ginger essence she'd had soaking all day in one of her big pans, and a hundred and one other things besides.

But still she stood there without moving, her eyes coming to rest on the neatly folded clothing she had finished that month. Folk just would not believe how little it cost her to make them, certainly not in view of what Horwood & Sons, Outfitters and Hosiers, sold them for.

Carrie walked across to the pile of clothing, stroking the soft material of the top garment absently. 'Exclusive design.' 'Original model.' That was how Mr Horwood had decided to market what he had called her 'line'. After what he'd considered a slow start, he'd recently announced himself well satisfied with the way things had picked up.

And it had all started from the day she had walked into the grand shop in the best part of Bishopwearmouth, inwardly shaking in her boots and outwardly poised. She told one of the shop assistants she wished to speak to Mr Horwood, and she could still picture in her mind's eye the way the beautifully dressed woman had eyed her from head to foot. The shop assistant's voice had been coldly superior when she'd asked *which* Mr Horwood madam was referring to. And from somewhere deep inside, the part of her that had reached out for life that morning on Penshaw Hill sprang up, giving her the courage to answer equally coolly that she meant Mr Horwood Senior of course.

Did madam have an appointment?

No, madam did not have an appointment but madam was quite sure Mr Horwood would want to see her.

Would madam like to explain what it was about?

Carrie had thought quickly before saying that the matter was private but greatly to Mr Horwood's advantage. And, amazingly, the woman had asked her to take a seat while she enquired if Mr Horwood was free.

Cuthbert Horwood had turned out to be a fat little man with a mop of grey, wiry hair which stuck straight up from his head like a brush. But it was his eyes, black, round and penetrating, that had unnerved her when she'd stood before him in his office five minutes later.

'I'm told you are about to inform me of something which is greatly to my advantage, Mrs Sutton.' His tone was not encouraging.

Her stomach was turning over like the hoops some of the bairns played with in the street, but she swallowed hard and said, 'Aye, that's right. I . . . I make things. Clothes. I knit and crochet.'

'And?'

'And I wondered if you'd like to sell them in your shop.'

'And this is the matter you led one of my staff to believe was of some importance? I don't like people wasting my time, young lady.'

'Neither do I.' Her head shot up at his biting tone. 'Probably because I never have enough of it.'

It clearly wasn't the response he expected. He stared at her, long and hard, and she stared back. She had nothing to lose now anyway.

'Show me.' He gestured abruptly to the large brown paper parcel she was holding, his voice impatient.

She unwrapped it on his grand mahogany desk, laying out the three items she'd brought as samples. They were favourites of hers: a crocheted sleeveless top in dove grey with matching cardigan, a cream and beige knitted dress, and a long-sleeved, waist-length jumper in midnight blue.

He picked each garment up, examined it closely but made no comment, and Carrie's confidence in the quality of her work took a nosedive.

After what seemed like an eternity, he leaned back in his big leather chair and raised his eyes to hers. 'You say you designed and made these?'

195

'Aye, I did.' Her voice was flat now.

'I like them. I like them very much.' His smile altered the hard face entirely. 'You have flair, Mrs Sutton. Panache, our London friends would call it. This is something that cannot be learned, it is here' – he rested a finger next to his eyes – 'and here' – he tapped his forehead. 'You clearly are an admirer of Coco Chanel, abandoning flamboyant fussiness in favour of a bold simplicity dependent on line, cut and quality.'

Was she? She had no idea what he was talking about. She'd vaguely heard of the Parisian designer who had led a revolution to make it 'chic' to dress like the poor in black or beige or grey, even adopting the workman's cap or scarf as an accessory, but fashion magazines were an expensive luxury she couldn't afford. She looked into the bright black eyes, sensing he knew something of what she was thinking and expected her to try and bluff it out. She cleared her throat, searching for the right words before she spoke. 'I'm not familiar with her work,' she said quietly. 'These are just my ideas, that's all.'

Again he stared at her for some moments. 'Then that is even better. May I ask you, Mrs Sutton, exactly what you are looking for here? A buyer who will pay well for any finished articles you wish to sell, or someone who will invest in promoting the clothing as an ongoing venture?'

All this clever talk. 'I'm looking for someone who doesn't think the two things are incompatible.' She was meeting the astute gaze head on now, and then, as he threw his head back and gave a hearty bellow of laughter, she continued, 'My husband is a miner, Mr Horwood. I'm not doing this simply because I think I can make a success of it but because I have to. I can't afford – *we* can't afford – to live on promises for the future. That doesn't pay the rent or put food on the table. I don't want to be forward but if you do like my clothes I would want a fair price for them, taking into account you have to make a profit too, of course.'

'Of course.' There was still a semblance of a smile on his face. 'In London's Regent Street a dress of wool lined with crêpe de chine would sell at something like fifty-five shillings, but this is Sunderland, not London. Would you be able to line your clothing, Mrs Sutton, where appropriate? Horwood and Sons cater for the discerning customer, and something like this dress and the top that goes with the cardigan would need to be lined.'

She nodded quickly.

'And some clients would like an edging of satin or silk to enhance an otherwise plain item of clothing. You do have a sewing machine at home?'

Now she lied without blinking. 'Of course.'

'Then I think we can come to some arrangement which would suit us both. You work alone?'

Again she nodded.

'That is not a problem at the present. If the line takes off we can reassess the situation.' And then, as though coming to some decision, he said, 'Can I offer you a cup of coffee, Mrs Sutton? And then we can thrash out terms and conditions.'

'Thank you.' Her head was whirling so much it was an effort to speak.

She left the shop some time later with a letter in her bag stating that Horwood & Sons were prepared to take her work and pay her handsomely for the privilege. She went straight to the Sunderland library to look up the word 'panache'. 'Flamboyant confidence of style or manner.' She read it twice before laughing out loud. From the library she called in at Tot Sewell's pawn shop and purchased a small sewing machine

197

with some of the money she had received for the clothing she had left with Mr Horwood.

Carrie came back to the present as Matthew bounded to the threshold of the room, saying, 'We've sorted some wood from the orange boxes in the yard but we need a bit more. Da said we'll get it tomorrow if there's time before everyone comes.' He didn't venture into the room, having learned long ago that thick leather boots and dirty hands didn't mix with delicate material and paper patterns. 'Mam, can I have a shive of bread and dripping to take up to bed?'

'You can't still be hungry, you've only just had your dinner.'

He grinned, all charm. 'I am. Please, Mam?'

Carrie shook her head at him, smiling as she did so. 'You've hollow legs, lad. Aye, go on, you know where it is, and just one piece mind. And then straight to sleep. We've a houseful tomorrow to celebrate you going into double numbers.'

'Aye, I am, aren't I?' It clearly hadn't struck him before. He stared at her and then said without any preamble, 'Is Uncle Alec coming?'

Carrie picked up a pile of clothes, turning away as she said, 'I'm not sure who's coming but I wouldn't be surprised,' the familiar sickness churning her stomach at Alec's name.

'Uncle Alec said he was getting me something right grand for my birthday.'

Now Carrie really had to control her voice. 'It's Aunt Margaret and Uncle Alec who buy you things, not just Uncle Alec.'

There was silence for a moment. Matthew stared at his mother. Why did she always have that note in her voice, the scratchy note, when she talked about Uncle Alec? She didn't have it with anyone else. He plucked up his courage and asked the question he'd been dying to ask for ages. 'Do you like Uncle Alec, Mam?'

'What?' Carrie was surprised into turning to face her son and by the expression on his face she saw that Matthew had the bit firmly between his teeth. It was at moments like these, when a kind of hardness came across the boyish features, that he resembled Alec the most. But she was not going to be drawn into discussing Alec with Matthew so she said, 'That's too silly a question to deserve an answer. Uncle Alec is your da's brother, isn't he? Part of the family. Now wash your hands before you get yourself that bread and dripping and I'll be up to say goodnight in a minute.'

'All right, Mam.' It was subdued but she pretended not to notice. '*I* like Uncle Alec.'

He shut the door before she could comment, leaving her staring across the room. She bit on her lip hard. Matthew, oh, Matthew. Where was this going to end?

It was another two hours before Carrie and David went to bed. Carrie did some baking and then she got David to help her reorganise the front room, but all the time her mind was dissecting the conversation with Matthew.

When she sat down heavily on the bed with a little sigh, David said, 'You're done in, lass, and no wonder. All this carry-on because of a birthday, as though you haven't got enough to do.'

'I wanted to do it.'

'Who's coming exactly?'

'Lillian and Isaac, Renee and Walter, and Ada of course. And Mam called by to say they're all coming, even Da.'

David nodded to this but said nothing. He had long since stopped hoping things would ever be right between him and

Sandy. Sometimes he got the feeling that Carrie's father would have liked to soften his attitude but Sandy was a proud man and any mellowing on his part would have meant losing face. True, Sandy answered him civilly enough these days but that was all, and David was in no doubt that this was only because he wanted access to his daughter and grandson. Both sets of grandparents worshipped the ground Matthew walked on; David had never thought to see his own mother so besotted with a child. Even with Alec he couldn't remember her being so indulgent.

The thought of his brother now moved David to say, 'Alec and Margaret, are they coming?'

'I don't know.'

'They haven't let you know?' That wasn't like Margaret. Alec's wife was a stickler for doing things properly.

'I never got round to inviting them.' Carrie rose from the bed and walked across to the dressing table. She picked up her hairbrush and began to brush her hair, seated on the little stool with her back to him. 'I dare say they'll call by.'

'You can bank on it. And what's the betting they'll have spent a fortune on Matt.' David's voice was resigned rather than annoyed and it suddenly irritated Carrie beyond measure. Probably because the conversation with Matthew was still burning in her mind, she turned abruptly.

'Do you think it's wise for them to come tomorrow? Margaret's last miscarriage was only two weeks ago.'

David shrugged. 'They wouldn't come if they didn't want to,' he said, beginning to undress.

Wrong. 'I'm not so sure Margaret wants to,' Carrie said carefully, picking her words. 'I think it hurts her to see Alec with Matthew and Veronica, and now Lillian's expecting. Surely you can see that's hard for her.'

'That's for them to work out together, lass.' David stretched, hard muscle moving under his shirt. 'You can't do nowt about it.'

'I don't think they work things out together, David.' She found she couldn't leave it alone. 'It's more a case of Alec deciding what he wants to do and Margaret falling in line.'

'That might be so, but it's still something for them to deal with surely.'

David's tone was so reasonable that for a moment Carrie wanted to throw the hairbrush at him. She was sure he still didn't really like his brother although he would never admit it, not when Alec had got him feeling so sorry for both him and Margaret – and, more powerfully still perhaps, when he could relate to how Alec was feeling about wanting his own bairn. She had thought for some time that Alec was aware of how David felt, that he got some kind of enjoyment from the knowledge. It was all part of the game he was playing.

Not for the first time, Carrie thought, he's dangerous, Alec Sutton. All that charm and attractiveness hid a heart that was as hard as nails. She knew he would never come out into the open and declare that Matthew was his, not while Mr Reed was alive anyway; he had too much to lose. But Alec could still hurt them all; in fact he *was* hurting them. If she was truthful, she knew David and Matthew would never be kindred spirits. Lots of fathers and sons weren't, but she wasn't imagining this deterioration in David's relationship with her son since Alec had made it his business to see more of Matthew.

She kept her eyes on David as she said, 'I think it would be better all round if we make it clear we don't expect to see Alec and Margaret so often.'

Startled brown eyes shot up to meet unswerving blue.

'They have lots of fancy friends and move in very different circles to us; it's not as if they're going to sit at home twiddling their thumbs. And all these presents for' – she had been about to say Matthew, but changed it to – 'Veronica and Matthew, I want them to stop, for Matthew at least. I don't like it, David. It makes me . . . uncomfortable. If they do have a baby we'd never be able to reciprocate.'

David had stopped undressing and was sitting with one leg in his trousers and the other out. 'What's brought this on, lass?' he said quietly, his eyes on her tense face.

'Brought what on?' She turned her head away to avoid his gaze. The tender concern in his deep brown eyes would prove her downfall one day, she thought painfully. She would blurt out more than she intended and in the process hurt David terribly. As the years had passed she had come to understand that David would be able to accept almost anyone as Matthew's father, but not Alec. And she knew this applied more, not less, since Alec had made his grand overture and the brothers had become friendly.

'This concern for Margaret,' David answered. He kicked off his trousers and pulled on his pyjama bottoms, and then came over to where she sat. He took the hairbrush from her, placed it on the dressing table, and then knelt in front of her, taking her fingers in his warm hands. 'Look, lass, it's dreadful the way things have turned out and I feel bad for her, course I do, like everyone else, but you can't take her problems on your shoulders.'

Carrie blinked. 'No, I suppose not.' She felt as though he was heaping coals of fire over her head. But she *did* feel deeply for Margaret when Alec was romping about with Matthew and Veronica, she told herself silently by way of exoneration. In fact, sometimes it had crossed her mind that Alec was being deliberately cruel to his wife when he made a fuss of the two children, punishing Margaret for being unable to present him with bairns of their own. 'But I would still rather we didn't see them so much.'

He pulled her to her feet and took her in his arms. Stroking her hair he said softly, 'If that's what you want, I'll have a word with Alec. I don't want to upset Margaret any more than you do, love.' He kissed her brow, his body hardening against hers and telling her of his need.

'I know you don't.' David didn't have an unkind bone in his body. 'If they just came occasionally rather than every Sunday it'd be better. I don't want the one day you don't work tied up with visitors all the time.'

His lips left her skin. 'There's more than one day in a week I don't work, lass,' he said bitterly.

Carrie said quickly, 'Oh, David, I didn't mean – I wasn't rubbing it in.'

'I know, I know.'

But the moment had gone sour and they both knew it.

Long after David had fallen asleep, Carrie lay wide-eyed in the darkness. She felt drained and she was dreading the next day.

David stirred once or twice, muttering something that sounded like her name and increasing her feeling of despair. He was born to have bairns of his own so why hadn't it happened? She just didn't understand it. Once or twice when she had been late her hopes had soared, only to plummet again within a day or so when she discovered she wasn't pregnant. There were folk like David's mam and da who had never really got on from the moment they were wed and yet could churn out babies like clockwork. She would give anything to be able to say to him, 'You're going to be a da.' She so wanted David's baby.

She twisted restlessly in the bed, her heart sore. She knew David's mam thought both she and Renee had decided to have just the one bairn because of their respective jobs. Olive had all but challenged her on it more than once, only backing down when she'd given her short shrift. Perhaps her own parents thought the same, but they would never interfere by saying anything. And it was ironic that in Renee's case, Olive was probably spot on. Certainly Walter had hinted to David more than once that things weren't right in the bedroom. But things were grand between her and David in that way, so why, *why* hadn't it happened?

She was no nearer an answer when she drifted off into a troubled sleep just as it was growing light.

Chapter Twelve

'It's good of you, man, don't get me wrong, but I'd have preferred you to clear it with me before you bought him the bike. His mam and me had told him he'd got to wait till he was older, that's the thing.'

'David, I had no idea.'

No idea. Carrie stood just outside her front door listening to David and Alec's low voices beside her as she waved to Matthew, who for the umpteenth time had just fallen off the brand new bicycle Alec had given him for his birthday. No idea, her hat. He'd planned this, probably for some time, and thinking back to last night she felt Matthew had had a jolly good idea what the 'grand' present was going to be too.

'Margaret and I just had this brainwave of getting a bike for Veronica and David's next birthdays.' Alec's voice went still lower as he said, 'I think it was because of the last miss, you know? She's beginning to accept she'll never have a bairn and this is her way of enjoying yours and Walter's, I suppose.'

'The bike was Margaret's idea then?' It was rare Carrie spoke to Alec directly and now, as she turned and met his eyes, hers icy blue, she saw he was taken aback.

He rallied immediately, smiling as he replied, 'I don't actually remember now.'

'Because that was what it sounded like,' she said, still unsmiling.

'Like I said, Carrie. I don't remember.'

Aye, and there were snowballs in hell.

'It doesn't matter now anyway,' David said hurriedly. 'And it's a beauty, Alec, but next time you're thinking of getting him a present as dear as that—'

'I'll check with you first,' Alec finished smoothly.

'I'm getting the hang of it now, Mam, aren't I!' Matthew had no skin left on his knees or his elbows, but his face was one wide grin as he limped towards Carrie, pushing the bicycle. 'It's canny.'

Carrie forced a smile. The bike was smooth and sleek and fancy, the gears, saddle and brakes the latest design. The paintwork was blue with silver lines and squiggles, and even the leather saddlebag looked as though it had cost a small fortune. Her da, along with Ned, Walter, Billy and the twins, were all standing at strategic points down the street, the idea being that the men were going to catch Matthew before he fell off the bike. None of them had succeeded so far. With this in mind, Carrie said, 'You're doing very well but don't you think it's time to have tea? Your grandas look as though their tongues are hanging out.'

'Aw, Mam, can't I stay out a bit longer? Veronica hasn't had her turn yet anyway.'

'You go in, lass, and start the ball rolling. We'll be in shortly.' David looked at her and smiled, his eyes saying, let it be for the minute, lass. Let's just get through the day.

'Just ten minutes then.' Carrie turned and stepped into the hall, and saw Renee at the bottom of the stairs.

'Shut the door, lass.' Renee waved at the open front door and whispered, 'I want a word.'

'What is it?'

All the other women were talking in the kitchen. Renee took her sister's arm and drew her into the front room which was set out ready for the visitors. She closed the door behind them. 'If Walter mentions anything to you about me being bad Thursday afternoon, just say something like you're glad to see me back to meself today. All right?'

Carrie stared at her sister. 'You were bad Thursday afternoon?' she asked in surprise.

'No, no, that's what I told Walter.' Renee's tone was impatient, and Carrie's hackles rose.

'If you weren't bad, why did you tell him you were?'

Renee moved her shoulders, saying under her breath, 'I took the afternoon off work, that's all, said I had to go home 'cos I felt ill with the monthly, but as luck would have it Walter saw one of the women I work with on the way home and she said she hoped I was feeling better. I got in after him and luckily I clicked on straight away he was up to something when he asked me if I'd had a nice day at work. He's never asked me that in me life. So I said no, not really, 'cos I'd felt bad and gone early but instead of coming home I'd called in to see you for a cup of tea and we'd got chatting.'

Carrie's voice was as low as her sister's when she said, 'What's going on, Renee?'

'Can't you guess?'

'I'm asking.'

'I wanted the afternoon off, all right? I work hard enough when all's said and done.'

'What did you do?' Carrie persisted.

'You mean who was I with?' Renee tossed her head. 'Well, if you must know it was Hughie.'

'Hughie? Not . . . you don't mean Hughie Fleming from the factory?'

'Aye.'

'But . . . he's married.'

'So am I, in case you'd forgotten.'

'No, I hadn't,' Carrie said tightly. 'Walter is David's brother, in case *you'd* forgotten.'

'And you're my sister so I should come first with you.'

This was Renee at her most brash, and now anger was replacing shock as Carrie stared into her sister's defiant face. 'Look, Renee, what goes on between you and Walter is nothing to do with me but how you've got the cheek to involve me like this I don't know. He's David's brother, family, and if you want to carry on that's up to you, I couldn't stop you no more than anyone else could when you've made up your mind to do something, but I won't be a party to it or lie for you.'

This was clearly not what Renee had expected. She swallowed twice. 'Don't be like that, lass.' She sounded agitated now, the cockiness she'd displayed so far disappearing. 'I'm not exactly asking you to lie—'

'That's exactly what you're asking,' Carrie interrupted furiously.

Renee gulped, her voice changing yet again. 'Please, lass, just this once. I've never asked you before, have I?'

It said volumes. 'So this has been going on for some time?' Hughie Fleming, the manager of the factory. Carrie had always liked him before this moment; he'd been a good boss to work for, friendly and kind, but now several things were fitting into place. The ease with which she and Lillian had got jobs at the firework factory on leaving school, Hughie agreeing to give her work at home before Matthew was born, Renee getting the promotion to forewoman . . . 'Were you carrying on before you were married?'

'No, honest, but I sort of knew he liked me and we'd have a crack together. I didn't let him . . . you know, till after I went back to work when Veronica was born. But he's nice, Carrie, and good fun, and his wife is a right old nag. Didn't want anything to do with him once she'd had the bairns. He says she only married him to have a nice house and a family. Used to lie back and think of England right from their wedding night. He says it was like making on with a stuffed pillowcase.'

'I don't want to know, Renee.'

'Oh, Carrie!' The irritation was back. 'Don't be so childish, it's not as if we're hurting anybody. No one knows. And I tell you, lass, having Hughie has kept me sane these last few years.'

'Do you love him?'

Renee looked at her, and for the first time her face held a touch of tenderness as she said, 'Aye, I do. It was a bit of fun at first, but now . . . Aye, I love him. He's generous and warm and funny, and he knows how to treat a lass.'

Carrie put a hand over her eyes, rubbing at her brow with her fingers before she raised her head. 'What about Walter?'

'What *about* Walter?' Renee tossed her head in the old way. 'I did my duty and gave him a bairn, didn't I, and he dotes on her and she on him. He's happy enough.'

'He's miserable, Renee. He's been miserable for years and you know it.'

'I don't care.' Renee wet her lips, digging her teeth into the flesh of the lower one. 'And I know how that makes me sound but I can't help that. He drives me round the bend, if you want to know. He's a right old woman, moping about the house when he hasn't got work and coming in tired and dirty when he has. I hate it; him, the pit, all of it.'

'You knew he was a miner when you married him.'

'It was different then. Look.' Renee paused, and there was a fawning quality to her voice when she said, 'Just help me out this once, lass, that's all I ask. I swear I'll never ask you again. Usually we cover ourselves fine but it was his birthday, and he'd had a row with his wife and she hadn't even got any of the bairns to make him a card . . . He had to go to Durham on business and I went along for the ride to cheer him up. I did, an' all,' she added with a wink.

Carrie didn't smile. 'I'm furious with you for involving me.'

'I know, I know.'

'Let's just hope Walter doesn't say anything to me.'

Carrie watched her sister's face stretch as she said, 'You wouldn't drop me in the mire?'

'I like Walter, Renee, and I've seen plenty of him over the years. Let's face it, he's round here almost as much as Veronica and for the same reason. He's lonely at home. You're my sister and I love you, but Walter feels like a brother, I tell you straight. And you're in the wrong in this, not him. You made up your mind you were going to lead him a dog's life once you'd had the bairn and that's the truth of it.'

'Plain speaking, is it?' Renee glared at her, anger turning her face brick red. 'Well, now I know.'

'Like I said, Renee, let's just hope Walter doesn't do any checking up.'

There was silence, a long, vibrating silence, and when Renee broke it her voice was a hiss. 'Thanks for nowt. I shan't forget this.'

'I hope you don't because I'd hate to have to say it all over again.'

Renee swung round and left the room, and for a moment Carrie thought she was going to bang the door but in the event she obviously thought better of it.

Carrie sank down on one of the dining chairs, her head reeling. Renee took the biscuit and then some, she thought angrily. To begin with, her sister's manner had been one of airy confidence that she would fall in with whatever Renee wanted, almost as if she was asking for a favour along the lines of leaving Veronica with them for a while or something similar. She wouldn't betray Renee, there'd never been any likelihood of that, but she hoped she'd managed to put the wind up her sister. It might bring her up short, although Carrie doubted it.

Hughie Fleming. Renee had been carrying on with Hughie Fleming for years and years; she could hardly believe it. Mind, thinking back she could remember Renee saying little things about him – that he'd married young, that he didn't get on with his wife, that he dressed really well, things like that. It would destroy Walter if he found out, and what about Veronica? In spite of the fact that her niece saw very little of her mother on a day-to-day basis, Veronica adored her mam. What a mess.

After a moment or two, Carrie rose from the chair and smoothed down her dress, taking a deep breath. This was turning into a day and a half and no mistake. Him out there with his grand presents, Renee carrying on with a fancy man and David's mam sitting in the kitchen with a face like a smacked backside because Ned had rolled home from the allotments after midnight well oiled.

Apparently the old miner who owned the plot next to Amos's, Benny Shield, had brought out a number of bottles of his homemade wine just as Ned had been about to leave.

'He must have bin hoardin' 'em for years,' Ned had whispered to her and David when he'd told them the reason for his wife's glowering face. 'Blackcurrant, rhubarb, gooseberry, sloes, he'd got the lot an' with his wife havin' just passed away he was feelin' a bit down. I said to him, "Benny, you're drinkin' to ease the pain of yours havin' gone an' I'm drinkin' to ease the pain that mine's still with me." By, like paint stripper one or two of 'em were; I've had the skitters all mornin'.'

Poor Ned. He was another one who was round here all the time because he didn't want to be at home, Carrie thought ruefully, which was another nail in her coffin as far as Olive was concerned. Renee had tipped her the wink a long time ago that their mother-in-law had been ranting and raving at both Walter and Ned for visiting Dock Street too often. 'I'm sure she thinks you're some sort of femme fatale,' Renee had giggled when she'd told her. 'Luring all and sundry into your kitchen.'

Carrie had laughed with her sister at the time but Olive's dislike of her had nevertheless caused her to lie awake for a good few nights afterwards. That had been five years ago. Now she accepted she would never do anything right as far as her mother-in-law was concerned, and that even Olive's adoration of her grandson was not enough to bridge the divide.

When Carrie entered the kitchen it was to see Margaret, still and quiet, her thin face as white as a sheet, listening to Olive expound on Alec's virtues of generosity and kindness. 'And he's promised your Veronica a bike on her birthday an' all,' she was saying to Renee. 'Did you know that? Still, fair barmy about them two bairns, he is. Nothing's too much trouble for them.'

Carrie stared at her mother-in-law. She was a cruel, hateful woman. She glanced at her own mother's uncomfortable face and then at Lillian and Ada who were positively squirming, before her gaze came back to Olive. David's mother knew exactly what she was doing to Margaret, turning the knife in the wound of her inability to carry her own child with devastating effect, whilst outwardly displaying the same ingratiating manner towards Margaret she'd always accorded 'Mr Reed's daughter'.

'Shall we see about getting the men in and having tea?' Carrie cut across what Olive had begun to say next with a coolness that was not lost on her mother-in-law.

'Aye, lass, I'll give 'em a call.' Joan was out of her seat like a shot, with Lillian close behind. And when Carrie ignored Olive's outraged face and said to Margaret, 'Could you put the kettle on for a fresh brew, lass?' she could almost see the steam rising from the top of her mother-in-law's head.

Olive had been holding court as she was wont to do given half a chance, Carrie thought grimly, but she wasn't going to get away with her spitefulness in *this* house. Carrie had lost count of how many times over the last years Olive had put the cat amongst the pigeons in some way or other, but she was in no mood for her mother-in-law's antics today. She caught Ada's eye and could tell that the old woman approved of her stand.

Margaret's gratitude at being given something to do was not lost on Carrie, and not for the first time she thought, that poor lass. It was clear Margaret never really felt included when the family was together like this, and Alec spoke to her as though she was less than the muck under his boots at times – and in front of them all, too. Carrie hated to think what life was like for her in that grand mausoleum of a house near Ashbrooke Hall in Hendon, which she and Alec had moved to three years ago. Margaret might have a housekeeper and maid, and a gardener three times a week, but Carrie wouldn't have her life for one hour for all the tea in China.

Renee must have been thinking along the same lines because now she rose to her feet and chatted to Margaret as the pair of them saw to the filling of the two big brown teapots Carrie had left ready at the side of the hob.

Even from across the room Carrie could see that Margaret's hands were shaking, and the nervous twitch – which had developed about the time of her fifth miscarriage – was very obvious today. So it was with a softening towards her sister that Carrie heard Margaret laugh weakly at something – no doubt outrageous and probably concerning their mother-in-law – Renee was whispering.

For her part, Margaret was praying that the afternoon would soon be over and she could go home. Home to Mrs Browell, the housekeeper, who had virtually taken the place of her mother the last years. She felt safe at home, less . . . conspicuous. And she was conspicuous in this gathering, however kind Carrie and Renee were, she told herself miserably. She wasn't like them, not in any way. Renee could laugh and joke about their mother-in-law and how dreadful she was, but she could never bring herself to do that. Olive Sutton terrified her.

When she was once again seated at the table opposite a glowering Olive, Margaret observed the way the other women spoke to each other. There was an ease, a familiarity that she envied with all her heart. Oh, they tried to include her time after time, she knew that, but she wasn't *one* of them, that was the thing. And without a child to bridge the divide, she never would be. She closed her eyes momentarily, the pain sharp.

After the first miscarriage, Alec had been so sweet to her, nothing had been too much trouble for him. It had been the same the second time, but after that he had progressively withdrawn from her. She was not imagining this. Sometimes he acted as though he thought she didn't *want* a baby and yet he knew this was not the case.

'Are you feeling unwell, Margaret?'

As Carrie bent over her, her voice low, Margaret shook her head quickly. 'I'm quite well, thank you,' she said with a smile. 'Just a little tired perhaps. I did not sleep soundly last night.' In fact she did not sleep soundly any night. How could she, with Alec turned away from her in spirit as well as body, and everything that had been so right at first now so wrong? But she *would* give him a child whatever it took, even if she had to lie in bed the whole nine months like the last physician had suggested. As Renee leaned across to talk to her, Margaret shut her mind to the little voice deep inside that whispered, ah, but *will* you be able to make him a father? Wishing for it is not enough.

Matthew's birthday tea was over and had been voted a great success by everyone other than Olive Sutton. David's mother had sat stony-faced throughout the afternoon and early evening, but her umbrage had not stopped her from filling her face, as Renee murmured to Carrie. 'I never believed in fairy stories when I was a bairn,' she added, 'but if ever there's a wicked witch, it's her.'

Carrie smiled faintly. It had been a long day with more than one surprise tucked in it.

'Me and Walter an' the bairn are off now, lass.' Renee leaned closer to her sister. 'And whatever you say, I know you won't let me down. You're not made like that.'

Carrie looked into the rosy-cheeked face and she really couldn't have said whether she wanted to slap Renee or hug her. In the event she did neither, merely saying, 'You hope.'

Her parents, along with Ada, Ned and a grim-faced Olive left after Renee and Walter, but Billy and the twins were playing cards with David, Matthew and Alec. The adults were letting Matthew win now and again, with Margaret helping him along.

Carrie left them grouped round the table in the front room and walked into the kitchen to clear away the debris of the day. She could hear laughter and Matthew's delighted squeal which meant he'd probably won another hand, but the sound brought no smile to her lips. She just wanted Alec to go.

When she heard someone behind her she turned quickly, expecting it to be Margaret offering help with the clearing up. Alec was shutting the kitchen door quietly behind him but the green eyes were trained on her face. Her tongue moved briefly over her upper lip before she said, 'Leave the door open, please.'

'All in good time.' He made no move towards her but leaned back against the closed door and crossed his arms over his chest. He looked very handsome as he stood there, his black hair and strong jawline complemented by the expensive shirt and tie he was wearing above well-cut twill trousers. As Carrie gazed into the hard face she thought, how could I have ever thought I loved this man, this selfish, vain, arrogant man?

'Well?' She kept her voice even and cool. 'I presume you're here for a reason.'

'Oh aye.' He let his eyes run over her face and then down to her body in a slow suggestive way which brought hot colour into her cheeks. 'I'm here for a reason all right.'

'Spit it out then.' Her voice was tight, her face equally so. 'I haven't got all day. They'll be wanting a bite of something and a drink in there in a minute.'

'I couldn't care less what they want,' he said pleasantly. 'No more than you care what I want.'

'I don't know what you're talking about.'

'No? Then David having a little word with me wasn't your idea?'

She stiffened, determined not to show any anxiety. 'We both thought a bike was too expensive a present—'

'I'm not talking about the bike,' he rapped out, then lowered his voice again. 'I'm talking about the little matter of my . . . insensitivity to poor Margaret's feelings in subjecting her to the company of Matthew and Veronica. "It might be better if you left it for a bit before calling again. Give her time to adjust after the last miss. She must be feeling it."' He mimicked David's voice sneeringly. 'David thought of that himself, did he?'

'Someone had to.'

He walked further into the kitchen, his eyes never leaving hers. 'Why don't you like me, Carrie?' he asked softly. 'I thought you did once.'

She had known this day would come, the day when he would mention what had happened between them, but she found she still wasn't prepared. Her hands were gripping her dress but her voice was firm when she said, 'I didn't know you then.'

'I thought we got to know each other very well.'

'One short encounter? I think not.' She heard herself dismiss the pain and anguish and horror of what had happened to her that night with inward amazement, but at the same time she instinctively knew that to show any emotion would be fatal with this man. He was looking for a chink in her armour. Now she came to think of it he had been looking for a long time.

'I married the wrong woman, didn't I?'

She hadn't expected this. Her brows came together.

'I thought I was going to have it all and do you know what I've got, Carrie?'

'Please, Alec, I've things to do.' She wanted to turn round and continue with what she'd been doing when he came into the room, but she found she didn't dare turn her back on him. He was in a funny mood, she hadn't seen this side to him before and she wasn't sure what was coming next.

'A big grand house with eight bedrooms and a separate wing for the servants – servants no less' – the self-mockery was acidic – 'and not one bairn in any of them.'

Carrie blinked. 'I'm sure Margaret feels it as much as you do.'

'Margaret!' It was insultingly dismissive.

'Don't be like that.'

'Like what?' He was standing in the middle of the room but she felt one wrong word or action from her would bring him to her side, and if he touched her she would scream. It wouldn't be the sensible thing to do but she couldn't bear the thought of his laying so much as a finger on her. 'She's a dried-up, barren stick of a woman and she drives me mad with her pills and potions and—' He stopped abruptly, running his hand through his hair so it stood up on end. 'You've no idea what it's like.'

He was pouting like a spoilt child. But then any resemblance to a child was swept away when he said, 'I could have had you' – again his eyes swept over her hair and face and body, but this time there was despair mixed with naked desire in his face – 'and we would have made a go of it. You've got guts, determination – look at how you've got on this far and you aren't finished yet, are you? You'll be in one of those houses overlooking Mowbray Park or out Hendon way before you're done.'

'David and I—'

'David!' He dismissed his brother in the same way he'd dismissed his wife. 'He's a nowt, a numbskull like Walter and my da. You'll have to drag him up by his coat-tails and you know it, same as I do.'

'Don't you dare talk about David like that.'

He stared into her angry face for some moments, the green of his eyes made all the more striking by the thick black lashes surrounding them, and then he seemed to relax, even smiling slightly as he said, 'Don't play the fond wife. We both know why you married David.'

As soon as she said, 'And why was that?' she knew she'd given him the opportunity he'd been waiting for.

'Because you were expecting my bairn.'

React, *react*. Get mad. Throw something. Her brain was sending messages but she felt numb.

'You handled him well, I'll give you that. But like I said, you've got guts. Did he really believe he was the father? Or was he so desperate to keep you he pretended to believe it?'

'He is David's.'

'No, Carrie, Matthew is my son. I've known it all along, long before he came "early". An eight-pounder two months early? Who did you think you'd fool? And that's why you don't want me round here, isn't it? You couldn't give a fig for Margaret's finer feelings. You're scared to death every time Matthew sees me, and why? Because he senses something, young as he is – a link between us, a bond that's a blood thing.'

'Uncle and nephew,' she cut in shakily. 'And you spoil him.'

'If I never gave him another thing, there would still be something there, there always was. He's mine, my son.'

'You wouldn't be saying this if you and Margaret had had bairns. Because of all that's happened you've convinced yourself Matthew is yours, that's what it is.'

'You can deny it until you're blue in the face but I know what I know. I was the first and the dates fit perfectly. He is mine. What I don't know is whether you convinced my poor sop of a brother he was the first.'

She gazed at him without speaking, hating him. Perhaps he saw something of this in her face or maybe her silence caught him on the raw, but suddenly he was at her side, his hands gripping her arms. 'I'm warning you, don't try and keep me away from him, Carrie. I need him. I have to see him.'

'Let go, you're hurting me.'

As she struggled his hands bit into her flesh even more. His voice was low as he said, 'I'll wreck your life if I have to, I swear it.' And then, as though someone had flicked a switch, his face changed and his voice became thick with emotion. 'I don't want it to be like this between us, damn it. I dream of you, do you know that? Night after night. I don't believe you're happy with David, you can't be.'

'*Let go!*' She jerked away with such force she hit her hip on the corner of the kitchen table. Her face blanched with the pain but her eyes were blazing as she said, 'You lay another finger on me and I'll scream the place down, do you hear me? And what will Matthew think of his precious Uncle Alec then? You can't prove anything of what you think because it's all make-believe, it's not true. And David *does* know he wasn't the first if you want to know, so you can't throw that at him. He might not have been the first but he *is* the father of my child, so there.'

For a second, just a second, she saw a flicker of uncertainty in his face, but then, as he stepped back from her, it faded. 'You're lying,' he said softly. 'Everything about you, the way you've been over the last years, tells me that.'

'You raped me, Alec.' She stared at him, the colour coming back into her face. 'Was I supposed to be glad to see you?'

'Rape's an ugly word.'

'It was an ugly act.'

'I don't remember it like that.' His voice was very soft now, even wistful. 'I remember it as something wonderful.'

He was trying to charm her! He actually thought he could turn on the spiel and she would fall for it. His arrogance was breathtaking. *'Get out of this kitchen.'*

'And I saw your face that day in Mam's house when I said I was going to marry Margaret. You knew then, didn't you? Maybe you'd even come to tell me, I don't know, but you knew well enough. And the next thing is you're married to David.'

He turned and walked to the door, and she prayed she'd remain strong long enough to conceal the trembling which was threatening to overwhelm her.

He glanced over his shoulder at her. 'Don't try and separate me from him, Carrie, because you'll regret it if you do. I don't give a damn about David or Margaret either. All I care about is Matthew . . . and you.'

'And Mr Reed?' She flung the name at him. 'What would Mr Reed do if you brought your ridiculous claim out into the open and hurt Margaret? You'd be out on your ear quicker than you could say Jack Robinson.'

'Maybe I'd consider it worth it.'

'Losing everything you've worked so hard for during the last ten years?' She forced a sneering laugh. 'Putting up with all you say you've had to put up with?'

'A husband has certain rights—'

'He would drum you out of town and you know it, rights or no rights. Every decent door would be closed to you and he'd make sure your name was dirt. All the money in the world can't buy back a reputation once it's gone. You'd perhaps be left with plenty in the bank but your life would be in shreds.'

221

Alec shrugged. 'If a man gets desperate enough there's no knowing what he'll do,' he said softly. 'So, think on, lass. All I'm asking is that you leave things as they are. The occasional visit from a loving uncle and aunt isn't too much to ask, is it?'

And he walked out of the room, shutting the door very quietly behind him.

'I might be wrong but I got the impression our Carrie wasn't overjoyed at Alec gettin' the bairn that bike.'

Joan glanced at her husband as she walked across the room. She pushed the kettle further into the coals before taking off her coat and hat. 'Why was that then?' she asked.

'You mean you didn't notice anythin'?'

Joan shrugged. 'There's always an edge when Alec and Margaret are there but then Alec's never got on with David and Walter, has he? You know that. And him rising in the world might be a thorn in David's flesh.'

'It's not David I'm talkin' about.'

'What affects David, affects Carrie. She's his wife, Sandy. They love each other.'

Sandy hunched his shoulders. David had ruined Carrie's life taking her down like that and here was Joan talking about love, but that was a woman all over. He didn't know a man alive who could fathom the way their minds worked.

Brushing the past aside for a moment, he returned to what was bothering him. 'The lass wasn't herself today, Joan, I'm tellin' you. I reckon Alec is tryin' to get his oar in.'

'With our Carrie, you mean?'

'Aye. I reckon he's sweet on her an' all this fuss he makes of Matt might be a means of gettin' his feet under the table.'

'Oh, go on with you.' Joan came over to him and put her

arms round his neck. Her voice was indulgent as she said, 'Look, m'lad, you might think the ground turns holy if our Carrie walks on it, but not everyone is of like mind. She's his sister-in-law and Matthew is his nephew, and likely he enjoys having a bairn to spoil. You know how things are with Margaret.'

'Aye, I do.' He gave her a look. 'You only have to see the pair of them together to guess at how things are behind closed doors.'

'I meant about them not being able to have their own babby,' Joan said reprovingly. 'What's the point in having all that money if he can't spend a bit on his brothers' bairns? He's perhaps thinking an uncle is all he's ever going to be.'

'So you think I'm worrin' unduly?'

'Aye, I do.' Joan rested her head against his shoulder.

He hoped she was right. Sandy said no more, but he couldn't rid himself of the feeling, which had been growing steadily for some months now, that Carrie was on edge about something. But she was a grown woman, a wife and mother, and gone were the days when he could sit her on his knee and charm away her tears with a slab of toffee or a bag of bullets, more's the pity. He sighed loudly. This business of having bairns wasn't all it was cracked up to be.

Chapter Thirteen

'They're stupid, the lot of them. Do you really think the government is going to listen to a load of ragtag and bobtail working men with their backsides hanging out just because they march from one end of the country to the other, carrying an oak box?'

'Over eleven thousand people have signed that petition.'

'So? What's the betting Baldwin won't even look at it when they get to London? It's just a waste of good shoe leather.' Renee glared at her husband, hands on hips and chin stuck forward.

'There's times I think you've forgotten where you've come from now you've got this forewoman's job,' Walter said grimly.

Renee tossed her head and threw herself down in the armchair in front of the range. 'Don't be daft,' she said, more coolly now.

'You were forever rabbiting on about the working man's rights when we were first wed, and now when there's families living on bread and gravy or going into the workhouse, and men topping themselves rather than having to face hearing their bairns crying with hunger or going through the means test, you say it's stupid to protest. You say *they're* stupid. I don't know how you've got the gall.'

'It was working *women's* rights I "rabbited" about,' Renee corrected without raising her head. She sipped at the cup of tea she had poured herself before the row had begun.

'Aye, well, like as it's the same thing in these times.'

'It's never the same thing. Men like you still think all a wife is good for is to stay at home and get their dinner, regardless of how intelligent she is.'

'An' you think you're intelligent, do you?'

'Aye, I do. Too intelligent to agree it's very bright to march all them miles to London in October when they'll be sleeping rough most of the time. Look how bad you were when you did the Durham march.'

'I didn't think you'd noticed.'

It was bitter, very bitter, and Renee looked up at him. 'Oh, for goodness' sake, don't start,' she said in a bored tone. 'By the way, I shan't be home till late tomorrow so I'll leave something cold in the pantry for you and Veronica. Me and a couple of the girls from the factory are going to the Empire after work. There's a new Laurel and Hardy on.'

'We can't afford it.'

'No, *we* can't but I can.'

Walter gritted his teeth. 'The bairn needs her boots mending and we're out of leather.'

'They'll do another few days.'

'They won't, her feet were blue when she came in earlier and it's been sleeting today. She needs—'

'For crying out loud!' Renee leaped up out of her seat, her voice high. 'If she needs them mending then go and buy the leather yourself.'

'There's nothing I'd like better and you know it.' The effort it was taking Walter to hold on to his temper showed in the veins

226

bulging on his forehead. 'But with only a couple of shifts last week—'

'You can't,' Renee finished for him, her voice scathing. 'Then you'll have to wait until I can, won't you? But I tell you one thing, Walter. I work hard for my money and like I've said before, it's not all going on you and Veronica. I deserve to get out of this house now and then.'

'Now and then? You're hardly ever in it. The bairn needs to see more of you, you're little more than a stranger to her.'

'Don't you come that, Walter Sutton.' Renee's head was pushed forward and she glared at her husband. 'Right from the beginning I said I didn't want bairns.'

'But she came.'

'Aye, she came all right and it was no accident, not on your part, was it? So you got what you wanted.'

'And I thank my lucky stars for her every day. I'd have been in the asylum living with you all these years if the bairn hadn't been around.'

'Believe me, I wouldn't have been around but for her. Who in their right mind would choose to stay with a weak-kneed scut like you! You're not a man, you're nothing! A nowt! All wind and—'

Walter moved without thinking and hit her. The blow propelled her backwards into the seat she'd just vacated. For a moment Renee lay there, stunned and silent, and then she scrambled to her feet, her hand to the side of her burning face. 'I hate you, do you know that?' she hissed. 'With every bit of me I hate you. I wish you was dead.'

'Mam?'

The voice from the doorway brought both pairs of eyes turning as one. Walter died a thousand deaths as he looked at his daughter's white face, everything within him crying out in protest. Veronica ran to her mother, burying her face in Renee's skirt and Renee looked him full in the face, satisfaction in every line of her body. 'Come on, me bairn,' she said, her voice softer than Walter had heard it in a long time and her eyes still watching his stricken face. 'This is no place for you. Mam will take you up to bed.'

And still holding the child against her, she led Veronica out of the room.

'You all right, man?'

Four days later David was standing with his father and brother outside Jarrow's Christ Church where two hundred marchers had just filed in for a special service, along with those wives and mothers who could attend. Beneath the threadbare clothes each man was as clean and fresh as soap and water would allow, newly shaven, their Sunday caps on their heads. Miss Ellen Wilkinson, the mayor, and other corporation officials had led the way, and the Bishop of Jarrow was taking the service.

There had been an air of suppressed excitement about the marchers as they went into the church, and this feeling had spread to the large crowd outside which included reporters and photographers and dozens of bairns. Walter, however, had hardly said two words since he had met his father and brother that morning for the walk into Jarrow. Billy and his father had intended to accompany them but at the last minute they had both got a shift at the colliery, and no one in their right mind ever refused work.

Now Walter turned to David, his voice low as he said, 'Aye, I'm all right.'

'What's up?'

'I said I'm all right.'

'Aye, and pigs fly. You middling or something?'

Walter stared at his brother, and then, as Ned began to talk to one of his cronies from the pit who had also made the journey into Jarrow to support the marchers, he said, 'I've had a do with Renee.'

'So, what's new?'

'This was different. I . . . lost me temper. I hit her, man, and the bairn, our Veronica, she walked in on it.'

'You struck her?' David knew quite a few men who used their wives for punchbags or wouldn't think twice about a cuff round the ear if they thought their spouse deserved it, but Walter was not one of them. Their da had brought them up never to raise their hand to a woman and he couldn't quite believe his brother had hit his wife.

'Don't look at me like that, man. I'm not proud of it. But she—' Walter broke off, shaking his head. 'Oh, what does it matter! I hit her and Veronica saw enough to know what had happened. She's had a job to look me in the face the last few days. What do you think I should do?'

David said nothing for a moment. There was the odd drop of rain blowing in the icy wind and it was freezing cold, but the look in Walter's eyes was bleaker than the weather. 'Talk to her,' he said at last. 'Your Veronica's a canny little lass. Explain it was a mistake, that you regret it—'

'I don't.' Walter's head had been hanging down but now he raised it, and David caught his breath at his brother's expression. 'I regret the bairn being upset but Renee deserved it, and more. I tell you, I don't know how I've kept me hands from her throat plenty of times. Only the thought of what would happen to Veronica has stopped me. She's a devil, David.'

A loud cheer signalled the fact that the service had ended and the marchers were coming out. David took his brother's arm and drew him to one side. 'Don't talk like that, man. It can't be as bad as that.'

'It's worse.' Walter was speaking slowly and quietly, and it carried more weight than any shouting. 'She thinks I don't know but she's been carrying on with someone for years, someone at the factory, like as not. I've walked the streets some nights when she's supposed to be out with some pal or other, looking for her and this bloke. I'm surprised I've not copped a good hiding, the number of courting couples I've disturbed in me time.'

David stared at his brother. 'That's daft, man,' he said weakly. 'I mean, I know things haven't been too good between you two for some time, but a fancy man?'

'I know, all right? Same as you'd know if it was you.'

There was a short silence which David was too shocked to break.

'I reckon he's got a car or a van or something, he must have or I'd have found them by now.'

'But . . .' David shook his head as though he'd been punched in the face. 'What would you do if you did find them?'

'Beat him into a pulp, do for him most likely. Her an' all.'

'You don't mean that.'

Walter screwed up his eyes as though they were smarting. Then he looked directly into David's and said, 'I do mean it. Oh, I mean it, man.'

There was a crab seller a few feet away, one hand on her hip, the other holding a basket balanced on her head. 'Nice boiled crabs,' she was shouting, 'ready to eat. Cr-a-bs, cr-a-bs, nice boiled crabs.' Men were streaming out of the church and the band struck up just feet away.

'Come over here, man, I can't hear meself think in this circus.' David pulled his brother clear of the crowd. 'Promise me you won't go walking the streets again,' he said urgently. 'Not without coming for me first. We'll go together if you need to try and find them, but promise me you won't go alone.'

'I don't do that any more.' It was weary. 'But thanks, David.'

'Why didn't you say anything before?'

'Would you have? If it'd been your Carrie?'

David wrinkled his face against the thought. 'No.'

'There you are then.'

The marchers and the harmonica band disappeared round a corner and the folk who weren't following them to the outskirts of town began to drift away in twos and threes. Ned came hurrying up, accompanied by a roly-poly figure of a man with a smiling pug's face. David recognised him from somewhere.

'I've bin lookin' all over for you two,' Ned said breathlessly. 'You remember Terry Proudfoot, lads? Amos's brother?'

'Oh aye.' David and Walter nodded to Terry who had moved down south when they were bairns.

Terry nodded back, his red-cheeked face smiling as he said, 'By, lads, I wouldn't have known you if I'd passed you in the street and that's the truth.'

'We're sorry about Amos, Terry,' David said and shook his hand. 'He was a grand man.'

'Aye, lad. Aye, he was.'

Amos had finally lost his fight with pneumoconiosis on the last day of September and his funeral was later that day.

'I'm taking our Ethel, Amos's wife' – Terry raised enquiring eyebrows at the three of them and they all nodded, although Walter and David hadn't known the name of Amos's wife – 'back south with me. Me an' Mildred have got a couple of spare rooms and we can make her comfortable enough, bless her.'

231

'Terry's done all right for himself,' Ned put in. 'Isn't that right, Terry?'

'Aye, well, I can't complain. It was hit an' miss in the first couple of years but the bairns mucked in and between us we've made a go of it,' Terry said. 'I'm in the automobile business, lads, on the used cars side. By, it's the way of the future and no mistake.'

'Four showrooms, Terry's got now. Isn't that right, Terry?' Ned was presenting the other man like a fairground show.

'Aye, four it is, right enough, and I'm thinking of a fifth come the spring. We all thought sales would drop a couple of years ago when they brought in this compulsory driving test lark, but not a bit of it, I'm glad to say.' Terry's face had lit up as he was speaking and it was clear to the three men watching him that he was passionate about his work. 'Mind, I can't see the need for this thirty miles per hour speed limit they've brought in, but if it's saving lives like they say it is, I don't suppose you can complain, can you?'

'No.' David could see from Walter's slightly glazed expression that his brother was feeling as lost as he was. None of them had even sat in an automobile, let alone driven one. 'I don't suppose you can.'

'London's changing, though, with all these traffic lights and whatnot, and I'm not too sure it's for the better meself.'

'Is that where you are now, London?' David interjected.

'Aye, that's it, lad, and it was the best thing me an' Mildred ever did when we took ourselves down there. I kept on at our Amos to come in with me, but he wouldn't. Stubborn old so-an'-so. He'd be sitting pretty if he had but you couldn't tell him anything. Mind, he thought the world of you, Ned.' Terry turned to David and Walter's father and gripped his arm. 'Right good to him you were and I'm

232

grateful. You all got time for a jar now the show's finished?'

David stared at Amos's brother. It was one thing to come and give the marchers a hell of a send-off like plenty of men on the dole or between shifts had done from as far as Newcastle and Sunderland because they supported their cause, quite another to view it as some sort of entertainment because you happened to be up north with some time to kill.

'Look, I'm getting a taxi back to town; why don't you three ride with me and we'll have a drink at the Grand,' Terry said jovially. 'I'm staying there while I'm up here and to tell you the truth I'd appreciate the company. The wife wanted to stay with our eldest who's just presented us with our first grandchild last week, so I'm all on my own and I've never been one for my own company. What do you say?'

'Aye, man, we'll have a drink with you.' Ned answered for them all, though he could see his sons were feeling uncomfortable.

Terry Proudfoot might have begun life as a miner's son in two rooms in a house at the Back of the Pit, but it was clear he had risen some way since then. His light grey check suit, highly polished black boots and black homburg were of good quality, as was the dark grey overcoat trimmed with fur at the collar. He wore his coat open, revealing the mound of a portly belly under the fine cloth. He looked prosperous and pleased with himself, and as far removed from the folk he'd once called his own as the man on the moon. Pawning the fire irons or bread knife, scrabbling for cinders on the tip or following the coal cart to pick up lumps shaken out by potholes or tram lines – what did Terry know about such day-to-day living? mused David as he and Walter followed the two older men down the street. Although he'd known it once.

Back in Bishopwearmouth, David made his excuses and left the other three outside the Grand. He told Ned he didn't relish the thought of entering the smart hotel dressed in his working clothes, whatever his father and Walter felt about it. He would go and have a tidy up at the allotment, spend an hour or two getting it ready for the next owner. Carrie was busy rushing through a special order the shop had asked her for, so he didn't want to get under her feet at home.

It was cold on the allotment, bitter in fact, but David found he was enjoying the physical work out in the open air, with an icy north-east wind blowing and the clouds scudding across the low sky. He had needed to do something after Walter's revelation.

He mulled over everything his brother had said as he cleared the hard ground of debris and lit a large bonfire. But once he was digging over the frozen earth, his thoughts moved on to the talk of war which was beginning to appear in the newspapers again. He had heard more than one miner say that Hitler could do whatever he liked if it brought in work. Everyone knew you couldn't have a war without coal – lots of it.

David straightened his aching back and stood with one hand resting on Amos's old spade, staring up into the grey sky.

Idly he watched a cloud shaped like a dog chasing one which could have passed for a cat. It seemed years rather than months since the Durham Miners' Gala in July. It had been a rare good day this year, not just because the sun had shone on the banners and bands, stalls and sideshows, but because they had all gone together – him, Carrie and Matthew, Walter and his family, Carrie's mam and da, Billy and the twins, and his own parents. Billy had brought along the lass he'd been courting for a while – a nice lass even if she didn't say two words the whole day

– and because everyone was together out in the open it had made things easier with Sandy somehow, less awkward. He remembered he'd thought at one point that he wished it could always be like this, everyone getting on and no sniping between Walter and Renee or his mam and da.

He shook his head at himself, lifted his cap and raked back his springy black hair before replacing the cap on his head. As he bent to start digging again, he saw his father and Terry Proudfoot come in through the side gate at the rear of the allotments. He raised his hand to them and his father waved back, and even from a hundred yards he could see the difference in his da's face.

He thought at first his father was well oiled. By, I hope he can hold it until the funeral's over at least, he reflected wryly, but then, as the two men got nearer, he saw it wasn't that. His da looked ten years younger, his face alive and his eyes bright. Ned was still some thirty yards away when he shouted, 'I'm glad you're still here, lad! Have I got some news for you.'

When his father reached him he didn't speak straight away as David had expected; he waited until Terry had come puffing and panting to their side. 'Tell him, Terry,' he said. 'Tell him what you said to me not an hour since,' and then before Terry had a chance to open his mouth, 'He wants me to go and work for him, lad, down south. What do you think of that?'

'Work for him?' David stared at his father. Terry was nodding enthusiastically, still trying to catch his breath. 'Doing what?'

'Lookin' after this new showroom he's openin' come spring, that's what. An' what's more, he's on about me havin' drivin' lessons with one of his lads an' havin' me own car.' Ned couldn't get the words out quick enough. 'Me with me own car, lad,' and he chuckled like a bairn.

'But . . .' David's gaze moved from one to the other before settling on his father's beaming face. 'You don't know the first thing about cars.'

'There's nowt he can't learn, lad, and me lads will see to it he gets a good grounding afore March. Besides, he'll be managing the new place for me, there'll be plenty of young wind-snappers doing the donkey work. I want someone I can trust in there, that's the thing. Someone I know won't be on the fiddle. Me lads see to the other places but there's only four of them so I was wondering what to do about this new one, and I owe your da, David. Ethel's been singing his praises since I got down here, saying how good he's been to her and Amos with the allotment an' all. Always popping stuff in and spending time with Amos. Not everyone bothers to do that nowadays, lad.' Terry shook his head sorrowfully.

'Aw, man, I was glad to do it.' Ned rubbed at his nose as he was apt to do when embarrassed. 'And a few bit veg is nowt.'

'Aye, but Ethel says it was the good stuff you gave them, Ned. None of the old rubbish. And when you managed to sell some veg if things went well, it was their pocket that saw the result. She said they had a job to get you to take a bit of baccy money. Without what you slipped them on the sly it'd have been the workhouse, according to Ethel, although why the daft pair didn't tip me the wink as to how things were I don't know. But that was Amos, stubborn as a cuddy and as proud as Punch.'

David was gaping at his father in amazement. He knew his da had sometimes managed to sell the odd few boxes of vegetables round the doors when there was a bit over – which wasn't often by the time he'd looked after Amos and himself and slipped Renee and Carrie some stuff – but he had always assumed his da had kept the money for the hard work he'd put in. And all the time he'd been looking after Amos and Ethel. Well, well. Talk about live and learn.

'So? What do you say?' His father's deep brown eyes, so like his own, were searching.

'Good on you, man, if you want to go.'

'Want to go? By, lad.' Ned couldn't go on but David saw that his shoulders had straightened and his head was up at the thought of a good regular job. His mother had stripped his father of every shred of self-worth in the last years, and it was only now, seeing the transformation in front of him, that he realised just how much it had hurt his da.

The thought of his mother made him say, 'What about Mam? What if she doesn't want to go? You know what she's like.'

There was a moment of silence which seemed to swell, before Ned said very softly, 'I shall be goin' alone, lad.'

'Alone?'

'Aye.' Ned wetted his lips. 'I've had me fill over the years, lad, an' that's the truth. She's treated me as less than the muck under her boots an' I can't stand the sight of her no more than she can stand the sight of me.'

Terry had turned his head away and was scuffing a clod of earth with his shiny boots.

'But . . .' David was at a loss.

'You think the less of me for it?'

'No, Da.' It was immediate. 'No, but I just can't take it in. Will . . . will we see you again?'

'Oh aye, lad, bless you.' It was Terry who replied. 'You and your dear wife and any of them who want to pay a visit will be made more than welcome, you rest assured on that. You just write and let your da know when you want to come down and there'll be train tickets provided, all right? On me. And that stands for as long as your da stays down south, which I hope

237

will be indefinitely. By, it'll be right grand to have someone from the old days to jaw with of an evening over a pint or two. The wife is forever in one or the other of the bairns' houses, and it'll be worse now our Nell has had her bairn. Be a magnet, that babby will. She's already spent a small fortune on kitting out the nursery for him as it is.'

It was another world. David knew he was probably staring gormlessly but he couldn't help it. Bairns up here were lucky if they top and tailed with umpteen others and had a change of clothing to their name, and here was Terry talking about fixing up the child's room and decking it out as though it was nowt. 'When will you go?' he asked his father.

'Straight after the funeral. Terry wants to get back and there'll just be time to see our Lillian before we catch the train. Walter already knows and I shall leave your mam to break the good news to Alec. They'll be able to chew me over all they like but I shan't be around to hear it. I shall tell her as I leave for the funeral and likely she'll clap her hands. It'll mean she'll probably go to Alec's which is what she's always wanted, the sun having always shone out of his backside.'

The three of them were silent for a moment, then Terry thumped David lightly on the shoulder and said, 'Don't forget, lad, whenever you want to pay a visit you'll be welcome.'

'Aye, thanks.' David nodded and turned to his father. 'I'll see you later then. At the funeral?'

'Aye, aye, you will.' Ned's voice was preoccupied now, as though he had already left. 'I'd best get home and get sorted then.'

'You do that, Da.'

David waited until the two men had passed through the side gate before he followed them out of the allotment. He needed to marshal his racing thoughts on the way home before he told Carrie his father's news.

By the time he reached Dock Street he was almost running. He burst into the front room only to find it empty. And then he heard his name called from upstairs. He walked back out into the narrow hall as Carrie descended from the bedrooms. For a moment as he saw her bright face he thought, she knows. Somehow she knows about me da and she's pleased for him. And he said, 'You've heard?'

'Heard?'

'About me da?' Her wrinkled brow told him he was on the wrong tack. 'If it's not me da, what are you looking so pleased about?'

'Tell me about your da first.'

So there was something. 'No.' He tapped her nose. 'You tell me.'

'It's the shop. Mr Horwood sent a message for me to go back with the driver when they came to pick up the order. I've just got back.'

'And?'

'And he's offered me a rise, a big rise. He wants me to just do specific orders for his best clients. Apparently quite a few of them are asking especially for me now, Mr Horwood says. There's a grand wedding in the spring and they've asked for me to do all the dresses. It's such an opportunity, David . . .' Her voice trailed away. 'Don't look like that.'

David made a huge effort. Carrie's words had caused a feeling of panic that was constricting his breath. She was beautiful, so beautiful, and she was going up in the world. He knew it as sure as eggs were eggs. And him? He was just an ordinary working man, and not even a white-collar one at that. There was nothing to hold her to him. Bitterness was like lemon juice in his mouth. He couldn't hold her, he knew that. He'd come to accept it slowly as he had watched her change from the young bonny lass he'd married, who had been little more than a bairn, into a strong-minded woman whose beauty took his breath away. 'I'm glad for you.' Even to himself the words sounded stilted. And then, because the light in her face was dying, he forced himself to say with more warmth, 'I am, lass. I'm really glad for you. It's just that I've had a shock the day. It's me da . . .'

David had left for the funeral twenty minutes earlier when Olive Sutton walked into Carrie's kitchen through the back door. In all the time Carrie had been married, her mother-in-law had never once paid an unexpected visit. Indeed, Carrie could count the number of times Olive had been to the house and they wouldn't have reached a dozen, being in the main for Matthew's birthdays, with the occasional Christmas or New Year thrown in. The move to Dock Street had been a thorn in Olive's flesh from the start; Carrie was well aware of this, and the fact that what really rankled with Olive was that the move had been funded by her own work.

Carrie's expression was guarded as she said, 'Hello, Mam. What are you doing here?'

Olive eyed her angrily. 'I've come to find out what you know about this idea Ned's got about moving down to London. And don't tell me you and David aren't in on it. Ned's forever in this house, along with others I could name.'

Carrie ignored this. 'I know as much as you, I expect,' she said quietly, carrying on with the task of lining a dish with pastry for the apple pie she was making.

'I doubt that, m'girl. And don't come out with the same story Ned did about this being something that's happened all of a sudden. This has been planned for weeks, hasn't it? Months, most likely. You've all been laughing at me behind my back. Do Renee and Walter know? And Lillian?' Olive didn't include Alec in the accusation of betrayal, Carrie noticed. She stared at the enraged woman; it was obvious Olive was holding on to her temper by no more than a thread.

'You'll have to ask Ned about that,' she said, her tone cool. 'As I understand it, he met Mr Proudfoot because of the funeral and—'

'I said I know the story that's been concocted, but Ned would never have the guts to do something like this without thinking about it for months. He's a spineless so-an'-so, always has been. No one knows what I've had to endure. We'd be like pigs in muck if it'd been left to him.'

Carrie was beginning to shake with anger inside but she kept her voice level. 'I think Ned is a lovely man.'

'I think Ned's a lovely man,' Olive mocked nastily. 'And in your book lovely men up and skedaddle and leave their family with nowt, do they? Nearly thirty-five years I've worked my fingers to the bone for that ungrateful scum, and what do I get?'

'Exactly what you deserve.' She hadn't meant to say it but her temper was up and for once she didn't care what her mother-in-law thought.

'So that's the way of it? I might have known.' Olive nodded, her head jerking on her thin neck.

'From the first day I came into this family I've never heard you say one kind word to him,' Carrie said hotly, 'not one, so what makes you think he would want to stay here when he's had an offer like the one from Mr Proudfoot?'

'I'm his wife, he's married to me—'

'No one knows that better than Ned, I should expect.'

Olive drew her body up as tight as a bow. 'You dare to speak to me like that! Scum from the bottom end, you are, and no amount of getting on will alter that. Little Miss Butter-wouldn't-melt-in-her-mouth. You set your cap at David, trapping him with the oldest trick in the world, but not content with him you make sure your own sister's husband is never off the doorstep, along with mine. No man's safe round you, Carrie McDarmount. You even encourage Alec through the bairn, playing on the fact that Margaret's worse than useless.'

The hot colour that had surged into Carrie's face drained away. Matthew? What did she mean by that remark? Surely Alec hadn't told his mother he thought the boy was his? 'I don't know what you're talking about,' she said shakily. 'Alec is Matthew's uncle. It's natural he'd want to see him.'

'Aye, and you're the mistress of natural feelings, sure enough.'

Olive didn't know, or she would have screamed the accusation at her right now, the mood she was in, instead of that last gibe. She had read too much into what had been just another nasty taunt. Gathering her scattered wits, Carrie said forcefully, 'I think you had better leave.'

'You're ordering me out of my own son's house?'

'Exactly.' Carrie held the livid green gaze and it was Olive who dropped her eyes first. 'He won't get away with it,' she muttered bitterly. 'Tell him that from me. I'll have him brought back, I'll get the police involved if I have to.'

It was an idle threat and Carrie didn't bother to contradict it.

'And I shan't forget the part you've played today, madam, or that son of mine. Taking Ned's side when any decent folk would have been horrified.'

'I asked you to leave.'

'I'm going, don't worry. There's nothing would make me want to stay here with you. It just amazes me Matthew has turned out as well as he has, having you for a mother.'

So saying, Olive exited the house the way she had come, banging the back door behind her with some force.

Horrible, horrible woman. Carrie drew in a shuddering breath, her legs suddenly weak. And the nerve of her, to come round here shouting and carrying on. To think she had even felt sorry for Olive when David had first told her what his da was going to do. Not that she didn't think Ned should go, not a bit of it, but to be left like that and everyone knowing . . . But she didn't feel sorry for the woman now. She looked at her hands which were still trembling and burst into tears.

By the time David returned to the house and Matthew came home from school, Carrie was in perfect control of herself. She had made up her mind that when she told David what had occurred with his mother, she would be calm and collected. It wouldn't help anyone if David knew exactly what his mother had said to her because he wouldn't stand for it and the row would just escalate.

When the evening meal was over and Matthew had been despatched to bed early, much to his disgust, she sat David down with a cup of tea in front of the fire and pulled one of the kitchen chairs close to his armchair. 'I need to talk to you,' she said carefully, 'about your mam.'

'Not tonight, Carrie.' David lay back with a deep sigh, stretching his long legs out in front of him. 'It's been a strange sort of day one way and another, and we can't do anything about Da going anyway. We'll talk tomorrow, all right?'

'She came here today.'

'What?' He sat upright. 'Me mam came *here*?'

243

'She was upset about your da going and she seems to think we knew about it beforehand, weeks ago.'

'That's daft.'

'I know that and you know it but she's made up her mind it was some sort of conspiracy.'

'What did she say?'

'Oh, she accused us of encouraging him, things like that. She . . . she was in a rage.'

'And she came here when she knew you'd be by yourself, with me and Da at the funeral.' He was staring intently at her wary face now, taking her by surprise when he said, 'Tell me exactly what she said, Carrie. Word for word.'

'I can't remember,' she prevaricated weakly. 'But we argued and it finished with me telling her to get out.'

'And you're saying you can't remember what provoked you to say that? Look, lass, I know me mam and she's a nasty piece of work. What did she say?'

It would be the end of any contact between them if she told him, and Matthew was fond of his grandma, as she was of him. 'I told you, I can't remember. She said things and I said things and it's all a blur now, mixed up.'

'Then I'll have to see about unmixing it, won't I?' He rose from the armchair as he spoke.

'Where are you going? Oh no, don't, don't, David. Let her cool down for a while, she's had a shock. Drink your tea.'

'Damn my tea.' He reached for his cap and muffler on the back of the kitchen door. 'And if you think my mother is going to cool down, you don't know her very well.'

It was a full two hours before the door opened again and he walked in, his cap and coat soaked with the icy rain that was falling. She stared at him and he smiled; his first words were about the weather. 'It's raining cats and dogs.'

244

'You saw her?'

'Oh aye, I saw her. Alec had left no more than five minutes before and she was in a stew because he hadn't offered to take her in, nor will he, if you ask me. He'll blame it on Margaret's nerves or some such thing, but the crux is he doesn't like her any more than the rest of us do. It just suited him not to get on the wrong side of her before, and with him being golden boy that wasn't difficult. Line of least resistance, that's Alec.'

'How was she?'

'Still spitting coals. I spat a few myself when she gave me the gist of what she'd said to you. Why didn't you tell me?'

'I didn't want you to go round there and fall out with her.'

'You have to be friendly with someone in the first place to fall out with them.' He was taking off his coat and cap as he spoke, and his mouth was hard and tight and not at all like her David's. 'Anyway, I haven't fallen out with her. I merely told her that when she's ready to come here and apologise to you she will be welcome in this house again, and able to see Matthew. That's all.'

'But she'll never do that.' She stared at him, her eyes deeply troubled. 'You know what she's like with me, she'll never eat humble pie.'

'Then that's that. The decision is hers, lass. She's brought all this on herself, not just this with us but Da leaving like he has. Why should any bloke have to put up with what he's had to put up with all these years?'

'I know, but—'

'No buts.'

'It'll cause so many problems, David.'

He had taken off his sodden shirt and was hanging it over the wooden clothes horse which he had moved close to the glowing range. The tone of her voice made him turn. He held out his muscled arms which were as strong and hard as the coal he hewed.

'Come here, lass,' he said quietly. When Carrie was folded into his embrace and his chin was resting on top of her head, he continued, 'If there are problems we'll face them together, all right?'

'But Matthew will want to see his grandma, you know how she spoils him and—'

David lifted her face with the tip of one finger and smiled at her. 'Together, all right? And that includes Matthew.' He kissed her thoroughly, and as she relaxed against the broad expanse of his chest she realised there was no other place she would rather be. David had become her rock and her fortress as well as her friend and comforter and lover. She loved him. Carrie's eyes opened wide. She wasn't sure when this love had crept up on her but it was there all right and it was real. He was part of her now, her other half.

Above his wife's head, David was smiling no longer. In his mind's eye he was seeing the pile of linen and patterns in the next room, and the typewritten letter on fancy headed notepaper which stated, in effect, that Mrs Carrie Sutton was destined to fly high.

There were going to be changes in the next little while, sure enough, he thought grimly, and this upset with his mam and da was the least of it.

Part 4

Rationing, Raids and Recriminations

1940

Chapter Fourteen

'What are you doing here at this time of day, Alec?'

'I've come to see you, of course, when I knew David was at the pit.'

The straight answer was unexpected and Carrie's face must have betrayed this, because Alec smiled, a wry twisted smile, before saying, 'I've been called up, Carrie. No reserved occupation, no bairns, barely married . . .'

'Don't.' She took a step backwards away from the scullery door where Alec had arrived unannounced a few moments before, the basket of dirty washing in her hands proclaiming her intent to visit the washhouse.

Alec gestured at the basket. 'Do you want me to carry that out for you?'

'No.' It was immediate. The thought of the two of them in the narrow confines of the brick-built washhouse wasn't an option.

In the four years that had passed since Matthew's tenth birthday, Alec had made it clear, in a hundred and one little ways, that he wanted her. The fact that she remained cool and slightly aggressive towards him didn't seem to deter him in the slightest.

'Have it your own way.' He walked further into the room, causing her to back out of the scullery and into the wider area of the kitchen, and then he said, 'Aren't you going to offer your ever loving brother-in-law a cup of tea before he goes off to fight for King and country?' His eyes were mocking her.

'Look, Alec—'

'No, you look, Carrie. You look for once.' He came close to her, not touching but near enough for her to smell the drink on his breath. Her nose wrinkled, and he said, 'Aye, aye, I've had a couple, Dutch courage to come and see you. Does that surprise you, eh? Alec Sutton, him that's risen as swiftly as a shooting star, needing to build himself up with whisky before he sets foot over your threshold? But it's true.'

Carrie said again, 'Don't,' but her voice was a whisper now. She hadn't seen him like this before. It was as though something had been stripped away from him, an outward veneer, and this unnerved her more than any passionate declaration of love could have done. But then that came too.

'I love you, Carrie.' And at her body's jerk of protest, he said again, 'I do. I love you. I suffer the torment of the damned knowing you're married to David, that he has the right to touch you, to make love to you—'

'*Stop it.*' Her voice was guttural, so harsh it checked the words spilling out of him. 'He's your brother, your *brother.*'

'And this is where I should say I love him and respect him and that if it wasn't for that I'd have followed through on what I said years ago.' It was bitter. 'But I don't love him or respect him, Carrie. Him and Walter allowing themselves to be brainwashed into going down the pit at fourteen makes me want to vomit. The only reason I haven't said and done this before is because I knew what you'd say if I did.'

'So what's different now?'

'I'm going away to fight and there's a good chance I won't come back. Men are being maimed, killed every day.' He

250

stopped, took a deep breath. 'It sort of brings everything into balance. Money, prestige . . .'

'You wanted all that very badly. If it wasn't for this war you'd still be the same.'

'Probably.' Alec tipped his head on one side as though he was considering what she'd said, and Carrie's breath stopped with the shock of how like Matthew he was in that moment. Or should she say Matthew was like him? she asked herself feverishly. 'Very probably,' he agreed softly. 'But it wouldn't make any difference to the way I feel about you. That's a thing apart.'

'You're mad.'

'About you? Dead right.'

'Stop this, Alec.' She stared into his face, the face which had woken in her the first stirrings of romantic love so many years ago, a love which had nearly caused her to throw herself into the river after he had trampled on it in the worst way possible. He had been handsome as a young lad but with maturity he was even more good-looking. And he knew it. Oh yes, he knew it all right.

'He's mine, isn't he?'

It was quiet, even tender, his eyes searching her face and allowing her to see the pain in his. She believed he was manipulating her for his own ends, using all this talk of love and that certain something he had with women to lull her into admitting he was Matthew's father. But even believing this, for one infinitesimal moment she was tempted to tell him the truth. It was enough to break the hypnotising power of the clear green gaze. 'No, Alec, he is not yours,' she said very steadily. 'David is his father.' And he was, in every way that counted. Who was it who had sat up with her every night for a week when Matthew was four years old and desperately ill with the measles? Who had fed her son, clothed him, helped him with his homework and taken him to the football matches Matthew was so passionate about? Who had tried to teach the boy right from wrong, applied discipline when Matthew needed it and a firm hand? It was these things that made a father, not a two-minute copulation.

'If I wasn't so sure in here' – he patted his jacket above his heart – 'I would almost believe you. You're getting better at lying.'

'Always the clever words.' She raised her head angrily. 'But I don't care what you think. Believe what you want, you will anyway. But I can assure you it's wishful thinking, and even that wouldn't have come about but for Margaret being unable to have bairns.'

Alec wetted his lips, then bit hard into the flesh of the lower one. It looked as if he was biting back hot words, but when he next spoke she realised this was not the case. His voice was low and rushed and highly embarrassed. 'I want you to know I'm sorry for what happened that night, or at least for the way it happened. I've never done anything like that before or since, it was the drink . . .' His voice trailed away. 'It was the drink.'

Carrie stared at him. She didn't trust this new tack, not from Alec. 'Four years ago in this very kitchen you denied you'd forced me,' she said stiffly. 'So what's changed?'

'Me.'

'Why?'

'Because I'm scared.'

'Scared?' Her brow wrinkled.

'You know as well as I do what some of those poor wretches are like that they got back from Dunkirk. Death would be a merciful release. Blinded, no legs, some with no limbs at all or burned beyond recognition.'

Carrie remained quiet, looking at him.

'Anything could happen, and I just wanted to say . . .' He shook his head. 'To go with a clear conscience.'

She had been leaning against the kitchen table, her bottom pressed against the wood, but now she pulled out a chair and sat down. Alec didn't move. She raised her head slowly after a few moments and looked at him. This was still all about him, she thought, her mind amazingly clear. If there hadn't been a war, if he wasn't going away to fight, he would never have said what he'd just said. He was like a bairn who said its prayers each night only because it was frightened something bad would happen to it if it didn't.

He swallowed. 'You don't believe I love you.' It was a statement not a question, but Carrie answered it anyway.

'If you didn't have this insane idea Matthew was yours you wouldn't be here,' she said quietly.

'I don't know what to say to that.'

'How about the truth?'

He stood looking somewhat helplessly at her and if it had been anyone but Alec she would have taken pity on them.

'All right, the truth is you're probably half right,' he said at last, his voice low and his gaze directed at the floor now. 'But only half right. Matthew keeps you at the forefront of my mind, of course he does, you're his mother, but that's only part of it.'

'I don't want to hear this. I'm married to your brother and I love him. Please go now.'

'Carrie—'

They both heard the back door open and when Matthew shouted, 'Mam?' she saw the change in Alec's face, the way it lit up, and she groaned inside. 'Mam, Brian Wilson's da's got an unexploded incendiary bomb, or so he says. Can I go and see it. I promise—'

What he would have promised Carrie didn't know, because as he stepped fully into the room and saw Alec standing to one side of the range he stopped abruptly, then grinned and said, 'Hello, Uncle Alec. What are you doing here?'

Before Carrie could say anything, Alec answered him. 'I've come to say goodbye, Matt. I'm going off to fight the Germans.'

He made it sound as if he was going to win the war single-handed, Carrie thought grimly.

'Really?' Matthew's eyes were like saucers; this was clearly another step up in the hero worship. 'Can I come and see you off?'

Again Alec pre-empted Carrie, probably because he anticipated her refusal. 'I'd like that very much.' He smiled warmly. 'And perhaps your mother would like to come too.'

'Won't Margaret prefer to have you all to herself at a time like this?' Carrie asked coolly, aware of Matthew's gaze flashing from her face to Alec's, and then back again.

'She's taken to her bed at the news.' It was flat.

'When do you leave?' There was absolutely no question of her seeing Alec off, but for Matthew's sake she had to give a viable excuse.

'Tomorrow morning.'

'I'm sorry but I have to be at the shop all morning. I have a special wedding presentation.' Carrie turned to Matthew. 'And didn't you say you were going up the allotment with your da for an hour or two before he goes on his shift?'

Matthew stared at his mother. How could she put a rotten old wedding presentation before seeing Uncle Alec off to war? He was going to fight for his country, he was a hero. Couldn't she see that? But she didn't want to. 'Da will come with me to see Uncle Alec off,' he said firmly, the look on his face as he spoke telling Carrie exactly what he was thinking.

The sound of his name being called from the backyard prompted him to turn to Alec and say, 'I'll go and tell him I'm not playing.'

'Not on my account, Matt. I'm just going.'

'Aw, Uncle Alec.'

'Come round later tonight if you want and we'll arrange a time for you and your da to be at the station. All right?'

'Aye, all right.' Matthew was all smiles again, and then as Brian called once more, he said, 'I'm going to Brian's then, Mam.'

Carrie nodded, her, 'Watch yourself,' automatic. When the back door had banged, Alec straightened from where he had been leaning against the wall at the side of the range.

'Don't try and stop him coming tonight or tomorrow, Carrie, or you'll regret it,' he said very quietly.

This was more like the Alec she knew. She made herself aggressive in both voice and manner, using it as a screen to hide her fear as she said, 'Here we go again. When are you going to see you can't threaten me, Alec?'

He ignored this as though she hadn't spoken. 'I'll tell him I believe I am his father and I'll give him all the dates to back it up, as well as the fact that he was supposed to be two months early. He's not a little bairn any more, he knows a bit about the birds and the bees.'

'You wouldn't.' She stared at him, her hand to her throat.

'I will if you try and thwart me on this.'

'What do you think his opinion of you will be if he knows what you did?'

'Like I said, he knows a bit about the birds and the bees now. I'll explain it was a wedding, we both had too much to drink

255

and one thing led to another. Of course with me being on the verge of getting engaged I couldn't let Margaret down, not over a mistake which incidentally I'll explain we both enjoyed.'

'*Get out.*'

'It wouldn't reflect well on you, would it? Lads have a thing about their mams being pure and above reproach. Funny that.'

'I said, get out.'

'I'm going, I'm going.' His voice was calm. He moved across the kitchen and into the scullery before he said, his hand on the back door knob, 'I meant what I said, I do love you.'

'You don't know the meaning of the word.' He could threaten her and in the next breath talk of love?

'If you had been halfway reasonable, this could have all been so different.'

'*You* talk of reason!' She glared at him, her face flushed with anger.

'So I'm going without your forgiveness?'

'You've never asked for it.'

'I'm asking now.'

'Fourteen years too late.'

'I see.' His voice was very soft and as his shoulders hunched slightly, Carrie told herself, don't fall for it, don't get taken in by the hangdog look. Two minutes ago he was talking of telling Matthew, which meant David too, and blowing everyone's world apart.

'Goodbye, Carrie.'

She couldn't bring herself to say goodbye or wish him well. Instead she inclined her head stiffly, her eyes on his face.

He turned, his shoulders straightening as he opened the door and then he was gone.

*　　*　　*

The next morning David and Matthew went to see Alec off at the station, and later that night, when David had returned from his shift at the colliery and they'd finished their evening meal, he said, 'You know, lass, I'm glad I went this morning. I've never got on with Alec as you well know, and there's not one thing we'd agree on if we sat and talked from now till doomsday, but I felt sorry for him this morning and that's a fact. All the other men had wives and bairns and mothers and goodness knows what, but he was standing all alone when we got there, and the look on his face . . . Well, it didn't look like Alec somehow. He was scared, Carrie. Scared out of his mind.'

He was expecting her to say something and she knew she had to respond, but she felt numb, strange. Eventually she managed to say, 'What about your mam? Why didn't she go?'

'I don't suppose she knows. She's never really forgiven him for refusing to have her when Da went, and I think Isaac is pretty firm with her, from what Lillian says. Isaac won't stand for any nonsense, that was one of the conditions of taking her in, so she can't throw her weight about like she used to. I think Lillian stands up to her and Mam has to toe the line, whereas at Alec's she was expecting to have the upper hand with Margaret.'

'Lillian and Isaac were marvellous to have her.'

'Aye, you can say that again. Every time we've been round there and I feel her giving me the evil eye, I think that.'

'She's civil enough.'

'Because Isaac's told her she'll be out on her ear if she isn't, and the only place then is the workhouse.'

The conversation continued along the lines of how well his da was doing down south, and Carrie kept it away from any mention of Alec for the rest of the evening, but once she was lying beside David in bed and his heavy regular breathing told her he was asleep, hot tears flowed down her face. She could not have translated her thoughts into words, nor could she have explained the pain that gripped her, but she felt desolate.

Chapter Fifteen

'Have you heard?'

'About the raid? Aye, lass. Bad business. They reckon the four lads who copped it in Laing's shipyard are all goners. It's a miracle there aren't more dead, considering fourteen bombs fell overall, but there're plenty injured, especially round the Royal. The Ali Baba Sauce factory is practically demolished, according to what I've heard, and Wreath Quay Road and Wreath Quay Lane were hit. They were aiming for the shipyards and the bridge, if you ask me.'

Carrie stared at David, who had just walked in from his shift at the colliery. There had been no bombs dropped on Sunderland in the first few months of the war, but since Alec had left, several had fallen, the first one in a field adjoining the Old Rectory in Whitburn, which had demolished a tithe barn and killed some horses. Up to yet, however, there had been no people killed, but a bombing raid at midday had changed all that.

'This is the beginning, isn't it?'

'Aye, well, we've got away light till now.'

They stared at each other for a moment more before Carrie said, 'I saw the Ali Baba Sauce factory this afternoon, David. If a bomb can do that to a big factory, a shelter would be no good if there was a direct hit, especially one like ours.'

'The chances of that happening are tiny, lass, now then, and ours is a darn sight better than one of the Morrison shelters which is all some poor blighters have between them and Jerry. Give me an outside one any day. I saw Sid White's the other night when I was on duty and called in to say his blackout curtains needing pulling, and it's nowt but an oblong box. They use it as a table most of the time but during a raid they all climb inside and pull mesh panels into place on the sides and ends. Mesh panels against the sort of blast we've seen evidence of in the last little while!' David shook his head disparagingly and walked through into the scullery to wash his hands.

The meal was ready and Matthew needed calling down from his bedroom, but Carrie continued to stand still, the agitation which had gripped her when she'd seen the destruction of the factory still strong. She knew their brick surface shelter in the backyard could withstand a considerable blast, but she wished they had a patch of earth so they could have an Anderson. These were half buried in the ground and made from six curved steel sheets bolted together at the top and with steel plates at either end, and then covered with earth. A front entrance with a blast wall to protect it and an emergency escape panel at the rear gave far better protection, in Carrie's view, than a brick box with a concrete roof which had the potential to crush them to death.

She glanced across at the emergency pack which consisted of a torch, cushions and blankets, and a flask which she'd fill before they all retired to bed. The pack had gone unused for months at the beginning of the war but the sirens had sounded in the dead of night more than once lately. She hated that sound. Oh, how she hated it. She'd never get used to it. And it was worse when David was on duty because then she worried that the explosions and thuds they could hear were where he was, as well as being scared of a hit on Matthew and herself. Not that she would have tried to stop David becoming an air raid warden, but she wished he'd been given their road to patrol, rather than one near Nelson Square some streets away and much closer to the river where industry lined the banks, an ideal target for the bombers.

'Something smells nice.' David walked back into the room, sniffing the air appreciatively in a way that always made Carrie smile.

'Harry kept a rabbit back for me.' Harry Forsyth, the butcher, had a contact who slipped him a few rabbits and the odd pheasant now and again, and since the war had begun he kept these for his favourite customers. This caused a certain amount of resentment among some of the old wives who frequented his shop, but no one dared complain or point out that it was supposed to be first come, first served.

Rationing was now part of life and the ration of bacon and ham per person per week was 4oz in total; other meat was rationed by price, a shilling's worth per week, so Carrie appreciated the elderly man's kindness. She had made a christening gown for his granddaughter some years before, and had refused to accept any payment when the daughter's husband had been killed while unloading crates at the dock days before the service. It seemed Harry didn't forget such things.

It took a bit of thinking to make 2oz of butter and cheese, 4oz of margarine and cooking fat, 3 pints of milk, 8oz of sugar and one egg a week – when available – plus 1lb of jam every two months stretch to provide filling meals for David and Matthew. But with Harry making sure that any sausage and offal – not rationed but scarce – came their way, and vegetables from old Amos's allotment, which Terry had passed over to David and Walter and was now tended by Matthew and Veronica, things weren't so bad. And David had made a long window box which he'd fixed along one side of the shelter, in which Carrie grew tomatoes. They hadn't gone to bed hungry yet. With stomach ache, certainly – there was a glut of plums at present and at twopence a quarter they ate them at every meal.

It was with this in mind that David now said, a twinkle in his eye, 'What's for afters, lass? No, let me guess. Fresh plums, stewed plums, baked plums or perhaps even plum crumble if I'm lucky.'

Carrie wrinkled her nose at him. 'Stewed plums,' she admitted.

'Just what I fancy.'

'Oh, you.'

'I'm not complaining, lass.' He pulled her to him. 'Just so long as you don't try any of these government recipes they're pushing. Carrot fudge and All-Clear sandwiches, who do they think they're kidding? And this so called Woolton Pie! One of the lads was saying his missus dished it up the other night and he asked her why she'd given him steak and kidney pie without the steak and kidney. Even the dog wouldn't touch it, according to John.'

Carrie tilted her head to smile up at him. If that had been David he would have eaten the potato, parsnip and oatmeal pie – named after Lord Woolton, the Minister for Food – without a word of complaint. She had served up the odd disaster in her time and on at least one occasion had been unable to eat the meal herself, but David would insist she was a 'grand cook' regardless. 'I've used our points this month on two pound of dried fruit,' she said softly, 'so there's sly cake for supper.'

'Now you're talking.' David released her as they heard Matthew's footsteps coming down the stairs. 'You know the way to a man's heart, Carrie Sutton, and no mistake.'

Oh, David. As Carrie walked across to the hob and began to

dish up the rich rabbit stew, crammed with chunks of potato, turnips, onion, parsnips and other vegetables, she told herself for the hundredth time that everything was all right. It didn't matter that Matthew insisted on writing long letters to Alec all the time or that her lad had become – her mind balked at the word selfish and substituted difficult. Not really. She and Matthew and David were all alive and well and in these times that was all that counted.

'Sit down, it's nearly ready,' she said to Matthew and a pair of bright, heavily lashed eyes in a face that was becoming more handsome with every month that passed smiled back at her.

'I've finished that book.' Matthew sat down at the table without acknowledging David beyond a quick nod and reached for a piece of stottie cake made with the coarse flour which was all that was available these days.

'Already?' Carrie's voice was cheerful even as she thought, he's so clever, it's a crime he'll be down the pit come September. She couldn't bear to think of it, her lad in that place. But he was a miner's son, and with the talk of ex-miners being brought back from the front to work down the mines, there was no way Matthew was going to escape his lot, not with the country's need for coal so critical.

'What book is that?' David asked pleasantly, making an effort to communicate with Matthew, as he always did. Some-times Carrie found herself wanting to say, it's no use, not with Alec brainwashing him drip by drip. Can't you see that? But she never did.

Matthew turned his head in the manner that was so like Alec's. '*A Farewell to Arms* by Ernest Hemingway,' he said coolly. 'Have you read it?'

Carrie stiffened. Why did Matthew do it? she asked herself

silently. He knew full well David hadn't read the book so why throw it in his face like that?

'No, I haven't read it, Matthew.' David's voice was just as cool now. 'Would you recommend it?'

As David held the boy's eyes, Matthew's gaze shifted, dropping to the piece of bread in his hand. He shrugged bony shoulders. 'I think it's good,' he said, a little shamefaced now. 'Uncle Alec thought I'd like it.'

Carrie pressed her lips together and shut her eyes for a moment. She had hoped that with Alec overseas his hold on Matthew would lessen but it seemed the indoctrination had been thorough. With some effort she said evenly, 'Is that what made you get that particular book out of the library?'

'I didn't.' Matthew raised his head, looking her full in the face as, with a touch of defiance, he said, 'Uncle Alec gave it to me as a present the night before he went to fight.'

Carrie blinked. Matthew had kept that quiet, as no doubt he did lots of things where Alec was concerned. Why was it that the more she tried to steer Matthew away from Alec, the more the boy gravitated to his natural father? Was it a blood tie? A recognition that went beyond the normal senses? Child for parent and parent for child.

But no, that didn't follow through. Look at Renee and their da, or Alec and his da for that matter. They couldn't stand each other. Whatever, all she knew was that in the weeks since Alec had been gone, Matthew had been like a bear with a sore head. She had even found herself encouraging him at one point to go and see his Aunt Margaret, thinking that the familiarity of the house that he had frequently taken himself off to in recent years, despite hot protest from her, might comfort him a little. That well-meant suggestion had caused the biggest row yet between herself and her son.

'I don't want to see her,' Matthew had said with youthful contempt. 'What on earth makes you think I would want to see Aunt Margaret? She's forever crying and going on about Uncle Alec not loving her. She drives him round the bend.'

'Did he tell you that?' Carrie's voice had been sharp and she'd held Matthew by his arms and shaken him slightly. 'Did he say that?'

'No, no.' The expression on her face had prompted the denial; Carrie knew he wasn't telling the truth. Matthew was fourteen years old at the end of the month and he would be starting work come September, but in spite of his outward appearance which could have led a stranger to think he was at least two years older, he was still just a young lad. Alec, however, had begun addressing Matthew as an equal, she had witnessed it on a number of occasions; he was appealing to the burgeoning man inside the boy, which made Matthew feel important and grown up, and what young lad wouldn't respond to that?

Carrie turned back to the stew, ladling out another bowlful. She brought two bowls to the table, placing them in front of David and a defiant-faced Matthew, and then fetched her own. When she was seated they all began to eat, Matthew with gusto, David quietly with the closed look on his face she hated. Carrie had to force every mouthful down.

When she couldn't stand the silence a moment longer, she said, 'Lillian's thinking of sending the bairns back to that couple they were evacuated to last year. She was round here in floods of tears this morning, not knowing what to do for the best but I'd still be surprised if she does send them.'

David sat back in his chair. 'Is she sure they'd have them back?'

Carrie nodded. 'She's kept in touch. With it being a farm

the bairns would eat well enough, that's for sure, and Lillian said they were kindness itself to them all. Luke still talks about his Aunt Ivy and Uncle Peter and all the animals, especially the farm cats. He had sorted out one of the kittens for his own apparently, before Lillian decided they were coming home. She said she made it clear to the couple at the time that she and the bairns were only leaving because we hadn't seen hide nor hair of the Germans here, not because they weren't happy or grateful to be with them.'

'I thought Lillian had jumped the gun in coming home herself,' said David soberly.

'Aye, well, that's as maybe, but when it was quiet here she wanted to get back to Isaac. She admitted today it's shown her she can't be in one place and him in another, even if it means she won't have Luke and Katie with her. You know what she's like. Anyway, this Ivy said she's prepared to take on the bairns without Lillian if that is what she wants.'

'*If* it's what she wants, but she had better be sure before she puts the bairns through leaving again,' said David quietly. He had not forgotten the sight which had met his eyes when he and Carrie had gone to see Lillian and the children off the previous September. Isaac had been unable to change his shift and was at work.

The platform was full of children from all over Sunderland, each one carefully labelled and clutching a bundle of belongings or a small suitcase, along with the square box which enclosed their gas mask. It had affected him deeply. It was something of an adventure at the time for those like Luke and Katie who were fortunate enough to have their mother with them, but most of the children had been pathetically alone, bewildered but trying to put a brave face on their confusion.

'Aunt Lillian said you could go along with Luke and Katie

if you want. She's checked with the farmer's wife and it would be all right.'

Even as she spoke, Carrie knew what Matthew's response would be. When the idea of evacuation had first been raised, her son had been adamant he was not budging from Sunderland, and nothing she and David said had persuaded him otherwise.

Now Matthew said, in tones of deep scorn, 'I am not a bairn, Mam, and I'm not looking after Luke and Katie.'

Matthew found three-year-old Luke and two-year-old Katie annoying most of the time when Lillian called by, besides which he and a bunch of his pals had decided it would be boring out in the country with no cinemas or League football. When half of the evacuees who had left the town were home again in the first couple of months of the year, everything they said seemed to confirm Matthew's suspicions and he had been even more determined he was not going to leave.

'All right.' Carrie nodded. 'But the offer is there if you change your mind any time, Matt.'

'I won't.' Matthew continued with his meal without looking at his mother, but inwardly he was fuming. His mam and da still treated him as if he was Luke's age half the time, and even now he'd left school and was due to start work with his da down the pit come September it didn't make any difference.

The thought of the pit brought a familiar sickly feeling rising in his stomach, but he told himself, as he had a hundred times before, it might not be as bad as he was expecting. Albert Burgham and Brian Wilson would be going down with him and if they could stand it, he could. His Granda McDarmount said it was the best time to be going down the pit; men were no longer being sacked for no reason or being put on short time. Suddenly the country had realised the importance of miners for the first time in years. His granda had also said that being down a mine was a darn sight better than being mowed down by Germans at the front, and Matthew agreed with him although he wouldn't have admitted it to a living soul. They might have thought he was one of these gutless conscientious objectors, like Edwin Cristelow's da. He knew a crowd of the lads from school had waited for Mr Cristelow one night when it was dark and had thrown rotten vegetables and stinking manure at him before running off. Edwin had never said a word about it. But then he wouldn't. Matthew reached for his cup of weak tea. The ration was 2oz per week and although he'd told his mam he'd rather have one good strong cup and then drink water, she never listened. The only person who ever listened to him was his Uncle Alec. He was a grand man. And he was fighting for his country.

'I'm done, lass, and I'd better get going.' David rose to his feet, wiping his mouth with the back of his hand. He was on duty and only had time to eat a quick meal when he was home from the colliery.

'Be careful.'

It was Carrie's stock warning every time he left the house and David smiled, ruffling her hair. 'It's me middle name,' he said, and turned to Matthew. 'Look after your mam till I'm back.'

Matthew gave a grunt which could have meant anything, and Carrie said quickly, 'He's going to the allotment with Veronica, aren't you, Matthew? There's some veg needs pulling and I could do with some runner beans.'

'Don't stay up there too late then.' David was never sure exactly how much work Matthew did. Young Veronica was her mother all over and built like a horse, and she always came back exhausted, but Matthew never seemed tired. The fact that Veronica worshipped the ground Matthew walked on made David suspect the work was not shared equally, even if the odd spot of profit was.

Matthew left the house soon after David, and as he bicycled towards the allotment he was humming to himself. The August evening was still warm after the heat of the day, the sky a blue expanse with just the tiniest cloud here and there.

Veronica was watching for him. As he dismounted and entered the side gate, she immediately threw down her hoe and ran along one of the narrow grass paths which separated the plots. She was breathless when she reached him. 'I've been here *ages*, Matt,' she said reproachfully.

'Got plenty of work done then I hope.' He grinned at her, ruffling her mass of short blonde curls in much the same way David had ruffled Carrie's earlier.

Matthew at fourteen was a head taller than his cousin, having shot up a good few inches in as many months, but Veronica, too, looked older than her age, her well-developed figure and general bulk suggesting she was sixteen if a day. Her face was not exactly pretty but it held a certain wholesome charm. 'It's a good job one of us does some work,' she said tartly. Then, when Matthew's expression changed, she added appeasingly, 'I brought some treacle toffee and fudge with me. Come on. Gran's friend gave me her whole sweet ration for the month when I dropped that box of vegetables off last night.'

'I thought we said we were going to start charging everyone except family.'

'Not Mrs Symcox, she's like family. Anyway, twelve ounces of sweets is more than we could have asked for in money.'

'I suppose so.'

Matthew let himself be persuaded. It was easier than arguing; besides, he could see that Veronica had already accomplished half the work they'd intended to do this evening.

At the small ramshackle hut he flopped down on one of the two orange boxes sitting outside and stretched out his long legs. 'I can't wait till I'm earning real money. A paper round is nowt.'

'Better than nothing though.' Veronica put a paper bag full of fudge in his lap. 'It's chocolate fudge, your favourite. And there's some tea in that flask but it's not very strong, I'm afraid.'

'It can't be worse than me mam's.' Matthew smiled at her, his good temper restored. Veronica was a canny lass.

Veronica smiled back, glad Matthew couldn't read her thoughts because she was thinking how wonderful he was. He was so handsome, she didn't know anyone as handsome as him unless, perhaps, their Uncle Alec. But Matthew's colouring was softer than their uncle's, warmer, and his face wasn't hard and square but more like his mam's, Aunt Carrie's. But it was a funny thing, and likely because Matt had spent so much time with their Uncle Alec, but sometimes she thought she could almost see Uncle Alec in the way Matt was. Not in his looks, not that, but how he was somehow. But then his da was Uncle Alec's brother and blood will out, as her mam often said.

The thought of her mother brought Veronica's face straightening. She didn't know what had got into her lately, she really didn't. She knew her mam laid great store by her job and she could understand that, with her not getting on with Da, but anyone would think it was Da's fault she had been put on short time at the factory. Perhaps it was because she didn't get the manager's position when Mr Fleming went off to the war. Poor Mr Fleming. Who would have thought he'd die of pneumonia just a month after going away, leaving his poor wife with all those bairns?

'What're these?'

Matthew's voice brought Veronica back to herself, and she grinned at him. 'I picked them up in the Old Market when I was doing me mam's shopping,' and she waved a casual hand at the pile of *Wizard*, *Hotspur* and *Rover* comics. 'There're lots of war stories in them.'

'Great.' If Matthew had been with any of his pals he would have curbed his enthusiasm. He and all his friends avidly read every comic they could get their hands on but it didn't do to admit to the fact, not at fourteen years old. 'Thanks, Vee.' He didn't offer to pay. Veronica was always buying him something or other, that's the way she was. He settled himself more comfortably, popped a piece of chocolate fudge in his mouth and opened the comic on top of the heap.

'M-a-t-t.' Veronica drew out his name in reproach. 'Come on, you can look at those later.'

'By, you're a slave driver, Veronica Sutton.'

'Aye, well, I have to be where you're concerned, Matthew Sutton.'

Matthew shook his head solemnly. 'Nag, nag, nag.'

'Oh you.'

Matthew got to his feet and looked up into the blue sky. He was silent for a moment, then he said, his voice now sober, 'Hark at the birds, and yet somewhere out there Uncle Alec is up to his eyes in it. Damn Nazis.'

'Don't swear.'

'Damn isn't swearing, not like some words anyway.' He scowled at her and rubbed his hand across his forehead. 'Aren't you worried for him?'

She did not answer him for a moment, and then she said, 'Not like you, I suppose.'

She came to stand near him and by unspoken mutual consent they both sat down now, side by side on the orange boxes. They sat in silence for some moments before Matthew said, 'It's so unfair, this war and everything. If it hadn't happened Uncle Alec would have taken me on in one of the shops, he said so. He was looking forward to it.'

Veronica nodded. This was not the first time he had spoken about it. Her voice soft, she said, 'You can still do that, when the war's over, I mean. It won't last for ever.'

No, it wouldn't, but in the meantime his uncle was risking life and limb on foreign shores and he had to go down the pit. 'Maybe.' He shrugged. 'Who knows though. If my da wasn't a miner I wouldn't have to go down the pit. Why couldn't he have been like Uncle Alec? He hasn't spent his life grubbing away under the earth, he's made something of himself. Look at him now, fighting for England. He's brave, he is.'

'Oh aye?' thundered a voice over their heads and a hand grabbed Matthew's collar. Veronica let out a piercing shriek and fell backwards off her box. She watched in horror as her father swung Matthew to his feet as easily as if the boy had been a wet rag. 'You saying your da isn't brave? Is that it?'

'Let – let go of me.' Matthew's face was turning a dark shade of red as his uncle's vice-like grip prevented him from breathing.

Walter ignored this and shook him slightly, like a terrier with a rabbit. 'You little scut you.'

'Da, Da, please.' Veronica scrambled to her feet and caught at Walter, her voice frantic. 'He didn't mean that, did you, Matthew? He didn't.'

'Well, did you?' Walter flung Matthew from him. He would have gone sprawling on the ground if the ramshackle hut hadn't been in the way. He steadied himself and glared at his uncle.

'He was just saying—'

Walter's hand made a sharp cutting action and Veronica

held her tongue. 'I heard what he was saying, lass,' he said grimly, without taking his eyes off the angry boy in front of him. 'You think your da has got the easy option, lad? Is that it? That Alec's away covering himself in honour and glory and your da is nowt but some sort of animal that "grubs" under the ground? By, you've got a lot to learn.'

Matthew stood tall and thrust out his chest. He was furious with his uncle for making him look a fool in front of Veronica. 'Uncle Alec *is* brave,' he said defiantly. 'He could be killed at any moment.'

'And you think your da couldn't?'

Matthew shrugged.

'I asked you a question.'

'Working down the pit is different.'

'Oh aye, lad, I'll give you that. Working down the pit is different all right. You work in places so low and filthy and dangerous you wouldn't put a dog in them, and once the shift is finished and you come up – *if* you come up, and there's plenty of poor blighters through the years who haven't – then you're on fire-watching duty or the Home Guard so you get it all ways.'

Matthew shrugged again, and this seemed to infuriate Walter more than any backchat. His voice was rough as he said, 'You don't know you're born, lad, that's the trouble with you. All these fancy opinions and still wet behind the ears. You're in for a shock in a week or two and no mistake. Or . . .' He paused, staring hard at the boy he had secretly never had any time for. 'Or perhaps you'd like a trip underground afore that, eh? See how your ideas hold up then.'

'I don't mind.' It was bravado, but not for all the world would Matthew let his uncle see that.

'That's settled then. And not a word to your mam, or your da for that matter. You hear that too, Veronica?' Walter knew she thought the sun shone out of her cousin's backside, something which had grown to irritate him more and more lately. 'I'll take you down tomorrow, it being your mam's day at the shop. The deputy knows you're starting after your birthday and I'll explain you're keen, eh? He can't wait, I'll say. Now, you get yourself off home, and you, miss,' he turned to his daughter, 'you're coming home with me.'

'Aw, *Da*. Matt's only just got here and—'

'No argument, lass. I'm not asking, I'm telling.'

Matthew gathered up the comics and walked off sulkily to his bicycle.

Walter called after him, 'Midday or thereabouts at the pit gates. All right?'

There was no reply, but then Walter had not expected one. He stood staring after the young lanky figure until his nephew had disappeared out of the side gate, silently admitting to a twinge of guilt now. He shouldn't have gone for the lad like that, but Matthew was such a blasted little know-all whilst knowing nowt. And the way the lad was about his da, it made his blood boil.

Strange, Walter thought, when you considered David was a miner through and through, but he couldn't see the lad making the grade somehow. There was what he could only describe as a weakness about Matthew and it was becoming more apparent, at least to him, as the boy got older. Of course Carrie and Renee and the rest of the womenfolk were like his Veronica, they thought Matthew could do no wrong. But regardless of all that, he shouldn't have gone for him. And then Veronica said exactly that. 'There was no need to be like that, Da.' Whereupon Walter promptly dismissed his pangs of conscience.

'No?' He looked at his daughter, the only thing in his life

that held any real joy for him, and his expression was dour. 'You think it right he runs your Uncle David down then? And it's not the first time I've heard him. The lad wants a damn good hiding.'

'He's missing Uncle Alec.'

'Aye, two of a kind they are.' It was not a compliment. 'And while we're on the subject of Matthew, I reckon it's about time you stopped coming up here with him. He starts work in a week or two and you'll have left school by Christmas. You're not bairns any more.'

'But what about the vegetables and everything?'

'Damn the veg.'

Walter admitted to a feeling of surprise when he saw Matthew waiting for him by the pit gate the following morning. He had expected his nephew to come up with some excuse or other to avoid doing what he didn't want to do. Matthew was good at that, in Walter's opinion. Of course there were some lads who were champing at the bit to follow their fathers down the pit, but Matthew wasn't one of them. Silly daft young so-an'-sos, their das would say, thought Walter, but nevertheless it was said with pride. It was born in some lads, that was the thing.

'You've come then.' Walter smiled as he spoke but there was no answering smile on Matthew's face. He just nodded at his uncle. So it was going to be like that, was it? Walter's mouth set. It suited him. He'd had a barney and a half with Renee this morning and was in no mood to wetnurse this little runt. Gone twelve, she'd got in last night, and stinking of whisky and cheap scent. She hadn't exactly been at home much right from when she'd gone back to work after Veronica was born, but the last few months were something else entirely. It was like she'd gone mental or something. And he'd got his suspicions about that an' all, oh aye. It seemed a mite too coincidental that this latest stage had started about the same time they heard the news about her boss from the factory.

'I'll do the talking when we're inside. All right?' Walter tucked his bait tin more securely under his arm as he spoke. He intended to stay down with Matthew for a couple of hours or so and then it wouldn't be long till his shift, so there'd been no point in leaving his sandwiches at home. Sandwiches he'd had to prepare himself, he thought bitterly. He'd heard some of his pals moan about what their missus had given them now and again, but he'd have been content with dry bread and water if it had been prepared by a wife who knew her place and function in the home.

'What've we got here, Walt?' An elderly man with blue marked skin and rheumy eyes was in the lamp house, and he gestured at Matthew as he spoke.

'This is my nephew, David's lad. He's coming down in a week or two when he reaches fourteen, but he wants to see what's what afore then so I'm taking him on a quick tour, as it were.'

'Thinks it's Blackpool down there, does he?' The man cast a watery eye over Matthew. 'Well, we've not much in sideshows an' such, lad, but you give the pit ponies half a chance an' some of them'll nip you harder than any seaside donkey. You heard about old Bronco?' he continued, turning to Walter while Matthew remained as still and silent as a block of wood.

'No, what's that then?'

'Took a chunk out of old Frank Armstrong's backside the size of a plate. Frank had gone into a quiet corner to do the necessary an' was bending over with his trousers round his ankles when the cunnin' blighter crept up on him an' sank his teeth into what he must have thought was his birthday

276

cake. They said you could hear Frank yell from here to Newcastle.'

'Serves him right. He worked with Bronco for a time and I reckon he brayed him once too often, and that one's an intelligent animal, he don't forget. And Bronco's a lamb with Geoff Pounder who's got him now. If you ask me, that horse has been biding his time for years for the right moment.'

'Aye, well, his patience was rewarded, sure enough. Just missed havin' Frank's weddin' tackle an' all, accordin' to them as saw it. They said Frank leaped so high he nutted himself on the roof an' then took off like a bat out of hell.'

'That'll teach him.' Both men were grinning now. 'He's a nasty bit of work, is Frank.'

'He is that. So, you're takin' the young 'un down. You'd better clear it with the deputy.'

'Aye, I will when I see him. It's no odds anyway, the lad's going to be coming down every day in a couple of weeks.'

'Here.' The lamp man handed Matthew a token and hung another one up on a long shelf behind him. 'Look after that, lad. Put it in a pocket without any holes in it. You lose that when you're comin' down regular an' you'll have the whole pit lookin' for you. An' if they find you alive, they'll murder you.'

Matthew nodded. He was too terrified to speak.

When he saw the cage he couldn't believe they were going down in it, but still he didn't speak; he followed Walter in and then hung on for dear life as it took off.

The two hours that followed were the worst of his life. When he first stepped out of the cage it wasn't as bad as he had expected. The area was larger than he'd thought it would be and relatively well lit, but then he was following his uncle down a road which got narrower and narrower as the roof got lower and lower, and all the time the light was being swallowed up by deepening blackness. In spite of his lamp Matthew kept banging his head and back on the roof and grazing his hands and elbows on the sides. And all the time the darkness grew, like a separate entity, until he couldn't see anything beyond the lamp, no matter how hard he tried. It was darker than the darkest night, blacker than the worst nightmare.

He saw men crawling like animals as they worked, some stripped to their underpants and some as naked as the day they were born, and all of them just a pair of white eyes in black faces and bodies. There were mice and rats and great shiny black beetle type insects with wings, and feelers as long as bootlaces, and the smell of coal dust was permeated by pony and human dung.

Above their heads the roof was held up by what looked to Matthew like the flimsiest of props, and with each creak he fully expected them to give way. He was led through doors and along tunnels past machinery, conveyor belts, chocks, winding machines, to a running commentary from Walter about blackdamp, in-bye, jowl, judd and a hundred and one other incomprehensible terms, until Matthew's head was spinning and his bowels felt loose and he wanted to be physically sick. He stumbled along almost blindly towards the end, the humid heat and stench and sheer thick black horror of it all pressing down on his mind until he just wanted to scream and run and run and run.

It will end, it will end. He kept repeating the words over and over in his mind through the whirling panic that at any moment the roof would come crashing down on their heads and they would be buried beneath millions of tons of slate, rock and coal. It will end, it will end . . .

He wouldn't have been able to tell anyone how they got back

to the main roadway and then the cage, but eventually he was going upwards and he was so thankful he had to fight back tears. There had been lots of banter between Walter and the miners who had been working, some of it spoken in such broad pitmatic by the oldtimers, it might as well have been a foreign language. This was another world. A world that had nothing remotely familiar about it and was typified by what Walter casually referred to as blacklocks. These bore no resemblance to the black beetles above ground; they looked like monster cockroaches and were as big as mice. Walter told him they were too big and nasty to ever come up out of the ground and that's why people didn't know about them. But he knew about them now, and this secret, terrifying, subterranean hell was where he would be every day in a couple of weeks' time. *What was he going to do?*

'So, there you are, lad.' Walter could see how pale his nephew's face was, even covered in coal dust, and there was something about the stiff way he was standing that prompted a softer tone than he had ever used to him before. 'It won't seem so bad second time round. You get yourself home and have a good wash afore your mam gets home, and then you'll have something to tell them both the night, eh? And your pals an' all. Stole a march on them, haven't you?'

The jerk of Matthew's head passed as a nod, and Walter stood and watched him walk away and out of the colliery gates. Well, he'd bet his last farthing Matthew wouldn't belittle his da's courage again; he'd been brought down a peg or two today and no mistake. Strangely, the thought brought no relief to the guilt Walter was feeling. Aw, to hell with it, he thought irritably. The boy had to see for himself and that's an end to it. Then he stomped off to the lamp house and Larry to while away the half an hour or so before his shift began.

Matthew found he had to concentrate very hard to keep the numbness that had enveloped him in place all the way home. He dared not think, not until he was safe in his bedroom with the door locked, where no one could see him if he let go of the flood of feeling that had built up throughout the endless time down the pit.

When he reached home he stood in the scullery for some minutes, his legs shaking, just gazing into space, before forcing himself to move into the kitchen. Again he stood for a while, holding on to one of the hardbacked chairs grouped round the table. He had thought he would cry once he was home, like he'd wanted to do in the cage, but curiously he found he was dry-eyed, the fear in him burning up the relief of tears.

After a moment or two he walked across to the range and lifted the big black kettle he'd filled with water before he'd left to meet his uncle this morning. He pushed it hard into the red glow. He would have a washdown in the bath and then see to his clothes, he told himself dully. His mam wouldn't be back from the shop for some time, it being a Tuesday, the day she saw individual clients by appointment.

When there was six inches or so of warm water in the bottom of the tin bath Matthew bolted the front and back doors and stripped off completely. It was only then that he saw his knees were skinned raw from the number of times he'd stumbled and fallen. The palms of his hands were in no better shape, and when he lathered up the bar of carbolic soap and washed his hair, the top of his head felt as if a cheese grater had been applied to it.

He sat in the water until it was stone cold, and when he rose to his feet he was stiff and every muscle ached. He walked naked to his bedroom where he pulled on a pair of trousers and a shirt. Then he returned to the kitchen and washed his clothes as best he could in the cold bath water. This did not even begin to lift the grime out of them, so he boiled some more water on the hob and rubbed and scrubbed until the black coal dust was gone, his sore hands smarting so much he had to hold his breath at times. But still he couldn't cry.

He hung his clothes on the line in the backyard, climbed the narrow stairs to his bedroom, shut the door after him and flung himself on the quilted bedspread that covered his narrow iron bed. His mam had made the bedspread and matching curtains and they were bonny. All his friends said he was lucky to have a room of his own, a room that had a square of carpet on the floor and a wardrobe and bookcase and shelving for all his toys and things. They all loved to come round to his house because his mam wasn't stingy with drinks and cakes, not like some. But then all his pals had brothers and sisters and, depending on the number, that meant they were hard-pressed. He was glad he hadn't got any brothers or sisters; he wouldn't have wanted to share this room with anyone or have little ones messing about with his things. His eyes alighted on the magnificent model of Sir Francis Drake's ship, the *Golden Hind*, which his Uncle Alec had bought him for his thirteenth birthday. It was perfect down to every small detail, and the present had been the envy of all his friends.

'Uncle Alec.' It was a whisper, a cry from the heart. 'Oh, Uncle Alec, please come back.'

But still he couldn't cry.

Chapter Sixteen

'What do you reckon then? Right pair of cards, these two, ain't they?'

Alec turned his head slightly in acknowledgement of the man who had spoken but he did not look at him, keeping his gaze fixed on the two red-faced and perspiring individuals on the makeshift stage. 'Aye, they're not bad.'

In truth, the duo was getting on his nerves. For the last half an hour they had been singing such songs as 'Hang Out Your Washing on the Siegfried Line', 'A Nice Cup of Tea', and other sing-alongs, cavorting about like a pair of loonies in their endeavour to get everyone to join in. In the absence of official entertainment, most of those present seemed happy to oblige, but Alec was not.

He shut his eyes for a moment, sighing deeply. Whenever he had imagined seeing a bit of the world – and he had dreamed of it more and more the last few years since Margaret had become so impossible – it had never been in the company of hundreds of his own sex. Most of them seemed to fill their time cursing and belching and passing wind of such intense toxicity that he felt certain the whole company would go up in flames one day. But he could take the smells, the exhaustion, the swill that passed as food and the lack of privacy better than some of the sights he'd seen. They went round and round in his head every time he tried to sleep, like that little Arab child this afternoon who had been in the wrong place at the wrong time and had got blasted to smithereens.

He opened his eyes and stared blindly ahead. Their commanding officer had congratulated them today on inflicting heavy losses on the Italian troops advancing across the Libyan border into Egypt, but Alec knew he wasn't the only one who couldn't get the picture of that young mother cradling the mangled remains of what had once been her son out of his mind.

The world had gone mad. He stretched his neck, flexing tired muscles. Stark staring mad. Every country he could think of seemed intent on killing, maiming or burning the occupants of another one, and all because one deranged rabble-rousing little corporal was intent on world domination.

The wind that seemed more prevalent in the evening lifted the warm dust at his feet into his eyes, and he swore softly.

The man at his side spoke again. 'You want to be thankful you're not neck high in mud. I went through the first war and nothing could be worse than Passchendaele. Me and my best mate joined up together and we'd covered each other's backs all through, then one night he went to relieve himself and never came back. We found him the next morning by his hand stretching out of the mud. He'd fallen off the boards, you see, and it had sucked him down. Lethal, that mud was. They say hell is hot and blazing, but I tell you, I've seen hell. It's thick and black and stinking and once it's got you, it don't let go. That's hell in my book.'

Alec couldn't take any more of this. 'I'm turning in.' He rose to his feet. 'See you.'

'No doubt about that.' The old veteran grinned up at him, his blackened teeth mere stubs. 'We're going to be slugging it out here for some time, you mark my words, but like I say, a few flies and heat and dust is nothing to that mud.'

A few flies? Alec just nodded before walking away. A few flies he could take, but the swarms that covered everything twenty-four hours a day were something else. They were the real enemy. You breathed them in, ate them, drank them . . .

He didn't go straight to his kit; instead he continued to walk into the shadows as though he intended to relieve himself. When he was some distance from where most of the men had congregated he stopped, put his head back and looked up into the dark sky in which a myriad stars were twinkling.

He was going to die out here. Die on foreign soil, probably with his guts spilled out in the sand and flies laying their maggots in him before he was even cold. Back home life continued as before. People were eating and drinking and loving as though nothing had changed. There were times lately when he wondered if he'd meet his end like Ted Stafford had. He'd suddenly gone berserk a few weeks ago and bolted out of cover like a rabbit with a fox on its tail, running blindly until he was shot by the enemy. There'd been nothing any of them could do but watch. And him with a young wife and a babby.

The thought of Ted's wife and child brought Carrie and Matthew into his mind before he could stop them intruding. He had found very early on in the mayhem that it didn't do to think of Carrie. It was weakening, draining; it brought too many things he'd left unsaid to the surface and tied his stomach into knots. She hated him. Funny, but it had only been since he'd been out here that he could accept that. That was the thing about staring death in the face: it stripped away any pretence or wishful thinking.

He screwed up his eyes tightly then opened them very wide and continued to stare into the velvet sky.

Matthew was his. His by the act that had alienated Carrie for ever, and his by Matthew's will too. His hand moved to the letter in the breast pocket of his uniform jacket. The boy had chosen to love him in spite of all his mother had done to keep them apart. And she'd tried, by, she had.

His face hardened and his gaze dropped from the sky to the scene about him. Whatever he'd done that night – and he wasn't proud of it, of course he wasn't, but she had been there with him at least part of the way – it wasn't right to try and keep him from his own flesh and blood. Not in times like these. And now Matthew was down the pit and terrified out of his wits, if his letter was anything to go by. He'd never have stood for it if he had been back home, whatever might have resulted from his interfering. Matthew was no miner, you only had to look at him to see that.

Alec swore, loud and long, but it didn't relieve the ache in his heart which had come into being when he had read Matthew's desperate outpouring.

'Hey, you.' An officer was standing some yards away, peering at him in the blackness. 'If you've finished, get back to the others. This isn't a Sunday school picnic, you know. There's a damn good reason why you're told to stay together.'

'Sorry, sir. I just needed a minute or two alone.'

The man moved nearer and Alec saw it was Lieutenant Strong. He liked Strong, all the men did, and they respected him. He might talk in a lah-de-dah fashion but that was the way he'd been brought up, no doubt, public school and the rest. But he cared about the men under his command and furthermore he was as brave as a bull when the chips were down, unlike some who were dab hands at sending their soldiers where they were chary of going themselves.

'Bad news from home?' the lieutenant asked.

'Aye, sir.' Well, it was in a way.

'Damn Jerries.'

'Aye, sir.'

'We *will* beat them, you know. Mussolini too.'

'Will we, sir?' Every man jack knew that with France finished they were facing two huge Italian armies, each with about two hundred and fifty thousand men, one here on the Libyan-Egyptian border and the other in Ethiopia.

'Definitely.'

'How . . . how can you be sure, sir?'

Lieutenant Strong paused for a moment, and then he said, 'I have a wife and two children. Do you have family?'

'Aye, sir. A wife and son.' He didn't hesitate.

'Well, every time the slightest doubt comes into my mind as to the outcome of this damn war, I think of Cynthia and my boys. I think of them under German occupation, of my boys being forced to wear the uniform of Hitler Youth and being indoctrinated by the Nazi machine. Then I know we will win. Anything less is not an option.'

There was silence for some seconds, and then Alec nodded. 'Yes, sir. I see.'

'Now you get back to your comrades, there's a good fellow.'

It was only when Alec settled down for sleep with a blanket on his lower half some time later that it dawned on him how instinctive his reponse had been to the lieutenant's question. And with the realisation came the knowledge that he had crossed a line tonight. Matthew was his son. He would defy Carrie and the rest of the world to say different, and when he got back home – *if* he got back home – things were going to change.

Chapter Seventeen

A sudden crackling from the wireless broke the silence, causing Carrie's head to rise sharply. There was going to be another air raid warning. The wireless always crackled when they switched the radio transmitters off. Carrie braced herself, and sure enough the sirens began wailing a second later.

The sound jerked her out of her chair by the fire where she had been putting the finishing touches to a silk and crêpe wedding dress that Horwood's van was collecting first thing in the morning. She hurried into the dark hall and shouted, 'Matthew! Matt! Quick! Get up.'

She had to repeat herself twice before she heard the thud which meant his feet had landed on the floor. Carrie darted back into the kitchen and grabbed the bag containing the torch and flask full of tea. 'Matthew!' she shouted again. 'Get down here.'

Since Matthew had been working down the pit he arrived home from his shift so dog tired it was all he could do to eat and then fall into bed, and Carrie was never sure he was really up and properly awake until she heard him coming down the stairs. Last week he had been half sleepwalking when he came downstairs and he still had a row of large bruises all down one side to prove it.

The heavy daylight raids over Britain had stopped at the end of September and the Luftwaffe were now mostly coming at night. Folk had barely had time to voice their delight that the Battle of Britain had been won – Winston Churchill's broadcast praising the RAF, 'Never in the field of human conflict was so much owed by so many to so few,' had raised cheers from those who heard it – before an onslaught of a different kind had begun. Not that they had it bad, Carrie thought now. Not like Coventry or London, poor things.

The thought of London brought David's father to mind and Carrie shivered. Night after night the Luftwaffe were blitzing London, and Ned had written to say he hadn't slept in weeks for the sound of bombs, anti-aircraft guns and the shrill bells of fire engines and ambulances.

David had written back immediately, suggesting that he get out of the capital for a while but Ned had replied that as far as he was concerned it didn't matter if you were north, south, east or west, if a bomb had your name on it, your time was up.

Carrie shivered again, wondering why the wail of the sirens always sounded so much more ominous when it was dark outside.

Matthew joined her a moment later, his hair ruffled and standing on end. He yawned long and loudly as he did up his trousers. Carrie handed him his jacket which was hanging ready on the back of a chair. 'I hope your da is all right in Nelson Square,' she said. 'I wish he was somewhere else than there.'

'You say that every time, Mam. Nelson Square is as safe as anywhere else.'

Carrie glanced at him but didn't respond to the irritable tone in his voice because she knew she *did* say it every time. But she couldn't help it. Instead she said quietly, 'You ready?'

'I suppose so.' He frowned at her, as though the air raid was her fault. 'Although why we have to keep going backwards and forwards to the shelter is beyond me.'

'You know why, Matthew, so don't start that again. It's safer.' She opened the back door.

'Huh.' He pulled in his chin. 'Safer than what? Safer than being down the mine every day? I doubt it.'

She said nothing more until they were in the shelter. She stared at him in the torchlight. 'I know you hate the pit, Matthew, but—'

'You don't know the first thing about how I feel, you couldn't. Not unless you'd been down there.'

'Matthew—'

'I know, I know.' His voice was resigned. 'Da is a miner and Granda's a miner and his da before him.'

'I wasn't going to say that. I never have, have I? I was going to say that perhaps you could do something else.'

'And be a laughing stock? Thanks very much. It would have been different if I'd never gone down in the first place but now I have, I can't just not go. And you know how it is with the war on. I'm a miner's son. I'm expected to do my bit.'

The last was so bitter Carrie winced. In the past few weeks since Matthew had begun work he had changed so drastically she felt she barely knew him. He never smiled, he never even spoke to her unless he had to. She didn't know what to do. Strangely, he wasn't so withdrawn with David, in fact she felt their relationship was better than it had ever been since he had gone down the pit. She just wished Matthew would talk to her properly, tell her exactly how he was feeling.

She watched him as he climbed into the six-foot single bunk bed she had bought from Binns for seventeen shillings and sixpence when the store had been advertising their special shelter furniture. With Matthew working down the pit she'd felt he needed something better than a chair to try and sleep in.

'Would you like some tea?' she asked quietly, sitting down on one of the three hardbacked chairs which, together with the bunk and a small table, made up the sum total of the furniture in the small structure.

'Mam, you can't call that brew we have these days tea,' came the muffled reply. 'And no, I don't want some. I just want to sleep.'

'All right. I won't talk any more.' After a moment or two Carrie switched off the torch and shut her eyes. As she sat in the darkness, her mind immediately began gnawing at the question that always nagged at her when she had time to think, which fortunately wasn't often because however much she agonised, she never got any nearer to an answer. Why hadn't she fallen for another bairn?

She didn't understand why it hadn't happened. It wasn't as if anything was wrong in that regard. She liked their making on, more than liked it. In fact, if she thought about some of the things David did under cover of darkness in their big double bed, it made her hot all over, but it was a nice heat. Sort of glowing. But in the last year she'd begun to give up hope that she would ever be able to say to him, you're going to be a da. It was so unfair on him after everything that had happened, but when she tried to talk to him about it he just said she was enough for him. Her and Matthew. But she knew Matthew was included to please her. Of course David wanted his own bairn, every man did, didn't they?

She hadn't felt able to discuss the matter with anyone, not even her mother, for a long time, and then one day when she was visiting Ada – the old woman's legs were now so swollen she was virtually housebound – it had all come spilling out, mainly because she had found out that morning that yet again there was no baby.

Ada had listened quietly and then patted her hand. 'Well, hinny, I know all about the disappointment each month an' the hopin' for the next. By, I tried everythin', I did. Someone told me you'd fall if you drank stout an' I fair lived on the stuff for a time, till Charlie got the idea I was turnin' into a soak. Mind, that was one of the more pleasant things. Someone else said if you slept with a peeled onion under your pillow you'd have a bairn within nine months; it was a good job Charlie had trouble with his adenoids an' couldn't smell a thing 'cos everythin' stank to high heaven. I tried smearin' me you-know-what with goose grease, wearin' a tassel of bairn's hair under me clothes, drinkin' a potion made with mornin' dew an' nettles, turnin' round three times before I got into bed of a night an' three come mornin' – you name it, lass, an' I tried it.'

Carrie's smile encouraged Ada to continue. 'Some bright spark said you had to lie with your legs in the air after. Now I've never been what you'd call a slip of a thing, an' tryin' to keep me legs up without Charlie catchin' on wasn't easy. He was a man who was always snorin' within seconds after, but there'd be me with me legs over me head an' me back breakin'. Damn near brained him once or twice when I slipped sideways. Nowt worked though.' And then Ada patted her again. 'But at least you an' David have got your Matthew, lass. That's a comfort to you both.'

Carrie had never wanted to confide her secret to someone as much as she did then but she just nodded, and since that time they had not talked of it again.

She must have been dozing when the explosion came but as her eyes flew open she knew it was Southwick way. She leaped up and opened the door into the backyard. The glow westwards

293

confirmed her fears. Two more ground-shaking thuds came shortly after she was out in the open, anti-aircraft fire providing a constant smattering in the background. Her mam and da and the twins! And Lillian lived in Wellington Street just off the Green. Billy was all right, he and his new wife of three months had taken rooms in Liddell Terrace not far from Palmers. Her mam had tried to dissuade Billy from moving there, saying it was too close to the quays with their cranes and industry, but it looked as though it had been safer after all.

'What's up?' Matthew joined her, rubbing the sleep out of his eyes.

'They've fallen Southwick way.' Carrie turned to him. 'Go back in the shelter, I'm going to see if your grandma and granda are all right.'

'Don't be daft.' Matthew caught at her arm. 'Not till the all-clear sounds.'

'I'm going now.'

'You're not, Mam. Da'll kill me if I let you, you know he will. Wait a few minutes. It'll probably all be over in a little while.'

'I'm going now,' she repeated frantically.

'Then I'm coming with you.'

Once they were running Carrie realised the night wasn't as black as it had seemed at first, although it was dark enough for her to miss her footing several times and nearly fall headlong. Matthew was just behind her and she could hear him panting and swearing but she didn't waste her breath to rebuke him for the cursing as she would have normally. Once or twice wardens and fire-fighters called to them but Carrie ignored them, knowing they would do their job and send her home if they could.

As they turned into Cornhill Terrace from Southwick Road it became obvious that James Armitage Street had not been hit. The relief Carrie felt was countered by the fact that the Green was lit up and a fire engine had just arrived. Two or three firemen unrolling hoses were visible as black silhouettes against the red glow of the raging fires. Carrie paused on the corner of James Armitage Street, not sure whether to take Matthew to her parents before she went to check on Lillian and Isaac and the bairns. She did not include David's mother in the thought.

As she stood hesitating, a voice said, 'Carrie? Carrie, lass? An' Matt? What are you doin' here? Why aren't you back home?'

'Oh, Da.' Carrie all but fell on Sandy's neck. 'I thought it might be you and Mam who'd got it.'

'I've told you before, lass. Only the good die young.'

Carrie saw the flash of his teeth in the shadows, but then his voice became sombre. 'I've come to check on young Lillian. With Isaac's da havin' died an' his mam livin' with the sister in Gateshead, I feel I owe it to Ned to keep an eye on the lass.'

'I'm coming with you.' Carrie turned to Matthew. 'Go to Granda's house and wait till we get back.'

'Mam, I'm not a bairn.'

'I know you're not.' Her voice softened. 'But your granny will be upset, you know she can't stand the bombing. Look after her.'

'Danny and Len will be with Gran.'

'They're fire-watchin' the night, lad,' Sandy intervened. 'An' your granny gets herself in a right old two an' eight about them an' all the rest of you. It'll put her mind at rest havin' you with her.'

'All right.' It was grudging, but Matthew turned and disappeared into James Armitage Street without further argument.

'I'd prefer you to go with him, lass.'

Carrie's answer to this was to begin walking towards the Green where more firemen, ambulance crew and rescuers were mingling with neighbours and anxious relatives. One bomb had ripped up thirty feet or so of pavement, a gas main, which had caught fire, and electricity cables, and another had scored a direct hit on a house. As they neared the scene, firemen working on the blaze suddenly shouted for everyone to get clear – they'd seen the chimney stack shudder. In seconds the chimney from pots to base collapsed with a resounding crash. Clouds of lime, dust and soot filled the air as the front of the building disintegrated, blotting out visibility for a few moments. Through the thick and heavy atmosphere came the sound of choking and coughing and children crying.

'Where do you think you're going?' As Carrie and Sandy made to pass, one of the firemen caught at Sandy's coat. 'There might be an unexploded bomb near that gas main. Why do you think we're evacuating the houses nearby?'

'We need to get to Wellington Street.' It was Carrie who answered. 'My sister-in-law lives there.'

'Oh aye? Go South Terrace way then and keep your heads down. There's no knowing if this is the end of it for the night.'

When they reached the house Lillian and Isaac lived in Carrie's heart was in her mouth. The house adjoining Lillian's had been all but gutted, and the ones either side had been partially demolished. Some locals from a pub opposite were busy pulling people from the wreckage of the gutted building. Miraculously, all were relatively unscathed apart from cuts and bruises in spite of having lived on the first floor of the house. The family with nine children who lived on the ground floor had been sheltering in the pub cellar when the bomb had hit so they, too, were unharmed. But the old couple who lived in the house on the left had been killed by a ceiling falling on them. The street door to Lillian's property was blocked by debris and rescuers were trying to ascertain if anyone was alive.

It was some twenty minutes before a way was made for Lillian and Isaac to pass their children through to waiting arms. They followed a moment or two later, with Olive Sutton bringing up the rear.

'Carrie! Oh, Carrie.' Lillian burst into tears at the sight of her friend, causing Luke and Katie, who had been grizzling with shock up to that point, to give way to full-blown howls.

'It's all right, lass, it's all right. You're safe, all of you.' Carrie had Lillian in her arms and was all but holding her up.

'I should've sent them away. I knew I should've sent them but I kept thinking another week wouldn't hurt.' Lillian was clutching her so tightly Carrie knew she'd have bruises come morning.

'You can still send them, I don't think the farm's going anywhere. But for now you're all unhurt and that's the main thing.'

'Me things. All me things are ruined.'

'They can be replaced in time. People can't.' Lillian was shivering uncontrollably, and Carrie said, 'Look, you're coming home with me, all of you, and we'll see what's what in the morning, all right? For now you need a nice strong cup of tea and bed. Right, Isaac?' She turned to Lillian's husband and he managed a shaky smile.

'Sounds good to me, lass. We'd just finished the last of our tea ration as it happens.'

'That's the way, lad.' Sandy clapped Isaac on the back so hard he took a step forwards. 'Spit in the Nazis' eyes, damn 'em.'

'And me?' Olive Sutton stepped from behind Isaac, her voice tight and her eyes gimlet hard. 'You including me in all this?'

'Of course, Mam.' Carrie made a huge effort to speak warmly. 'You're very welcome.'

'Crowd you out, won't we?'

There was a clear note of satisfaction in the words, and as Carrie held Olive's gaze for a moment, she groaned inwardly. Crowding out was the least of her troubles if her mother-in-law was moving in.

'Not at all,' she said quickly. 'We'll sort things out as we go, eh, Lillian?'

'This is so good of you, lass.'

'You'd do the same for us.'

'Aye, I would. I would that.'

'We can go to Margaret's,' Olive interjected. 'They've lots of room, as you well know.'

It was Lillian who now rounded on her mother, her voice sharper than Carrie had ever heard it. 'Margaret is not well, *you know that*. Her father has had to engage a nurse to be with her most of the time since Alec left. She's gone all to pieces worrying about him.'

'All the more reason to be with family, to take her mind off things.'

'I don't think it would work like that.' Carrie stared her mother-in-law straight in the eye. 'She couldn't cope. Even a brief visit exhausts her these days.'

'Huh.' Olive drew herself up ramrod straight and despite the fact she was covered in brick dust and her hair resembled a busby, she cut an intimidating figure. 'What do you know about it? All this molly-coddling by everyone. That's why she's in the state she's in, if you ask me.'

'This is not the time or the place to discuss this,' Carrie said shortly. 'The bairns need to be settled.'

'Carrie's right.' Isaac bent down and lifted his children into his arms. 'Let's get the bairns out of this.'

'Here, lad, give Katie to me.' Sandy took the little girl, while Carrie kept a protective arm round Lillian who was now trembling violently with shock. Supporting each other in this way, with Olive Sutton following behind, they walked away from the ruins of what had been Lillian and Isaac's home.

Chapter Eighteen

The last week of February saw Wearside gripped by severe winter weather, the worst in living memory according to all the oldtimers. Power lines were brought down by the weight of snow and ice, trams and buses struggled to run any sort of service at all, and the bombing raids continued most nights. The room where Carrie worked was given over to Lillian, Isaac and their little ones, and Matthew's room was occupied by Olive, which meant Matthew was sleeping on a put-u-up in the kitchen. Carrie felt her life had been turned upside down but she could have coped with it all quite easily – it was Olive Sutton who was the real thorn in her flesh.

Carrie was now working as a volunteer in one of the day nurseries that were springing up wherever funding could be found for them. There was a vital need for women to work in munitions factories, tank and aircraft factories, civil defence, nursing, transport and other key occupations in order to release men for the armed forces. The responsibility for nursery provision was shared between the Ministry of Health and local authorities, but some officials were proving obstructive. There was still widespread antipathy to the idea of mothers with young children working, and this, together with the grudging release of the necessary funds and facilities, meant the nurseries already in place were desperate for volunteers prepared to work without a salary.

Carrie now rose at half past five every morning in order to leave the house at half past seven with Luke and Katie, for whom, by volunteering, she'd gained places at the nursery. This left Lillian free to take a job in the same steelworks as Isaac, where she was immediately put on cutting shell cases. Having lost everything in the bombing, and with their house under order to be knocked down because it had been rendered unsafe, the couple were anxious to save every penny they could in order to buy essential furniture and move into rented accommodation. On Lillian's first shift a red-hot shaving of steel hit her across the face and loosened her teeth, necessitating an hour in the Sunderland infirmary and many stitches, but she was back at work the next day – badly bruised and hardly able to open her mouth, but back at her machine.

Carrie normally arrived home at half past four in the afternoon after her eight-hour stint at the nursery and she did this three days a week. The other three days she worked at Horwood & Sons in a small stuffy room which had been provided for her. She arrived at eight in the morning and left any time between six and nine at night. In spite of the long hours, cramped working conditions and poor lighting which made her eyes ache and her head pound, she much preferred these days and she was grateful that the talk of clothing rationing had not come to anything as yet. On the days she worked at the nursery she saw too much of her mother-in-law in the afternoon for it to be comfortable.

Despite broad hints from Lillian and Isaac that with Katie and Luke now in nursery six days a week, Olive was free to find work herself, she seemed determined to resist the call to take employment. This meant she saw far more of Matthew than

Carrie did, especially when Matthew was on the 6 a.m. shift and got home at just after two in the afternoon. Carrie would often walk in to find the pair of them settled over a cup of tea and a plate of girdle scones or sly cake, despite the number of times she had pointed out to Olive that rations were short.

Matthew had always liked his grandmother: she indulged him to the point of stupidity, but lately his affection seemed to have grown. Indeed Olive was the only person he really spoke to. The brief rapport he'd had with David when he first started down the pit had evaporated since his grandmother had arrived in the house. Carrie was aware of all this, and suspected that Olive was conducting some sort of murmuring campaign directly against her, but she had no concrete proof and deemed it wisest to say nothing rather than risk alienating Matthew.

This finished abruptly in the last week of February. Carrie had just got home with Luke and Katie whom she'd sent through to the kitchen which was warm from the range. She was standing in the scullery, taking off her hat and coat which were thick with snow, conscious that her feet were like blocks of ice and that one of her boots was leaking. Through the scullery door she heard Luke say loudly, 'That's not fair, *I* want one,' and then came the sound of a ringing slap, followed by howls from the little boy.

Carrie fairly leaped into the kitchen. 'What's the matter?' Luke flung his small body against her legs and buried his head in her skirt. 'Did you smack him?' Carrie demanded. 'What did he do?'

Olive and Matthew were sitting at the kitchen table, and as Olive raised her head and looked straight at her, Carrie thought, you haven't changed a bit, not a bit. Olive was still the dominant, cruel woman she'd always been; the meekness she'd shown after Ned's leaving and during her years with Lillian and

Isaac was no more than a thin façade. Olive was staring at her with an expression that proclaimed she thought she was looking at something unclean, something beneath her notice. The rage that her mother-in-law had brought to the surface once before was kindled again now.

'Did you smack him?' Carrie repeated, her tone cold and her face white with anger.

'Aye, I smacked him.'

Katie had joined Luke and was nestling into Carrie like a tiny fledgling seeking security in the feathers of its mother.

'Why?' Carrie asked.

'Because he won't take no for an answer, that's why. Lillian's spoiled him.'

'Luke is a very well-behaved boy.' Carrie had a hand on each of the children's heads but her back was straight and her chin was up as she glared at the woman who hated her. 'And I repeat, what did he do?'

'He wanted a scone.'

It was Matthew who answered her and his voice was low but cool, with a quality to it that notched up Carrie's anger even further. 'Well? What's wrong with that?' she asked, ignoring the fact for the moment that in making the girdle scones her mother-in-law had probably used the last of the currants for the month, something she'd specifically asked her not to do.

'Your son' – Olive placed a slight emphasis on the last word as though pointing out that Carrie's loyalties should be with Matthew and not Luke – 'has just endured another day down that hellhole, and I baked for him, not Lillian's brat.'

'Don't you dare call Luke a brat.' Carrie knew this confrontation had been coming from the moment Olive had stepped into her house months before, but she'd never imagined the showdown would arise over something as trivial as a girdle

302

scone. 'And you've no right to refuse him a scone. Of course he wants one, it's only natural. He's hungry and he's three years old, besides which the food in this house is for everyone. You say you made them for Matthew. You haven't had one then.'

Olive's sallow face flushed. 'Luke doesn't know his manners,' she said, ignoring the question. 'Spare the rod and spoil the child, that's what the good book says.'

'Don't quote scripture at me, not in these circumstances.'

'Now look, Mam, Gran didn't mean anything,' Matthew chimed in, his tone protective, and the thread which had been holding Carrie's patience since her mother-in-law's arrival in the house snapped.

She turned to her son, her tone icy as she said, 'No, Matthew, *you* look and you'll see we all pull our weight in this house except your grandmother. No one is entitled to special treatment, do you understand me? Your father works just as hard as you do, and the steelworks is no picnic for your aunt and uncle. I work all the hours God sends and I'm thankful for what it brings in, but the point is we *all* work. We all pull together. We all share whatever there is. There will be no more cooking when I'm not here.'

'I see.' Olive had tucked in her chin and was fairly bristling. 'Miss High-and-Mighty with the fine job laying down the law as usual. Well, let me tell you, girl, I brought four bairns into the world and sacrificed any idea of a job outside the home to look after them properly. But not you, oh no. First of all you trick my lad into marrying you and then it's no more bairns, regardless of what he wants.'

For a moment Carrie couldn't believe Olive was saying these things in front of Matthew. She glanced at his face and saw that the story of her tricking David into marrying her was not a new one. In her haste to assure her son the accusation was

303

untrue, she spoke without weighing her words. 'There was no question of my tricking David, as well you know, and there's nothing more I'd like than to give him a bairn – another bairn,' she corrected in the next breath. The slip steadied her, taking the edge off her anger. She couldn't afford to let Olive get to her like this.

'David! He'd say black was white to please you.' Olive did not give Matthew a chance to speak, but then, on the last words, her voice died away as though her mind was elsewhere. She stared at Carrie, her face working for a moment, but whatever she had been about to say was never voiced. She simply got up and headed for the door. 'I'm going to my room.'

Carrie's face was pale. Had she given herself away with that remark about giving David a bairn, or was she imagining the speculative look she thought she had seen in Olive's eyes?

'You didn't have to go for her like that. She's had enough to put up with with Granda leaving like he did.'

Carrie glanced at Matthew as she ushered Katie and Luke to the table. 'Have you ever bothered to ask yourself *why* a nice man like your granda would do such a thing?' She seated each child on a chair and put a scone in front of them. 'Well, have you?' she asked again. 'It might have escaped your notice but she led him a dreadful life.'

'Is that what he said?'

'It's nothing to do with what your granda said or didn't say. I saw it with my own eyes. And what about your Uncle Alec? He didn't want her with them, did he? Have you ever asked him why?'

'Because of Aunt Margaret. He told me so.'

Matthew had an answer for everything and all supplied from one source, or maybe two with Olive putting in her two pennyworth. Carrie's gaze rested on Luke's ear as the little boy cupped it in his podgy hand for a brief moment as though it was hurting, which no doubt it was. It was pillarbox red. When she said, 'I'll get a warm flannel for your ear in a minute, Luke,' Matthew rose abruptly from the table.

'That's all you're bothered about, isn't it?' he said bitterly. 'Luke and Katie, Aunt Lillian, Da – everyone but me.'

'Matthew, that isn't true.' She was deeply hurt and it showed in her face, and for a moment Matthew looked down at his feet, his face reddening.

When he looked up again, he said very quietly, 'It's true, isn't it, about you and Da having to get married because I was on the way.'

Carrie's voice was even quieter. 'I'm not going to lie to you, Matthew. The only thing I would say is that no one *has* to get married, one chooses to in the end. I chose to marry your da as he did me.'

'Who knew?'

'Knew?'

'About me. About you being . . .' He waved a hand.

'Only your Gran and Granda McDarmount, that's all. They're still the only ones who know for sure. We said you came early to everyone else.'

He was standing very straight, his back rigid. 'You don't think that fooled anyone, do you?'

What could she say to take that look off his face? When had Olive started whispering her newsmongering? How long had he been drinking in her poison? 'We wanted you. We wanted you very much, Matthew. You have to believe that.'

He stared at her for a long moment. 'I'm going round to Brian's and I shan't be back for dinner. We're going to the pictures.'

'Don't go like this. Please, let's talk.'

305

She was wasting her breath. He grabbed his coat and cap and didn't stop to put them on before he left the house.

Carrie stood staring after him. Had he believed that last lie? She had told him she wouldn't lie to him but she'd had to; she couldn't have let him go without saying something to reassure him. She pressed her eyeballs with her finger and thumb, her head throbbing. She hated David's mother. How could Olive have told him, her own grandson, such things? It was cruel.

'Aunt Carrie? 'Nother one?'

When she looked down, Luke smiled up at her disarmingly, his baby mouth smeared with crumbs. It didn't seem two minutes since Matthew had been that age but now he was all but grown up. The pain in her head intensified. And he didn't like her. Her boy didn't like her. She had read dislike in his eyes before he walked out of the house.

Carrie cut open two more scones mechanically, put a smidgen of jam on each and placed them in front of the delighted infants. Should she have lied to Matthew and assured him he was conceived after her marriage to David? No, he had known. There hadn't been the slightest doubt in his face or voice. It hadn't been a question so much as a statement.

She drew in a shuddering breath, feeling sick to her stomach. This was the end as far as her mother-in-law was concerned, she wasn't tolerating Olive in the house one more hour after this.

She bent down to the children. 'Sit still and eat your scones and I'll be back in a minute. All right?' Then she straightened, drew in another breath and smoothed her dress. She walked with measured steps into the hall, pausing for a moment and glancing upwards before she began to climb the stairs.

When Olive reached her room, she did not walk across to the bed or to the chair standing to one side of the window. Instead she reached to the top of the narrow wardrobe and brought down the big cloth bag she'd put there.

She had no intention of remaining in this house until David got home from his shift just after ten, she told herself. He was a deep one, was David. Of all her children she had never been sure what he would do or say next. She wasn't sure if he was capable of physical violence, but when he was informed of what had occurred here today and what she had told Matthew, she wouldn't put it past him.

She took her clothes from the wardrobe and the small chest of drawers, and folded them into the cloth bag. She stared at it for a moment. It hadn't taken long to pack all her wordly possessions, she thought bitterly. She'd had to sell all her furniture, apart from a few of the best bits which she had taken with her to Lillian's, and they were now under a pile of rubble.

Oh, to be reduced to this. *Her*, who had always prided herself on her lovely home and nice things. And there was that cocky little madam downstairs, who had been dragged up in the bottom end, with this bonny place.

The thought of Carrie brought her plumping down on the bed. She'd always thought Matthew was the image of Alec in his ways and mannerisms; perhaps that was why she had taken to the boy. The way he had of looking at you sometimes, his mouth, his smile especially, but until now she just hadn't put two and two together. But then who would? Her Alec, with that scum of scum. Olive screwed her thin buttocks into the bed in protest. But what man wouldn't take it if it was offered on a plate? And that's what would have happened, sure enough. Little baggage. She was a sly one, Carrie McDarmount. Olive had never allowed herself to think of Carrie as a Sutton.

But perhaps instead of putting two and two together and making four she was making ten here. Olive thought back to

Carrie's face when she'd talked about giving David a bairn, and shook her head slowly. No, she wasn't. She'd bet her life she wasn't. And the way the little scut had tried to cover up. She would never have twigged if Carrie hadn't done that, but she'd been rattled, flummoxed, and it had been plain to see. And if David wasn't the father, it had to be Alec with the bairn so like him.

When Olive heard footsteps on the stairs she braced herself for the knock at the door, but instead Carrie walked straight in, her face grim. She glanced at the bag on the bed. 'You're leaving?'

'Aye.'

'Good, because you're not welcome here any longer.'

'I never was.'

Carrie did not deny this. Instead she said, 'You've got a cesspit for a mind, do you know that?'

'Because I call a spade a spade?'

Again Carrie didn't respond to the taunt. 'I hope God can forgive you for what you've said to Matthew because I can't, and I know David won't. Now please go.' She stood to one side of the door and waved her hand towards the landing.

'I'm going.' For one moment Olive was inclined to throw her suspicions into Carrie's face just to see her reaction, but she restrained herself. Now was not the time. There were more ways of killing a cat than drowning it, and she would use this to better advantage if she didn't let on for the moment. Her time would come.

She stalked past Carrie with her head held high and marched down the stairs, the cloth bag in her hand. Carrie followed her into the kitchen. Luke and Katie were still seated at the table and they looked at their grandmother with big eyes, sensing something was very wrong.

'You and your sister.' Olive turned on the threshold to the scullery where her coat and hat were hanging. 'One a big blowsy tart who will go with anyone and doesn't care who knows it, the other acting so pure and holy but just the same under the skin. I've had the measure of the pair of you for years.'

Carrie stared at the face twisted with spite. 'I think it is high time you left,' she said steadily.

'Truth always outs, girl. Don't you know that?' Olive grabbed her hat and rammed it on her head, then pulled on her coat.

'I've done nothing I am ashamed of.'

'More's the shame on you then.' So saying, Olive opened the back door and stepped out into the raw afternoon which was already growing dark.

For just a second Carrie was tempted to ask her mother-in-law where she intended to go, but then she just let her walk away out of the yard. She didn't care where Olive was going so long as it was away from this house. Her presence had been a constant strain on everyone from day one, everyone except Matthew, that was.

Carrie closed the door and went back into the kitchen. Lillian's children were sitting as quiet as mice, cowed by the grim voices and the way their grandmother had glared at them when she'd come downstairs. The sight of the small frightened faces brought a swell of emotion in Carrie's chest, which could have led to tears if she'd let it. Instead she forced a smile and said brightly, 'Who's going to help me get dinner ready? I need someone to scrub vegetables.'

Normally the tots loved any such activity and Katie shouted, 'Me! Me!'. But Luke, a year older, said solemnly, 'Where is Granny going?'

'She's going to live with someone else, Luke.'

'For ever?'

'And ever and ever.' Carrie brushed back a lock of his hair as she spoke. 'Do you mind?'

The little boy shook his head, looking up at her with big brown eyes. 'Me an' Katie don't like Granny,' he whispered confidingly. 'Do we, Katie?'

Katie obediently shook her head.

'She's got hard hands,' Luke said revealingly.

And a hard heart.

Olive walked swiftly and with purpose once she was clear of the side roads which were heavily banked with snow and almost impassable in places. She knew exactly where she was making for, and now she was on her way she told herself she should have done this weeks ago. Anything would have been better than living under that baggage's roof, and why should she be dictated to by Carrie and David and the rest of them anyway? Alec was her son and it was about time he did something for her. That wife of his all alone in that great big house with a housekeeper and maid and goodness knows what. There was plenty of room, and no one had actually approached Margaret on the subject as far as she knew. She'd put it to her straight that she was prepared to come and stay and Margaret could do away with having to hire a nurse. She'd look after Alec's wife.

It was beginning to snow again, and as the flakes began to whirl and dip about her, driven by the raw north-east wind, Olive said to herself, a night like this and being cast out by my own son's wife. By, it's come to something. But Margaret was a different kettle of fish to Carrie; she could handle Margaret.

Olive did not consciously think here that Margaret was frightened of her, but the thought that followed flowed from

310

the belief. Give it a day or two for her to settle in and she'd find out what Margaret knew about Alec and Carrie. Because there was something there, she'd swear it. Now that the possibility of Matthew being Alec's child had reared its head, so much fitted into place. Carrie had always tried to keep Alec away from the bairn, fearing, no doubt, that David would cotton on he wasn't the father. She was a loose piece all right. Olive pursed her lips. Renee was bad enough but there was something about Carrie that had spelled trouble from the first time she'd laid eyes on her. Even as a bairn she'd had the menfolk buzzing about her like bees to a honeypot. Men were such fools.

In all the time that Alec and Margaret had lived in the better part of Hendon, Olive had been invited only twice – once for Christmas five years before and again when a large party had been organised by Margaret for her father when he reached the grand age of sixty-five. The occasion had not been a success. Margaret had been fraught with anxiety and she had communicated her tension to her guests, with the result that the party had been awkward and strained.

It was quite dark by the time Olive walked through the tall iron gates set in a high stone wall bordered by laurel. She was panting heavily now with the weight of her bag, and as she marched up the long drive she was hoping Margaret's father was not visiting. She had been disappointed in him when she'd met him on Alec's wedding day, and her opinion of him had not improved on the two subsequent occasions she'd been in his company. Olive considered him to be coarse and abrupt and not at all as someone in his position ought to be. This opinion was heavily flavoured by the fact that Arthur Reed did not suffer fools gladly and had made his opinion of Olive blatantly obvious. Since Margaret's mother had died a few years before, he had become even more taciturn with people he did not like, and he definitely did not like Olive.

When Olive knocked on the big oak front door set in the middle of the large double-fronted house, it was opened almost immediately by a tall thin woman of middle age or beyond. She was dressed in a light grey dress with sparkling white collar and cuffs. Olive knew her to be the housekeeper, Mrs Browell, and as though she was a daily visitor, she said, 'Where's the maid? Surely it's her job to see to the door.'

Freda Browell peered at her for a moment. 'Mrs Sutton? Madam has not informed me you were expected.'

Olive did not reply to this until she had stepped into the wide spacious hall. She stood for a moment, glancing round at the thick wall-to-wall carpeting and expensive embossed wallpaper. Then, planting her bag firmly on the floor, she said, 'No, she wouldn't have, Mrs Browell,' before repeating, 'where's the maid?'

'Gone to work in a munitions factory like all the young things.' It was said with unconcealed disapproval. 'One just cannot get the staff since this wretched war, Mrs Sutton. Madam has advertised for weeks now since the agency were unable to help but all to no avail, and what can you expect when bits of girls can earn more than they ever dreamed of a year or two ago? I said to madam the other night, what are we going to be left with when the war is over? Once a young lass's head is turned, it stays turned, and I can't see the majority of them returning to work in service. Even the nurse has taken herself off this week.'

Olive did not care what the housekeeper could or could not see and her tone made this perfectly clear when she said, 'Kindly take my bag to one of the spare bedrooms, Mrs Browell. Is Mrs Sutton in the drawing room?' On her first visit to the house she had made the mistake of calling this room the sitting room and it had been the housekeeper who had corrected her, albeit tactfully. But Olive did not forget a slight and that was what she considered Mrs Browell's correction to be.

'Madam is in the dining room. I was just about to serve dinner.' Freda Browell had stiffened in both voice and manner.

'I'll join her.'

Olive watched the housekeeper's eyebrows give the slightest movement upwards. But Freda Browell had been in service since she was thirteen years old and she wasn't about to argue with her mistress's mother-in-law, even if she did privately consider her to be an upstart who was as common as muck under her airs and graces.

'Very good, Mrs Sutton.'

Very good, Mrs Sutton. Olive didn't move until Mrs Browell had picked up her bag and begun to walk up the stairs which were situated halfway down the hall. Thinks she's the real mistress here no doubt, Olive thought sourly, what with Margaret forever taking to her bed. Olive had heard Alec expounding the housekeeper's virtues on more than one occasion, saying she ran the house like clockwork and that since Margaret's own mother had died his wife relied on Mrs Browell more and more. Well, those days were finished if she had anything to do with it. She had blamed Alec for not having her to live with them when Ned skedaddled, at least at first, but the more she'd thought about it, the more she had been convinced it was Mrs Browell and Mr Reed bringing their influence to bear. Neither of them liked her and she knew why – they thought she was too close to Alec, had too much of an influence on him. And it was true he had always listened to her – would he be where he was now but for her guidance when he was a lad?

Olive squared her bony shoulders and brought her sharp chin up. With Lillian bombed out and Carrie having told her she wasn't welcome under David's roof, Margaret couldn't refuse her a bed. And if Walter and Renee were mentioned, she would make it quite clear she wouldn't dream of soiling her conscience by living under that baggage's roof. Those McDarmounts, she had known there would be nothing but trouble when her lads took up with them.

The dining room door opened. Margaret froze when she saw her mother-in-law in the hall, and the chaffing she had been about to voice to Mrs Browell at the delay in dinner being served died on her lips. For a moment she couldn't believe her eyes, and then Olive marched up to her and said briskly, 'And how are you this evening, Margaret?'

'Fairly well, thank you, Mother-in-law', she managed to respond. 'But . . .' She hesitated. 'What are you doing here? Not that it isn't nice to see you of course, but I had no idea you were coming. Have you eaten?'

'Mrs Browell is serving dinner for two.' Olive managed to make it sound as though it was the housekeeper's suggestion.

'Oh, I see. How . . . nice. But with the weather so inclement . . .' Margaret's voice drifted away.

Olive said evenly, 'Mrs Browell has taken my bag to one of the spare rooms, Margaret. I may as well tell you that Carrie has made it abundantly clear I am not welcome with them any more, and as you know, Lillian is staying with them for the present. With Renee being Carrie's sister I obviously can't go there.'

'You . . . you mean . . .' Margaret took a deep breath, her sallow, thin face flushed with nervous colour. 'You want to stay here?'

'I understand the maid and nurse have both left to do war work.' Olive seated herself at one end of the large dining table which was set for one with silver cutlery, fine glassware and a damask linen cloth of exquisite design. 'Poor Mrs Browell is having to run this house and look after you single-handed.' Again she made it sound as if it was the housekeeper who had suggested she stay. 'It seems a good time for me to help out, don't you think?'

Margaret felt the trembling inside communicate itself to her hands and she tucked them in her lap. 'But, Alec . . . I mean, it would be up to him.'

'Alec is not here, Margaret.' Olive spoke in a tone that suggested she thought Margaret was dense or confused. 'But I am sure he would want his mother to look after his wife in such difficult circumstances. We're family, aren't we? And at times like this, family should look out for one another. Who knows what tomorrow could bring, what with the raids and all? I'm sure his mind would be put at ease if he knew I was here.'

Margaret wondered what her mother-in-law would say if she knew her son had stated he would rather cut his own throat than have his mother live with them. But Alec wasn't here, and she couldn't stand up to this dreadful woman by herself.

'Don't worry, dear.' Olive gave a twist to her lips which could have passed for a smile. 'I'm more than happy to stay for a while so don't you worry your head about it a minute longer.'

Margaret was saved having to make a response to this by Mrs Browell, who entered the room without any ceremony and laid another place at the table in front of Olive. Then she left the room again. The door had barely closed behind her when Olive said, 'That woman takes liberties, Margaret. You really ought to be firm with her.'

'Mrs Browell?' Margaret was stung into rare retaliation. 'She's a friend, not just a housekeeper.'

'Ah, well, there's the root of the problem, if you don't mind me saying so. If you let servants think they're in with the door shut, it breeds over-familiarity.' Olive spoke as though she was used to dealing with a whole household of servants.

A familiar wave of weakness came over Margaret; it always assailed her in Olive's presence, and she knew she wasn't strong enough to tell Alec's mother to leave. She glanced down at the white damask tablecloth helplessly. What was she going to do?

It was now three days since Olive had come to stay and Margaret thought she was beginning to go mad. Of course there were those who said she was mad already, what with the injections for her nerves and the treatment she had undergone at private clinics in the last few years. But she had known she wasn't all mad, even in the worst of her depressions. But now . . .

She glanced across at her mother-in-law who was seated on the other side of the roaring fire in an armchair identical to the one she herself was sitting in. Olive was doing her best to alienate Mrs Browell, and if the housekeeper left, Margaret knew she wouldn't be able to go on. If only her father wasn't in bed with this wretched influenza, she could have asked him to call and take care of things. There wasn't a man or woman alive who could intimidate him. He would soon tell Olive Sutton she was taking too much on herself.

As though her mother-in-law had picked up her thoughts, Olive now said, 'You should have listened to me this afternoon when that little madam called, Margaret, and refused to allow her over the doorstep. Daring to come here bold as brass when she threw me out of her house. And why would any of them think I'd want to go and stay with Walter and Renee?'

'I thought it was kind of Carrie to come here and tell you what had been proposed.'

'Kind?' Olive sat up straight, her back tight against the chair. 'I can see she's took you in, girl. If Walter and Renee are so keen to have me with them, why didn't they come themselves and suggest it? Eh?'

'Carrie said Walter is working extra shifts and Renee is ill in bed with the influenza.'

'So she expects me to go there and keep house while that big fat lazy sister of hers lies on her back all day? I wasn't born yesterday, whatever Carrie McDarmount might think. I've got her measure all right.'

'I've always found Carrie to be most pleasant,' said Margaret stiffly.

'Oh aye, she can be pleasant, especially with the men, if you get my drift.' Olive raised thin eyebrows meaningfully. 'But she caught her toe when she found out she was expecting Matthew. But with David in the wings offering to marry her she knew she was all right. It's not many men that'd take on a flyblow but perhaps he thinks the boy is his, although I doubt it. Matthew and David have never got on, but then you know that.'

'I . . . I didn't.' Margaret was highly embarrassed and it showed.

'No? You surprise me. I thought it was obvious to everyone. The boy has nothing in common with him, that's the thing. Nothing at all.' Olive paused a moment but when Margaret said nothing she continued, 'But like I said, if Matthew isn't David's, it's not surprising they don't see eye to eye on anything.'

Margaret's brow wrinkled. She was aware Olive was putting a wealth of meaning into her voice but she really didn't see where this distasteful conversation was leading. She cleared her throat. 'This is really none of my business,' she said feebly.

317

'Of course it is, you're Alec's wife, aren't you?' And then Olive shut her mouth with a little snap, only to open it again to say, 'Oh dear, I've said too much. It was that glass of wine at dinner. I'm not used to alcohol. But I've always maintained that blood outs in the end.'

Margaret had a puzzled little frown between her eyes.

For crying out loud, thought Olive, do I have to spell it out for her? Plain as a pikestaff and as thick as two short planks. Alec certainly didn't marry her for her looks or her brain.

Olive relaxed back in her chair. 'I'm glad we've had this little talk though, it's cleared the air, so to speak. I can't be doing with secrets, not in a family, leastways, and I suppose you've always wondered, knowing how Carrie worshipped the ground Alec walked on at one time.'

What on earth was the woman talking about? Margaret smoothed a fold in the skirt of her dress in order to break the hold of her mother-in-law's intense gaze. Carrie had no time for Alec, she behaved quite differently with him—

The penny dropped and her hand became still, her eyes frozen on the material beneath her fingers. Olive was saying that Alec and Carrie had . . . *No.*

For a moment she thought she had spoken out loud but when Olive remained silent, she knew the shout had been in her head. Her mind raced. You've always known he didn't love you, always, and here's the answer. And look how he is with Matthew. He's not the same with Veronica, he's not. All the time you've told yourself it's because Matthew is a boy and he can relate better to him, but it's not that. You've seen him looking at Carrie in that certain way. All right, he looks at lots of women and women look at him, but Carrie never does. Never. She avoids him. She dislikes him. And why? Because he got her pregnant. It must have been about the time Alec proposed marriage. Oh no, no, I can't bear this. I can't bear it. And she's so beautiful, so bonny.

Margaret raised her head and met Olive's eyes, and what she read in them provided confirmation. For both women.

Oh aye, the lass knew all right, it was written all over her face, Olive thought with some satisfaction. Perhaps she'd always suspected something wasn't right but hadn't tumbled. Well, you wouldn't, would you, in the normal run of things and her thinking the lad was David's son, but this should put a spoke in Carrie McDarmount's wheel. Thinking she could come here and pretend to be concerned about Margaret. Her card was marked now. If she knew one thing about Margaret it was that she was besotted with her husband; Carrie would find the door closed against her if she took it into her head to try and cause more trouble. Suggesting she should be packed off to Walter's like a sack of taties! Olive sniffed loudly. Carrie must think she was daft.

'Well, I'm for bed, lass.' It was the kindest tone Olive had ever used towards her daughter-in-law, but Margaret was unaware of it. Her mind was still grappling with the enormity of tonight's revelations.

'What? Oh, yes . . . Goodnight.'

It was vague, but Olive did not take offence. Margaret had plenty to think about now, and no doubt many things which had occurred over the years would take on a new meaning – as they had done with her when she had first realised the significance of it all. It was amazing but sometimes you completely missed what was right under your nose.

It was snowing again when Margaret stepped out of the house two hours later. Olive and Freda Browell had long since retired and Margaret had been in her quarters for over an hour, but she had spent the time sitting on her bed staring vacantly into space. Now she stood in the snow like someone dazed, looking first one way and then the other as though she did not recognise where she was. In spite of the severe weather she was wearing no hat and coat, and her shoes were more suited to the drawing room than the conditions outside.

When she began to walk down the drive she moved slowly, her lips working as though she was talking although no sound left her mouth. In the white empty street she turned to face Seaham, and then her steps became more purposeful. In the months following her engagement to Alec and before their marriage, they had often borrowed her father's horse and trap and taken a picnic to Seaham. It had been a nice drive and they had rarely met anyone they knew, unlike the times they had stayed in town or ventured on the beach at Seaburn, Roker or Whitburn, and since her marriage Margaret had often looked back on those times as the happiest in her life.

By keeping to the coast road Margaret was able to avoid meeting anyone in the blackout, flitting through the whirling snow with a speed which would have amazed her doctors. When she reached the first stretch of beach, however, she received a shock. The sands were protected by barbed wire and anti-aircraft guns; naval guns and barrage balloons were in the harbour. She was just approaching the harbour when someone called to her, and a member of the Home Guard and two women in khaki uniforms appeared out of a building to her left.

'Where do you think you're going, love?'

It was the man who spoke and his voice was kind, but Margaret couldn't answer him except to say, 'It's all so different, nothing is the same.'

One of the women came closer to her. 'You're frozen, lass. Where's your hat and coat?' she said, just as kindly.

Then the sirens began to sound.

'Here, you come with us.' The man caught hold of her arm but Margaret surprised him and herself with the speed and force with which she shook herself free.

'Don't,' she said. 'I have to find him.'

'Find him? Find who, love?'

'My husband. He's here. I need to talk to him.'

She saw the three glance at each other, and then another man, an elderly one this time, in Home Guard uniform joined them. 'What's up?'

The first woman said, 'She's looking for her husband,' but the other one made a gesture with her fingers against the side of her head.

They thought she was mentally disordered. Margaret stared at them. All she wanted to do was find Alec and ask him . . . What was it she needed to ask him? She couldn't remember now but it was important. She knew it was important. 'It's important.' She spoke to the older man. 'It's very important.'

'Course it is.' He smiled at her, his soldier's cap already coated with a layer of snow. 'So why don't you come and tell me all about it in this nice shelter we've got, and then perhaps we can go and find your husband once this little lot is over. How's that? He might even be in the shelter for all we know.'

'Might he?' Margaret smiled. She hoped so.

They were just feet from their objective when a high-pitched whistling sound caused Margaret to glance upwards. The elderly veteran flung himself over her, pulling her and himself to the ground.

The shelter received a direct hit and exploded, throwing

321

up debris and burying Margaret and her valiant oldtimer under bricks and rubble. Within fifteen minutes firemen had uncovered the bodies, but unlike those in the shelter, Margaret's and the old gentleman's were whole and largely unmarked. There was no sign of life.

Chapter Nineteen

'I shouldn't have left her side. I knew she wasn't herself, I should have slept on the couch in her bedroom and kept an eye on her.'

'Mrs Browell, don't blame yourself. You were marvellous to her, wonderful. Everyone knows that. Come on, please. You'll make yourself ill.' Carrie found she was virtually holding the housekeeper up as they walked away from the graveside, and she signalled to David who was a few yards behind her to come and take Mrs Browell's other arm.

As he reached them, Freda Browell gave way to racking sobs. 'Miss Margaret, oh, Miss Margaret. What am I going to do? She wasn't just a mistress to me, she was more like the daughter I never had. And Mr Sutton told me he knew I'd look after her while he was away. What's he going to say to me now? And we don't know how he is. And then there's Mr Reed. What's happened, Mrs Sutton? Everything has changed. It's terrible, terrible.'

Carrie could give little comfort because she agreed with her. It had been a terrible shock to them all when they'd received the news that Margaret had disappeared, apparently in the middle of the night, and then within twenty-four hours the police had called with the grim news that they suspected they had found Margaret's body at Seaham. Mrs Browell had been in such a state she hadn't been able to accompany Olive to identify the body, but David had gone with his mother while Carrie and Lillian had sat with Mrs Browell at the house. And then, before Olive and David returned, a telegram arrived. It informed them Alec was a prisoner of war.

Mr Reed, who had collapsed with a suspected heart attack at the report of his daughter's disappearance, did not live to hear the news of her death confirmed; he passed away with a second massive attack just hours after the first. Two deaths, which made Alec a very rich man, but what good were all the riches in the world if a man was incarcerated in one of those terrible camps they were reading about in the newspapers? Carrie shivered, but it was caused by a chill within rather than the bitter wind cutting through the bleak cemetery.

And now Olive had declared herself to be permanently in residence at the Ridings, Alec's house, telling all and sundry she intended to keep it functioning as normal so it would be just as Alec remembered it when 'the dear boy comes home'.

Olive was very much the mistress of the occasion today, Carrie thought, glancing over the head of the weeping Mrs Browell and watching as Olive talked to the local vicar, for all the world as if she was the lady of the manor. And Mrs Browell must have been thinking along the same lines because she raised her tear-washed face and said brokenly, 'I'm sorry, Mrs Sutton, but I can't stay on at the house, not with Mr Sutton's mother. She's made it very plain she thinks I ought to look for alternative employment, and to be truthful I would have anyway. I . . . I can't get on with her.'

You and the rest of the world. Carrie nodded, saying, 'I understand, Mrs Browell.'

'Miss Margaret wasn't the same after Mr Sutton's mother walked through the door,' Mrs Browell continued, wiping her face with her handkerchief. 'I might be saying it as shouldn't, but I can't help it. That woman scared madam to death, her nerves went all to pieces the last few days before she . . . before . . .'

'Come on, Mrs Browell. Let's go back and have a hot cup of tea, yes?' Carrie gently led the sobbing housekeeper to the waiting car which had formed part of the long black funeral cortège. David and Walter were executors of Margaret's will in Alec's absence, something Alec had arranged when he had suspected his call-up was imminent, and so all the family were going back to the house – much to Olive's chagrin.

Margaret's will was very simple. In the event of her dying before her beloved husband, she left everything to Alec, with a proviso that the sum of five hundred pounds be given to Mrs Freda Browell whom she considered her dear friend and companion. Freda was also left some fine pieces of jewellery, and a small terraced property in Bishopwearmouth. She could either continue to rent it out as was currently the case, sell it, or live in it herself.

'That's it.' The solicitor looked round at them all, his glance taking in Freda Browell who was holding on to Carrie's hand very tightly and looked rigid with shock. 'The bulk of the estate is Mr Sutton's, but there is a paragraph which states that both Mr and Mrs Sutton have agreed that Mrs Browell is welcome to stay on at the Ridings as housekeeper for as long as Mr Sutton lives on the premises. If you take this course' – he now was speaking directly to Mrs Browell – 'an adequate allowance will be made each month for you to keep the house in order for Mr Sutton's return. Otherwise we will shut the establishment until further notice.'

Carrie dared not glance at David or any of the others, but when Renee brought out a handkerchief and pretended to blow her nose, hiding her mouth in the process, she knew that her sister was enjoying the position Olive now found herself in as much as she was. In one fell swoop, Margaret had given Mrs Browell the upper hand in a way she could never have envisaged when the will had been drawn up. Olive's goose was well and truly cooked. If she wanted to stay on in Alec's house she would have to stomach a large helping of humble pie.

Even in her grief Mrs Browell clearly appreciated the irony of the turnaround in her and Olive's circumstances because she said quietly, 'Could I let you know what I intend to do in a few days' time, Mr Greer, when I've had a chance to reflect? Of course if I decide to stay on here some help would be useful' – a strangled sound came from Olive – 'but I'm really not sure.'

Renee glanced at Carrie at this point and Carrie read her sister's face like a book. She was applauding Freda's stance.

'Of course.' The small man rose to his feet, brushing an imaginary spot from his immaculate jacket as he said, 'I will take my leave but not before I offer you all my condolences again. Mrs Sutton was a truly fine and gentle soul, a lady in every sense of the word.'

'Yes, she was. Thank you.' As the oldest brother present it was Walter who replied.

When they all left a little while later, it was Mrs Browell who saw them out, her mantle already one of gracious host. Olive was standing just behind her and looked as if she was going to burst a blood vessel when Mrs Browell said to Carrie, 'Thank you for being so supportive,' and took her hand. 'Whatever I decide, I do hope we can keep in touch, Mrs Sutton, and if I stay on here, you and the rest of the family are welcome at any time, any time at all.'

They were halfway home in the taxi cab when the sirens sounded, and within minutes the whole sky was filled with lights and bombers, the flares so bright it seemed like day. But for once Carrie welcomed the diversion, if not the actual raid itself, because Matthew had just been voicing his opinion of events. 'Fancy Aunt Margaret giving Mrs Browell the right to stay at the Ridings,' he said peevishly, 'instead of Gran. That's not fair. Gran said Mrs Browell was going to go and that I could go and stay with her if I wanted, seeing as it would make more room at home for Lillian and everyone. Nothing ever works out for me.'

Part 5

Truth Will Out

1944

Chapter Twenty

Carrie felt her heart begin to thud so hard it actually hurt her chest as she stared at the calendar on the kitchen wall. She must have made a mistake surely. She counted the days again, and then once more. Then she walked over to the rocking chair to one side of the range and sat down, her legs weak.

Two periods. She had missed two periods now; the second had been due over a week ago. Admittedly she had been the odd few days late in the past, but never anything like this. And she had been feeling off colour for a couple of weeks and had been sick three mornings in a row. Why on earth hadn't she cottoned on before?

And then she answered herself. Because the thought of having another bairn hadn't crossed her mind in months. The last year had been so busy, she hadn't had time to think, let alone brood about a baby.

The first half of 1943 had seen parachute mines, firepots and incendiaries rain down on Sunderland incessantly; large areas of the town had been flattened and many lives lost. Even David and those working underground hadn't been safe; a bomb had dropped down the mine shaft in one colliery and sealed the fate of dozens of men. After this Carrie hadn't known which was worse, David and Matthew and her father and brothers working down the pit when a raid was on, or being above ground where fire-watching and warden duties were proving more and more dangerous.

Carnage and destruction had become a way of life, and there was barely a family in the whole of the north-east who had not lost loved ones to the onslaught. But all that had occurred the year before, and since the previous summer no more bombs had fallen and the barrage balloons that had arrived within days of the last two heaviest raids had been hardly used.

This cessation had been too late for two of Carrie's loved ones, however.

Early in March 1943, a parachute mine had exploded virtually in Ada's backyard. The warden who had been patrolling the area said he saw an orange flash and an explosion, and when the rescue services reached the house they found a large crater next to where Ada's shelter had been. Ada had been found crushed into the ground with her cats in her arms, and Carrie's only comfort was that her friend had died instantly.

A week later the bombers were back, and this time it was Isaac who was killed. Lillian's husband had been engaged in fire-watching duties when a row of houses close to the North Dock shipbuilding yard had been hit and all but flattened by several 500kg bombs. Isaac, two Special Constables and a warden had tunnelled into the wreckage at a point where they could hear children crying. After an hour's hard work they succeeded in reaching two girls, sisters, the eldest of whom was only six years old. The children had been trapped under a stout kitchen table, which was what had saved them; it had provided a three by five foot shield against falling debris.

When the little girls had been safely handed to waiting neighbours, Isaac and one of the Special Constables attempted to reach the mother who was clearly seriously hurt but still alive. Working in a space no more than a foot or so high, they had just uncovered the woman's legs when the rest of the house collapsed, burying both men and the injured woman.

Lillian had broken down at the funeral, and Carrie – still struggling to come to terms with the loss of Ada – had suggested that she and her children come and stay for a few days. After several weeks Lillian still hadn't been able to face the thought of returning to the rented property she and Isaac had shared for the last two years, though, and so it was agreed that Carrie's front room would again become a permanent bedsit. After a while Lillian had begun to pull round, her depression lifting a little.

It had been over the Christmas period, some months later, that Lillian had admitted to Carrie that her despair in part had been due to the prospect of Olive seeing Isaac's death as a means to moving in with her, should she rent a property or rooms of her own.

'I could manage Mam when Isaac was here, he wouldn't stand any nonsense from her and she knew it, but now . . .' Lillian gazed at her friend with tragic eyes. 'She'd be up to all her old tricks and the bairns are frightened to death of her as it is.'

'Look, lass, there's a home for you and the bairns with us until you decide otherwise,' Carrie said stoutly. 'Your mam might not like being Mrs Browell's skivvy but it was her choice, and she was lucky to get offered a roof over her head after how she'd been. David and I want you with us, all right?'

Lillian had cried and hugged her, but Carrie had noticed her friend had gone into the new year with a much more positive frame of mind, and now – a full twelve months after Isaac's death – she was almost her old self again.

Carrie now rose from the rocking chair, deciding she needed a fortifying cup of tea. A *baby*. Oh please, God, let me be right about this, please don't let it be another false alarm or

333

something like that. But it wasn't, she just knew it wasn't now that the idea had taken shape. She walked over to the range, lifted the kettle which was already full of water and placed it on the hob before resuming her seat once again.

She lay back in the rocking chair, her hands going over her flat stomach in a protective gesture. She felt pregnant now that she thought about it; the sickness and deadening tiredness she'd suffered the last couple of weeks were just the same as she'd felt early on with Matthew. That should have given her a clue if she'd stopped to think. Oh, David, David, a baby. *Your* baby. But would he be pleased, the way he had been lately?

The thought brought her up short. Make the tea first, she told herself. One thing at a time. She sat at the kitchen table and drank two cups in a leisurely fashion, one hand on her stomach, despite the fact she had to see about getting the dinner on.

Things had been . . . difficult between them lately. And then she bowed her head. More than difficult. Last autumn she had suggested they find a house where the ground floor could be designated a work area – a sewing room, fitting room and eventually, perhaps, a sales room. Of course they would need a bigger place than they already had, maybe even shop premises with a flat above, and at least one girl to assist her. But she'd be her own boss – *they* would be their own bosses, because she'd suggested David leave the pit and be part of the enterprise. She had expected him to be enthusiastic. She knew he had never really liked her working for Mr Horwood so she thought he would be all in favour of her working for herself. But he hadn't wanted to consider it or even talk things over with her, and the row that had followed had been short but unpleasant.

He had been unhappy since then, sort of closed in on himself, and the gulf between them had widened with each passing month. It frightened her. Again Carrie touched her stomach but now with a nervousness to the gesture. The loss of the old David had shown her just how much she loved him, and she did love him, so much. But she wasn't sure if he loved her any more. When they made love now it was different, *he* was different.

She shut her eyes, resting her chin on one hand, her elbow propped on the table. All their married life he had constantly told her how much he loved her in the warmth of their bed at night. He'd said she was beautiful, amazing, all sorts of things, things which could never be voiced in the cold light of day, but he didn't do that any more and the loss was more than she thought she could bear at times. But she wouldn't beg him to love her. Her eyes opened again and they were misted. She would never do that. But with a baby on the way she needed to find out where she stood – and before she told him she was expecting.

She rubbed her hand across her face and stood up. She walked across to the rack where the potatoes were, but then her gaze alighted on the pile of fabric and old clothes sitting on a chair against the wall. The rationing of clothing had been introduced in June 1941 and it operated according to a point system whereby a person could buy one complete new outfit a year. This had meant her hours at Mr Horwood's shop had gradually seen a reduction, until she was only working there one day a week. However, the 'make do and mend' order of the day had meant her own knitting and dressmaking expertise had been called on more and more by friends and neighbours.

Women's magazines were packed with handy tips on how to turn an old lace curtain into a 'dashing little bolero' and a blanket into a beautiful swagger coat, but Britain's new race of working women didn't have the time or skill to make the clothes. Very quickly Carrie had found she was having to refuse orders. Space was at a premium with Lillian occupying the front room, and what with her work at the nursery and at Horwood's shop, she was pressed for time too. Her hand rested on some parachute silk which a prospective bride had asked her to make into a nightdress and matching negligee. If David had been willing to move, she could have finished at Horwood's and perhaps reduced her hours at the nursery to concentrate on their fledgling business. It would be a success. She *knew* it would be a success and now was the time to do it so that when the war was over – and pray God that would be soon – she would have built up a loyal clientele who would continue to buy from her when fabric was more plentiful again.

The back door opened and she turned, expecting to see Lillian with Luke and Katie. But it was David who entered, bringing a gust of icy-cold March air with him.

'Hello.' Ridiculously her new knowledge had made her shy. 'I didn't expect you yet, I thought you and Walter were staying up the allotment till dinner time.' David was working the 6 a.m. to 2 p.m. shift at the moment, which meant most of his afternoons and evenings were free.

'The ground's like iron.' Their gaze held for a moment. 'You can smell the snow in the air and the sky's so low you can reach up and touch it. We're in for a packet, I reckon.'

Carrie nodded. 'There's tea in the pot if you want some. Mrs Fearn paid with some of her ration coupons for those grey trousers I cut down into a skirt for her lassie, so we've extra tea and sugar this week.'

'I could do with a cuppa.' He sat down at the kitchen table and poured himself a mug of black tea. Carrie filled a bowl with enough potatoes for dinner and brought them across to the deep white square sink to scrub and peel.

She was aware of him sitting in brooding silence and could feel his eyes on the back of her neck, but she didn't look at him. At one time, just a few months ago, he would have kissed her if no one else was here when he came in.

'They've asked for extras to work the night shift; some of the Bevin boys claim they're sick with the flu.' David's voice was mordant. Ernest Bevin had brought in a scheme whereby lads of eighteen who were eligible for call-up were sent down the pit instead of into the forces if their name began with a certain letter, and most miners were loudly vocal in their condemnation of what was a desperate measure to increase output.

'You don't think they're really sick?'

'Sick of the pit but that's all. Most of 'em are terrified of the dark, of the machines, of being cooped up miles underground, and of us most likely. They've no background in the pit, they do the least amount of work possible and even that's not handled properly. They're a danger, that's the thing. A danger to themselves and everyone else. They don't understand the way things are done, and why should they? Most of 'em are office boys or something similar. Anyway, I've said I'll work tonight.'

'You have?' Carrie turned to face him now. 'Walter too, I suppose?' They normally worked together if they could.

'Aye, he'll be there.'

Why had he said he'd work an extra shift, and the night shift at that? As the war had dragged on, coal had become even more vital and Bevin had increased wages and improved working conditions as far as possible. David now averaged four pounds a week or more, a sum undreamed of before the war. But the pits weren't any safer and there were more accidents every day because of the extra shifts and the inexperienced newcomers. Carrie didn't pause to consider her words. 'I don't want you to go, David.'

David did not reply to this. His voice softer than it had been for some time, what he did say was, 'You look tired, lass. You're on the go from morn to night, it's time to cut back on a few things.'

There was silence between them for a moment, and then, her voice as soft as his had been, she said, 'Don't go. Stay with me.'

Stay with me. What the hell did that mean? David stared at the woman whom he loved more than life itself. There had never been a time when he hadn't been aware of her existence; she had grown up with him, she'd been part of his childhood and youth, and his love of her had made him a man. He had been married to her for eighteen years and in all that time she had never once told him she loved him. Did she know that? He gazed into the great blue eyes set in a face which still had the power to turn his knees to jelly. Probably not. Oh, she had returned his physical love, he had no complaint there, and he knew from what some of the lads down the pit said that not all women were as generous with their favours as Carrie was. Some of them had to beg, demand or threaten to get their conjugal rights even once a month, and that after the priest or vicar was brought in to remind the wife of her duty before God. But Carrie always welcomed him, her body as generous as her spirit.

But generosity or gratitude wasn't love. His stomach muscles clenched. She filled her life with a million and one things – was that because he wasn't enough for her? And bringing Lillian back to live with them – had that been the act of an unselfish friend or did she want his sister in the house to avoid being alone with him more than she had to be? Damn it, he didn't know. And he couldn't ask her. He was too afraid of what the answer might be, or that she would lie. He had felt he'd had his answer to some of the nightmares which plagued him when she told him of her plans to set up her own business, but now he wasn't sure if he had jumped the gun in assuming this bid for independence was the beginning of the end of their marriage – a marriage which had begun in desperation on her part. Any port in a storm.

'I have to go, I've already said I will.' He finished his tea in one gulp. 'But I won't do any more extra over the next little while if that makes you feel better.'

She stared straight into his face. 'We have to talk, David. We can't go on like this.'

He nearly said, like what? But his innate honesty wouldn't let him dodge the issue, even though his guts had twisted into a knot. 'Aye, I know.' And then, as they heard Lillian and the children's voices in the backyard, he added, 'But not now. Tomorrow, all right? We'll talk tomorrow.'

'I'll stay home. I'll say I'm sick.' And she most likely would be come breakfast time, she thought with a thread of black humour.

She watched him wet his lips before he said, forcing a wry note into his voice, 'Aye, well, it'll be something to look forward to once the shift's ended.'

There was something in his face which made her want to press him close to her and bring her face to rest against his but she restrained herself. And the next moment Luke and Katie were running into the kitchen, cheeks as cold as iced silk and their button noses as red as cherries.

Matthew was on the afternoon shift so it was Carrie and David, Lillian and the children who sat down for dinner. When they had eaten and the washing up had been dealt with, Lillian was in and out of the kitchen and her room, putting Luke and Katie to bed, drying out the children's coats and boots which had got soaked during the day, preparing the packed lunches she and the children took each morning, and a hundred and one things besides. There was no chance for a private word with David. Not that she could have said anything really, she told herself as she watched him pull on his jacket a little while later. They needed to thrash things out properly and that couldn't be done in a hurry. But one thing was for sure, she wasn't prepared to go on like this, skirting over the surface of life. However painful, she needed to know how he felt. She had thought they had something good together, something precious, but if he didn't feel like that any more she would not try to hold him or use the baby to keep him. Her heart thudded into her throat but she lifted her chin and smiled at him as he came to kiss her, something he'd always done before leaving for the pit, except these days, since she had put her plan to him, it was just a peck on the cheek.

Tonight, however, he stopped in front of her and looked down at her for a long moment before he spoke. 'Try and get an early night, you look done in.'

She nodded but did not speak. She wanted to ask him again not to go to the pit, but knowing what his answer would be she remained silent.

They could hear Lillian quietly singing a lullaby to little Katie who had been fretful all evening, and Carrie was horrified to find the sound brought tears pricking at the back of her eyes. She couldn't have said if they were for Katie and Luke who would have to grow up without the love of the wonderful man who had been their father, for Lillian, for David, or even for herself and the unborn child, but as she stood staring at him a stillness settled on them both, a stillness which grew with every passing breath. It seemed a long time before his head slowly lowered to hers, and then he was kissing her, really kissing her, and she kissed him back with an uninhibitedness she'd only shown before in the privacy and darkness of their bed. He was speaking her name against her lips and it was a caress in itself; more endearments followed as he took her face between his hands and showered kisses over her brow, her eyes, her cheeks, her mouth . . .

'Oh, I'm sorry.'

Lillian's voice brought them jerking apart. Carrie whirled round to see her friend standing in the doorway and she found herself saying somewhat inanely, 'David's leaving for the pit.'

'I didn't— Katie wants a drink of water.' Lillian clearly didn't know where to put herself. 'I'll come back in a minute.'

She had gone before Carrie could say anything more, and as she turned to look at David again she saw he wasn't smiling as she had half expected but was still watching her intently. 'I have to go.'

No you don't. Don't turn up, say you were sick tomorrow. It might make things awkward with one man short but that doesn't matter. But David wouldn't do that. He had given his word and he would stick by it. She nodded. 'Be careful.'

'You too. Remember a shelter's only a shelter if you shelter in it.'

This had been their stock goodbye at the height of the bombing, and Carrie smiled as she said, 'There hasn't been a raid in months and months. Hitler's got bigger fish to fry than Dock Street.'

'You never know, just keep your wits about you. Disaster strikes when you least expect it.'

He drew her gently to him again as he spoke, but this time kissed her lightly on the lips before almost immediately putting

341

her from him. He walked across the room, pulling on his cap low over his eyes.

He didn't look back in the scullery; he opened the back door and stepped out into the bitter wind and driving snow, adjusting his muffler closer round his neck as he walked across the yard. At the gate he did look round as though he knew she would be standing on the back step.

He did not speak. He simply raised one hand to her, and as he stood there he looked very big and broad and strong in the whirling snow. And then he turned, closed the gate and was gone.

Carrie stood quite motionless for a full minute, staring out into the whiteness. It was a blizzard. The thought dissipated the last of the stillness, and with its going her heart began to beat faster.

She should not have let him go. She should have stopped him. Suddenly it was so clear. She ran to the gate and looked frantically up and down the back lane, calling his name. But the only answer was the howling of the wind through the spinning snowflakes.

Chapter Twenty-one

'Walt, where are you going? I thought you were doing the extra shift along with your David and the rest of us.'

'Aye, I am.' Walter nodded at the man who had spoken. He had downed a pint with this pal and a few other miners over the last couple of hours, not because he had particularly fancied a drink but because Renee had told him she'd be out all evening when he had called in at her place of work earlier to tell her about the extra shift. He hadn't believed her explanation that she was going dancing with some of the girls she worked with, but since Veronica had got involved with the Land Army and gone down south, he'd ceased caring what his wife got up to. Or that was what he told himself anyway.

'Well, lad, I hate to point out the obvious but the pit's this way.' The other man crooked his thumb over his shoulder.

Walter grinned. 'I know, I know, I ain't lost me marbles yet. I'm peckish though. There's just enough time for me to nip home and get a bite to bring down with me if I'm sharp about it.'

He turned as he spoke and walked away from the public house which was situated close to the colliery entrance. He crossed Southwick Road a moment later where the end of Pilgrim Street began.

He'd have been happy to leave the pub an hour ago when

that bunch of GIs had walked in, he thought morosely as he walked through the whirling snow, his head down and his collar up. With their snazzy uniforms, endless supplies of forgotten luxuries and smart Yankee chitchat, the lot of them thought they were the cat's whiskers. He didn't know one woman who hadn't been bowled over by the American soldiers, or one man who wasn't convinced that the parties they hosted on their bases for the local bairns, where they plied them with ice cream and fresh fruit and chocolate bars, weren't just a ruse to get into the women's drawers.

Overpaid, oversexed and over here. It might be a phrase bandied about in the pit by one or two smart alecs, but by gum it was true. He just hoped there wasn't an American base close to where Veronica was if the local lasses hereabouts were anything to go by. A pair of nylon stockings and some nail varnish or perfume and they were anybody's. Look at young Dick Allingham, poor devil. Comes home on leave to find his wife five months gone and him not having been around for going on nine. Like he'd said in the pub, what could you do when the GIs were earning nigh on three pounds ten shillings a week and a British soldier just fourteen shillings? The lasses went on like the ugliest Yank was a film star.

His house was situated halfway down Pilgrim Street and as Walter opened the front door it was all in darkness. He didn't bother to put the light on, feeling his way down the hall and walking through into the quiet kitchen where the glow from the range gave the slightest of illumination. The kitchen was furnished very well, as was the rest of the house, but Walter didn't notice his surroundings. He walked across to the bread bin and fetched out half a loaf of the grey, rough-grained bread everyone ate now. He had just entered the pantry where he knew a large shive of spam pie and some cold potatoes were residing, when he thought he heard the front door open.

The days had long since gone when he and Renee called a greeting to each other as they entered the house, so he continued putting the food into his bait tin. Then he stepped back into the main part of the kitchen, expecting his wife to walk through the door any moment. But she didn't. He cocked his head. He could hear voices in the front room, or Renee's voice at least and her unmistakable gurgle of a laugh. Just hearing that laugh had had the power to make him rock hard at one time but now it merely irritated him. Perhaps she had been telling the truth for once about going out with a friend or two; she'd recently had the front room done up with a new three-piece suite and fancy sheepskin rug in front of the fireplace, and no doubt she was showing it off now. She rarely bothered to make sure the pantry was stocked but the house always had to be immaculate.

He turned the collar of his coat back up, made sure the lid was firmly in place on his bait tin and prepared to leave the house by the back door, knowing Renee wouldn't appreciate him looking in on her and one of her pals in his working clothes. It would spoil the effort she'd taken with the front room.

He actually had his hand on the back door when he heard the laugh. A man's laugh. He froze, then turned round very, very slowly. He walked out of the kitchen and into the hall, and he was a foot or so away from the front room door, which was open a chink, when he heard a male voice say, 'You're one swell dame, you know that, don't you? One swell dame.'

Walter's mouth dropped open.

'You're not so bad yourself.' Renee's voice held a husky note now and the tone was familiar.

He knew what he was going to see when he pushed open the door to its fullest extent, but still the sight of the two naked bodies writhing on the sheepskin rug in the mellow light of one oil lamp was like a punch in the stomach. 'What the hell are you doing with my wife?' he bellowed.

'*Holy cow!*' The man who jumped to his feet was hardly a man at all, he didn't look a day over eighteen, but even stark naked he was every inch a GI with his perfect haircut and tanned skin. He was also acutely embarrassed. He grabbed his trousers and attempted to put one leg into them. In his panic he fell over against the sofa.

In contrast Renee just stood there, making no effort to cover herself. It was the American who, having managed to scramble into his trousers, threw her dress at her, saying to Walter, 'Hey, man, I'm sorry. I'm sorry. She said she was a widow.'

'I am.' Renee held the dress against her body which was still as magnificent as when Walter had first made love to her in their courting days. 'I've been a widow for years and years, haven't I, Walter? Your husband doesn't have to die for you to be made a widow. Didn't you know that?'

'You whore.' His gaze was fixed on Renee and her brave stance faltered a little as she took in the simmering rage at the back of his eyes. 'To bring one of them into my home.'

'Look, I didn't know, OK? She said—'

As the American approached him, Walter's right fist shot out, making hard contact with his square chin. The American reeled backwards and Renee screamed. He recovered his footing and stood with a hand to his jaw, staring warily at Walter.

'You've already told me what she said.' Walter's eyes didn't leave Renee. 'Now get out.'

'OK, OK.' He didn't bother to put on the rest of his clothes but gathered them up along with his socks and shoes and scuttled out past Walter.

Renee didn't say another word until they heard the front door slam, and then, with a coolness that worked like petrol on the flame of Walter's anger, she said, 'Poor boy, you've frightened him now,' and she pulled on her dress without bothering with her underclothes which were scattered about the cord carpet. 'He'll catch his death out there.'

'How many have you brought back here when I've been working?'

'What?'

'You heard me. How many?'

'Oh, for goodness' sake, Walter.'

She actually made to walk past him but he caught her arm, wrenched her round and threw her back into the room.

'How many?'

He didn't move but Renee backed away further. She turned her head away and muttered, 'He's the first, I swear it.'

She was lying. He knew it without a shadow of a doubt. He could feel himself shrinking at the knowledge that the neighbours must know what she had been up to. Nothing went on round these parts but that the whole street weren't aware of it. They'd all be talking, the old wives gossiping over the gate in the backyard and the men chewing him over as they sat in the pub of an evening. Poor old Walt, couldn't keep his missus satisfied, have you heard? Has 'em back to the house now, she does, bold as brass. Be a red light in the window before long, you mark my words. He had heard them with other folk; he knew how they would be. There would be the jokers whose comments would become cruder and cruder depending on how much beer or encouragement they got; worse, there would be those who felt sorry for him. Does he know? No? Well, someone ought to put him in the picture, poor blighter. I'd want to know if it was me.

But no one had.

'You whore.' This time it was a low snarl. 'In our bairn's home, in my home—'

'Yours and Veronica's! Oh aye, you might well say yours and Veronica's. That's the way you've always thought, isn't it? Right from her birth I've been pushed out of the picture.'

'Don't you come that. It was you who went fair barmy when you found out you were having her, it was like old Nick himself had lain with you. And after, you wanted nowt to do with me. Nowt to do with me but plenty to do with that Hughie Fleming. Thought I hadn't twigged, didn't you, but I'm not as daft as you think. And what was he? A two-bit manager in a tuppenny-ha'penny factory, but he had the time for larking about and having a tumble, didn't he? Poncing about in his neat little suit, the damn upstart.'

'Don't you call Hughie an upstart.' Renee seemed to swell with anger. 'He was ten times the man – twenty – that you are.'

'He was nowt. They're all nowt. Any man who takes another man's wife—'

'Oh, don't come the holier than thou act, not you. Anyway, you'd be none the wiser if you'd done what you said and gone on the night shift with the rest of your beer-swilling, foul-mouthed cronies.'

'That's all I am to you, isn't it?'

They were staring at each other, their gazes locked and their mutual hate snaking between them, and when Renee spoke she fairly hissed the words at him. 'You want to know what I think of you? You really want to know? Then I'll tell you. You called Hughie nowt but he was a man, a real man, something you've never been. You grub about under the earth all day like a repulsive insect and even when you've bathed you still smell of dirt. It's in your nails, your ears, the crevices of your skin

348

like those blue marks that cover you. You disgust me, do you know that?' She had moved close to him in her rage, her angry features now thrust to within a foot or so of his white face. 'I hate you, Walter Sutton. I hate the look of you, the sound of you, and my flesh creeps if you touch me—'

The sound Walter made cut off Renee's voice. It was not human, and his face did not resemble the quiet, melancholy, dull man she had lived with for nineteen years. She did not have time to reflect that she had pushed him too far because in a flash his hands were round her neck, squeezing the breath out of her.

She clawed at the iron grip, she kicked and fought until she lost her footing and brought them both falling to the floor, but still Walter did not loosen his hold, not even when Renee's heels began to scrabble convulsively and an engorged tongue protruded through her lips.

It was a full minute before Walter's hands relaxed their death grip, and then he continued to kneel by the body for some moments more, his breath coming in rasps and his eyes glazed.

The fire his wife had lit earlier was blazing now, the fancy guard in shining brass which Renee had bought to protect the new sheepskin rug waiting to be put in place. When a burning coal rolled on to the hearth and came to rest against the edge of the rug, Walter stared at it, watching as the pale cream wool began to blacken and smoulder.

By the time he left the house by the back door the rug was well and truly alight. He kept on walking through the fierce blizzard, his pace steady, the bait tin in his hand. He had to report to the colliery for his shift. That was as far ahead as he was thinking for now.

* * *

349

'You cut it fine, didn't you? Good job Tom Burns is on, another deputy would have seen to it you were fined a good whack for being late. Andy Blyton for example. He fines you for breathing, he does.'

Walter nodded to the man who had just spoken to him but said nothing, which wasn't like him. David stared at his brother as the cage took them downwards. Walter looked like death warmed up.

'Aye, well, for every overman or deputy who's a pain in the backside, there's one like Tom who's right canny.' Another man joined in the conversation. 'Little Dickie Cowan gave him a mouthful the other day, cheeky little so-an'-so, but Tom just clipped his lug and told him to watch his mouth. There's more than one who'd have reported him to the office. Sixteen, Dickie is, and thinks he knows it all.'

'Aye, I know the lad. Cocky little runt. Gives me a headache, he does.'

'It's a pain in the arse he gives me, man.'

Under cover of the laughter David said quietly, 'You all right, Walt? You look rough.'

'Aye, I don't feel too good. Gyppy belly, that's all.' He had killed her. Dear God, dear God, help me. What had possessed him? Why hadn't he just turned round and walked out like he'd done a hundred times before when she went for him? But he hadn't known before that she was bringing Yanks back to the house. He hadn't meant to do it, not kill her. He'd just wanted to stop her saying those things, things which always made him feel less than a man. Oh, Veronica, Veronica. A wave of sickness swept over him and he wanted to vomit. What was he going to say to his bairn?

He raised his eyes and glanced at Sandy who was over the other side of the packed cage which had just jolted to a stop.

Renee was Joan and Sandy's bairn like Veronica was his. He squeezed his eyes shut, letting some of the others push past him into the roadway, and when he opened them again Sandy was in front of him. Like David, he commented, 'You don't look too grand the night, Walt. You all right?'

'Aye, aye.'

With David on one side of him and Sandy on the other, Walter began to walk in-bye, and Sandy, speaking directly to Walter as he always did when the two brothers were together, said, 'You heard owt from Ned recently? London's taken a hammering in this war and no mistake.'

Walter shrugged. 'He was all right the last time he wrote, back in February.' He would have to say something, he couldn't keep this up. He felt sick, he couldn't breathe. Oh, Renee, Renee. Veronica . . .

He stumbled, and David said, 'Steady, man, steady. You don't want to brain yourself before you get to the face.' His voice was wry.

Walter managed a weak grin. He'd tell them after, not down here. You needed to keep your wits about you, especially now when the increased need for coal to fight the war meant they were cutting deeper and deeper into the wall of the face. The cutting machines that had been introduced over the last ten years saved a lot of blood, sweat and toil but they produced a constant cloud of coal and stone dust. And you couldn't hear yourself think with hard steel blades slashing and screeching against stone and pneumatic drills hissing and hammering. But he wouldn't mind that today. He didn't want to think.

The deputy was waiting for them as they approached their place of work, and he nodded a greeting at them. 'There's been more pockets of gas released the last shift than I've noticed in a long time, lads. It's collecting under the roof

351

with the poor ventilation we've got this far in, so watch yourselves.'

'Damn the gas, Tom. It's the dust and muck in me bait that bothers me. The missus does me right proud an' all; I wouldn't dare tell her I can't tell if she's given me caviar or best steak.'

'You should be so lucky, Alf.'

'You wouldn't like caviar anyway, man. Give me a nice bit of cod with plenty of batter any day.'

'Oh aye? You're something of a connoisseur of caviar, are you? Goes with the dinner suit an' bow tie you're wearin', does it?'

As Walter listened to the lads chaffing each other, he thought, that was me yesterday. And now everything had changed. He'd done murder. *He'd murdered his wife.* His stomach turned right over and the bile came up into his mouth. He rested one hand against the wall of the face. 'You go on a minute,' he said. 'I'm feeling—'

But he never got to finish the sentence. One moment David and Sandy were looking at him, the next there was a noise so loud it came out of the top of his head and he was flying through the air, men tumbling about him as clouds of dust hit his face and eyes and filled his mouth and nose. He landed hard on his back, arching up over a piece of sharp rock, and as the pain hit he knew he screamed but then he lost consciousness and didn't know any more.

David hit the ground, landing on his front, and in the same moment he was aware he was on fire. He could hear other men screaming and tearing at their burning clothes and he rolled over and over in an effort to put out his own smouldering jacket and trousers. Some of the men had already stripped down to their underpants, boots and knee pads because where

352

they were working was the hottest place in the pit, and he didn't like to think what the flames had done to them.

When he was sure his clothes were out he lay still, and he became aware that there was a roar in his ears like a giant waterfall. He thought his eardrums had burst. It was blacker than pitch, no light at all. A measure of hearing returned and he could make out groans and cries around him. He felt as dizzy as when he'd gone on a pirate's ship at one of the miners' galas.

'Walter? Walter, man?' As he tried to rise to his knees the pain he'd felt in his leg intensified, telling him it was broken, but he fought it, calling again, 'Walter?'

'Is that you, David?'

It was Sandy's voice that answered him, and David gasped, 'Sandy? Where are you?'

'Here.' The next moment a hand touched him and he realised Sandy must have landed right next to him in all the mayhem. 'It's a bad 'un, lad. There's plenty not movin' who were a bit further on. Look, we've got to try an' get back to the cage. The roof's down. Did you see Billy earlier?'

'Billy? No, is he doing the extra shift?'

'Aye, but I don't know where he's workin'. Likely his section's all right. By, you can taste the gas, man, we've got to get out of here. This might not be the end of it.'

'I can't go without Walter.' David was crawling now, touching bodies which either groaned or remained ominously silent, but within seconds he came to the roof fall and his way was blocked.

There were one or two other men stumbling about and they obviously had the same idea as Sandy and were trying to orientate themselves in order to go back the way they had just come. There were three men able to walk, of whom

Sandy was one, and two others, like David, who were injured but able to crawl. They checked the bodies on the floor for heartbeats and found only one who was still breathing. When he stirred, saying, 'Renee? Renee?' David's heart leaped out of his chest.

'Walter? You all right?'

The answer was a muffled groan, and then his brother said, 'I can't move, man. David, David, I can't move.'

'Don't worry, you'll be all right.' He crawled towards the sound of Walter's voice, reaching out with his hand until he touched his brother's face.

'We've got to get moving, lads,' said one of the other men.

'Aye, you go on,' Sandy answered him. 'Me an' David'll bring Walter.' If Walter couldn't move, ten to one his back was broken. Getting him out would be slow and difficult; there was no point in holding everybody up.

The others crawled off, keeping as low as they could in the thick, dust-filled air. Some minutes later, when they'd managed to drag Walter's inert body a few yards, the roof collapsed.

When the noise and dust had settled, Sandy was surprised to find he was still alive. He had to cough and spit several times before he could croak, 'David? David, man?' There was similar coughing and choking at the side of him. 'You got Walter there?'

Two voices answered him, and the brief elation they all felt at still being alive was quickly extinguished by the realisation that they were trapped in a pocket of air; the roof had come down in front of them and to the rear. There was no way of knowing how far ahead the others were or if they were clear.

Sandy had been half expecting the fall after the force of the explosion. Everyone knew the roof on this stretch had been weakened by continually dripping water from the North

Sea above, and the extensive undercutting of latter years and constant firing hadn't helped. The props, however well they'd been put up – and some were useless, thanks to the Bevin boys – could only take so much, and even the biggest of them, some so heavy it might take two men to lift them, could splinter and snap like a matchstick. It didn't take much, and the explosion had been more than a little bang.

Every miner knew that in a fall, whatever else was happening, you could be sure the oxygen was running out. Every time someone breathed, they used up what little air was left and replaced it with carbon dioxide from their own lungs. It was an inescapable fact, and no one could help it.

'They'll come for us.' David's voice was bracing despite the agony his leg was giving him. He didn't add, pray God they'll be in time, but they all thought it.

'Aye, they'll come all right. I just hope them in front of us got clear before the roof fell,' Sandy said quietly.

'Aye.' David cleared his throat. 'Thanks for staying back with us, Sandy. You could've been long since gone with the others.'

'I'd never have been able to look me lass in the eye again if I'd left you,' Sandy said gruffly in reply. 'She thinks a bit of you, does Carrie.'

The roof above them creaked and stretched, and they became silent. A little while later David said, as though Sandy had just spoken, 'I dunno about that.'

'What?'

'Carrie thinking a bit of me.'

'Don't be daft, man.' It was Walter who spoke and his voice was weak. 'She thinks the world of you, a blind man could see that.'

'Maybe.'

'Maybe?' Sandy's voice carried a note of irritation and something else which was sharper. 'It was her thinking a bit of you that got her—' He stopped abruptly. 'Oh, to hell with it. It's all water under the bridge now.'

But it wasn't. David's eyes strained in the darkness which was blacker than anything above ground. Even with the blackout, the darkness above was never complete like it was down the pit. He'd often heard folk say they couldn't see a hand in front of their face when their blackout curtains were drawn and the lights were off. More than once he'd been tempted to tell them they didn't know they were born, but he never had. Unless they came underground and switched off the lamps they wouldn't know what he was on about anyway.

The roof settled itself a little more, the sound prompting David to say, 'Look, Sandy, there's something I want you to know.' He suddenly couldn't bear the idea of going to meet his Maker without coming clean with Carrie's da. 'Matthew, well, it's not like you think.'

'It never is, lad.'

'No, what I mean is, he's not mine. Matthew isn't mine.'

The silence was intense, and again it struck David how completely they were entombed. And then Sandy's voice came, tense and low. 'What the hell do you mean, he's not yours?'

'Carrie was . . .' Damn it, how did he say it? 'She was forced, the night of Renee and Walter's wedding.'

'You're tellin' me—' Sandy stopped abruptly. His voice rose as he went on, 'You're sayin' my lass was taken down against her will? My Carrie? You're mad, the explosion's addled your brain.'

'I'm sorry, Sandy.' Something in David's voice stopped further protest.

356

'Who?' Just one word but David was glad he couldn't see Sandy's face.

'I don't know.' And then as Sandy made an exclamation of disbelief, he said, 'I swear I don't know, Sandy. She . . . well, she might have told me if I'd pressed her, but to be honest I didn't want to know. I was prepared to take the bairn on but I felt if I knew who the father was he'd forever be there looking out of its face.'

'I can't believe it.' But Sandy's broken voice told the other two men he believed it only too well. 'I knew somethin' was wrong that night. Well, you saw the state she was in, lad. An' after, she was never the same, never. By, a bit lass, that's all she was. I'd hang for the filthy scum if I got me hands on him, even now. What man'd do that to a bit bairn?'

David made no reply to this, and after a moment Sandy said, 'Why didn't she tell her mam an' me?'

'She was confused, scared, ashamed.' David moved slightly and the searing pain in his leg almost made him pass out. After a moment he was able to say, 'She might have told you though after we'd married if I hadn't told her I didn't want anyone to know the bairn wasn't mine. I . . . I can't explain it, Sandy, but taking Carrie and the baby on was all right, I'd have walked through coals of fire for her for ever and a day, I still would, but . . .' He swallowed. 'Other folk knowing . . .'

'Aye, well, I can understand that, lad, aye, I can. I think I'd be the same, although I don't know if I'd have been big enough to do what you did.'

It was all the recompense David wanted for the years of being treated like a leper by this man who had once been like a father to him.

Sandy went on, 'I should've known you weren't the sort of lad to take a lass down on the side.'

357

David protested. 'How? You were told I was the father and I'd got her into trouble. I'd have reacted like you. You love her, course you were angry. But . . . I wanted to set things straight, once and for all.'

The three of them knew what he was saying. The chances of their being rescued before the air ran out were minimal. They had all been part of rescue teams in their time, and the pit was chary about giving up its prizes once they had been marked.

There was silence for a few moments, and then Sandy said, 'I'm glad you've told me, lad. It's eaten me up over the years, the thought of you doin' the dirty on me. Joan used to give me gyp over thinkin' that way, tellin' me I was puttin' meself before our Carrie, but it wasn't like that, not really. You were – are – a son to me an' I thought I knew you through an' through. It appears I did after all.'

The sound of Walter's laboured breathing was audible in the quietness that followed, and when he spoke, both David and Sandy felt a sense of relief because his voice dispelled the intense emotion that had been quivering in the small space. Their relief was shortlived, however. 'I need to say something an' all. I found Renee with a bloke, one of them GIs. I've done for her.'

Walter's words were cut off by a gurgle in his throat and he coughed, or tried to cough. The sound was painful, and David's arms were about his brother by the time the rasping gasps were over. 'Lie quiet, man, don't try to talk.'

'Did . . . did you hear me?'

'Aye, I heard you.' David's voice was quiet, embarrassed. 'You found Renee with someone.'

'One of them Yanks. They were sporting on the rug like a pair of newlyweds.'

'Walter, man, we don't have to hear this.'

358

'I've killed her, Sandy. I've done for her.'

'You don't mean it.' This was from David and said in a tone of incredulity threaded with horror.

The sound of shifting stones and rubble told them Sandy was moving, and then he, too, was kneeling by Walter. 'You've killed her? Not just knocked her about?'

'She . . . she was screaming at me, saying things. I wanted to shut her up, that was all, but . . . Man, I didn't mean to do it.'

'What about the Yank?'

'He'd skedaddled after I hit him.'

A curse vibrated in the darkness but it was from David, not Sandy.

'I was going to tell you once we were up.' Walter's voice was hoarse and straining, each word an effort. 'She . . . she's been with lots, it was that Hughie Fleming from the factory to start with. I . . . I dunno but something just snapped tonight. One minute she was shouting and the next me hands were round her neck. I just kept pressing and pressing.'

David made a sound deep in his throat but there was still no reaction from Sandy, not until Walter gasped, 'I'm sorry, Sandy. Man, I'm sorry, I'm sorry.'

The stones shifted again, and then Sandy said, 'She was my daughter but she was your wife, lad, an' I won't pretend I hadn't heard whispers she was being a mite free an' easy, but then half the flamin' womenfolk are. It's the stockings an' all, it's turnin' their heads. But I didn't know she was actually . . . Look, are you sure she's not just unconscious or somethin'?'

There was a plea in the words, but Walter couldn't respond to it with anything except the truth. 'She's dead, Sandy.'

'Oh, man, you fool.' David's voice was thick. 'You'll go down the line for this.'

'There's only one place I'm going, little brother, and I reckon it won't be long.' Walter coughed again, the gurgle more pronounced, and as he tried desperately to get his breath, David's arms still tight round him, Sandy spoke.

'You know we've never got on, Renee an' me, but I wouldn't have wished this for all the tea in China. That said, I can understand how she could provoke you to doing somethin' silly, lad. She could get me riled up quicker than a pig in a poke, an' but for her mam gettin' between us more than once I'd have done somethin' I'd have regretted. But to think of her going like that, it's hard. We haven't spoken in years, you know that an' all, but nevertheless she was my daughter an' she was a bonny little lass as a babby.'

'I'm sorry.'

'Aye, I know you are, lad. I know you are.'

Whether Sandy would have said different if Walter wasn't fighting for his breath, David didn't know, but when in the next moment his brother began choking, he was aware of Sandy helping him hold Walter up a little. The sound was terrible, it seemed to fill their space. David said frantically, 'Bend him forward, that might help.' There was a rattling from Walter's throat, and something warm trickled on to David's hand. He realised it was Walter's blood. 'He's drowning in his own blood.' David was crying now, almost delirious from the pain in his leg as he tried to manipulate Walter forward.

Sandy said, 'Easy, lad, easy. He's gone, let him down,' but David found he couldn't let Walter go. His arms tightened round his brother.

'No, no. Dear God, not like this. Don't let him die like this.'

'There's nowt you can do, lad, an' happen it's for the best after what he's told us. This way he won't have to face being shut up an' knowin' what's at the end of it, 'cos ten to one it'd be a hanging job.'

'That's assuming we're going to get out of here.'

'Aye, there is that an' all.'

Silence reigned for a few minutes as they both tried to come to terms with what they had heard and Walter's death. After a while David gently laid his brother on the ground and shifted himself into a more comfortable position. The movement shot fire through his broken leg and he bit his lip to stop himself groaning out loud.

'This is going to hit young Veronica hard,' Sandy said. 'It's enough her mam and da both going, but to know it was her da that did her mam in. She'll never get over it. It'll ruin her life.'

David said nothing. What could you say to something like this? he asked himself grimly. He felt the darkness was pressing in on him; it was thick and heavy and he didn't dare ask Sandy if he thought the air was running out because he didn't want to know the answer. Walter dead, maybe the rest of their shift too if they hadn't got clear when the roof came down, and he wasn't going to have the chance to say goodbye to Carrie. To tell her one last time he loved her. Suddenly it didn't matter a damn if she loved him like he wanted her to, all that mattered was that she knew what she meant to him. He'd been a fool the last months, a proud, stupid fool, but he couldn't turn back the clock and he couldn't put things right.

'David, you awake?'

Sandy's voice was urgent and David knew he was really asking if he was unconscious. 'Aye, I'm awake.' He knew exactly how Sandy felt. The thought of being all alone down here without anyone to talk to didn't bear thinking about. 'Just trying to conserve air like they always tell us to do.'

'Damn that. There'll either be enough or there won't, an' us talkin' won't make that much difference. Look, man, I've been thinkin'. I got the impression Walter's told no one else what happened.' David gave a grunt of agreement. 'Well, if he hasn't an' if no one saw him leave the house, who's to say he did Renee in? It could've been anyone, couldn't it? That Yank she was with for instance. I'd heard she was spreadin' it about a bit; it could be any number of blokes who might have been to the house.'

David was feeling light-headed, and he was sure the air was going. 'Meaning?'

'Meanin' we say nowt if we get out of here. Sayin' anythin' can't help Renee but if we keep quiet maybe Veronica'll never know. Eh? What do you say?'

'What if they put someone else in the frame? This Yank for instance?'

'That's different. But this way it'll spare Veronica an' make it easier for the family. The women are going to have enough to deal with with losin' Renee an' Walter.'

'Aye.' It was all theoretical anyway. They were never going to see the light of day again. He hoped Billy was all right where he was, and it wasn't likely the twins had put their hands up for an extra shift. They were too busy doing the rounds of the local dance halls come evening, seeing what they could pick up after the Yanks had had their choice, or going to the Regal or the Gaiety for the same reason. Damn it. David shut his eyes, his head swimming. Why the hell had he agreed to work tonight? It wasn't as if they were desperate for the money.

David and Sandy talked for some time more, both men secretly amazed at how easily their old relationship had been restored and each one regretting the loss of all the years between. After a while, breathing became more difficult, and by unspoken mutual consent they became quiet, sitting now with their shoulders touching in the pressing blackness.

Was Alec still alive in that prisoner-of-war camp? David's mind was wandering and half the time he wasn't sure if he was awake or asleep. They hadn't heard a word since the notice that he had been captured, but that didn't mean anything, not in this war. Wicked so-an'-so's, the Nazis, if even a quarter of what was being reported was true. Matthew talked of him less now, but he had the idea the boy thought of his uncle just as much.

Matthew . . . David rested his head against the hard rock, a consuming tiredness taking hold. He wished he could have been more of a father to the lad; he wished they could have got on better; he wished he'd had a bairn of his own, just one. Oh, Carrie, Carrie. Remember the good times, the times we've laughed and loved, not the last months . . .

His body slumped a little, settling into the rock face beside that of his father-in-law who was now quite still.

Chapter Twenty-two

The crowd at the pit gate was thick despite the fact that the weather hadn't let up in the last hours and the blizzard was still raging. There were no hysterics or weeping and wailing among the women, who made up the greater part of the assembly, and the bairns were silent, the men grim-faced. At times like this the mining community thought as one; there was no need for words.

Carrie was standing with her mother and Billy's young wife either side of her; Matthew, Danny and Len were behind her, but she could take no comfort from their presence. Renee was dead, and David, her da, Billy and Walter might be too for all they knew. It seemed impossible but it was happening, and her conscience was crying so loud in her ears she couldn't hear anything else. She hadn't told him. She hadn't told David about the baby, but it was more than that. In the last few hours she hadn't been able to hide from the fact that she had taken David's love, expected it, treasured it and yet never once had she told him how much she had come to love him. And why?

She moved her head in the dull grey light of early morning, the wind so raw it cut through any amount of clothing like a knife. Because she had always held something back from him, some last commitment which would entail saying the words, I love you. Once they had been said, once she had told him how she had come to feel for him, she would become vulnerable again, open to rejection and being used, discarded. But that was stupid, so, so stupid. It was David who was her husband, David who loved her, not Alec. And David would never behave like Alec had done all those years ago.

She had thought she was over the rape. She raised her eyes and stared unseeingly. She thought she had put it behind her years ago that day on Penshaw Hill, but now she understood that a residue of fear had persuaded her that the love she felt for David was really gratitude mixed with tenderness and deep affection. But it wasn't. It was true love – full, mature and achingly real.

When they had brought what remained of Renee out of the charred shell of the house, Carrie hadn't at first been able to take in the fact that her sister was dead. A house fire, a stupid, senseless house fire, after Renee had come through all the bombing without a scratch. As Carrie had stood there weeping with her mother and a couple of the neighbours who had come running to fetch her, it had struck her how unhappy her sister had been. And Renee had been unhappy, deep in the heart of her. How could you be anything else when the person you were bound to, the man you'd promised to share the rest of your life with, was barely more than a stranger living in the same house?

Standing there in the swirling snow, Carrie had counted her blessings, and the main one was David. And then, with the smoke still curling in the sky and the acrid smell in their nostrils, someone had come running to tell them there had been an explosion at the pit.

Fear and panic gripped her. What would she do if David was dead? She must have made a sound in her throat because Matthew spoke from behind her, his hand on her shoulder.

'Don't worry, Mam, it'll be all right. The rescue team has sent word they're on the point of breaking through the first fall and they can hear knocking.'

His voice was gentler than it had been for years and if he had spoken like this in the normal run of the mill Carrie would have been delighted. Matthew had become increasingly withdrawn and morose of late, his bad humour always worse when he had visited Olive at Alec's house. She knew he was missing Veronica, but the last time his cousin had come home for a few days, Carrie had got the impression they had quarrelled, although when she had tentatively put it to him he had not been forthcoming.

Now, however, his mellowing brought her no warmth or comfort. She felt numb and icy-cold, but she forced herself to reach up and put her hand over his for a moment in a wordless gesture of thanks.

It was another hour before the first batch of survivors, one of whom was Billy, came up. These men, along with several other sections, had been working in a different area to where the explosion occurred but had been cut off by the fall in the main road. They were all unharmed and to a man they wanted to stay and work with the rescue team, whose most urgent job was to establish a fresh-air base and get the ventilators operating again as they moved forward to the explosion site. It appeared the roof had come down in several places, and there was no knowing how many men were still alive.

Billy's wife fell into his arms, and Carrie hugged her brother and wept tears of relief, but the strange sense of unreality that had come over her in the last hours increased rather than decreased with the knowledge that some of the men were safe. It somehow emphasised the fact that those who were trapped were in an increasingly bad way.

Joan clung to Billy as though she would never let him go. She seemed to have aged twenty years since they had brought Renee's body out of the house. And when the first rescue team was due to be relieved and she realised that her two youngest sons and her grandson intended to be part of the second, she wanted to stop them.

'They're all miners, Mam,' Carrie reasoned with her, 'and Da's down there, along with David and Walter. You have to let the twins and Matthew go, don't you see? They need to do this, they'd never forgive themselves if they didn't go.'

She happened to glance at Matthew as she finished speaking and found her son's eyes hard on her face. Something in his expression caused a chill to sweep over her. He didn't want to go down, he was only going because the other men would think it bad if he didn't. She stared at him, her stomach turning over as she read the resentment her words had caused. And then his gaze dropped and he turned away to answer something Len had said, leaving Carrie more shaken than ever. He didn't care about David and the others, not in his heart of hearts. The only person he really cared about on God's earth was Alec. She closed her eyes, sickness rising up into her throat. She couldn't pretend any longer. He'd gone from her. Somehow in the last years he had gone from her as completely as if he was one of the lads who had been lost in the war. She muttered an excuse and hurried away to find a privy where she was violently sick. Her stomach twisted into knots as she strained time and time again.

Don't let me lose the baby, Lord, not on top of everything else. When she had finished, her legs were trembling so badly she had to sit for a while. Whatever happened, she wanted this baby more than ever. If she never got to tell David he was going to be a father, she could at least raise his son or daughter in the knowledge that their da had been the most wonderful man in the world.

It was twenty hours later when the rescue party reached the first of the men who had been on David's shift. The mine had taken all of them, crushing them under the stone and coal they had mined each day of their lives.

One by one they were slowly uncovered and then gently stretchered away on their last journey in the cage, their fellow miners holding them as tenderly as they would their own bairns. Now and again an agonised groan would rend the air as a father or brother or son recognised his own, blood crying out to blood, but otherwise the job was done in almost total silence, a silence more consecrated than in any church. Hard-bitten veterans might be crying like babies but no sound would pass their mouths, the only indication of their grief the streaks of wet clean skin in coal-blackened faces.

As a ragged dawn began to break, Carrie sank quietly on to the snow in a dead faint. Only then did her mother come to herself a little. Joan took Carrie home and persuaded her to eat. Afterwards she wrapped a blanket round Carrie where she had fallen into an exhausted sleep in the rocking chair, and sat quietly by. Two hours later both women were back at the pit gate.

When the last man from under the roof fall had been brought up, word came filtering through to those at the gate that the current rescue team were going to press forward. Carrie and her mother turned as one and stared at each other.

They weren't there. The three of them, Sandy, David and Walter, weren't there. That must mean they were together somewhere surely. So there was still hope. They didn't say this out loud, it wasn't necessary – both women were of like mind.

The hours ticked on. Danny and Len finished their stint with the rescue team and joined the two women and Billy, who had come back to the pit gate after a meal and a bath. Matthew went home to bed, declaring he was spent. Carrie was surprised to find she didn't mind his going; in fact she would have gone further than that and said she was relieved if she had been capable of rationalising how she was feeling. The only people she wanted round her were those as desperate as she was.

At midday, when a weak, watery sun was shining for the first time in days, word came through that they had reached a second fall just yards behind the first and were on the point of breaking through. Because a small section of roof had held between the two falls, the going was more dangerous and slower than ever. The remaining section of roof needed shoring up and propping, and although every man on the team knew time was of the essence, they also knew any mistakes could mean they and their fellow workers were the next victims.

Through all the hours and hours of endless waiting, the time had never crept by so pitilessly as in the next little while. The blizzard had died and the world about the pit gates seemed clean for once. The covering of white on the rooftops and the glistening carpet coating the streets seemed to mock the events of the last forty-eight hours, and among the remaining folk at the gates none was more aware of this than Carrie herself. The cold white brilliance made her tired eyes ache and, ridiculously, she found herself remembering a Sunday the previous summer when she and David had taken a picnic and walked into the surrounding countryside. They had left just as it was growing light and had returned when it was dark, and David had been in his element, showing her figwort, cinquefoil, thyme, wood geranium and all sorts of other flowers and plants.

They bought a drink of milk from a farm. The cowshed was

warm and stickily scented with milky magic, and the farmer's wife, who seemed to take to them, pressed two freshly baked ham pasties into their hands, refusing any payment when they tried to offer her some coins. They ate their picnic in a sun-drenched meadow close to a small pond, and again David brought her alive to the shimmering silver-green and blue dragonflies hovering close to the still surface, when all she had seen at first was murky water. He pointed out water crickets moving in slow motion on long legs, making her laugh when he called them aquatic clowns on stilts.

Oh, David, David. All that love of nature, of life, couldn't be buried in the tomb of the pit. When he died it ought to be as an old man, and then with the sun and wind on his face or the velvety darkness of a cool night.

They had made love lying on a fragrant bed of grass and wild flowers, and it had been the first time in seventeen years of marriage that she had seen him engorged and erect. She'd seen him naked before when he bathed in the tin bath in front of the fire, but never like that day when he had worshipped her with his body and his mouth. He'd had to persuade her to take her clothes off, but once she had succumbed she'd felt as giddy as a schoolgirl although terribly shy – until, that was, he'd begun to make love to her.

An expectant rustling among the crowd and her mother's fingers tightening on her arm brought Carrie back to the present. Word had come. They had reached them, and at least one was alive.

She did not think or breathe or move – or so it felt – until one of the rescue leaders was standing in front of them. She knew this man; one of his sons had been in the same class as Matthew at school and another had recently married. The first battered body to be brought to the surface some hours before had been that of the second lad. Carrie stared into the exhausted face, and she couldn't take it in at first when he said quietly to her mother, 'Your husband is alive, Mrs McDarmount.' Then he turned to her. 'David too, lass.'

'And Walter?' It was Billy who spoke.

The man shook his head. 'I'm sorry.'

Walter would never have to be told about Renee now. Somehow Carrie could more easily comprehend that Walter was gone than that David was alive, perhaps because it was too miraculous, too wonderful to be true. 'My husband . . .' Her voice emerged as a croak and she had to clear her throat and try again. 'My husband and Da. Are they hurt?'

'Your da's relatively unscathed, cuts and bruises and the like. David's leg's in a bad way and he has a nasty cut on the back of his head. He's lost a lot of blood but he's young and strong. He'll pull through, lass.'

She was being given a second chance. Her world had exploded into hundreds of pieces but against all the odds she was being given a second chance.

And at that moment Olive said behind them, 'Well! And no one thought to tell me what was going on then! If it wasn't for them talking in the queue when we were waiting at the butchers I'd be none the wiser even now.'

Carrie heard her mother give an audible groan. She bit her lower lip before she turned and said, 'Hello, Mam.'

'Don't you "Hello, Mam" me like butter wouldn't melt in your mouth. Why wasn't I told about this?' Olive's head was poking forward, her green eyes, as round as aniseed balls, alive with hate as she stared at the object of all her venom. Carrie looked back steadily and for a moment she wondered if she should tell this terrible woman that the rest of the family, even her beloved Matthew, had agreed they didn't want her at the pit gates. She shrugged. 'Everyone knows. We assumed you'd hear and please yourself if you came or not.'

'If? *If?* Why wouldn't I want to be here? David and Walter are my lads, in case you'd forgotten.'

'Do you want to know what the news is on "your lads"?' It was Carrie's mother who spoke, anguish for the loss of Renee making her voice sharp with the woman she saw as an unnatural mother.

Olive's sallow face took on a pinker tinge. By, they were upstarts, the McDarmounts, every last one of them. She could remember a time when you could set your clock by Sandy McDarmount acting the cuddy on a Friday night when he'd had a drop. Dancing and singing enough to wake the dead, he'd be, and now here was Joan acting as though she was Lady Muck. She hoped Sandy had got his just deserts in this little lot; here's one who wouldn't miss him. Scumbags, the lot of them.

'Well?' Olive looked Joan in the eye. 'What is the news?'

'David and my da are all right,' Carrie said quietly, 'but Walter . . . I'm sorry, Mam.'

Olive blinked. So her firstborn was dead. She knew she would be considered odd if she admitted to the fact that she felt very little one way or the other. In truth Walter had irritated her from the moment he could toddle. He had been his da all over, that was the thing, and David perhaps more so. Maybe if she had married the sort of man she felt she had been destined for, someone who appreciated her taste for the finer things of life and who would have given her her own home, bought and paid for, and a good going on, she might have felt differently about her bairns. As it was, the more she had come to despise Ned for the weak-livered nowt he was, the more the feeling had rubbed off on his bairns somehow. Except Alec. Alec had been hers from the moment he had been born. Even after this little baggage in front of her with the angelic face and loose ways had beguiled him, Alec had still been her boy.

Olive raised her pointed chin, her eyes like cold green glass. 'It's no secret Walter and I didn't see eye to eye,' she said stiffly, 'but he was my bairn, Joan.' Then, glancing about her, she added spitefully, 'And where's your Renee? Shouldn't she be here, at least playing at being the good wife?'

'Don't you dare talk about my sister like that.' Carrie's eyes were flashing now. 'Renee can't be here, there was a fire at the house and—' She found she couldn't go on; her heart was crying, oh, Renee, Renee. I can't believe I'll never see you again. Renee had been so full of life, so vibrant. And then all other thoughts faded as she caught sight of her father in the distance. He walked out of the yard flanked by two of the rescue workers, and she and Joan flew to his side. He put an arm round each of them and said, 'All right, all right, don't take on so. Here I am, right as rain.'

Joan was sobbing into his chest, oblivious of the arid smell of sweat and coal dust, and over her mother's head, Carrie said, 'David?'

'He's coming, lass, but prepare yourself. His leg's pretty bad. We thought he'd just broken it but it's a bit of a mess. He passed out when we moved him and it's probably the best thing. The doctor's with him and they're taking him straight to the infirmary. You can go with him if you want.'

If she wanted? 'Oh, Da.' She reached out and touched her father's face. 'I'm so glad he was with you if this had to happen. And poor Walter.'

'Aye, poor Walter.'

'Sandy, we've lost Renee.' Joan hadn't planned to tell him like this but she found she needed him to know and she couldn't wait. 'It was an accident, a fire in the home. They . . . they think it started in her front room.'

Sandy's jaw bones worked against his skin before he said, 'Our Renee? Oh, lass, lass.'

Carrie froze as a stretcher was carried through into the yard, with a doctor walking by the side. For a second she felt unable to move, and then she made to push past into the yard. A policeman who was on duty at the gates caught at her arm. 'Sorry, lass, but you can't go in there.' She yanked her arm away with such force he had to steady himself as she slipped past him and ran to David.

The policeman must have followed her because she heard one of the rescue team say, 'Leave her be, it's her husband.' Her whole being was caught up with the man lying so deathly still. It was David and yet not David, because even in sleep or when he was resting or reading one of his botany or wildlife books, life emanated from him. 'He'll be all right?' Her voice was high as she looked at the doctor.

'Yes, yes, don't worry. I've given him something to make him more comfortable for the journey to the infirmary, that's all.' Carrie was kneeling in the snow beside the stretcher, stroking David's hair back from his brow, the tears coursing down her face, and the doctor said, 'Come along, my dear. The sooner we get him there, the sooner we can begin to mend that leg of his. I assume you're coming with us.'

Carrie did not answer because David had begun to stir. He opened his eyes very slowly as if it was a great effort. He stared at her, almost as though he didn't believe what he was seeing, and when she said, 'Oh my love, my love,' his reply bore this out because he murmured, 'I didn't think you were real.'

'I'm real.' Oblivious of everyone, she took his face into her hands and kissed him gently on the lips. Her tears wet his cheeks as she whispered, 'I love you, I love you,' over and over again.

He lifted his hand to her and she grasped it with both of hers, frightened by the whiteness of his face beneath its coating of coal dust. 'I'm coming with you, I'm never going to let you leave my side for a second again,' she whispered fiercely.

The corners of his mouth lifted slightly. 'That's going to make for some interesting times ahead,' he murmured. His heavy lids closed again although his hand continued to hold hers tightly.

Chapter Twenty-three

Olive Sutton sat rigidly in the ambulance, her gaze fixed on Carrie as she sat looking down at David. David had not opened his eyes again, nor had he spoken, but when Carrie had tried to withdraw her hand from his to climb into the ambulance, his grip had tightened until it hurt, and so they had remained joined together.

As for Olive, it wasn't maternal feeling that had made her insist on being allowed to accompany her son and his wife to the infirmary. She had already worked herself up into a cold fury at being ostracised before she reached the colliery, but the altercation at the gates followed by the sight of Carrie and David's reunion had maddened her. She was consumed by burning resentment and rage at her daughter-in-law. She had told herself so often that Carrie McDarmount was the cause of her losing her home and everything she had ever wanted that she now believed it totally.

Blubbing all over him as though she had never looked at another man in her life! Olive's teeth were clenched together so tightly her jaw was paining her. And him, daft as a brush about her, the low, common, brazen hussy. Well, he wouldn't have his rose-tinted spectacles on much longer if she had anything to do with it, Olive told herself grimly. She had always promised herself she would see her day with the McDarmount sisters, and it appeared God wouldn't be mocked. He had taken Renee to her just deserts, and now it was up to her to do her bit and see Carrie got what was coming to her. And she would do it, by, she would. There was talk of the war ending soon and she wanted the baggage long since gone by the time Alec came home. David might be a fool, but when he knew Carrie had tricked him into marriage and that he had been playing da to his brother's child for eighteen years, that would be the end.

The ambulance thudded over a pothole in the road, one of many caused by the intensive bombing last year. David stirred and moaned, and Olive's eyes narrowed as Carrie murmured, 'It's all right, dear, it's all right.' She wouldn't be 'dearing' him much longer if she did but know it, and once David had thrown the chit out, someone would need to keep house for him and Matthew.

Olive straightened her back, staring straight ahead now. And that would suit her, she'd had enough of Freda Browell to last her a lifetime. When she thought of the humiliations she'd endured at that woman's hands, treating her employer's own mother as little more than a skivvy. But she'd see her day with that one too, once her boy was home. Oh aye, Freda Browell would get short shrift all right. And what was the betting that with Margaret gone and Alec having no other bairns, he'd see fit to take Matthew into his home?

She sat picturing the years ahead. Once Alec was home from the war and had sent Freda packing, she and Matthew would leave David and move in with him. She would be mistress of her own home again, and what a home.

Time had a way of making truth out if you were patient enough, and she had been waiting for the right opportunity to speak her mind for more than a little while. Even if Carrie denied it, David only had to look at the boy with eyes unclouded

378

by his obsession for the McDarmount girl to see Matthew was Alec all over. And weak and low as he was right now, without the physical side of his love for the chit paramount, he'd see all the more clearly. She'd have a word with him as soon as he was settled, she wouldn't delay. And after all, it was kinder in the long run for him to know, wasn't it? The truth never hurt anyone.

As it happened, it wasn't possible for either Olive or Carrie to speak further with David that day. On their arrival at the infirmary, another doctor examined him while the two women sat on hardbacked chairs in the corridor outside, and he decided to operate immediately. Carrie just had time to kiss a drugged David goodbye before he was whisked out of sight. The first doctor remained with them just long enough to tell them to come back that evening although David might not be conscious by then.

He wasn't, and the following evening, on the dot of visiting time, Matthew and Carrie stood waiting in the area outside the small side ward where David had been placed for the present, and Olive joined them.

'Hello, Gran.' Matthew smiled at his grandmother and Olive smiled back.

'Hello, lad.' Olive offered her cheek for a dutiful kiss and totally ignored Carrie, who stared at her mother-in-law for a moment before giving a mental shrug.

When the visiting bell rang, Matthew stepped forward and opened the door for the two women. As Carrie entered the dismal, green-painted room, her eyes went immediately to the bed. While they had been waiting they had been informed by a brisk, no-nonsense nurse that Mr Sutton was due to be moved to the main ward tomorrow if he'd had a comfortable night, and that Doctor was pleased with his progress. But when Carrie saw the cage over the bottom part of the bed, her heart came up into her mouth despite the encouraging words.

She walked over to the bed, Olive and Matthew following her. David appeared to be asleep. The face on the pillow was as white as the sheet beneath it, but then the eyes opened and it was David looking at her, his lips parting in a smile. 'I've been waiting all day to see you,' he said, his voice sounding the same as always.

Carrie did not speak because she was finding it impossible to form coherent words; with an unintelligible murmuring she bent over him and kissed him in a way which made words quite superfluous. His hands pulled her down on to his chest so she was sitting on the bed with her upper body on his, and they remained like this, their lips joined, until a sharp little cough reminded Carrie they were not alone.

She pulled away, saying, 'Matthew and your mam . . .' but David caught her again and placed one more hungry kiss on her mouth.

Colour was hot in her face when she turned to look at Matthew and Olive. Matthew was smiling somewhat embarrassedly, but she saw immediately that Olive had taken exception to the show of affection. Carrie continued to sit on the edge of the bed, her hand in David's. 'Come and say hello, Matthew, and bring that chair closer to the bed for your grandma.' She turned back to David, her voice soft as she murmured 'I thought I was going to lose you.'

'Not me, lass. I'm built like a homing pigeon and my home is where you are. You couldn't lose me if you tried.'

Matthew approached the bed and punched David lightly on the shoulder. 'You all right then?'

'It has to be said I've been better, lad.' There was a remnant of a smile, but it faded when Olive came to the bedside.

She stared down at him for a moment before she said, 'You pulled through then.'

'Aye, Mam, I pulled through, thanks to Carrie's da.'

'Him? What did he have to do with it?'

'He helped me with Walter. But for Sandy we'd have been back at the original fall or buried under the one that took the others. Either way I'd be a goner.'

Olive did not comment on this but her chin came down into her neck. Her hands were joined on the handle of her big black handbag which was resting on the slight mound of her stomach beneath the grey coat she was wearing, and she continued to survey her son silently for a moment before she said, without any preamble, 'She's made a monkey of you. You know that, don't you?'

'What?'

'Your lady wife with her fine ideas about going up in the world. She found herself in a fix all them years ago and then along came you, bright-eyed and bushy-tailed, and before you knew where you were you were pulled in so fast it made your head spin.'

The look on his face cut off her flow of words but only for a moment. She had waited too long to have her say and nothing was going to stop her now.

'Did you ever really believe he was yours?' She gestured with her thumb at Matthew. 'After he was born, I mean?'

'Stop this. He's ill—'

'He's Alec's,' Olive went on remorselessly. 'Open your eyes, man, and see what's in front of you. She was carrying on with your brother and that's why she married you, to conceal the fact she was expecting Alec's child. You were a means to an end, that's all. That's all you've ever been and ever will be to a woman like her.'

She had to deny this, she had to stop it. The command was in her head but Carrie was gripped by paralysing shock.

'She took you for a ride, she took us all for a ride. No doubt she meant to trap Alec into marrying her but with him being betrothed to Margaret, he likely gave her the cold shoulder, and so she looked around for another pansy. And there you were.'

David's gaze moved away from Olive's face, his eyes resting first on Carrie and then moving to Matthew who was standing stock still. David knew his mother was speaking the truth; he had buried it deep in his subconscious from the beginning because he wouldn't have been able to stand living with the fact that the baby was his brother's child. And he would have killed him for forcing her. If he had known for sure, he would have gone down the line for Alec.

Even if there had still been any doubt in his mind, the look on Carrie's face confirmed that his mother was telling the truth, the vicious old witch.

His hand tightened on Carrie's but he did not look at her or at Matthew because the boy's face was painful to behold. He kept his gaze on the woman who had borne him, speaking slowly and quietly as he said, 'There are no secrets between my wife and I, there never have been. You can't hurt us, Mam, don't you know that by now? You can't touch us, and the reason is because you're not worth that much' – he clicked his fingers – 'to me or the rest of the family.'

'Don't you dare talk to me like that, your own mother.'

'Mother?' David shook his head slowly. 'You might have been the woman who brought us into the world, but you were never a mother. Even the most primary of God's creatures are better mothers than you to their offspring.'

'She's poisoned you against me.'

'No, Mam, you did that job yourself years before Carrie and I got wed. Right from a bairn I can remember wondering why my mam wasn't like other mothers. You never kissed or cuddled me or even gave a kind word, and the only contact I can recall is a clip round the ear. But shall I tell you the person I most feel sorry for? Alec. Because you smothered him, you took a normal lad and turned him into a male version of you. How me da stood it all those years I'll never know, because I tell you straight, I couldn't have.'

'Your da? You dare hold your da up to me after what he's done? Abandoning his family—'

'The only person me da left was you, and you know it. He stuck you until we were all grown up and could fend for ourselves and then he went, and every single jack one of us wished him well. He's got a woman down in London, you didn't know that, did you? A nice woman, kind, who lost her husband in the first month of the war and thinks Da is the bee's knees. He's happy for the first time in his life, Mam.'

Olive stared at her son, her face working. 'I don't believe you,' she said at last. 'He wouldn't. We're still married.'

'Believe what you want.' David's voice was weary now. 'But it's the truth and there's not one of us who blames him.'

Olive turned without saying another word, and when the door had banged behind her, David lay back on his pillows, sweat forming in beads on his brow. Carrie bent over him, patting his white face with a handkerchief she had dampened with water from the glass on his bedside locker, and when his breathing had steadied again she lifted his head for him to take a few sips of water.

Matthew had stood quite still while all this was going on, and it was only when David was resting again, eyes shut, that he spoke. 'Is it true? What Gran said about Uncle Alec being my da?'

David's eyes opened and he looked at the stiff face of the boy he had always tried to be a father to, and what he saw there caused him to close his eyes again.

Carrie couldn't answer for a moment. Her worst nightmare had come true.

'I asked you a question, Mam. Is Uncle Alec my real da?'

Carrie put one hand on the iron bedstead for support, her mind searching for a way to tell him. In the end there was only one way to say it. 'Yes.' She knew she might lose both of them, Matthew and David, but things had gone too far to prevaricate.

They looked at each other, Carrie and her son, and in answer to what she read in his face, she said, 'But it wasn't like she said, Matthew, you have to believe me. I was fifteen years old, I'd had too much to drink at your aunt's wedding and—'

She was talking to the wind. He had turned on his heel and gone, banging the door after him so hard it shook the room.

'Leave him.' She would have gone after him but David's voice from the bed caught her. She looked down at him. His eyes were open, his expression tender. 'Leave him for now, lass, he's got a lot to take in. He'll be back and then you can explain, but for now he's all riled up and likely wants to hurt someone. He'd say things he'd regret and that'd help no one.'

'Oh, David.' She stared at him, unsure of what he was really feeling. 'I'm sorry. I'm sorry it was Alec.'

'So am I, lass, for you. It was bad enough he did what he did, but for you to have to see him, for him to be my brother and part of the family . . . I'm surprised you ever took me.'

'It was the best thing I ever did.' Her voice was shaking but

384

strangely she found she couldn't cry; the look in Matthew's eyes as he had stared at her prevented the relief of tears. 'You saved me.'

'Saved you?'

'From doing something silly; from having to go away; from never getting over what Alec did.'

'Come here.' He held out his hand and she sat down beside him again, the trembling which she couldn't control communicating itself to him through her fingers.

'You helped me to find real love, David, but . . .'

'But?'

'I don't know why you love me like you do,' she said, a bewildered note in her voice.

'Because you're the other part of me, the beautiful part. Because you're all I've ever wanted and will ever want. Without you I'm nothing, lass, and I know it. That's why . . .' He paused, and then went on, 'That's why I've always been scared you'll look at me one day and see me for what I am. An ordinary bloke.'

'Oh, David, David.' Her arms went around him, her lips covered his, and they moved in tiny burning kisses to his brow, his eyes, his cheeks, his chin, before coming back to his mouth. 'I love you, I love you so much it frightens me. I've loved you for years but I didn't dare say it.'

His love had unblocked the dam, and now both their faces were wet, their tears mingling, and it was a long time before she drew away and sat up, their hands still joined. 'I've got something to tell you,' she said softly. 'Something good.'

'It can't be better than hearing you say you love me.'

She looked at him, at his dear, dear face, and in spite of all that had happened that day she relished the moment. 'We're going to have a baby, you're going to be a da.'

For a moment she thought he hadn't taken it in because his expression didn't change, and then a look came over his face which humbled her. He reached out his arms and she fell against his chest, and together they lay quiet for a moment before he said, in a tone of wonder, 'My cup runneth over, lass.'

Part 6

Homecomings and Departures

1945

Chapter Twenty-four

The man who stepped out of the train in Central Station had grey hair which was quite white at the sides above his ears, but almost every female head turned for a second glance as he made his way through the milling crowd. He was in uniform but this wasn't what drew their eyes; the war had only been over a month in Europe, and Japan was still to be subdued, so men in uniform weren't an uncommon sight. It was the startling good looks of the man which were so striking, despite his extreme thinness which bordered on emaciation, that and the way he held himself as though he was somebody.

The sun was shining as he emerged into Union Street, the scene of devastation some years before when a couple of bombs had hit the railway station and blown a carriage out through the roof, the carriage wheels and part of the station roof ending up in the window of a sports goods store. Today, however, the only sounds came from the moving traffic and shoppers, the mellow sunlight bathing the scene in homely ordinariness.

Once the man had hailed a taxi cab, given the driver his address and settled himself inside, the evidence of intensive bombing by the now defeated enemy became more apparent. Large areas of the town were going to need rebuilding; rubble and the burnt-out shells of buildings that had once been factories and houses seemed to mark every corner.

In the privacy of the taxi the man's shoulders slumped, and when he raised a hand to his brow, wiping the beads of sweat which had gathered there with a crisp white handkerchief, the taxi driver said, 'You all right, mate?'

'Yes, thank you.' It was stilted, as though the man wasn't used to the sound of his own voice, and this was true to some measure.

He had lost count of the weeks and months he had been incarcerated in solitary confinement in the tiny wooden hut in one of the most exposed parts of the camp. He would be there still if it was not for the liberation of the camp because one thing was for sure, the commandant had expected him to die in there, a warning to other prisoners. Freezing cold at night and as hot as hell in the day, with the minimum of food and water to keep him alive one more day, he had been the commandant's showpiece of what would happen if anyone else was foolish enough to 'interfere with camp procedure'. But he had never regretted the action which had led to his confinement, not once.

'Been away long?' The taxi driver was nothing if not persistent.

'A while.'

'Bet it looks different, eh?'

'Aye, it does.'

'Still we showed 'em in the end, didn't we? Old Churchill called Hitler a bloodthirsty guttersnipe, but that's too good for the so-an'-so in my opinion. Doin' away with himself like that, the lily-livered coward. I'd have liked to have seen him and that Eva Braun strung up by their heels like they did to Mussolini and his mistress after they'd shot 'em.'

Alec looked at the back of the taxi driver's head. He wanted to ask if that would have helped the hundreds of thousands who had died from starvation, typhus, typhoid and tuberculosis in the concentration camps, or whether it would have sent a message to the commandant's wife who'd had a lampshade made from tattooed human skin. But he didn't. He had got out of the habit of talking, and if you had not been there and seen the things he'd seen with your own eyes, the futility of such meaningless revenge wouldn't be comprehended anyway.

For days on end that psychopath in charge of the camp had had Lieutenant Strong staked out on the parade ground under a burning sun, and what had the lieutenant's crime been? He had picked up one of his men who had passed out during morning inspection which had gone on for hours in the extreme heat.

On the fifth night, under cover of darkness, Alec had crept and wormed his way across the parade ground to where the blistered body lay, and when it had become apparent that the lieutenant was near the end, he had done what his officer had asked him to do and ended the man's ordeal by holding his hand tightly across the lieutenant's nose and mouth, praying with him as he did so. And then the guards had found them.

The taxi driver, offended by the lack of patriotic fervour that had greeted his words, lapsed into silence, leaving Alec to his thoughts.

He was glad he'd managed to get to see the lieutenant's family as he had promised him he would. They had been just as he had thought they'd be, both boys the spitting image of their father and his wife an attractive woman with sad eyes. After telling the lads their father had died a hero, he had then lied through his teeth to Mrs Strong, assuring her that her husband's death had been quick and painless. It was the last thing he had been able to do for the man who had become his friend.

'Here we are then.'

The taxi driver's voice brought Alec out of his musing. The vehicle was passing through the gates and then it slowly scrunched its way up the pebbled drive to the front of the house.

After he had paid the driver and the sound of the taxi's engine had faded away, Alec stood for a while just looking about him in the dappled sunlight. Birds were singing in the trees and the May blossom still scented the air with its sweetness, despite it being the second week of June. If he shut his eyes he could imagine it was just as he had left it an eternity ago, but the once pristine lawn, smooth as a bowling green, now held regimented rows of vegetables; only a small border of grass remained.

All this was his now, and plenty more besides. The thought brought no rush of excitement or pleasure; in fact no emotion whatsoever stirred in him. It had bothered him at first, this lack of feeling since his release from the box which had been his cell for endless months, but now he hugged it to him. He did not want to feel, not ever again.

He had not been popular with his doctors when he had insisted on discharging himself from the hospital he'd been brought to on his arrival in England. He had only stayed three weeks. His detachment from feeling was beginning to be breached by some of the poor devils in there, and he had wanted to be by himself once more. And so he had left, travelling first to Kent to fulfil his last act of respect to Lieutenant Strong, after which he had found a little bed and breakfast place deep in the countryside, where he had slept and eaten and walked the days and nights away, in that order.

The camp commandant had been a law unto himself and had allowed no letters in or out of the camp, and only on his release did Alec discover he was a widower, and that his family had received no word as to whether he was alive or dead since he had been taken prisoner.

He informed the appropriate officials that he would like

notification that he had survived the war to be forwarded to his family and that he would be returning to Sunderland in due course; he had been adamant that no information should be given regarding the date of his arrival in England or the location of the hospital he was being taken to. With the exception of perhaps Matthew, there was not a person in the world who cared if he was alive or dead, and after four long years maybe even Matthew had changed.

The sun was warm on his head; the last two or three weeks had been unseasonably hot, which was just as well, Alec reflected with dark humour as he walked to the front door. A walking skeleton didn't look so bad with a tan, and the last couple of weeks out in the fresh air had taken away the deathly pallor which had so shocked him when he had first looked in a mirror after his release.

The front door was not locked when he tried the handle, something which brought home the fact that Margaret was no longer there. Her nervous disposition had meant that both the front and back doors had had to be locked at all times. Poor Margaret. He tried to feel regret at her passing but his life in this house was so remote now, it could have belonged to another person in another lifetime.

He entered the house and was standing in the hall, amazed at how nothing had changed, when he became aware of a presence on the perimeter of his vision. Half turning he looked towards the stairs and there was his son, but he saw instantly that the boy had been replaced by a man.

Matthew stood staring at him, one hand resting on the banister halfway down the stairs and the other hanging limply by his side. Alec was just as taken aback. It was a moment or two before he said, 'Hello, Matthew,' and he was surprised to find his voice sounded quite normal.

'Da?'

The voice did not belong to the tall, broad-shouldered man standing looking at him, it could have come from a child, but as Matthew took the last few stairs in a great leap, his voice was loud and deep as he shouted, 'Da! It's really you!'

Da? Alec found himself enveloped in a bear hug, his mind completely blank except for that one small word. Da. Not Alec. Not even Uncle Alec. Da.

When Matthew drew away, Alec saw that his son's face was wet, but until he tasted the salt on his own lips he wasn't aware he was weeping himself.

A strange racing, churning feeling flowed through him; it was threatening to drown him. To avoid being swamped by it, he forced himself to try and speak but no words would come. And then Matthew said, his voice now just above a whisper, 'I've been here every minute I've not been at work since they told us you were all right. I knew you would be, somehow I just knew. I never stopped believing you'd come home.'

He couldn't let himself go, not now, not in front of the lad. He put out his hand, much as a blind man might do, and said, 'I need to sit down,' but his voice broke on the last word and his eyes were blinded by tears.

Somehow he found himself sitting in an armchair in the drawing room some minutes later, a glass of whisky in his hand and Matthew directly in front of him on a stool he had pulled close. 'I . . . I'm sorry.' The ice of protection had started to melt and it was pouring out of his eyes still, in spite of all his efforts to control himself.

'Don't be. We – us here in England, I mean – we've heard a bit of what went on in some of the camps. Was . . . was it very bad?'

'Bad enough.'

Matthew waited for more, but Alec did not go on. He took a handkerchief out of his pocket and rubbed at his face, then stuffed it back in his pocket before finishing the whisky in one gulp. 'I think I need another one.' It was wry.

Matthew rose and refilled the glass without comment, and it was only when Alec had drank half of it that he lay back in the armchair with a sigh, his eyes still fixed on Matthew. 'I didn't expect any sort of welcome, apart from maybe Mrs Browell, that is.'

'She's out shopping with Gran.'

Alec did not comment on this. 'Out there in the hall, you said . . .' He pulled in air through his nose. 'You called me da.'

'Well, you are, aren't you?'

'She told you?'

'Yes. No.' Matthew shook his head, running his fingers through his hair from his brow to the back of his neck. 'It's a long story.'

'I've nothing but time and I want to hear it.' Alec reached out and grasped one of Matthew's hands. 'She never admitted to me you were mine but I always knew it. What made her tell you?'

'Gran, I suppose.'

'Gran? You mean my mam?'

Matthew nodded. 'It happened like this . . .'

Alec had finished the whisky by the time the story was told. He sat forward in his seat when Matthew said, 'And I ran out of the hospital and went home and cleared out my things. I slept on a pal's bedroom floor for a couple of weeks and then Mrs Browell said I could come here till you got home. He came round to see me when I moved here.'

'He?'

'David.'

The name was said with such bitterness that Alec stiffened.

'He said it happened on the night of Aunt Renee's wedding, that you and Mam were drunk and that you . . . you took advantage of her. Did you?'

Alec's face was grim and his voice low when he said, 'I'm not proud of that night, Matt, but it was a wedding and the drink was flowing. I came home and your mam and Aunt Lillian were acting the cuddy. Lillian went to bed and . . .' He shrugged. 'One thing led to another.'

'But you didn't know afterwards. That she was expecting.'

Alec stared into the young face. It was true he hadn't realised Carrie was pregnant with his child until after she had married David, but once he had cottoned on, it had suited him to keep quiet. And he had made sure in the days and weeks that followed that she understood he wanted nothing more to do with her. Those were the facts. Should he admit to them? He might lose Matthew if he did and he knew now he couldn't bear that.

And then Matthew made up his mind for him. 'I hate them,' he said, 'the pair of them. Him pretending to be my da and her knowing all along it was you and trying to keep me from you. I'll never forgive them, never.'

'Whoa, lad, whoa.' A voice in his head was saying, look at how he's taken it, he's one hundred per cent for you, don't do anything to spoil it, but it was overshadowed by another which argued, you've told yourself that if one thing and one thing alone has come out of the madness and depravity of the last years, it's that you know yourself at last. He had started to grow up the day he had shot his first German, a young, fair-haired boy who hadn't looked old enough to shave, and the process had been completed the night he had crawled out to Lieutenant Strong. 'It wasn't like that, see this clearly.'

'I am.'

'You are not.' Matthew was staring unblinking at him and it took all his courage to say, 'It wasn't six of one and half a dozen of the other that night, Matt. Your mother was verging on sixteen and had never been out with a lad. I was a man of twenty and had already sampled a few women. David is right, I did take advantage of her and I didn't stop when she wanted me to. It was the drink, and I've never behaved like that before or since, but that doesn't excuse what I did. Afterwards I was more concerned with my own plans for the future than her. David married her and he is the one who has brought you up.'

As Matthew went to speak, Alec raised his hand, saying, 'Let me finish. I can't pretend I'm happy Carrie didn't want me around but I can damn well understand it, and you're old enough to understand it too.'

'He knew he wasn't my da, he told me so.'

'And you give him no credit for accepting you as a son?'

'No. He did it because he wanted her, and she kept me from you out of spite. Dress it up how you like but that's the truth. And now they've got their own bairns they wouldn't want me around anyway.'

'What?'

'They've got twins, a boy and a girl. They were born just before Christmas. I thought you knew, that someone would have told you.'

Alec didn't say, how could anyone have told me when I haven't been in contact with any of you? It had been his decision not to write or telephone before he came home, just as he had decided to keep his whereabouts undisclosed once

397

he was back on home shores. What he did say was, 'Is there anything else that's happened I ought to know about?'

'You know about Aunt Margaret and Mr Reed?'

'Yes.' A solicitor's letter had informed him he was a rich man.

'Isaac was killed when he was fire-watching. He saved two children; it was in the *Echo*. And Aunt Renee, she died in a fire in her house, and Uncle Walter in an accident down the pit the same day.'

'Walter?' He couldn't imagine his brother had gone. Not solid, dependable Walter.

'And—' Matthew stopped abruptly, his voice quieter when he continued, 'And Granda. He came through the Blitz but the doodlebugs got him last year. Him and his friend and his friend's wife, they all copped it.'

His da. Now he would never have the chance to try and put things right. He closed his eyes and leaned back in the chair. He felt very tired suddenly, so tired it was an effort to breathe. He'd had this experience time and time again since he had first been lifted out of the hut by Allied soliders and carried to the makeshift medical centre. He knew they had thought he wasn't going to make it because he'd heard them talking, but he had proved them wrong. At first it had been the promise he'd made to Strong to go and see his wife and boys that had kept him fighting, and then it had just seemed the right thing to do, in spite of the fact that there were days when his mind longed for the peace of oblivion. No memories, no pictures in his head of unmentionable atrocities, no screaming nightmares, just . . . nothing.

But he had Matthew now. He opened his eyes as his whisky glass, half full again, was pushed into his hand.

'Drink this, Da.'

Da. He said it so naturally, as if he had been thinking it for a long, long time. He looked down at the whisky. There were some at the hospital who had their wives or pals bring in booze every day just to get through. Without it they couldn't sleep or face the world. He handed the glass back to Matthew. 'Thanks, but I've had enough. Is there anything to eat in the house?'

'Eat? Oh aye, you know Mrs Browell. Gran hates it because she can do better pastry than her with the bitty wholemeal stuff we're still getting.'

'My mother is living here?'

Matthew nodded.

For a moment Alec felt like asking for the drink back. His mother here. Saints alive. Well, that was not going to continue. He could afford to make some sort of provision for her and he would do so, she was his mother after all, but as for her living under his roof, that was out of the question. He didn't like the part she had played in all of this, even though the end result had been Carrie acknowledging Matthew was his.

He smiled at his lad. 'Well, son, shall we go and raid the larder?'

And Matthew grinned back at him. His da was back, he could hardly believe it. He had waited so long for this day. And now there was no one to stop them spending time together. It would be the end of him having to go down the pit, he knew that. When he told his da how he felt, that'd be it. And whatever he said about *them* – he always referred to his mother and David as them in his mind – it wouldn't make any difference. He had been forced down that hellhole first and foremost because the man he'd been told was his da was a miner, and all the time his mam had known. She had *known*.

*　　*　　*

The next morning Olive was sitting, straight-backed and thin-lipped, in the hall, her big cloth bag at her feet. Matthew was with her. Alec had just gone to run the car round to the front of the house. She fixed her grandson with gimlet eyes as she said bitterly, 'It's come to something when I'm carted off like a sack of taties.'

Matthew moved his shoulders uncomfortably but said nothing. His father had spent some time talking to him about what he was going to do and why, and for the first time in his life he was seeing his grandmother without rose-coloured glasses.

'There's your da owning umpteen houses round about the town, from what I can make out, and he's not even setting me up in one on me own. Oh no. I'm going to be a tenant like Joe Bloggs off the street and sharing with others. His own mother. Do you know what he said to me last night? Behave yourself.' Her voice rose with outrage. '*Me!* Behave yourself, he said, or the other couple of tenants might make life difficult.'

'You'll be all right, Gran.'

'Will I? Huh.'

Olive would have said more but Alec opened the front door at that moment. He surveyed his mother for a moment before he said, 'Pick up your grandmother's bag, Matthew, and we'll be off. Have you made your farewells to Freda, Mam?'

Olive's chin rose a notch. Made her farewells indeed! If he thought she was giving that woman a further chance to gloat, he was very much mistaken. She stood up and strode to the front door by way of answer, brushing past Alec without a word.

She sat in the front seat of the car, her body rigid and her eyes staring straight ahead. She'd never thought she'd say it, but Alec was just like the rest of them, ungrateful to the core. But now she knew where she stood and one thing was certain: she wouldn't care if she never clapped eyes on any of them again.

Chapter Twenty-five

Carrie stood gazing at David who was fast asleep in his armchair. The two babies in his arms were also slumbering although every so often one or the other of them would make a little sucking motion with rosebud lips. They were such happy bairns, and bonny. Philip already had a crop of light brown curls, but poor little Melanie was still as bald as a coot. Not that she would have dared to put the 'poor' in front of Melanie's name if she was talking to David, she reflected wryly. As far as he was concerned, his children were the bonniest, brightest and most perfect little angels who had ever been born. He had been a wonderful father to Matthew from the first, but whether it was because he was older, or this was the second time round, or simply that deep inside it was different because he knew the twins were flesh of his flesh, he had a confidence in handling the infants that he had never had with Matthew. Then again the circumstances were so different now.

Carrie glanced round the kitchen, her face now sombre. If only she could have given Matthew a start like this. Matthew's crib had been an old drawer, and although she had loved and appreciated Ada, that front room in the house at the Back of the Pit had been poky and dark and depressing. And there had been no question of having her firstborn in hospital like she'd done with the twins – the five guineas this had cost would have seemed like a fortune nineteen years ago.

It had been wonderful to be free from the worries of rationing, laundry and housekeeping for a while, and with the twins turning out to be model babies who woke on the dot every four hours for their feeds and slept the rest of the time, she had come out of the hospital feeling rested and ready to tackle life again. And how she had needed that.

Carrie left the kitchen and walked back to the front room where she resumed her seat at the sewing machine. She had gone to check whether David required help with the babies but she might have known he would be fine, she thought fondly.

After the accident at the pit, David had needed several operations on his injured leg and had been in and out of hospital like a yoyo. For a time it had been touch and go whether amputation was the only answer, but the doctors had worked a minor miracle and the shattered bone and torn flesh had eventually healed enough to take his weight. But he had been told that the leg would always be stiff and unbending, which had effectively put an end to his life down the pit.

During this time, Lillian had decided to share a house with a widowed friend of hers from the steelworks, who had children the same age as Luke and Katie. Lillian had insisted that with twins expected, life was going to be hectic enough without in-laws always around, besides which her going would give Carrie her workroom back which she was going to need now that no wage would be coming in from David for the foreseeable future.

Carrie did not argue against Lillian's decision too hard. Her friend was adjusting to Isaac's loss at last, and since Lillian's pal at the steelworks was in the same situation as Lillian was and all the bairns got on well, Carrie felt it was a good move.

When Lillian moved out, Carrie set about establishing her workroom, letting folk know she was working from home. She and David had decided to deposit his compensation money from the pit straight into the bank to join the nest egg she had laboriously saved over long years; they would touch it only if absolutely necessary, something Carrie was determined would not happen.

She soon found she had accepted more work than one person could realistically cope with, especially since the person in question had discovered the baby she was expecting was in fact two. When she asked Miriam, Billy's wife, if she would like to work a few hours a week for her, Miriam had jumped at the chance. And no one was more surprised than Carrie when her mother offered her services.

'I've been taking in washing and such for years, lass, to make ends meet, as you well know,' Joan said when she called round to see her daughter the morning after Carrie had spoken to Miriam. 'And I tell you, I've had me fill of steaming rooms and damp clothes everywhere. There's enough of them anyway with your da and the lads. The thought of coming to work for you would be like a tonic – that's if you want me, of course.'

Carrie had wanted her and within days it was clear to the three women that this was an ideal set-up. Joan had a flair for the work, and although Miriam was merely adequate, she was eager to learn. And Carrie paid well.

David's final operation took place eight weeks before the twins were born, which meant he was out of hospital and as mobile as he was ever going to be when Carrie brought Philip and Melanie home. During the weeks leading up to the birth, they had discussed their future. Carrie had put forward a variation of her earlier proposition. How about, she asked David, if they followed through on her suggestion to buy shop premises with a flat above, but along with the workroom and salesroom they designated another part of the building for David's use? He could buy, mend and sell secondhand sewing machines, irons, crimping machines, small hand mangles, goffering irons and other equipment.

She had been both relieved and thrilled with his enthusiasm for the idea, and it had gone some way towards easing the ache in her heart that had been present since Matthew's abrupt departure from the house. But in the dead of night, when David was asleep, she often cried scalding tears, lying awake for hours in spite of being exhausted. Three times she had called to see Matthew, swallowing her pride with some effort when it became clear Olive was gloating over the estrangement. The first time Matthew had spoken to her just long enough to tell her not to call again, and the next two times he had flatly refused to see her. She had written many letters but had heard nothing in return and had no way of knowing if he'd opened them. She feared he had ripped them up unread.

She knew he felt she had grievously wronged him in concealing the fact that Alec was his father, and had compounded this crime by trying to prevent anything but the most minimal contact with his 'uncle', but she couldn't truthfully say she wouldn't do exactly the same if she had her time over again. And he did not seem prepared even to try to understand how difficult it had all been for her. David told her over and over again that Matthew would come round in time, but as the weeks and then the months passed, she had become increasingly frightened. And then they had heard Alec was alive and coming home soon.

Alone with her thoughts, Carrie found she couldn't concentrate on the task in hand – Miriam and Joan had long since gone for the night. She rose and moved restlessly to the window to look out into the twilight. She had lost Matthew to Alec. She rubbed her hand over her aching eyes. Since Matthew had gone, she had begun to feel such hatred for Alec it scared her.

When she looked up, her thoughts seemed to have imprinted themselves on the glass because Alec was staring back at her.

She shut her eyes, then opened them very slowly, and when only her dim reflection looked back at her she put a hand to her racing heart. A moment later the doorbell rang.

Carrie's nails were digging into the palms of her hands as she left the front room and walked into the hall. Just before she opened the front door she lowered her head, saying to herself, you knew he would come to crow that it's all worked out his way, but don't let him see how much you're hurt. Don't give him that satisfaction. Be cool and remote.

She opened the door.

'Hello, Carrie.'

When she had imagined this meeting – and she had imagined it many times since they had received word via Mrs Browell that Alec had survived the war – Carrie had never dreamed she'd be lost for words. She had changed her hypothetical response many times as she tried to predict what Alec might say, but she had never considered she would be incapable of speech.

She had thought it was the thick window glass which had changed his face a little but she saw now he really was as thin as he'd appeared a few seconds before. There were deep lines carved in his face which had not been there four years earlier, and his countenance had taken on a rugged quality. He was still as handsome as ever but in a different way, and he looked bigger, although terribly gaunt, and every day of his forty years.

'May I come in?'

Still unable to talk, Carrie swallowed before standing aside and gesturing with her hand for Alec to come in.

In the hall he turned and waited for her to shut the door. She was more beautiful than he remembered. Alec's heart was thumping so hard he wanted to put a hand to his chest but he restrained himself. How many times had he pictured her in his mind the last four years? Hundreds, thousands. He had hugged the image to him every day he had been in solitary confinement, unable to stand upright or move about in the container and wondering if each day would be his last. Carrie had stood for home, for everything wholesome and beautiful and good in a world gone mad. What would she say if he told her that? But of course he never could, he had forfeited the right to do so twenty years ago. She was David's. He had lost the chance of true happiness, first through blind lust, and then because he had been too stupid to see her worth. He was a fool. He had always been a fool.

It was with some effort that Carrie said evenly, 'David is in the kitchen if you would like to go through.'

'Thank you.'

She expected him to walk ahead of her, but when he didn't move she passed him. He was aware that she was careful that no part of her body came into contact with his.

When Carrie opened the kitchen door, David was awake and sitting up, probably woken by the doorbell, his stiff leg stretched out in front of him. Both babies were still fast asleep in his arms.

There was a moment when his eyes met hers, and then his gaze went to the man behind her. David stared at his brother and Alec stared back, his face impassive, but whatever reaction Alec was expecting, it clearly wasn't the one that followed.

'Hello, Alec,' David said quietly. 'We've been expecting you.'

'I . . . I felt I needed to come.' Alec was speaking in a formal manner and had made no move to step over the threshold into the kitchen.

Carrie had gone to stand behind David's chair, one hand resting on her husband's shoulder, the other gripping the hard back of the rocking chair. She felt slightly sick, mainly because this new Alec was an unknown quantity. David inclined his head, and he did not smile when he said, 'You will have to excuse me not standing up but as you can see, my hands are full.'

Alec allowed his gaze to fall on the sleeping babies, and no one would have guessed from his expression that the sight of them pained him. 'I heard about the twins. They're bonny.'

'Aye, they are.' David paused, then said, 'Come in, Alec. Carrie was just about to make a brew and what we've got to say to each other will be better over a cup of tea.'

Carrie turned away towards the range without speaking. She didn't want Alec sitting in her kitchen drinking tea with them. But the sight of him had shocked her, his gauntness proclaiming its own story, so she put the kettle on the hob then turned and looked at the two men.

Alec pulled a chair from under the table and seated himself.

'When did you get back?' David asked.

'Yesterday.' Although the impassivity was back, Alec was twisting his hands which were hanging between his legs, and he must have become aware of this because he suddenly stopped and thrust them into his pockets.

Now David asked the same question Matthew had done. 'Was it very bad?'

And Alec replied in much the same fashion as he had before. 'It was no picnic.'

He had changed. How he had changed. In fact he didn't seem like the same man. Carrie was feeling more and more disturbed as the seconds ticked on. The brashness, the swashbuckling cockiness, everything that had made him Alec seemed to have gone, and in its place was – what? Carrie found she couldn't put a name to it.

Alec raised his eyes to Carrie's white face. 'I want to say at the outset that I asked Matthew to come with me tonight,' he said flatly, 'but he refused even though I made it clear I felt he should. I told him if anyone has been wronged in all of this, it certainly isn't him, it's you.'

Carrie did not contradict him. Part of her mind was saying, don't trust him. He's a master of manipulation. Look at how he wheedled his way in with David all those years ago just to get near to Matthew.

'I would agree with that.' David's voice was still quiet. 'And there's something *I'd* like to say at the outset. If Carrie had told me the night of Walter's wedding just who it was who had attacked her, I'd have killed you and been happy to take the consequences. And if it wasn't for the war and what you've been through, I still might have done it. As it is, us fighting would only damage any reconciliation between Carrie and Matthew.'

Carrie noticed David did not include himself in the equation and it saddened her. To a certain extent, he had shared her pain and grief over Matthew's leaving but there had also been an element of relief, though she knew he would never give voice to it. David and Matthew had never really got on. All excuses aside – and she had told herself plenty through the years – the relationship between her husband and his brother's son was the same as the relationship between David and Alec. Chalk and cheese.

Her gaze moved from David to Alec. She spoke rapidly. 'Have you told Matthew the circumstances which led to him being born, because he flatly refused to hear it from either of us when we tried.'

'Aye, I have.'

She didn't believe him and her face spoke for her.

Alec sighed, raking his hand through his hair which was now so grey. 'Believe me, Carrie,' he said very softly, 'I have. He accepts I wronged you but . . .'

'But what?' she asked tightly when he paused.

'He is more my son than yours.' When she would have protested he raised his hand. 'What I mean by that is he's looking at all of this purely in terms of how it affects him, without considering anyone else. He's selfish, like I was at his age. Like I was until the last few years, in fact. I just hope it doesn't take a war to wake him up to the fact that the world doesn't start and finish with him. That said . . .' His eyes dropped from hers now. 'I can't pretend I'm sorry the truth is out at last. I knew he was mine, I felt it in my bones. He is my son and I need him.'

'So do I.'

'You have another son, a daughter too.' The green eyes were looking straight into hers again and she saw they were moist, which took her aback. 'Not to mention David. You could go on to have more bairns. As for me, Matthew is the only child I will ever have.'

'How do you know that? You're free now, and wealthy. You'll meet someone—'

'No, I will not.'

A long, steady breath escaped David, and Carrie turned to look at him.

'What are your plans?' he asked.

Why was he asking Alec what his plans were? She wanted her son back, couldn't he see that? Didn't he care? Couldn't

409

David, of all people, understand that she could go on to have ten, twenty, fifty bairns but she would still grieve for Matthew if they weren't reconciled? But they must be, they must.

David was aware of Carrie's stiffly held body and hurt eyes, but for the first time in his life he felt he really understood his brother. Alec loved her. It was there in his rigid control, in his eyes, in his voice, and this was Alec the man, not Alec the spoiled lad.

But Carrie was his. David glanced at her. He knew that now. And with the knowledge came pity for his brother.

'I'm taking him into the business as a partner.'

'That's unfair.' Carrie spoke hotly now, her eyes burning. 'You're buying him, you've always tried to buy him.'

'He hates the pit, Carrie. No, he doesn't just hate it. It terrifies him, scares him senseless. For four years he has suffered the torment of the damned, and if I can take him out of it I will and damn what you or anyone else thinks.' And then Alec grimaced. He reached into his jacket pocket and said, 'Could . . . could I have a glass of water?'

'You're ill,' said David as his brother pulled a small pill container out of his pocket. Carrie filled a glass and handed it to Alec who took a pill and gulped at the water. His face had lost all colour and it was a few moments before he spoke.

'It's nothing, it'll pass.'

Was this a trick? Carrie would have liked to think so but in all honesty she couldn't. Alec was ill, ill and broken. She stared at him, and when a vestige of colour returned, she said, 'What's wrong?'

Alec shrugged. 'A number of things. They'll ease in time.'

They said nothing more as Carrie mashed the tea and then poured each of them a cup. She placed the sugar bowl in front of Alec.

'He will come round in time,' Alec said. 'I'll make sure of it. Just . . . just give him a bit of breathing space for a while.'

'A while? You mean you don't want me to see him.' Carrie stopped and covered her eyes with her hand, and when she heard David stand up she turned blindly into him, taking one of the twins while he continued to hold the other. 'He hates me, doesn't he?' she said into David's chest.

'Of course he doesn't hate you.' Alec cleared his throat. 'It's just that he's resentful and confused and needs sense talking into him.'

'Then why won't he let *me* talk to him and explain how things happened and why I did what I did?' There was silence for a moment, and then Carrie made herself face Alec. 'Will he be living with you?' And when Alec nodded, she added, 'And your mother?' Fat chance of any reason coming to the fore while Olive was whispering in Matthew's ear.

'No, not my mother. She's . . . gone elsewhere.'

'Oh?' This was from David.

'I've put her in one of the terraced houses I own in town.'

'I bet she's as pleased as Punch about that.'

Alec raised wry eyebrows but made no comment on this. 'A few months and Matthew will be looking at all this differently. A new job and a different kind of life will work wonders, you see if it doesn't.'

When David gently agreed with his brother, Carrie almost rounded on the pair of them and spoke her mind. But she bit back the words. They wouldn't understand. She felt as though Matthew had gone from her for good and right at this moment it was more than she could bear. At least before Alec had come here tonight her hate for him had sustained her in her worst moments of missing Matthew. She had found hate was very akin to love in its strength. But now she had seen Alec again, that support had been knocked away. This was not the same man who had left for the war. Even then, although Alec had been frightened out of his wits, there had been an arrogance that had reminded her of his indifference in the days and weeks after he had raped her. Now nothing of that remained.

As though to emphasise this, Alec said, 'Carrie, I'm truly sorry. Please believe me.'

It was on the tip of her tongue to ask whether he was sorry about raping her or about Matthew rejecting her, but as she looked into the world-weary face she said nothing. She did not know it but she was experiencing a feeling similar to David's, its main ingredient being pity.

But this was still Alec, change or no change. With this in mind she merely nodded tightly as she struggled to take control of her racing emotions.

She would think about all this later when David was asleep and there would be no one to see if she wept. For the moment she had to be strong. And if what she had begun to suspect this last week or two was true, she would need to be even more determined not to give in to her fears that Matthew would never talk to her again. Everyone knew that weepy mothers produced weepy babies. But she did so hope it was just the one this time.

Chapter Twenty-six

Over the next months many changes took place in Carrie's life. Just six weeks before her next confinement was due, she and David invested all their savings in a property across the river in Holmeside.

The three-storey property, which consisted of shop premises on the ground floor and family accommodation on the upper two, needed extensive refurbishment due to war damage. Although this meant they acquired it at a reasonable price, they nevertheless had to take out a hefty mortgage. It took a little effort on Carrie's part to persuade David to take the plunge. His motto had always been 'Neither a borrower nor a lender be', but she finally convinced him that a mortgage was quite unlike being in debt, more a way to advance their future and that of their children.

Continuing shortages meant that the basic food ration had not changed with the end of the war, but the government recognised the importance of nutrition in pregnancy and expectant mothers were entitled to an extra pint of milk a day, extra fresh eggs and a packet of dried egg every eight weeks. They also received an extra half meat ration and had first claim on bananas and oranges when they were available.

Some of this made Carrie feel rather uncomfortable, especially when she was pushed to the front of the queue if there were oranges in the shops. The extra nutriment must have paid off, however, because when Edward Walter Sutton made his way into the world, he weighed in at a hefty ten and a half pounds. When David came into the hospital room to see his new son, after several hours of pacing the hospital corridors and smoking his way through a packet of Woodbines despite the fact he didn't smoke, Carrie informed him in no uncertain terms that she never wanted to see another orange in her life.

They finished renovating the property and moved into their new home exactly four months after Edward was born. David did most of the work himself and took great satisfaction from it, while Carrie wielded a paintbrush with gusto and proved herself to be a dab hand with finishing touches.

By the end of the year they knew the business was going to succeed and prosper. Every time Carrie tucked the children into bed at night, she thanked God that her two youngest sons would never know what it was to work miles beneath the earth. They had a family business now and she was determined it would go from strength to strength. And she never ceased to ask the Almighty to soften Matthew's heart towards her. Although Alec kept them informed via Lillian of all he and Matthew were doing, the boy still refused to relent and come and see his new siblings and herself, not even at Christmas or on New Year's Eve.

At the end of January the temperature all over Britain plummeted. Snow fell continuously, accompanied by vicious gale-force winds from the east. Twenty-foot drifts transformed the landscape, turning the country into a huge, white maze. The River Thames froze over, coal boats were icebound in north-eastern ports and snow closed roads and railways as effectively as if they had been bombed.

Where the armies of Hitler had failed, the forces of winter

succeeded, bringing the country to its knees. Three hundred major roads became impassable, cutting off England from Scotland and the north from the south. The RAF dropped food supplies to the shivering and starving inhabitants of isolated communities, and in Sunderland the streets were plunged into darkness as electricity failed. The young and fit raided the nearest coke tip or walked out of the town into the countryside where they foraged for logs in the frozen woodland.

With electricity to households turned off between 9 a.m. and midday, and again from 2 p.m. to 4 p.m., Carrie's main concern was keeping her three children, especially little Edward, warm and comfortable. They all moved into the sitting room of the flat above the shop to live, eat and sleep, in an effort to keep that one room warm. Although the three bedrooms, like the sitting room, all had open fires, there just wasn't enough coal to go round. Timber of all kinds, from old furniture and pallets to disused railway sleepers, became highly sought after as fuel. Water had to be collected from a tap in the road, and sometimes Carrie queued for more than half an hour for two bucketfuls.

At long last, on the ides of March, the thaw began. But the ice and snow melted into torrents, rivers overflowed and flooded homes. A great storm in the middle of March spread the floodwaters far and wide, and although the property in Holmeside was not affected, Carrie heard through Lillian that Alec and Matthew had had to move out of the house in Hendon for a short period.

The harsh winter was followed by a cruel spring and everyone suffered, but in April the New Look burst over Britain like a fashion bomb as Christian Dior unveiled his unashamedly romantic 'corolle line'.

Carrie was captivated by the full mid-calf skirts, wasp waists, plunging necklines and batwing sleeves, and she gambled that there were plenty of women who had worn service uniforms or factory overalls, or who had donned the thick socks, sweaters and breeches of the Land Army, who were now sick of utility clothing and the make-do-and-mend ethic.

She commandeered Lillian, who was still smarting at losing her job at the steelworks now that the war was over and the men were back, into working for her full time, and asked her mother and Miriam to increase their hours. And then she went into overdrive, producing modified versions of Dior's designs at various price levels.

She knew the venture was risky and she wasn't sure if Sunderland was ready for chic fashion, but she was as sick as anyone of serviceable and practical clothing. All her married life she had worked her fingers to the bone, first with home work from the firework factory, then working for Horwood's and at the nursery, along with continuing to make cheap items from home and building her reputation as a good seamstress with neighbours and friends.

And that had been fine then. It had given her a good grounding for what she intended now, and also provided a standard of living they'd all benefited from. But with the purchase of the shop which had more space than they'd ever hoped for, she wanted to see if she could achieve a dream which had always been on hold in the back of her mind – that of opening her own dress shop.

She didn't intend it to be purely an exclusive and pricey one like some in the town, although the upper range of what she would sell would be both those things. She wanted anyone and everyone to be able to afford something, and for those who wanted to be dressed for a specific occasion, she would start by selling them a good foundation and work outwards.

By the end of the summer, which had been as hot as the

winter had been cold, she knew the gamble had paid off. Women from all walks of life knew what they wanted, and it was to surrender to the delicious rustle of taffeta or the caress of silk and lace. They had worked hard in all sorts of occupations during the war and had proved that women were every bit as good as men, hadn't they? And there was more to life than leaving school only to become a housewife, Britain's new breed of working women told themselves. It was high time to take a step away from the kitchen sink. Those who wanted to spend their lives scrubbing and donkey-stoning the front step were free to do so, but women had brains and ability and it was not unfeminine to use them, as they'd been told in the past.

David's side of the business, although not as financially productive as Carrie's, was also doing well. The children were all happy and healthy. They saw plenty of Carrie's parents, along with Billy and his family, and Lillian and the bairns. Danny and Len were engaged to two sisters and due to have a double wedding the next year. Everything in the garden was wonderful, in fact, Carrie told herself at least once a day, and she could make herself believe it if she didn't think of Matthew. But she did. She thought about him a great deal.

She knew David was worried about her. He was forever telling her to slow down and take time off, but by packing twenty-five hours into every day and working so hard she fell asleep as soon as her head touched the pillow, the worst of the ache in her heart was kept at bay. Every time she went into town or to the beach with the bairns, or to the cinema, her eyes searched for one face. It was never there.

And then at the end of September two things happened in quick succession, the first having a direct bearing on the second. Late one Saturday afternoon, when David had taken the children to the park and Carrie had just sent everyone home and shut up shop, Veronica came to see her. A very grown-up and remote Veronica, with hard eyes and a somewhat brittle smile, and clothes which Carrie could see immediately were both expensive and well-cut. Renee's daughter had not come back to Sunderland after the war but had made her home with a Land Army friend, whose parents had a big house in London.

'I'm going to be married, Aunt Carrie.' Veronica smiled as she spoke, and Carrie was struck by how much she resembled Renee. 'He's the brother of my friend, an accountant in the City. He has a wonderful job and we're buying a gorgeous house that overlooks Richmond Park. Gerald says I can furnish it exactly how I want, what do you think about that?'

Over a pot of tea and hot girdle scones, Carrie let her niece talk for some time about her plans and then, when Veronica stopped for breath, she said, 'Are you happy, Vee?'

'Happy? Of course I'm happy. I'm . . .' She hesitated, then burst into tears.

Carrie leaned forward and touched Veronica's arm gently, and when the girl turned into her she held her and rocked her much as she would have done little Melanie. It was a while before Veronica was all cried out. Carrie wiped her face and poured her another cup of tea. Then she said softly, 'What is it? What's wrong?'

'Oh, Aunt Carrie.' Veronica gulped, rubbing her nose in a childlike gesture which made her seem very young despite the carefully applied make-up and styled curls. 'It's . . . it's nothing, not really. Wedding nerves, I suppose.'

With an intuition born of her love for her son and for Renee's daughter, Carrie said, 'Is it something to do with Matthew, Vee? You can tell me, really. I know you quarrelled the last time you were home on leave.'

'He told you?' Veronica raised wide eyes.

'Not in so many words.' Carrie did not add that Matthew had not really talked to her for some time before their last altercation. 'But you haven't been back since so that speaks for itself. Do you want to go and see him? Is that it?'

Veronica said nothing, she only shook her head as two more big tears spilled out of her eyes and rolled down her cheeks.

'Is it something Matthew said? Something he did?'

This time Veronica slowly nodded. Carrie waited now, and after a moment or two, Veronica said, 'It was about my mam.'

'Your mam?' This was unexpected. Carrie had known Veronica was sweet on Matthew, she had followed him around like a devoted puppy from the moment she could toddle. Carrie had thought that perhaps Matthew had told the girl her feelings were not reciprocated, something along those lines.

'He said . . .' Veronica gulped. 'He said my da likely wasn't my da, that it could be someone else.'

'*What?*'

'We . . . we'd got friendly, you see, just kissing and that sometimes, but when I came home that time I wanted to know if . . . well, if we had a future I suppose. Lots of lasses like Matthew and I just wanted to know where I stood.'

'I can't believe he said that. It's not true, I know it isn't true. Where on earth did he get it from?'

'Gran.'

'Gran? Gran Sutton?'

'Yes.'

'And you argued about that?' She could understand it. Of course Veronica would defend her mother, but how could Matthew trifle with the girl's affections in the first place? Veronica had always been quite open about her feelings for

Matthew but a blind man could have seen Matthew didn't feel the same way.

'He said everyone knew my mam was . . .' Veronica hesitated again, her voice a whisper as she said, 'loose.'

'Oh, lass.' Carrie's heart went out to the girl. 'Look, Vee, your gran is a nasty, bitter, twisted old woman and she never liked your mam or me either. I know for sure your da was your da, all right? Renee was my sister and she told me everything. *Everything*.'

Her niece raised tear-washed eyes. 'There's more, Aunt Carrie. He said Gran had told him my mam was carrying on with . . . with all her sons at one time or another. She said . . . she said she wouldn't like to guess who exactly had fathered me because it could have been any one of them.'

Carrie stared at Veronica, her mouth agape. She couldn't believe that David's mother was capable of such unmitigated venom. But yes, she contradicted herself in the next moment, yes she could. Olive had always hated Renee and she had never taken to her granddaughter like she had to Matthew. If Olive had been worried they might get together then Carrie could easily imagine her making up some story to stop it. Her precious Matthew defiled by Renee's daughter, that's the way she'd look at it. And if nothing else, it set the picture perfectly for her revelation about Alec being Matthew's father. Two sisters, bad blood. She could just hear Olive saying it. The old witch. The evil old witch.

'Veronica.' Carrie put her fingers under her niece's chin and brought her face up to meet her gaze. 'Your mother never carried on with Uncle Alec or Uncle David.' Veronica's eyes flickered and Carrie knew she was going to have to say more if Veronica was to believe her. 'She never carried on with anyone until long after you were born. Then, well, your da and her started having problems and Mr Fleming, you remember Hughie Fleming from the factory? He and your mam fell in love. And she did love him, lass. It wasn't a fleeting thing or anything like that. I know it doesn't make it right, but there was only Hughie.' There had been at that point, Carrie told herself. Veronica didn't have to know it all, just enough to convince her that Walter was her father. 'No one knew about it except me because like I said, your mam told me everything. Do you believe me?'

Veronica stared at her, looking deep into Carrie's eyes, and then her face changed, becoming softer, lighter. 'You're sure, Aunt Carrie?'

'Lass, on my bairns' lives, I know Walter was your father.'

'So I'm not Matthew's half-sister then?'

'You are cousins, lass. That's all.' She put out a hand and stroked the silky smooth skin, wiping away the dampness from Veronica's face. 'Your gran had no right to tell Matthew lies like that, but sometimes I think she's not right in the head. Now.' Her voice became brisker. 'Does that alter anything concerning Matthew and this other young man?'

Veronica dropped her head to one side. Her voice was shaking when she said, 'No, not really, Aunt Carrie. Matthew . . . he was so cruel that day. He knew how I felt about him.' She raised her head. 'I've never been much good at hiding my feelings, have I?'

'Not much,' Carrie said, hugging her.

'I've thought about it a lot and after a while I realised it suited him to tell me at that point. He doesn't love me, not in that way. I . . . I think I'll always love him, but Gerald is nice and kind and I like him.'

'But you might meet someone else some day, lass. Someone you can feel about like you did Matthew.'

'No, I won't.' Veronica's tone was certain and very matter-of-fact. 'And I don't really want to feel like that again, Aunt Carrie. It's too . . .'

'Painful?'

Veronica nodded. 'Gerald worships the ground I walk on and that's very nice, but he's also funny and clever and gentle. I'll always know exactly where I am with him and he won't break my heart because he can't. But I'll be a good wife to him.'

'I'm sure you will.' Carrie felt terribly sad. Veronica was still just a young lass but youth had fled from her. She could have been thirty, forty, the way she was talking. How could Matthew have been so insensitive?

Because he is Alec as Alec was at that age.

The answer shocked her, the thought coming like a bolt out of the blue.

'I must go, Aunt Carrie. I want to call in and see Aunt Lillian and the bairns before I catch the train, and Granda and Grandma. Thank you.' Veronica flung her arms round Carrie in one of the impulsive gestures Carrie remembered from the past, and as she hugged her back, she thought, you can be proud of her, Renee. She's a grand lass.

'You'll come to the wedding, you and Uncle David and the bairns?' Veronica was smiling now and she didn't seem like the same girl who had walked quietly into the flat an hour before. 'I'll send out the invitations nearer the time of course, but I would like you to come.'

'Of course we will.' The two women hugged again, and Carrie said, 'Your mam and da would have loved to see you get married. They both loved you very much, you know.'

'Thank you, Aunt Carrie, but I think we both know that you had more of a hand in bringing me up than Mam.' It was not said with rancour. 'Mam was the sort of woman who should

422

never have had a bairn, but I know Da thought the world of me. He was lovely, my da.'

'Aye, he was, lass.' Again Carrie felt overwhelming sadness.

When David returned and the children had been bathed, fed and tucked up in bed, Carrie told her husband of Veronica's visit.

'I think she had finally nerved herself to come and find out the truth,' Carrie said gently as she finished telling the tale. 'But it must have been eating away at her like a canker, poor lass.'

David stared at her, quite unable to speak for a moment or two. Then he said, 'Someone'll swing for my mother one day, you mark my words. She'll go too far and someone will do for her.'

They didn't have to.

When Carrie and David went round to the house where Olive lived to confront her with her lies, they couldn't make anyone hear at first. Eventually, with the help of a neighbour who lodged upstairs, they forced the door. It was the smell that hit them first, that and the flies.

Olive Sutton had clearly been dead for some days; it looked as if she had collapsed and tried to crawl to the door before she died. She had been in some pain judging by the marks her broken and bloodied fingernails had made on the floorboards where she lay.

Carrie stared in shock at the remains of the woman who had hated her from the day she had first set eyes on her, and her first thought was, she died as she lived, alone and unloved, and no one, not even Olive Sutton, should have such a terrible epitaph.

Chapter Twenty-seven

Two days before her mother-in-law's funeral, Carrie saw to it that a letter was delivered to Alec. It enclosed a note for Matthew. In her letter to Alec she explained what she had heard from Veronica and exactly what she had written to Matthew. She stated she would not be going to Olive's funeral, regardless of what folk thought; it would be the height of hypocrisy given what she felt about the woman and her manipulative evil ways. She made it clear she was disappointed by Matthew's part in all of this, and she felt he owed his cousin a written apology for his insensitivity. The letter to Matthew was the hardest thing she had ever had to do, but although David tried to tell her she didn't have to send it, she knew differently in her heart. She owed it to Veronica and even more so to Renee. Her sister might not have been the best of wives and mothers, but she did not deserve to have her name blackened in such a fashion.

On the morning the letter was sent, Carrie found herself quite unable to work as usual. The last few months she and David had employed Danny's fiancée, who was a trained nanny, to come and take care of the children each day from nine to five, although Carrie often sent the girl home early because she wanted more time with the children. Their baby kisses and hugs were balm to her sore heart like nothing else could be. And today, more than any other, she needed that comfort.

She didn't know if the letter would forever alienate her from her son, but she thought it might be the final nail in her coffin as far as Matthew was concerned.

After telling Danny's delighted fiancée she could have the day off, Carrie spent the morning quietly with her children. She prepared a light lunch of cold meat and salad for everyone as she normally did, and when David, her mother, Lillian and Miriam had gone back downstairs again, she put the twins down for their afternoon nap and spent some time with Edward before he, too, went down in his cot.

In spite of how wretched she was feeling inside, she forced herself to sit down at the desk in a corner of the room and begin looking at some correspondence that needed attention. She dealt with it automatically, and when it was finished she rose and paced the sitting room.

Her mind was filled with images.

Matthew as a chubby, smiling baby with soft downy hair and dimpled hands. Matthew curled up on top of the covers in his narrow iron bed in a pair of blue flannelette pyjamas she had made for him. Matthew standing very still and stiff with a quivering bottom lip as she left him on his first day at school. Oh Matthew, Matthew, Matthew.

Her sadness was pressing in on her, causing an ache in her heart which would have been a moan had she expressed it. She loved him so much, didn't he know that? But he must, he must. Then why was he punishing her like this?

And then she took hold of herself and came to a standstill. 'Enough, enough,' she said out loud. 'You can't make him love you or forgive you, and if this letter is the final severance, you did what you had to do.' But it was little comfort.

Half an hour later the twins woke up and she brought them into the sitting room to play. When David walked into the room, Philip and Melanie immediately made a beeline for him. Over their heads and without any preamble, he said, 'Matthew and Alec are downstairs asking to see you. Shall I tell them to come up?'

'Oh, David.' She stared at him, her eyes wide. 'How do they seem?'

If he had spoken the truth at this point he would have said, 'Grim.' As it was, he shrugged. 'I'm not sure, but I think it might be wise for your mother to take care of the bairns for a while.'

Carrie's hand went to her throat. 'All right, but ask Mam to come up here and take them after we have introduced them to their brother.' She was not going to apologise to her son for her other children, neither was she going to spirit them away as though she and David had done something shameful.

David nodded.

'You'll stay with me?' Carrie asked in a tone which immediately brought him to her side. 'When they come up?'

'Of course I will.'

Her throat swelled at the love in his eyes, and she held on to his hands for a moment before he went downstairs. She must not let emotion get the better of her now. She had to carry this off whatever happened. She was not going to snivel or beg or plead. She had done nothing wrong except to love Matthew with all her heart and soul from the moment he was born.

Footsteps on the stairs outside warned her they were here. David was the first one to enter the room. Alec followed him, then her mother, and Matthew made up the rear. The twins, sensing the atmosphere and a little over-awed, clung to Carrie's skirt instead of running to their grandmother as they would normally have done.

'Hello, Alec. Hello, Matthew,' Carrie said, before bending down to the twins. 'This is Uncle Alec and your brother, Matthew.' Two little bewildered faces stared up at her. 'Say hello.'

Two heads buried themselves in her skirt, and now Joan bustled across, saying briskly, 'I'll take them down to the girls for a minute or two, you know how they love that. Come on, my pets. A little bird's told me there's a tin of fudge downstairs. Shall we go and find it?'

She had said the magic words and the twins trotted off quite happily, leaving Alec and Matthew standing just inside the sitting-room door. Carrie looked at them. The contrast in their colouring was stark, otherwise she was looking at two peas in a pod. Matthew had changed considerably in the last year and his father's genes were now strongly in evidence. She forced herself to say politely, 'Sit down, both of you. Would you like a cup of tea?' even as she wanted to run across the room and take Matthew's stiff body in her arms and beg him to listen to her.

'No tea, thank you.' Alec made no move to take the proffered seat, and neither did Matthew. David moved closer to Carrie and took her elbow in his hand. They stood facing the other two.

'Matthew has something to say to you, Carrie.'

Alec glanced at his son and, on cue, Matthew spoke up. 'I'm sorry that I repeated the things Gran said to Veronica and I'll write and say so. I should have checked with you before I said anything.' He was looking at her and speaking as though to a stranger. Nothing she had experienced this far was as painful. She couldn't speak, and after a long pause it was David who responded.

'I hope you know it was a pack of lies.'

Matthew nodded, his acute embarrassment becoming obvious for the first time when he stammered, 'I . . . I didn't know how Gran was then.'

This was awful, worse than she could have imagined. She shouldn't have written to him. Her eyes moved from her son's red face to Alec's, and the green eyes were waiting for her. He cleared his throat.

'We were planning to come and see you even before we got your letter,' he said quietly.

Something in his voice brought Carrie's heart racing. Whatever Alec was going to say she was not going to like it, she could tell.

'My health has not been too good this winter. My doctor has advised me I should think about going somewhere warm.'

'You're going on holiday?' She was surprised, she had thought he was going to say something terrible.

'Not exactly, no.' Alec cleared his throat. It was clear he was finding this difficult.

Carrie saw Matthew glance at him, and then he said, speaking directly to her, 'The doctor said he wouldn't survive another winter and spring like the one we've just had, that's the truth of it. What he went through has weakened his chest too badly.'

Carrie stared at Matthew, her head whirling. What were they saying? She wanted to ask them to make themselves clear but she didn't want to hear the explanation.

David drew Carrie more closely into his side. 'Do I take it you intend to leave the country?'

Alec nodded. 'I've sold the business, the properties, everything,' he said quickly. 'There's no point in being the richest man in the graveyard, is there?'

Carrie was frozen, her eyes locked on the face of her son. He was going away, and not just to another part of the country

429

but to another part of the world. She wanted to ask a hundred questions but couldn't force one past the lump in her throat.

'We're going to travel for a while.' This was the first spark of animation Matthew had shown. 'France, Italy, most of Europe, and then we're going to America.'

'America?' David looked past Matthew to Alec. 'Why America?'

'I've a friend there, in California. He wants me – us' – he corrected himself with a quick smile at Matthew and the intimacy and easy comradeship hit Carrie like a punch in the solar plexus – 'to go into business with him. I thought it was just talk when we spoke of it in the camp; you dream to keep yourself going in those places, but a couple of months ago Marvin contacted me and it appears he's serious. It seems the perfect solution.'

The perfect solution? Carrie said, very quietly, 'When do you leave?'

'In a few days' time. We want to get away before the bad weather.' Matthew was more subdued now, his eyes holding hers.

Carrie wasn't aware of her stricken expression, but when Alec said, 'We'll let you have our address once we're settled of course, we mustn't lose touch,' she stared at him as though he had spoken in a foreign language. With every fibre of her being she wanted to fling her arms round Matthew and hug him tightly, she wanted to beg him not to go, not to leave her without hope. Because she knew and he knew that this was what they were talking about. America, the other side of the world. She might never see him again.

She took a deep breath, glad of David's arm round her. 'I've always only wanted your happiness, Matthew,' she said in a low voice. 'I hope in time you will understand that.'

'I know.'

She saw him take a deep breath, and then he said, 'Don't take on, Mam, this is what I want. It's . . . it's the best thing all round.'

No, no it wasn't. She continued to stare into his beloved face but she couldn't speak, and then as she saw him move forward and hold out his arms, she went into them like a homing pigeon.

'I'm sorry, Matthew. For not telling you, for the pit, everything.' She was conscious of how tall he was as he held her, how broad, but with the tears streaming down her face she couldn't see clearly. She loved him so much it was a physical pain in her chest.

'I know,' he said again.

She could feel his heart beating as he held her. Her head rested in the hollow of his throat and she could smell the fresh clean fragrance emanating from his shirt. Freda Browell obviously took pride in the laundry. It was a ridiculous thought for such a moment.

She had to control herself, she had to make it easy for this young man who was now six inches taller than she was and who had already left for foreign shores in his mind. She hugged him one last time before willing herself to step away. She drew her handkerchief from her pocket and wiped her face. 'Will I see you again before you go?' she asked shakily.

There was a slight pause and then Matthew said, his voice a little gruff, 'We're travelling down to London tomorrow morning and spending a few days seeing the sights before we go.'

She nodded, unable to answer.

'Carrie?' As her gaze swung to Alec, he said, 'I'm sorry.'

She wanted to shout at him. She wanted to tell him he was

taking her boy, her firstborn, and that it wasn't fair. None of it had been fair. But as she stared into the pale, drawn face of the man watching her, she knew this was not the Alec of twenty years ago. That man had gone, and the one standing in his place was not a monster. What she read in his eyes enabled her to say, 'If the doctor has said you must go, you must go.'

Alec's eyes roamed over her face. 'I promise you if there was another way I would take it, but contrary to how I felt before I came home, I've found I want to live. I would prefer it to be in England but beggars can't be choosers.'

Carrie found she could look at him without inwardly flinching for the first time since that night when she had been fifteen. 'Hardly a beggar.'

'Not in terms of wealth, no.'

She understood what he was trying to say, but then, because she couldn't hold the words back, she said, 'But you have Matthew.'

'Yes,' he said, 'I have Matthew. And you have David and your family.'

When it was time, they all walked downstairs together. On the doorstep the men shook hands, and as Matthew bent and brushed her forehead with his lips, she said, 'I love you. I always have and I always will. Remember that if nothing else, won't you?'

He looked down at her and for a moment the boy was back. The little lad who used to rush in from school shouting for a shive of bread and dripping, his words spilling out as he told her about his day, or the sleepy child cuddled into her as she told him a bedtime story.

'I'll remember,' he said.

For a heart-stopping moment she thought he was going to

say he loved her too, but then he turned and walked away from her with Alec, and but for David holding her up she would have crumpled to the floor.

A moment later she had pulled herself together sufficiently to straighten. She would not let the last image he had of her be one of pathos. There would be time for tears later, all the time in the world, in fact. But oh, if she never saw his face again . . .

She watched as Alec and Matthew reached the large car parked at the side of the road, and it was Alec who turned to wave before climbing into the passenger seat. This was it, they were going. She held herself rigidly, her eyes fixed on her son.

Matthew had actually started the engine and the car was beginning to move when suddenly it stopped and all became quiet again. Her heart thumping a tattoo, Carrie saw him say something to Alec who nodded, and then he was coming towards her again. She wanted to fly to meet him but she didn't, and when he was in front of her she remained quite still.

'I'll write, Mam. I promise.'

'You promise?'

'Aye.' His voice was gruff. 'Don't worry.'

She inclined her head at this because once more she couldn't speak but then his arms were round her again, briefly this time, and the gruffness was more pronounced as he said, 'Goodbye, Mam. I love you.'

Carrie watched the car drive away through a mist of tears. She blinked furiously, becoming aware for the first time that she was holding on to David's arm with all her might. 'Do you think I'll ever see him again?'

David did not know the answer to this, but he said, 'Of

course you will, love,' his voice warm as he brushed a strand of hair from her damp cheek.

She had to believe that. And she had to keep believing it in the long months and years ahead.

David moved her into him, encircling her body with his arms, and he echoed her son's words as he said, 'It'll be all right.'

Oh, she loved this man. Carrie looked into the concerned brown eyes and reached up to stroke his face, oblivious of passers-by. As long as David was at her side she would be able to bear whatever came. The love of her children might wane, but never his. Matthew was gone from her, and only time would tell if he would keep the promise he had made. But she had hope, and she would cling to it, that and her David's love. The most precious thing.

Candles in the Storm

Rita Bradshaw

A fierce storm is raging when Daisy Appleby is born into a fishing family, in a village north of Sunderland, in 1884. When her mother dies from the fever a few years later, it falls to Daisy to run the household and care for her family. Life's hard: the sea barely yields a living, and then there's always the anxious wait for the menfolk to return . . .

In the storm that takes her father and two brothers, Daisy risks her life to save a handsome young stranger from certain death. Although William Fraser is captivated by his spirited, beautiful rescuer, his rich and arrogant family despise Daisy. A tangled web of lies tears the couple apart, and Daisy must overcome tragedy before she can find her destiny . . .

Acclaim for Rita Bradshaw's novels:

'If you like gritty, rags-to-riches Northern sagas, you'll enjoy this' *Family Circle*

'Catherine Cookson fans will enjoy discovering a new author who writes in a similar vein' *Home and Family*

'Rita Bradsaw has perfected the art of pulling at heartstrings, taking the emotions to fresh highs and lows as she weaves her tale' *Sunderland Echo*

0 7472 6709 X

headline

The Urchin's Song

Rita Bradshaw

Growing up in the 1890s amid crushing poverty in Sunderland's East End, Josie Burns is no stranger to dirt, cold and hunger. Every day Josie and her younger sister are sent out to beg by their brutal father, but Josie has a special gift – a beautiful voice. By singing in the rough dockside pubs, Josie earns enough for her father to leave them alone.

When Josie is twelve years old, she learns that her father has sold her older sisters to his evil friend, Patrick Duffy, to work the streets. Josie flees to Newcastle, obtaining refuge with a kindly mining family, but for Josie even this sanctuary is not free from pain or the long arm of Patrick Duffy.

Josie is drawn to the music halls, but the road to success is not an easy one. Josie must fight for what she believes in before she can find true happiness.

Acclaim for Rita Bradshaw's novels:

'If you like gritty, rags-to-riches Northern sagas, you'll enjoy this' *Family Circle*

'Catherine Cookson fans will enjoy discovering a new author who writes in a similar vein' *Home and Family*

'What an emotional rollercoaster ride of a book! It grabs your attention from page one and does not let go until the end' *Sunderland Echo*

0 7472 6708 1

headline

Now you can buy any of these other bestselling
Headline books from your bookshop or
direct from the publisher.

FREE P&P AND UK DELIVERY
(Overseas and Ireland £3.50 per book)

Across a Summer Sea	Lyn Andrews	£5.99
A Pocketful of Silver	Anne Baker	£6.99
Candles in the Storm	Rita Bradshaw	£6.99
The Pride of Park Street	Pamela Evans	£5.99
Strolling With The One I Love	Joan Jonker	£6.99
Out With The Old	Lynda Page	£6.99
Pride and Joy	Dee Williams	£6.99

TO ORDER SIMPLY CALL THIS NUMBER

01235 400 414

or visit our website: www.madaboutbooks.com

Prices and availability subject to change without notice.